UNDER A SPELL

"Do you feel that?" I hissed over my shoulder to Will.

My skin started to prick and I could feel the sweat start to bead at my hairline. My heartbeat sped up, the thrum of a solid ache in my chest.

"There's something here," I whispered, shaking my head. I clawed at my chest and pressed my palm against my quick, steady heartbeat. I was finding it hard to breathe. My eyes stung and every muscle in my body perked, then stiffened. I felt like I was walking into something—something cold, something with icy fingers that walked down my vertebra bone by bone. Something evil . . .

Books by Hannah Jayne

UNDER WRAPS

UNDER ATTACK

UNDER SUSPICION

UNDER THE GUN

UNDER A SPELL

PREDATORY
(with Alexandra Ivy,
Nina Bangs and Dianne Duvall)

Published by Kensington Publishing Corporation

UNDER A SPELL

The Underworld Detection Agency Chronicles

>―•―○―•―<

HANNAH JAYNE

k

KENSINGTON PUBLISHING CORP.

http://www.kensingtonbooks.com

KENSINGTON BOOKS are published by

Kensington Publishing Corp.
119 West 40th Street
New York, NY 10018

All Kensington Titles, Imprints, and Distributed Lines are available at special quantity discounts for bulk purchases for sales promotions, premiums, fund-raising, and educational or institutional use. Special book excerpts or customized printings can also be created to fit specific needs. For details, write or phone the office of the Kensington special sales manager: Kensington Publishing Corp., 119 West 40th Street, New York, NY 10018, attn: Special Sales Department, Phone: 1-800-221-2647.

Kensington and the K logo Reg. U.S. Pat & TM Off.

ISBN-13: 978-0-7582-8112-8
ISBN-10: 0-7582-8112-9
First Kensington Mass Market Printing: August 2013

eISBN-13: 978-0-7582-8113-5
eISBN-10: 0-7582-8113-7
First Kensington Electronic Edition: August 2013

10 9 8 7 6 5 4 3 2 1

Printed in the United States of America

To my first teacher: my big brother, Trevor.
Looking forward to all the chapters to come.

Chapter One

"You want me to do what?"

In all my years as the only breathing employee at the Underworld Detection Agency, I've been asked to do a lot of things—hobgoblin slobbery, life-or-death, blood-and-flesh kind of things. But this? This took the cake.

Pete Sampson leaned back in his leather chair, and though I usually beamed with pride when he did that—as I had been instrumental in getting him back into head of the UDA position—this time, I couldn't. My stomach was a firm, black knot and heat surged through every inch of my body as he looked up at me expectantly.

"I really thought you would be excited to visit your old stomping grounds."

My knees went Jell-O wobbly then and I thumped back into Sampson's visitor's chair. I yanked a strand of hair out of my already-messy ponytail and wrapped it around my finger until the tip turned white.

"Excited? To return to the source of my deepest angst, my inner-turmoil—to the brick walls that can only be described as a fiery, brimstony hell?"

Sampson cocked an eyebrow. "It's just high school, Sophie."

"Exactly."

Most people would say that high school is the most traumatic time in their lives—myself included. And since in the last few years I'd been shot at, stabbed, hung by my ankles, almost eaten, and sexually harassed by an odoriferous troll, *most traumatic* took on a whole new significance.

"Isn't there anything else we can do? Anything I can do? And I'm talking human sacrifice, demon sacrifice, total surrender of my Baskin Robbins punch card."

"Sophie," Sampson started.

"Wait." I held up a hand. "Are we sure we have to go in at all? And why me, specifically? I mean"—I rifled through my purse and pulled out a wrinkled business card—"it's been a while since you've been back at the Agency, Sampson. See?" I slid the card across the desk to him. "It says right there: *Sophie Lawson, Fallen Angels Division.*" I stabbed at my name on the card as though that would somehow give my title more emphasis. "Does this case have anything to do with fallen angels? Because if not, I'm sure there are other UDA employees who would be excellent in this investigation. And then I would be able to really focus on my current position."

Granted, my position more often than not found me pinning a big baddie to a corkboard or locked in a public restroom san clothes, but still.

Sampson stacked my business card on top of a manila file folder and pressed the whole package toward me.

"You should go in because you know the high school."

"I'll draw you a map." I narrowed my eyes, challenging.

"And because everyone else around here—" Sampson gestured to the open office, and I refused to look, knowing that I would be staring into the cold, flat eyes of the undead—and the occasional unhelpful centaur. "Well, everyone else would have trouble passing. Besides, it's not like you're going in alone."

"I'm not worried about that. And hey, I'm flattered, but there really is no way I'm going to pass as a student."

Though I'm only five-five (if I fudge it, stand on a phone book, and stretch), often wear my fire-engine red hair in two sloppy braids, and have, much to my best friend's chagrin, been known to wear SpongeBob SquarePants pajama bottoms out to walk the dog, it had been a long time since anyone had mistaken me for anything more than a fashionably misguided adult.

"You're not going in as a student. You're going in as a teacher. A substitute."

I felt as though all the blood in my body had drained out onto the brand-new industrial-grade carpet. Because the only thing worse than being a high school student is being a high school substitute teacher.

My left eye started to twitch. "A substitute teacher?"

My mind flooded with thumbtacks on desk chairs and Saran Wrap over the toilets in the teacher's lounge. Suddenly, I longed for my cozy Underworld Detection Agency job, where no one touched my wedged-between-two-blood-bags bologna sandwich and a bitchy band of ill-tempered pixies roamed the halls.

"A substitute teacher," I repeated, "who saves the world?"

Sampson's shrug was one of those "Hey, pal, take one for the team" kind of shrugs and I felt anger simmering in my gut.

"You can 'teach'"—he made air quotes that made me nauseous—"any class you'd like. Provided it's in the approved curriculum. And not already assigned."

I felt my lip curl into an annoyed snarl when Sampson shot me a sparkly-eyed smile as if being given the choice between teaching freshman algebra or senior anatomy was a tremendous perk.

"If this high school isn't about to slide into the depths of hell or in the process of being overrun by an army of undead mean girls, I'm going to need a raise. A significant one," I said, my voice low. "And a vacation."

Sampson nodded, but didn't say anything.

"So," I said, my eyebrows raised, "why is this so dire?"

"Do you remember last year when a body was found on the Mercy High campus?" Sampson asked.

My tongue went heavy in my mouth. Though I was well-used to the walking undead and the newly staked, the death of a young kid—a breather who would stay dead—made my skin prick painfully. I nodded.

"That's what this is about?

Sampson didn't answer me.

"Her name was Cathy Ledwith, right?"

It had been all over the papers—a local student mysteriously vanishing from an exclusive—and, before that day, safe—high school campus. A week later, her body was discovered dumped near Fort Cronkhite, an old military installation on the Marin side of the Golden Gate Bridge. Though the story was told and retold—in the *Chronicle*, the *Guardian*—and the Mercy High School campus was overrun with reporters for the better part of a semester, there weren't a lot of details in the case. Or at least not a lot were leaked to the press.

"That murder was never solved," Sampson said, as he slid the file folder over to me.

"Didn't someone confess? Some guy in jail? He was a tweaker, said something about trying to sacrifice her." The thought shot white-hot fire down my spine, but I tried my best to push past it. "I still don't see what this has to do with the high school. Or with me having to go into it. I followed the case pretty closely"—I was somewhat of a *Court TV* or pretty much anything-TV junkie—"and I don't remember any tie-back. I mean, the girl was found in Marin."

"She was dumped in one of the tunnels at Battery Townsley."

I shuddered. "People go through there all the time."

"It was a hiker that found her. Her killer obviously wasn't concerned about keeping Cathy's body a secret."

I winced at the mention of Cathy's "body."

"I still don't understand what this has to do with us—with the Underworld. Everything about it screams human. Cathy was human—someone even recognized a van, right? Very few of our clients drive vans."

Sampson gestured to the folders and I swallowed slowly, then looked down at them. Directly in front of me was a black and white photo of a smiling teenager—all perfect teeth and glossy hair—and it made my stomach roil even more. My high school picture was braces doing their darnedest to hold back a mouthful of Chiclet teeth and hair that shot straight out, prompting my classmates to announce that my styling tools were a fork and an electrical socket. I yanked my hand back when I realized I was subconsciously patting my semi-smoothed adult hair.

"What? The prom queen—?" I stopped and sucked in a sharp breath when my eyes caught the headline plastered over the photo: MERCY HIGH STUDENT MISSING.

I scanned quickly.

Mercy High School student Alyssa Rand disappeared Monday afternoon. Erica Rand, Alyssa's mother, said that she last saw her daughter when she boarded the number 57 bus for Mercy as she always did; teachers confirmed that Alyssa attended her classes through the lunch period, but she did not show up for afternoon classes. Police are taking student statements and a conservative approach, unsure yet whether to classify Alyssa as a runaway or an abductee.

I looked up, frowning. "I don't understand. I mean, it's horrible, but we don't even know if she's really missing."

"She is, Sophie."

Sampson pressed his lips together and sighed, his shoulders falling in that way that let me know that he wasn't telling me everything. "There has been talk of a coven on campus."

Relief washed over me and I sort of chuckled. "Sampson, every high school has a coven on campus! It's called disgruntled teenage girls with black dye jobs and too much angsty time on their hands pretending to read tea leaves and shoot you the evil eye." I waved the article in my hand. "I don't see how one has to do with the other."

"When Cathy Ledwith was found last year, she was in the center of a chalked pentagram. Black candles at the points."

I licked my suddenly dry lips. "They didn't mention that in the paper or on the news." There was a beat of silence where Sampson held my eye; finally, I rolled mine with a soft of snorting laugh. "Wait— they think it was witchcraft? Have you seen *The Craft? Teen Witch?* Pentagrams and candles is Freak Out Your Parents With Wicca 101. The killer probably found the pentagram left over from some kids calling up the spirit of Heath Ledger and dumped the body. Convenient, unfortunate, but convenient. "

"The police considered that, but she had an incantation carved into her flesh."

I blinked. "Carved?"

"I consulted both Kale and Lorraine."

I sucked in a breath, willing Sampson to stop talking. Kale and Lorraine are the Underworld Detection Agency's resident witches. Kale had recently been run over by a car but spent her downtime controlling the elements, and Lorraine was the most powerful Gestalt witch the Green Order had seen in decades. She was also a top Tupperware saleslady, and if anyone knew a true incantation— or, for Lorraine, how to burp a lid— it was these ladies.

"They both confirmed that the incantation was legitimate. The killer also drained her blood." Even Sampson winced and my heart seemed to fold over on itself. I chewed the inside of my cheek and found myself praying that all of that had been done postmortem.

Sampson went on. "From the looks of it, Cathy Ledwith's killer was trying to summon a demon— and not a good one. This isn't just over-the-counter witchcraft."

"Oh." The word came out small and hollow, dying in the cavernous room.

"As I mentioned, Cathy's body was found seven days after she went missing. It was obvious that her attacker wanted—or needed—her to be found on that day."

"I don't understand. How do you—why—how do they know that?"

"According to the police report, an anonymous call came in at 7:07 that morning."

"Seven-oh-seven on the seventh day?"

"Of the seventh month."

I frowned, resting my chin in my hands. "Maybe

her killer is just OCD. Did anyone explore that angle?"

It was silly, but I knew the significance of sevens—and I knew the demon Cathy's murderer was calling.

"Seven is divine. Seven-seven-seven is—"

"Satan." The word took up all the space in the room and I found it hard to breathe.

Everyone knows 6-6-6 as the devil's "call" sign—or they think they do. And while it does have true significance—mostly in movies, fiction, and speed metal songs—it is more like a pop-culture high-five to the Prince of Darkness. The trio of sevens is the summoner.

My heart was throbbing in my throat. I knew the answer, but still had to ask. "Do they think the other girl—"

"Alyssa."

"Alyssa, do they think she—that she may have been abducted by the same person?"

Sampson's hulking silence was answer enough.

Something tightened in my chest, and Sampson, his enormous cherry wood desk and his entire office seemed to spin, then fish-eye in front of me. I gripped the sides of my chair and steadied myself.

"We want you to go into Mercy and see what you can find out about this so-called coven."

"Are they even rela—"

Sampson held up a hand, effectively silencing me. "They're related, Sophie. There's no question.

Students who knew Cathy confided that she had, in fact, been bullied by a group of other students. Haven't heard the same about Alyssa but it's a good possibility."

A memory wedged in my mind and I was fifteen again, awkward, terrorized, cornered in a Mercy High bathroom by a selection of mean girls with Aqua Net hair and slouchy socks. I could feel the sweat prick on my skin again, the nauseous way my stomach rolled.

"The police—aren't they working on this?"

Sampson nodded slowly, then laced his fingers together in front of him. "They are."

"But?"

"They don't have a whole lot to go on, either. But that's not what we're concerned about."

"We're concerned about potential witches."

"I can't help but believe there is a supernatural element in this case, Sophie. The carving, the state of the body. The police aren't going to look at things like that. If there is a new coven brewing . . ." Sampson let his words trail off, his dark eyes flicking over me.

"I don't get it, Sampson. If there were a coven—a coven full of *real* witches, wouldn't we know about it? I mean, it's kind of what we do." I pointed to the plaque behind Sampson's head. "It's right there in the name, Underworld *Detection* Agency."

The stern way Sampson's brows snapped together as he crossed his arms in front of his chest let me know that he wasn't enjoying my light banter-slash-attempt to do anything other than this assignment.

"Yes, Sophie, I know the name of the agency. But witches are among our least adherent of clients."

I felt my mouth drop open. "Really?"

"Check the books. We don't have a lot."

"I thought that's because there aren't a lot."

"There are thousands. Likely hundreds of thousands in California. We've got Wiccan factions, a group of Druids up by Humboldt."

"And what? They don't consider themselves 'Underworldy'?"

Sampson blew out a sigh and nodded his head. "Something like that. If there is a new coven in town—even if it's an old, under-the-radar one—we likely wouldn't have known."

"So really, I have to go out to Mercy and see what I can detect?"

Sampson smiled and jerked a thumb over his shoulder. "Yup, detect. It's right there in our name."

I rolled my eyes and pushed myself out of my chair. "Okay. I'm going to run upstairs and get the briefing from the police department. Kind of nice, I guess. They work on the physical, we pick up the metaphysical." I nodded again. "Kind of like a Batman-and-Robin kind of thing."

Sampson stood. "No, not like that all. We're

strictly working our angle on this. We're not trying to find the girl, we're trying to find the coven."

A bolt of something shot through me. "So my job is to stand by and look for flying brooms and eye of newt while a girl is missing?"

"The police are going to find Alyssa. They're going to find Cathy's killer. Our job is to make sure that if there is a coven involved, if anything has actually been summoned—or anyone is looking for girls to use as future sacrifices—we stop it. We're doing this on our own. Do you understand that, Sophie?"

I crossed my arms in front of my chest and studied the office supplies on Sampson's desk.

"Let the police do their job. You need to keep your nose out of the physical part of this case."

Sampson eyed me and I broke his gaze, finding myself touching my fingertips to the tip of my nose. I didn't stick my nose into things.

For me, it was pretty much a full-body kind of stick.

"I need your word, Sophie."

"Okay, fine. You have my word." Even as I nodded my agreement, my mind was racing: check evidence. Read autopsy reports. Wear black. Break into something. I wasn't exactly lying to Sampson; I was simply covering all my supernatural bases. You'd be surprised how often a banshee shows up in a file folder.

I walked out of Sampson's office feeling as

though I had just sealed my fate. Each step back toward my office made my stomach sink lower, even as I edged around the hole in the linoleum where a wizard had blown himself up (eons ago—was anyone ever going to get around to that?). I was about to hightail it into the ladies' room when I realized that part of the reason for the upswing in my stomach acids—and nausea—was standing on a chair, legs akimbo, facing me off in the hallway. I immediately started breathing through my mouth.

Steve.

Steve was our resident troll—resident, in that he was an independent contractor who never seemed to leave the confines of the Agency. Troll, as in, well, troll. He who resides underneath bridges, asks ridiculous questions, and desperately wishes to deposit his little troll babies deep in my lady parts.

He's grey and vaguely scaly, is constantly showing off his tufts of lichen-green chest hair, and has a cache of dirty jokes and bad pickup lines that would make any honky-tonk or used car salesman envious. I should say that I have a soft spot for the little guy—he is mostly harmless (that stench did kill a few flowers) and he had been instrumental in saving my life. But the spot that was soft for him was growing a little harder each time he "bumped" into my backside or left me love notes that frankly should have started "Dear Penthouse Forum," rather than "My Dear Sweet Sophie's Legs."

Steve grinned salaciously when he saw me, and

he suddenly jumped off his chair, pushing it to the side.

"Steve thinks Sophie looks distressed."

Also, Steve always referred to himself in the third person. I'm not totally sure that that's a troll thing—I'm pretty sure (hopefully) that it's purely a Steve thing.

"Would Sophie like to tell Steve all about it?"

I swung my head—and pinched my nose. "No thanks, Steve. It's nothing." I continued down the hallway and Steve trotted next to me, finally picking up speed and pushing his chair in front of him. He bumped it into my calves, jumped on it, and laid his swamp hands on my shoulders. "Steve is a very good listener. And he will give you massage. . . ."

Steve dug his thumbs into the meat above my shoulders, leaving two wet spots on my blouse.

"Soph—I mean, *I* appreciate the sentiment, but like I said, I can handle this one." I tried to squirrel out of his grasp, but for three feet of lichen and swamp slime, he had an impressive grip. I softened, slightly, as he cocked his head and listened intently to me, his coal-black eyes registering nothing but sweet concern as his fingers moved little circles up toward the top of my shoulders. "Steve knows where a lady carries her stress. Steve studied reflexology."

"Hey. HEY! Hands off you little swamp creep!"

Apparently, in Steve's world, ladies carried most of their stress in their breasts.

Steve jumped off his chair and took off running down the hall.

"I'm going to call HR on you, you little pervert!"

I pushed open the ladies' room door and turned the tap on cold, ready to plunge my whole head in the sink. The back of my neck was clammy and sweaty and my cheeks were flushed midlife-crisis-Corvette red. I settled for splashing water on my face instead of the dunking, as I was trying to present a more sophisticated, less stained Sophie Lawson.

"Okay," I said to my reflection. "Everything is going to be okay. I'm in charge. I'm in charge." I pushed wet, floppy tendrils of hair behind my ears, wiped the mascara from under my eyes and gave myself the tough-as-nails, sexy chick stare I'd been working on.

"Yeah," I purred. "I'm in charge."

With my self-confidence damp but re-inflated, I turned for the door, and busted directly into Vlad LaShay. His black eyes were wide, his lips set in a hard, thin line. Gone was his usual king-of-the-underworld swagger; in its place was something that I had never seen on any vampire, let alone this one: fear.

"Vlad, this is—"

Vlad grabbed both my shoulders in his cold hands and walked me backward back into the ladies' room, glancing nervously over his shoulder every few feet.

"You've got to hide me," he said finally.

"Who am I hiding you from?"

"Kale."

My eyes shot around the room. "You realize that this is the girls' room, right? And that in addition to being pissed off by you, she's a girl? Who could very possibly have to pee at any given moment?"

Vlad grabbed the trashcan and pulled it in front of the door. "I don't plan on staying in here all day. I need you to sneak me out of here, and then keep Kale distracted long enough for me to get out of the office and into the elevator."

Aside from being the demon clearinghouse for everything that went bump (or groan, or splat, or bite) in the night (think DMV with longer lines and check boxes that included dead, undead, and other), the Underworld Detection Agency had also recently become the hotbed for hormonal ancient teen-vampire-slash-teen-witch activity.

It was like the *Jersey Shore* house with fewer suntans.

At the center of this week's activities were apparently Vlad—Nina's nephew, my boss, and the acting head of the Vampire Empowerment and Restoration Movement—and his ladylove (or something), Kale. The fact that Vlad was an immortal sixteen-year-old (now a hundred and thirteen years young) meant that he had ruddy pink cheeks and had perfected that wholly teenage boy look of both scrutiny and complete indifference. The fact that he was my

boss made it awkward that he had been couch surf-
ing at my place for the last twenty months and technically had the power to fire me, but apparently not
the power to pick up his socks. The fact that he was
involved with—nay, head of—the Vampire Empowerment and Restoration Movement meant that he
dressed like a less appealing combination of Count
Chocula and had every polyester Dracula costume
ever sold. Kale, his paramour—or now, predator—
is a teen witch who is firmly entrenched in our intern
program under a powerful witch-cum-Tupperware
saleslady named Lorraine. Lorraine works in the
billing department so five days a week Kale answers
phones and gets training on accounts receivable,
QuickBooks, and how *not* to make it rain in the
Underworld Detection Agency break room.

Several exceptionally soggy bologna sandwiches
let me know that she wasn't exactly great at the
latter.

"If I'm going to hide you from cute little Kale"—
eighteen, chronologically and supernaturally, with
a bunch of wince-inducing piercings, bright blue
hair, and an unsavory attraction to the trembling
vamp in front of me—"you're going to need to tell
me why."

Vlad shot yet another glance over his shoulder.
"There's no time."

I hopped up on the sink and examined my nails.
"I've got all the time in the world."

"Fine! Fine. Kale heard that I may have had a

little incident with a certain female vampire at one of the VERM meetings."

"You may have had?"

"All right, I had, okay? I'm sixteen, willpower isn't exactly my strong point."

"You're a hundred and thirteen and, technically, my boss."

"Are you going to argue what I am and am not, or are you going to help me?"

"Why do you need me? Can't you just have someone take her out shopping or something? I mean, Kale has a temper. A bad one." I shuddered.

"That's why I need you." Vlad's eyes were so earnest that I couldn't help but soften to his plight. "You're magic immune, so if she tries to fry or filet you, nothing will happen."

In addition to being one-hundred-percent human and the one and only breather down here in the Underworld, I also have the uncanny ability to *not* be affected by magic. Though vampire stealth, banshee death screaming, or a witch's magic might have been more convenient, being immune to the aforementioned fileting and frying had come in handy more times than you'd think.

"Fine." I hopped down from my perch and shoved the garbage can away from the door, just before it barreled open and I caught a face full of it.

"Crap! Nina!"

Nina's eyes were wide—coal black, like her

nephew's—and her hand slapped over her open mouth. "Did I get you?"

"It's not too bad," I mumbled.

She began jumping up and down, tiny little soundless hops as vampires have no discernible weight. "So, so, is it true? Is it true?"

"Is what true?"

"That you're going back to high school! You get to relive all your high school fantasies! The football games, being crowned prom queen . . ."

"It's refreshing to know that in the eight years we've lived and worked together, you haven't retained a single memory about my high school torment. Or, as I like to call them, The Dark Years. No football games, no prom queen. No twirling memories."

Nina rolled her eyes. "I know, I know—it was all bullies, headgear, and a grannie that played mahjongg with a pixie. Boohoo. Some of us didn't even have that."

I took Nina in and felt no sympathy for her. She was tall and ballerina slim with glossy black hair that hung down her back in gorgeous waves that nipped at her tiny waist. Her eyes were wide and deep set; her nose was a cute little ski jump, and her lips— ruby red and pursed right now—were perfect and heart shaped with a pronounced cupid's bow that led men to stare and follow. Where my legs were stumpy and shoved in tights like sausage casings, hers were long and toned, her marble skin exposed and completely flawless.

And, as a vampire, she would forever remain that way.

In addition to being that frustratingly flawless, Nina is my office mate, my roommate, and my very best friend. She also happens to have the fashion prowess of every dead couture designer in the world, and fangs that could shred a grown man to ribbons should she have the inkling to do so (or wasn't bound by UDA-V bylaw not to). But right now, she was really pissing me off.

"I kind of hate you right now."

Her black eyes skipped over my full sink, up to my pink cheeks, to the damp paper towel I was pressing against my forehead.

"You couldn't make the rent without me. So, spill. I need all the details." She hopped up on the counter and positioned herself with her back against the mirror, legs stretched out on the granite. She glanced over her shoulder at her non-reflection, bared her fangs and smoothed her hair.

"Can you actually see anything in there?"

"No." She produced a lip-gloss from some secret spy pocket sewn into her vintage couture—this one, I knew, was a Gaultier—and pursed her lips, doing a perfect gloss job. "But old habits die hard."

Seeing as the last time Nina was able to see her reflection petticoats and powdered wigs were in fashion, the "old habits" quip struck me. My "old habit"—a perfectly pointy love triangle that included a delicious fallen angel and a just-as-enticing Guardian—was something I hoped to put to rest as soon as possible.

God, I hoped I never came back to life.

"Sampson is making me relive this hell."

"Relive? Hell? You have an amazing opportunity, Soph."

I groaned. "I know, I know, prom queen."

"Don't be silly; you're not prom queen material."

Um, thanks?

"What I mean is, you have this amazing opportunity to mold young minds. To really make an impression on these girls." She stuck out her lower lip. "I need some sort of legacy like that. Something to leave behind."

"You're immortal. You are the legacy."

Nina shrugged, appeased, and went on. "You'll be immortal, too—through these girls. Think about it: they'll carry the memory of Ms. Lawson with them for the rest of their lives."

My stomach lurched and bile rose at the back of my throat. "For the rest of their lives?"

They could remember my phenomenal failure for the *rest of their lives.*

"I don't think I can do this."

"Can we get back to me, please?" Vlad wailed from the toilet seat he was sitting on.

Nina cocked a brow at me. "What's he doing in here?" Then, to Vlad, "What are you doing in here?" She waved her hand at him when he tried to answer. "Never mind. Kale's looking for you." She turned her eyes back to me—intense, fixed. "And you have to do this. A girl's life depends on it. Your life depends on it. And besides, you get to do a little 'Hot for Teacher' with Alex in the teacher's lounge."

My spine straightened and something zoomed through me, landing solidly in my nether regions. Alex—fallen angel, delicious, earth-bound detective and me in the teacher's lounge? Maybe there was an up side to this thing.

"You didn't tell her where I was, did you?" Vlad wanted to know.

I chewed the inside of my cheek. "Yeah, well Alex and I seem to be a little less 'Hot for Teacher,' a little more 'Me, Myself and I.'"

Nina frowned. *Do over*, she silently mouthed.

"Did you tell Kale where I was?" Vlad shouted, stomping across the restroom's pink tiles.

Nina glared at him, her eyes narrowed and nearly flaming. "No. But I'm thinking I should, you dirty little undead Hugh Hefner. How dare you cheat on Kale!"

"Allegedly."

Nina cocked an eyebrow and I got out from in between them, fairly certain that at some point, lightning bolts would start shooting from her eyes or fangs would sink into undead flesh. Suddenly, a Mercy

High coven and a possible kidnapper/murderer on the loose didn't seem quite so terrifying.

"Allegedly?" Nina spat. "You've got two options, Vlad. Take your chances with her or take your chances with me."

Vlad widened his stance and narrowed his eyes at his aunt, whose glare was still stone cold. They stared like that for a full, silent beat before Vlad huffed and went for the door. "At least I know Kale won't behead me in my sleep."

"And don't you forget it!" Nina yelled at the closing door. When she turned her eyes to me, she grinned. "I can't believe you get a do-over. I mean, I get a lot, but you! You're, you know, you!"

"I'm investigating a past murder and the disappearance of another girl and whether or not a new coven is responsible. I'm not going all *Never Been Kissed*, Neens. This is serious."

"Ohmigawd!" Nina clapped a dainty hand over her open mouth. "How completely adorbs would it be if, during all the doom and gloom of your stupid detective work, you totally fall for the music teacher or something?"

"Nina . . ."

"Fine. The Spanish teacher, whatever." Her eyes had gone glassy and she was fluttering around the bathroom, apparently lost in some sort of in-her-head musical soundtrack. "And you'd get your first kiss out on the football field in front of everyone!"

Now I was snarling. "I've had my first kiss. I've gone all the way—you know that."

"Half this floor knows that."

I narrowed my eyes, hopeful they were shooting daggers. Nina might be my very best friend and, she might have the ability to kill me with one soft press of her pinkie (or fang), but she was often the most supremely annoying person—undead or otherwise—I've ever known.

"Okay, okay, I'm sorry. I was just having a little fun. Why are you so uptight? It usually takes you, like, ten chapters to get really upset over a murder."

I let out a long sigh. "It's not the murder I'm upset about. I mean, don't get me wrong. I'm very sorry for the girl who got murdered last year and I will absolutely not stop until we bring Alyssa home safe but, but . . ."

Nina put a hand on my shoulder and even though it was ice cold, the gesture warmed me. "It's okay, Soph. Whatever you have to say, it's okay."

"I. Hated. High school."

A slick smile made its way across Nina's perfect porcelain face. "Do over . . ." she sung.

I bit my bottom lip to stop its trembling and let Nina's words wash over me. But I couldn't stop the tears that bubbled and clung to my lower lashes.

"And . . . you know how I told Alex—I told Alex I loved him?"

Nina sucked in a deep breath—which was purely

for show as vampires don't breathe. "I've heard about it incessantly."

"Now I've barely heard from him in weeks. Weeks!"

In my mind, I wear kick-ass black leather and wield a sword while taking down the rogue demons (and occasional big baddie human) in the Underworld. In actuality, I am a blubbering, blotchy-faced mess in the Underworld Detection Agency ladies' room.

"It's probably nothing, Soph. And even if it is, it's not like he dumped you after you had sex or anything. He dumped you after you told him you loved him. That's saying something."

I crossed my arms in front of my chest and cocked out a hip. "It's saying what, exactly?"

I could almost see the cogs in Nina's head spring into action as her eyes widened. "It says you're great in the sack."

I was about to respond when Nina went back on her dreamy rampage. "Imagine the things you can teach those girls, Sophie."

"Really?" I glanced at myself in the mirror, saw my blotchy, snotty reflection staring back at me, and sighed. "I'm somewhere in the neighborhood of thirty living with two vampire roommates, working in an organization that immediately calls me when the toilet roll needs refilling or when a corpse turns up. What, exactly, should I be teaching those girls?"

Nina opened her mouth, but I stopped her, holding up an index finger. "And don't say I could teach them about being great in the sack."

Chapter Two

My heart was thundering in my ears even before my clock radio started blaring something awful and upbeat. I sat bolt upright, eyes wide open and feeling like I'd stared at the ceiling all night—mostly because I had. Murder, I could handle. I wasn't especially fond of it, but I was the kind of girl who found corpses and evil like a Kardashian could find paparazzi and Apple Bottoms jeans. But high school chilled me to the bone.

I took a leisurely shower, tossing an entire canister of "Soothing Lavender" bath salts over my head hoping for some Prozac-like relief. It made my head feel like a nicely scented gravel pile, which calmed me enough to allow me to remind myself that I was an adult. That I was no longer that horrible-haired, buck-toothed, scared-of-her-own-shadow girl. I was Sophie Lawson and I kicked supernatural—and the occasion natural but unsavory—ass. I was feeling sassy and confident until I caught a glimpse of the clock and stopped dead.

"Shit!"

I was an adult Sophie Lawson with a heap of wet spaghetti hair boring a damp spot on the back of my blouse, not a speck of makeup on, and exactly eighteen minutes to make it to my first day at Mercy High. I bit my lip, one foot in the bathroom where pretty, pale pink cheeks, under-eye concealer, and sleek, straight hair lay, the other aiming toward the front door and respectable punctuality.

I blew out a sigh, grabbed a morning Fresca and my purse, and decided that my supermodel return to Mercy High School would have to happen another day.

It's not like there was anyone I was expecting to impress at an all-girls high school, right?

"Whoa, love. You're out of here like a Tasmanian devil."

I was chest to chest with Will Sherman, my floppy hair snapping his cheek with a wet smack. He wore his sandy hair just long enough to let a few strands flop over his forehead, making any red-blooded woman willing to sell her soul to push those few strands out of his hazel, gold-flecked eyes. He had the lean, muscular build of a soccer player and an accent that made panties drop, and he lived across the hall from me. Also, he was my Guardian——but not in an "until I'm eighteen" or *50 Shades of Grey* kind of way; he simply was the man in charge of defending me against anyone who might seek to gut me, quarter me, burn me alive, or perform any other such unfortunate activity. And for all of this, all I had to do was house a supernatural vessel that held all of the human souls of the world that were stuck in a kind of limbo. It is—or I am—called the Vessel of Souls and it is an artifact that the angelic and evil planes desperately fight over—kind of like a Hatfields-and-McCoys kind of thing that could destroy the world and possibly enslave all humanity. And it was in me. No one is quite sure why, but my guess is some half-naked diaper-wearing cherub thought it would be a hoot to hide the most valuable thing in creation in the spirit of a San Francisco woman who would rather just say a few Hail Marys while eating a donut than spend her life dodging all manor of weaponry—even if it did come with a drool-worthy Guardian.

I jumped back and blinked at Will, then blinked again. "You look fantastic. Like Professor Plum or something."

Will beamed, opening his arms to show off the crisp pale blue button-down he wore under his tweed jacket, and I took the opportunity to sweep my eyes over the nice way his chinos hung on his hips, the way his blazer did nothing to hide his broad, strong shoulders, the way that button-down clung to his taut, sinewy chest.

"Wait!" He held up a silencing hand. "You haven't seen the best part." Will rifled through the battered leather briefcase he was carrying and slid on a pair of heavy, dark-rimmed glasses. With his usually bed-headed muss of sandy brown hair combed back from his forehead, he had a distinctly David Beckham-does-Harvard look, and I wanted to sit down and learn everything he had to tell me.

"Sophie?"

Will was leaning into me, and I felt a blush rush over my cheeks and made a mental note to pray for my overactive imaginary libido to dry up and stop turning me into a puddle of ooze every time Will shot me a grin or a view of one of his pecs.

"No, right, you look terrific. Why?"

"Work. Isn't this what all the good professors are wearing?"

"You're working as a professor? That's funny, because I'm going in to my old high school as a substitute—" I felt all the color drain from my face. "You're my help."

Will fell into step beside me. "With all due respect, love, I'm not the help, I'm the Guardian." He said it as though he was channeling Superman, but I was still flummoxed.

"Sampson is sending you in to keep an eye on me, isn't he? He doesn't trust me!"

Will scratched his head and pulled the downstairs door open for me. "Uh, no, I believe he doesn't trust whatever wiggy it is that's running around the high school, disappearing girls and carving them up." He flashed a quick grin and waggled his car keys. "Shall we take Nigella?"

I nodded dumbly and Will led me to Nigella, a thousand-year-old, half-rusted, half-funky maroon Porsche with Pepto-pink interior that he insisted was a classic.

"We're a team, you know."

"Hey, how come you get to be a professor and I'm just a substitute teacher?"

Will sunk the key into the ignition and Nigella coughed to life. "It's the accent, love. Makes Americans think we're brilliant. So, what's on your lesson plan?"

"You have a lesson plan? Where'd you get a lesson plan?"

"I made it." He paused. "Let me guess—you assumed I was just born your Guardian."

"No." *Yes.*

I was up to speed on Will's involvement by the time we rolled into the Mercy High staff lot. Alex was up for the job, but having been out of organized education since slates trumped binder paper, both he and Sampson thought Will would be a smoother fit. According to Sampson, Will was there to investigate, to see what else he could turn up, but I couldn't help but feel that his presence on campus was little more than a babysitter for an investigator that Sampson had no faith in.

All eyes were on me the second Nigella sputtered to a stop. The faculty lot and the student lot were separated only by an elbow-high cyclone fence, a sea of shiny, new-model haves on one side, a mottled bay of slightly dented have-nots on the other.

My heart slammed itself against my rib cage in what felt like a desperate attempt to escape as I snapped Nigella's door shut, hitched my shoulder bag and my chin, and met Will on the sidewalk. I could already feel the heat pricking at my upper lip and my ears were already buzzing with the whispers I knew were coming: *Special Sophie . . . the freak of Nineteenth Street. . . . Look at the freak. Look at the freak. Lookatthefreak.*

I reminded myself that I had come a long way, that I was the teacher now, that I was helping to solve a murder and possibly take down a wily coven of supernatural evil. A crime fighter couldn't be a freak.

I threw my shoulders back, and suddenly I didn't feel like the blistering center of unwanted attention. There were no whispered hums, no more eyes . . .

Because they were all on Will.

At first Mercy students littered the grand lawn, making their leisurely way toward the main building. But just like *that* every girl stopped, sucked in a collected breath, and straightened, shoving out best assets—breasts, hips, taut teenage butts—and turning their heads toward Will.

"Are you fucking kidding me?" I spat.

Will didn't need to say a word. The grin he

tossed over his shoulder at me was flattered, smug, and dancing on my last nerve.

"You just remember we're here solving a crime, okay? We're here to find a missing girl."

Will interlaced his fingers, outstretched his hands, and cracked his knuckles, the universal sign (in my dictionary) for sleazy old man leering at young girls.

"Fine, man whore. If saving a poor little girl's life doesn't get you, just remember that statutory rape laws are strong in San Francisco."

Will just shook his head as though I had uttered an interesting anecdote about higher education or Pippa Middleton.

"Hi."

"Hi."

"Hi."

Our exchange—my admonishment, his rebuttal— was interrupted by a trio of schoolgirls in their knife-pleated Mercy skirts, their chests straining against their crisp white shirts and sweaters, the high, round breasts of padded bras and youth. I felt myself snake my arms across my chest and curl into my A-cup.

"Are you the new teacher?" the ringleader asked. She was dead center, smoked-sapphire blue eyes glued to Will, black hair Pantene perfect, heart-shaped face flawless.

"We both are," I said, trying to break the girl's Spock-like mind control.

"I'm Fallon," the girl said. She grinned, blinding me with her blue-white teeth, a perfect line of Chiclets that would never dream of going buck or hanging on to a thread of spinach at a dinner party.

"This is Finleigh and Kayleigh." Fallon acknowledged each girl with a miniscule shake of the head before squirreling her way in between Will and I and threading her arm through his. "I can show you where the admin building is."

"That would be lovely, cheers."

The other two—Finleigh and Kayleigh, equally as uninterested in me as Fallon was—slapped perfectly manicured hands over their mouths and giggled.

"OMG, cute!"

"English. Love!"

I rolled my eyes and followed Will and his entourage to the front doors of Mercy High School. They walked in as though they weren't walking through the gates of teenage hell, as though the memories of being bullied and harassed just for existing weren't still fresh enough to make my stomach fold over itself.

"Here goes nothing," I said, stepping over the threshold.

Spires of hell fire didn't shoot up through the ultra-waxed linoleum. Scary circus clowns didn't circle me and point, and nobody stopped to give me a body check or a disdainful once over. Maybe things would be different.

I sniffed.

Maybe not.

It's amazing how the smell of a high school hallway never changes. The janitors can try, they can swap out the district-issued lemony-fresh cleaning products for summer-rain-scented potpourri, but the underlying stench of scuffed linoleum, spiral notebooks, and teenage angst embeds itself in every loop of nondescript carpeting, in every inch of every number-two pencil, and in every rusted, dented corner of every locker of every high school in the world. Mercy was no different.

The girls deposited Will and me at the administration offices, where we were greeted by Heddy Gaines, school secretary—her little carved wood veneer nameplate placed prominently on her desk.

Heddy looked like every school secretary in every high school teen angst-slash-comedy ever made. She had a beige bouffant that was spun like cotton candy with perfectly rounded bangs that barely licked her forever-surprised red-brown brows. Her face was warm and matronly, as was the lacy Peter Pan collar on her dress, as she shoved a little cut-glass bowl of hard candies toward us. As I took a grape candy—and took her in—there was a tiny niggling at the back of my mind. Did I remember her? Her eyes flitted over mine, then went to Will. She offered us a practiced smile, her orange-red lips pressed tightly together.

"May I help you two?"

I stepped forward. "We're the new teachers," I hiss-whispered, and one of Heddy's eyebrows went up even more than usual.

"Teachers?" she hissed back.

"Heddy, Heddy, I've got them."

The gentleman speaking strode over to us, his tie flopping on his chest. He jutted out a hand. "Principal Lowe," he said, shaking my hand so heartily I thought it'd snap off at the wrist.

For every inch that Heddy looked stereotypically secretarial, Principal Lowe looked atypically principal. He was tall, eye to eye with Will, with close-cropped salt and pepper hair and pale blue eyes that were kind, but rimmed with clear exhaustion. He was slender enough to make me suck in my gut, and his navy-blue suit—white button-down shirt, sans tie—gave him a cool but approachable edge. I vaguely wondered when Lowe had taken over, wondered if it was directly after the cranky old woman who had been the principal when I'd attended Mercy. Principal Stockman had lived up to her name as if it were an honor. She was built like a fireplug with a shock of fuzzy, blue-grey hair, turned-down eyes and a perma-scowl. Or, maybe the scowl was only for me. I shifted now in Principal Lowe's visitors' chairs, remembering the hundred or so times I had sat here, shrinking in Principal Stockman's shadow as she told me that "girls will be girls" and that if I'd just ignore the mean girls' comments, they would eventually forget about me and move on.

In my freshman year that had seemed like sound advice. By senior year I knew it was a crock of shit.

"I really appreciate you both coming out here," Lowe said, his pale eyes moving from my face to Will's. "And Ms. Lawson, I understand that you are a Mercy High, uh, alumna, is that correct?"

I shook my head quickly, then cleared my throat. "That is correct, sir."

Lowe and Will both broke out into smiles. "You can call me Edward, Ms. Lawson. You're not in any trouble here."

I felt a hot blush warm my cheeks and the smile dropped from Edward's face.

"Well, not in here. But out there"—his eyes flashed to the halls behind us and he shook his head—"I'm not so sure."

I suddenly snapped into information-gathering mode and pulled my notebook and pen from my shoulder bag. Every cop seemed to have his own black leather flip-open notebook—Alex kept his in his back pocket—and I knew professionally, I would need my own. I couldn't exactly find the model the cops used, but found that my Target stand-in with the glittery, big-eyed unicorn on the front cover still got the job done.

"Do you have any additional information you can give us, Edward? Anything at all about either of the missing students or any suspicions about your current class?"

Edward blinked at me blankly and Will put a soft hand on my knee. "What she means is, is there anything we should know before going out there?"

Edward shuffled some papers on his desk before handing one each to Will and me. "You'll be teaching English Two, Ms. Lawson, and Mr. Sherman—"

"Will, please."

"Will, thank you. You'll be teaching American History."

I let out a yip that was half nerves, half amusement. "He's teaching American History?" I jerked a thumb toward Will. "He's English."

"With all due respect, love, we English have a pretty good working knowledge of what's happened here in the States. We did own you and all."

Edward cleared his throat and we both snapped back to attention, caught bickering in the principal's office.

"You'll each be teaching four classes a day with two free prep periods. You don't start until after lunch today. The lessons are already prepared for you and left in each of your rooms. You have free rein of the building for your investigation." Lowe pulled two keys from his top desk drawer and handed one to each of us. "But of course, you'll keep your true intentions for being here from the student body. The girls were quite stirred up when the uniformed men were on campus. I don't know what kind of *CSI*-type havoc they'd wreak if they knew two undercover FBI investigators were here as well."

Lowe grinned and I smiled back, impressed. *FBI investigators, huh?* I made a mental note to thank Sampson for giving us a decent cover; the last time I went to investigate some supernatural bumps at a house in the Marina, Sampson told the lady I was an exterminator and I wound up with a tetanus shot and a vague certainty that her demon spider had laid a dozen eggs in my left nostril.

Lowe shrugged, his slim shoulders hugging his ears. "I wish I could give you some more information, some direction about the girls or the administration. Everyone here is like a family. I can't imagine . . ."

"So, I believe our—FBI boss, Pete Sampson— told you what we're investigating?"

"Of course." Lowe nodded. "The possibility of a coven."

"Yes." I nodded back, flipping over my notebook in a bid to look uber FBI-like. "Do you know which students are a part of it?"

Edward swung his head and stiffened. "If there even is a coven. All the girls have been pretty tight lipped about their clubs and activities off campus. But I've heard the murmurs in the halls."

"We met three girls earlier. Kayleigh—"

"Finleigh and Fallon," Lowe finished. "They're like the three Musketeers."

"Yes. Are they—is Fallon perhaps part of the murmuring? She seems sort of . . ." I let my words trail off, hopeful that Edward would get the message without me having to say that the pubescent bombshell seemed a bit witchy.

"Fallon? No. She's a star student here. Very friendly and helpful. Heads up the blood drive every year."

I shifted in my seat. Nina was in charge of the blood drive at the office, but it was less a good-citizen thing, more of a lunch-truck thing.

I instinctively didn't trust Fallon. And I swore to myself it had nothing to do with her perfect curves or the lascivious way she rolled her tongue over her bottom lip while hanging on Will's every accented word.

"Fallon helps out a lot of students—especially new ones. High school can be pretty intimidating—especially here."

Didn't I know it.

Lowe turned us out into the hallway and my heart was thudding. Our footsteps echoed through the deserted corridor and I couldn't help thinking about the green mile, a prisoner walking toward their death.

"Brings back a lot of memories, huh?" Will said. "Bet you were rollicking around here with your pigtails and your high-heeled shoes."

I felt my upper lip curl. "I was going to high school, not a fantasy porn shoot. And my memories weren't all good. I'm pretty sure if there's witchcraft around here, it's going to be right out in the open."

"Why would you think that?"

I got a flash of my fifteen-year-old self, dwarfed by a backpack and a headgear, being Ping-Ponged between the popular girls as I tried to make my way to my locker.

"Just a gut thought."

I pulled the file Sampson had given me from my shoulder bag as we walked the hall in silence.

"Here," I whispered. "This is Cathy Ledwith's class schedule. These two are Alyssa Rand's from the last two years. Anything significant?"

"Yes. Absolutely. American teens are sadly behind in math. Look at this—juniors. Geometry One. A shame."

I glared at Will, but kept the fact that Geometry One and I had shared more than a few tearful years together a secret. "No. I meant any crossover classes or teachers."

He scanned the sheets. "They both took art with Mr. Fieldheart in 6B. Both third period last year, Alyssa second period this year. Both took Honors English in their junior year, both with the teacher you're replacing."

"Okay, okay, that gives us something to go on."

Will handed me back the pages. "What, exactly, does it give us to go on?"

"I haven't figured that out yet. Let's go upstairs and check out room 6B."

We climbed the stairs and peered into classroom 6B, where a ring of girls sitting at easels turned to glare at us and no one adamantly jumped up and tried to turn us into toads.

"So much for your walk-around-and-stare-at-things plan."

"I have other plans."

"And they are . . . ?"

Saved by the bell.

Break time at Mercy High was a flurry of plaid skirts and high-pitched chatter, everyone stuffed shoulder to shoulder in the lunchroom as the weather outside rolled from an almost-blue to a definite, angry-looking gray.

Will branched off on his own and I paced the cafeteria aisle, infinitely glad that I could cross my arms in front of my chest rather than have to balance a tray while working to keep my eyes locked forward, away from the bullies of my youth. I kept my head slightly cocked, hoping to hear incriminating words pop from the multitude of conversations about clothes, nails, and this week's pop star du jour, but conversations faded the closer I got, only to start up again as I passed. At the back of the cafeteria, I spotted a girl, sitting at a table full of students who had left an empty ring around her, a solid indicator that she was alone.

"Hey there," I said with a wave.

The girl's eyebrows appeared over the top of a book and then her dark eyes, small, darting. She pressed a fuzzy strand of deep brown hair behind one ear.

"Can I help you?"

I cleared my throat and reminded myself that I was the adult there, so my first instinct to fall all over myself and hide my head in my turtleneck sweater was not a good one.

"My name is Soph—Miss—Ms. Lawson. I'm going to be substituting here for a little while. Are you waiting for someone?"

The girl's eyes swept over the ring of empty seats. "No." She went back to reading.

"Mind if I sit?"

"It's social suicide."

I batted the air. "Been there, done that. So . . ."

"So."

"You are?"

The girl sucked in a deep breath and laid her book down flat. She narrowed her eyes at me and shrunk her hands into the sleeves of her sweater. "Are you really a teacher?"

My heart started to thud and I surreptitiously looked around for Will, then attempted to send him a telepathic *Abort! Abort!* message. I had been undercover all of two hours and was already found out.

"Look, I'm not on drugs, all right? If you're the

sober companion or whatever, you're at the wrong table."

Relief crashed over me. "Sober companion? Me? No. No, I really am a—a teacher. Substitute. Totally. Here to teach. Things."

The girl blinked at me, her dark eyes sizing me up, taking me in, and finally spitting me out. "Miranda."

I blinked back. "Miranda?"

"I'm Miranda. Why are you sitting here?"

"Oh, well, I—" I picked at a dried lump of something with my thumbnail. "I just saw you sitting here and—"

"No," Miranda groaned. "Why are you here in the cafeteria? Most teachers don't interact with us unless it's on the lesson plan."

"Oh." I straightened. "I guess I don't really have anything in common with most of the other teachers."

Miranda looked at me and nodded, her expression blank. She went back to her book.

"So, other than reading, what else is there to do around here?"

She lowered her book a few inches and cocked a brow, not quite understanding. "The usual, I guess. Basketball, soccer, clubs."

I pounced. "Clubs! What about the clubs?"

Miranda slid a bookmark into her book and eyed me. "Regular clubs. French club, Spanish club."

"Oh," I said, nodding. Miranda rattled off a few

more of the basics—astronomy club, a branch of Amnesty International, Lock and Key Club.

"Are there any others?" I asked. "Like, maybe not sanctioned by the school?"

"I don't know what you mean."

I thought fast. "When I was in school, there were all the regular ones, too, but then sometimes some girls would start their own clubs—like stoners or—" I licked my lips, pausing. "Band."

Miranda sat back, a reproachful look on her face. "You read the paper, huh? You want to know if there's a coven here—if we're all a bunch of crazy-assed teenage witches, killing the prom queen."

I was taken aback by the cutting judgment in Miranda's reply, but did my best to chuckle it off nonchalantly. "Well, no. I wouldn't think that you'd kill—I mean, no, but yeah, of course I read the paper. But the coven? I don't believe that. Not for a second. There were always girls in my grade who wore torn black fishnets and Doc Martens with their uniforms. A little black eyeliner and everyone thought they were witches."

Miranda didn't say anything and I felt pinned under her gaze. Finally, I relented and dropped my voice. "Do you know anything about any covens on campus?"

"No. I'm pretty sure you're safe—no one's going to turn you into a goat." She stacked her books and slid a hand under them, then stood up. "I've got to get to class."

Miranda left me sitting alone at the lunch table, feeling just as stupid as ever.

"Well, love, ready for this?" Will sunk into Miranda's abandoned seat.

"Ready for what? We've checked out half the school and asked around and"—I made an O with my fingers and eyed Will through it—"zero."

"Speak for yourself."

"You found something?"

Will laced his fingers behind his head. "The geezer in the office agreed to lend me some yearbooks. I thought I would do a little research, see what I could scratch up."

"The geezer?"

"The old bird."

I frowned. "Heddy's not a geezer. She's . . . seasoned."

Will shrugged and produced a bag of Skittles, picking out the orange ones.

I leaned forward. "So, did you find anything?"

I prayed Will would whip out last year's yearbook, open to the photograph of last year's coven, complete with names and addresses, so I could skirt Mercy High and leave these hallowed halls back in my nightmares where they belonged.

"Not yet. She's getting them together for me." Will cocked his head and the bell rang. He grinned and downed his whole bag of Skittles while my stomach dropped into my groin and threatened to expel everything I'd eaten in the last twenty years.

"Looks like we got some classes to teach. You okay? You're looking kind of green."

I just nodded, somehow certain that opening my mouth would lead to a spew of vomit or one of those blood-curdling banshee yells. *Who ever thought it was a good idea to let* me *teach people?*

My heart thundered in my ears as I stood up and followed Will. I closed my eyes and thought of Nina, of her glistening eyes as she danced around and told me these girls were lucky to have me. I was the adult.

"*I'm* the adult here," I whispered under my breath.

"What's that, love?"

"Uh, I'm just, uh, thinking about the case."

Will stopped and turned to me, the back of his hand softly brushing over my cheek. His eyes held a sympathetic softness that I had never seen and my body started to melt into him. "Don't be nervous, love. The girls are going to go crazy for you." His voice dropped; it seemed slightly choked. "How could they not?"

He gave me a half smile, and when his soft palm left my cheek I was acutely aware of what wasn't there.

Will left me in the hall with my traitorous body piqued, every synapse and nerve on high would-you-make-a-goddamn-decision-already alert. Which is why I nearly choked on my tongue—and launched my big-girl briefcase through the window—when I walked into my classroom and was met by thirteen pairs of made-up eyes, some curious, some scathingly judgmental, most bored.

I got through my first class without throwing up or making a complete fool of myself. I think I may have even passed as a semi-decent substitute teacher. The lunch bell rang at the same time Will knocked on my door frame.

"So," he said, jamming his hands in his pockets. "Did you get through your morning classes okay, Ms. Lawson?"

The way Will's lips curved over my name sent an inappropriate bolt of lightning right through me. "It was fine," I stammered. "You?"

"Fine." We stood there in an awkward beat of silence.

"We should finish our tour of the school, see if we can find anything."

"Aha. This side of the school is the evil side. Cauldron in the gymnasium. Flying monkeys in the lockers." He grinned, produced an apple from somewhere, and took a huge bite.

I couldn't figure out whether I wanted to smack him or lick the tiny dribble of apple juice from his lip.

"Come on."

We made the rounds, poking in empty classrooms and nonchalantly trying to overhear student conversations, ears piqued for anything suspicious, anything that sounded remotely like a teenage girl firmly entrenched in the dark arts. We learned that someone named Carlie was a slut, that no one used Facebook anymore, and that the boys from St. Ignatius were so sex-starved, they would buy you anything if you showed them the top of your boobs.

"I don't know," I said to Will. "I kind of think this might be a dead end. We should be out looking for Alyssa, not playing around here."

Will may have answered me, but I couldn't be certain because all sound was drowned out by the screeching wail of the fire alarm.

"Drill?" I yelled.

"Don't think so," Will said, shoving by me. "It's outside."

Heavy plumes of smoke were choking the clear glass windows.

"It's coming from the faculty lot," Will said, breaking into a run.

"I'm coming with you."

Will looked over his shoulder. "It's just a fire, love."

"Could be supernatural. Could be a hellfire."

"Just come on!"

When Will wasn't guarding me and my amazing ability to seek out people who wanted me dead, he was a bona fide San Francisco fireman. I could have left him to it—probably should have—but I was half expecting a dragon to be on the other end of that huffing fire.

Heddy and Principal Lowe met us at the bottom

of the stairs, Heddy thrusting a fire extinguisher into Will's hands.

"We've made an announcement to the ladies that they're to sit tight. The fire is out there, at the Dumpster. There's no danger of it reaching the school."

Will and Lowe went running toward the door and I followed behind them, panting like a puppy.

Note to self: focus on cardio this month.

The Dumpsters sat between the back lawn and the faculty parking lot. I briefly considered rolling my car up against the flaming Dumpster, using it as a fire wall, and, once it was heroically charred, claiming the insurance money. But alas, I was too much of a good girl and Will already had the fire extinguisher aimed, huge white clouds choking out the black ones snaking from the box.

Within minutes the whole thing was extinguished. A cheer went up from the girls pressed against the window; they hugged and shot thankful googly eyes at Will as though he had saved a bus full of puppies rather than a Dumpster full of now-charred cafeteria waste.

"Any idea on the cause of the fire?" Principal Lowe wanted to know.

Will handed him the expelled extinguisher and hiked up on the edge of the Dumpster, looking inside. "I won't be able to really get in there until the smoke clears and everything cools off."

"Okay, okay. I'm going to tell the girls that everything is fine. Will, I'll take charge of your class for the rest of the hour, and Sophie, Heddy can look in on yours."

I waited until Principal Lowe disappeared through the front of the school before tugging Will's shirtsleeve. "So?"

"So what?"

"Does anything about the fire look suspicious?"

"Other than the fact that garbage rarely bursts into flame on its own? No, not really, though I won't be able to tell until the heat dies down."

I sighed. "We don't have that kind of time! Here." I snapped a branch from one of the trees lining grass. "Use this."

"As what? A bippity-boppity?" Will bobbed the twig wand style.

"God! Do I have to do everything?"

I snatched the twig out of his hands and threw my weight against the rim of the Dumpster, the toes of my dress shoes thunking and squeaking on the dirty metal. "Can you at least give me a hand?"

Will gave me a good hard yank and I situated myself next to him on the side of the Dumpster. With my twig held fishing-pole style and our legs dangling into the Dumpster, we would have made a lovely—though twisted—Norman Rockwell painting.

I leaned slightly forward, stretching out one leg. "It's not hot anymore." I poked my stick into the blackened rubble and fished out the remains of something that had once been white. I pulled it closer to me, then delicately touched it with my index finger.

"Oh, see, not hot at all."

"That's brilliant, love." He snatched my catch from the end of the stick, gave it a cursory look, then tossed it back in the box. "You've found a sock. Notify the queen."

"Shut up, Will. We need to see what it was that started the fire. If there are witches here, they must be lighting candles. Maybe they tossed one in the trash."

Will cocked a brow, lips pressed together. "No one is dim enough to throw away a lit candle."

I craned my head, scanning the debris.

"You might want to watch yourself, love. It's a bit moist out here—"

Will may have finished his sentence. I wasn't sure, because I was face-first in yesterday's cafeteria lunch, my ears, I was fairly certain, clogged with some sort of maggot-type brain eating insect.

"Ugh! Oh, God!" I kicked and dog paddled my way through a mass of spaghetti, then found my footing on a garbage bag filled with something hard.

"Find any clues?" Will's grin was smug.

I grabbed a handful of spaghetti and tossed it at him.

He dodged it. "Now that's just mean!" He leaned down and offered me a hand. "Come on, out with you. There's nothing in there but garbage. Probably some of the tough birds were out here smoking."

I tried to move toward him, but something was wrapped around my right foot. "I'm stuck on something."

"It's probably a Salisbury steak or something. Shake it off."

"I can't. It's stuck. It's got me."

A little niggle of panic shot through me as I unsuccessfully tried to free my foot. My heartbeat sped up. I truly never considered my demise could be at the behest of a three-day-old hunk of cafeteria meat.

Will hopped into the Dumpster with me, though he landed on a spaghetti-free, solid-looking bag across from me. "Take my hand and I'll pull you free."

"What if it's some kind of animal? What if it eats my leg?"

He clamped down on my wrist. "I'm willing to risk that."

I gritted my teeth while he yanked; my foot came free and so did I, barreling into Will's chest and laying us both out on a black garbage bag, ash raining down around us like snowflakes.

"Still have your foot?"

I yanked my leg up and examined it. "It wasn't Salisbury steak," I said, yanking the cloth wrapped around my foot. "It was this."

Will pulled us both to standing and climbed out of the Dumpster. I followed him.

"And what exactly is that?"

"It's fabric. Or the remains of fabric." I turned the charred remains in my hands. "Here's a zipper. Oh, and a tag."

Something broke inside of me.

I felt my whole face blanch, felt my chest tighten as my heart seized up. I gripped the fabric, holding it so hard that my nails bored into my palms.

"It's—it was—a skirt. From a uniform. A uniform from here." I licked my impossibly dry lips. "Will, someone was trying to burn this uniform."

Will blinked at me, then disappeared back into the Dumpster.

"What are you doing?"

"I'm looking for whatever else remains of that uniform." He paused his mad shuffle through the trash, but didn't look at me. "Or whoever owns it."

I gently laid the remains of the once grey tweed skirt aside, touching the fabric gently as though showing this inanimate object a moment of tenderness could soften the blow for its owner.

"Find anything yet?" I asked, once I got back in the Dumpster.

"No. I don't know if that's bad or good." He stepped back. "This is where the fire was centered. See that?"

He pointed to a blackened circle, then toed the small mountain of grey-white ash in its center.

"I was here when I found the skirt," I said, using my hands to dig through the spaghetti. The stench was overwhelming—burnt plastic and garbage— but I was so focused on finding the rest of the charred uniform—and hopefully not the girl who had worn it—that I didn't care.

"Wait." My hand closed around something soft and I pulled. A stretch of fabric that used to be white slid through the debris. I winced. "It's a blouse. Part of it."

Will leaned in. "It's not burned."

"No. It's torn." I rubbed my finger across the sodden, frayed edge of the shirt and pulled back when something sliced across my flesh. "Ow!"

"Something get you?" He took my hand in his and rubbed the tucked tail of his shirt over my thumb. "You're bleeding. That's not good."

"What got me?"

Will took the fabric scrap from my hand, then produced a small, filthy pin attached at what looked to be the shirt's collar. He rubbed the muck from the pin and I could see that it was made of a cheap gold fashioned into a tiny lock with a key inside.

I took the fabric and examined the pin. "It's a Lock and Key pin. It's a club on campus. Every member gets one of them."

I laid the piece of fabric on the end of the Dumpster, smoothing it out and shining up the pin. It glinted in the sunlight and my heart ached. Lock and Key was a club you had to be admitted into—

only students with the best grades and community service records were allowed and it looked great on Ivy League applications. When I was at Mercy, Lock and Key was basically a country club for the already perfect, a tiny golden promise to keep the classes pure.

"What's this?" Will yanked something then stood upright, offering it to me. My heart thudded.

"It's a girl's shoe."

His face was sallow, his eyes glassy and rimmed with red. "You found a sock earlier."

Tears pricked behind my eyes, but I wouldn't let them fall. "Keep searching."

We worked in frenzied silence, tearing open bags and tossing aside contents, and when there was nothing left to go through, we climbed over the side of the Dumpster one last time. I laid the shoe next to the remains of the skirt and blouse.

"Well, there was no body in there, so I suppose that's good."

"And we don't even know who this skirt belonged to. It could be anyone. We should still report it to the police, though. Call Alex?"

"Sure," I said, trying my best to convince myself. "But the whole thing could be nothing at all. Just common . . . uniform . . . burning."

Will's eyes flashed. I appreciated him not trying to rush me to the obvious.

"I mean, this shoe could be—" I stopped, biting off my words, keeping them back with my gritted teeth. Though the sole was melted completely on one side, it was untouched on the other. Untouched by fire, at least.

"Alyssa," I whispered. I fingered the name drawn in fat letters and decorated with ballpoint ink stars and hearts. "Someone was trying to get rid of evidence."

Chapter Three

I was congratulating myself for nearly getting through my first day at Mercy while my last class of the day was filing in. I went to turn around and found myself nose to cosmetically perfected nose with Fallon.

I cleared my throat and gripped my briefcase so tightly that I could feel my fingernails digging little half-moons into my palms.

Think, Sophie, THINK!

My mind sprung into action and I pasted on a grin, then relived—in rapid succession—every humiliation I had ever suffered in these halls, at the hands of girls in identical skirts.

I felt myself start to tremble.

You're the grown-up.

I quickly whipped up a memory of staking a big baddie vampire, of defeating a couple of crazed psychopaths, of having the super-popular-girl luck of seeing a fallen angel *and* a Guardian naked.

I was pretty kick-ass.

"Are you mute or something?"

The snark in the comment—and Fallon moving toward her seat—thunked me back to the classroom and I blew out a sigh.

"No, sorry, ladies. I was just thinking about when I was a student here at Mercy." A few girls leaned forward, a few raised their eyebrows, showing vague interest. Fallon whipped out a file and went to work on her right hand.

"My name is"—I paused, scanned—"Ms. Lawson, and I'll be taking over for the time being while Mrs. Prusch is on medical leave."

"You mean in the nuthouse."

I was beginning to recognize Fallon's voice with every part of my body. Just the sound of her spitting words poked at my stomach.

"Shut up, Fallon." The mumbled quip came from a girl sitting in the front row. I smiled.

"Hi, again."

Miranda looked up at me. Sitting in front of me at her desk, she somehow looked much smaller than she had in the cafeteria. She didn't greet me, just went back to her book. I scanned my girls, then looked back at Miranda.

In real life, she was pretty. She had deep olive skin with thick, black brows and a head of fuzzy, dark curls that rolled over her shoulder. In high school world, however, she may as well have been wearing a kick-me sign: she was enviably thin (from a thirty-three-year-old's point of view) with curves that the mean girls would call fat. Her curls were gorgeous and natural but neglected and unruly (similar to my own, which had earned me the quaint nickname Electric Head), and she bore the high school equivalent to leprosy: a decent case of acne that peppered her nose and chin.

"I had the pleasure of meeting Miranda at lunch today." I looked up, thinking my connection to the obvious outcast would make her seem adult and cool. But the mention of her name—as if it were the punch line of some untold joke—caused a quiet ripple of laughter through the classroom. I felt myself bristle, then grabbed Mrs. Prusch's role book and went through the hallowed high school ritual of butchering the students' surnames and, in this decade of Ja Net (pronounced *Jenae*), Niola, Suri, and Jacita, their first names as well.

Didn't anyone name her kid Jennifer anymore?

"Uh, Kayleigh?"

"Here." A strawberry blond raised her hand as if it weighed eight hundred pounds and her one-word response would be the last she'd ever utter.

"Finleigh?"

Kayleigh's neighbor to her right gave me a finger wave and a dazzling smile.

"And . . . so—I'm sorry, I'm not sure how to pronounce this."

Big blue eyes rolled backward like a slot machine.

"It's pronounced *so-fee*," the other girl sandwiching Kayleigh groaned. "Sofeigh."

I wouldn't have believed it if it weren't there in ballpoint and white. "Interesting. I've just never seen it spelled that way."

Sofeigh gave me another eye roll and then exchanged the are-you-kidding-me gaze with Fallon and the other 'eigh-ers. I felt sweat beading at the back of my neck.

You're the adult, Sophie.

"Okay." I snapped the roll book shut and slid up on the front desk à la every sexy actress playing a teacher in every film I'd ever seen. "We're talking today about *The Scarlet Letter.* Who wants to explain to me a little about the book?"

A heavy silence washed over the room and every eye was turned on me, every pair blank.

Where is a swirling vortex of hell when you need it?

The bell rang and it was the single most sweet, welcome sound that I'd ever heard. The girls were up with laptops, iPads, and English books packed, iPhones whipped out and already in mid-text before the thirty-second bell ceased.

"Remember to read the Prufrock poem in its entirety," I said to the backs of their heads. I could have raised my voice or rapped my hand on the desk to get their attention, but truthfully, watching the herd of teenage girl heads filing en masse out the door took my breath away. Their desertion of my classroom was a thing of pure beauty.

Until I noticed it wasn't completely deserted.

"Everything okay, Miranda?"

Miranda was hunched at her desk, shoulders sloped, massive waves of frizzy curls tenting whatever it was she studied. She looked up, surprised. "Is class over?"

I nodded silently, and though I knew should do something teacher-ly and admonish her for reading during my lecture, I felt a certain kinship for her, could understand the overwhelming desire to dip into an artsy world when the real one echoed with monikers like Super Dork and Forever Virgin.

I smiled softly at her. "So, was it as bad as I thought it was?"

Miranda looked up from the paper she was doodling on with a shy smile. "No."

I held her eye and a blush warmed her cheek; she broke my gaze and studied her notebook. "Well, kind of."

I bit my lip. "And to think the only thing I was worried about subbing here at Mercy was . . . well, you know." I watched Miranda's eyes for any new flicker of recognition/witchcraft/avoidance. She just blinked at me, her face blank.

"You know, the kidnapping?" I paused, breathing deeply. "And the other stuff we were talking about earlier."

Miranda nodded her head, solemnly. I tried a more nonchalant tactic, sliding up onto my desk, letting my legs dangle. "So, did you know her?"

Miranda went back to doodling, a blanket of hair hiding her expression. "Alyssa? Or Cathy?"

"Either," I said, my heartbeat starting to quicken. "Or both."

She continued moving her pencil across her paper, not bothering to look at me. "Alyssa was in this class. Fallon's sitting in her seat right now."

"Fallon took over Alyssa's seat already?" I tried not to gape.

Miranda just shrugged, pushed a lock of hair between her lips and sucked on it. "I didn't *know* know Cathy, but she's kind of a legend here now."

"A legend?"

"You know," Miranda made air quotes. "'The girl who was sacrificed.'"

"So that's what kids here think? It was a sacrifice?"

Miranda raised her eyebrows in the universal sign of "duh" and went on. "Because of the pentagram. And the stuff carved into her."

I swallowed sour saliva, hating the image the word "carved" brought up. Then I straightened. "How did you know there was something carved into her skin? I don't remember seeing that in the paper."

"Welcome to Generation Internet."

"So . . . do they think it was witches, because of the carvings? Or Satan worshippers?" I tried to force a lightness into my tone—as light a conversation about a dead girl and human sacrifice could be, anyhow.

Miranda dropped her pencil and perched her chin in her hand. "Do you know that there has never been even one bona fide instance of Satanism or Satanic sacrifice in San Francisco?"

I did know that, unfortunately, and could have corrected Miranda—there's never been a documented case of true Satanic sacrifice in all of the U.S. But I just played dumb.

"Wow. Well, what about the witch stuff? I heard some of the girls saying that maybe the—what was carved—was, like, a spell."

Miranda didn't answer and I rushed on. "When I went here, there were always a few girls messing with that stuff. You know, pentagrams and charms and stuff." I stifled a manufactured oh-how-silly chuckle. "There was even a rumor about a coven on campus."

Miranda carefully closed her notebook and laid her pencil on top. My throat went dry and a shot of adrenaline zinged through me.

"Yeah. You told me that already."

Of course it couldn't have been that easy.

The sun was beginning to dip and gray fingers of darkness stretched across my classroom when Will came across the hall and knocked on my open door frame.

"Ready to head out?"

I looked around my empty room as though some sort of clue or explanation would pop up, but there was nothing. I sighed and pulled my bag over my shoulder. "I feel like today was a total waste. I floundered in front of three classes and we're no closer to finding Alyssa."

Will pulled Alyssa's burnt clothes—which were now carefully packed in Ziploc bags—from his satchel. "We found her clothes."

"So now we know that she may or may not be dead. Great." I held my thumb and forefinger a smidge apart. "I stand corrected. We're this much closer to finding out some information about Alyssa."

"What did Angel Boy have to say about it?"

"What? You mean Alex?"

Will shook his head slowly. "What'd he have to say about the uni?"

I paused, fairly certain I was wearing one of my most attractive deer-in-the-headlight looks.

"You did call him, didn't you?"

"Not exactly."

Will cocked a brow.

"Not at all. I thought you'd be happy about that. You hate 'Angel Boy' and the police and all."

Will crossed his arms and pinned me with a fatherly expression that oozed disappointment. "It's evidence, love. You're supposed to report all findings of any significance to the brass. And I never said I hated the angel. I just find it hard to like someone who tried to kill me."

I wrinkled my brow. "*You* tried to kill Alex."

"Did I?"

"And I'm not deliberately hiding evidence. For starters, I'm not sure how significant a burning Dumpster—"

"With the uniform of a missing student—"

"—is. And secondly, I've been rather busy here, investigating. There are a lot of students to interview, Will. Lots of crevices and rooms on this campus to check out."

Will rolled his eyes.

"And also I forgot."

I could see Will suppressing a groan so I rushed on.

"But it's not like that's going to make any difference. Like I said." I pinched my fingers together again. "That much closer to finding Alyssa."

"We're a little bit more than that much"—Will imitated my gesture—"to finding her kidnapper."

My eyebrows rose. "How so?"

Will sauntered down the aisle of desks and plopped himself down in one toward the back of the room, kicking up his professor shoes on the desk kitty-corner from him. "We know that the garbage goes out on Monday mornings."

I flipped a desk around and sat it in. "We do?"

"Okay, I know that the garbage here goes out on Monday mornings. So we know that Alyssa's clothes had to have been dumped within the last twenty-four hours."

"And that means?"

Will blew out a sigh. "I thought you were the crime-fighting expert and I was just the attractive sidekick."

I felt myself bristle and let out and audible growl.

"It means that whoever dumped Alyssa's clothes more than likely has a connection to the school."

"Of course—" I was about to summon up my best "duh" expression, but Will held up a silencing hand.

"I mean other than as a hunting ground."

I felt a hot blush was over my cheeks. "Go on."

"Why would your perp—"

"Unsub," I corrected, feeling the stupid need to contribute something of merit.

"Why would your unsub"—Will eyed me as he said the word—"return to the scene of the crime just to light up his victim's clothes? He could have done that anywhere."

"Maybe he was trying to make some kind of statement?" I bit my lip, considering. "A burning uniform . . . maybe his statement is that high school is like the burning fires of hell?"

"You know, you could really use some therapy for all those non-repressed memories."

* * *

My head was spinning—and throbbing—by the time I snapped Nigella's door shut and trudged up the steps to my apartment.

"Same time tomorrow?" Will asked as he sunk his key into the lock.

I shook my head. "I need to run some errands tomorrow so I'll take my own car. But I'll see you."

Will gave me one of those exceptionally manly head nods before disappearing into his apartment. I pulled my own keys from my shoulder bag and was about to unlock my door, but I stopped, cocking my head to listen.

Music was thumping through my front door—a weirdly cheery electronica beat. I would have chalked it up to one of Vlad's super-vamp bands, but this particular song lacked the recorded-in-a-coffin timbre and any lyrics bemoaning an afterlife pox that included Sookie Stackhouse and the *Twilight* cast.

"Vlad?" I pushed my key into the lock and was surprised when Nina's dark head popped up from behind my open laptop. She was stationed at the dining table, papers spread all around her, a spiral notebook thick with black scrawl in front of her. She grinned when she saw me.

"So, what do you think?" she yelled over the beat.

"About what?"

"This!" Nina stood up and did a series of funky club moves that probably looked great with low lighting and a severe buzz.

"What is that? And"—I gestured to her cira-1980s full-body snake motion—"what is that?"

She clicked the volume button off and we were dropped into blessed silence—even though the electronica beat still throbbed in my head. "What is all this?"

"Okay, remember how I said that I needed something to really make my mark?"

"Because I'm a substitute teacher, enriching young minds to the point of complete and utter disdain for me? Yeah, I remember that."

"Well, this is it!" Nina flung out her arms in a measure of complete and utterly confusing joy.

"You're teaching the snake to a new generation of club dancers?"

Nina's sigh was so exasperated and so long I thought her chest would implode. "No, silly. Listen." She clicked the beat on again, started her little jig again, and again, I was baffled.

"What is it?"

"It's *UDA*," she crowed. "*The Musical!*"

"No," I said, my sheer terror pushing me backward. "Just . . . no."

Nina frowned, slammed my computer shut, and slumped down into a chair, chin in hands. "It wasn't exactly coming together like I wanted. Nothing rhymes with Underworld Detection Agency."

"Neens, you don't need a musical to make your mark on the world. You've made your mark on me. Doesn't that count for anything?"

Nina's eyes were soft and she took my hand, shaking it sweetly. "Oh, honey, of course that counts for something. Just not something for posterity. What do you think about a live action show based on my life?"

I sat down next to her. "Hey, I have an idea. Why don't you go back to your novel?"

Nina had had a short stint as a vampire romance novelist. Her book was awful, contrived, and a bloody love note to herself, but on the plus side, it wasn't set to music.

"No, Soph. That was good, but this is different. I want to help. I want to make people really *feel.*"

I kept the empathetic smile on my face, thinking that the release of *UDA: The Musical* would make people feel something, all right. "How do you feel about interpretive dance?" I suggested.

Nina considered if for a second before smashing her hands against her open mouth. "Oh my God. Oh my God, I'm so awful! Here I am lamenting about myself and my contribution to the world when you're back from your first day as a crime-fighting substitute teacher!"

Sophie Lawson: Crime-Fighting Substitute Teacher. That's a failed book title if I ever heard one.

"How was it?"

I kept that smile pasted on my face for as long as possible, certain the second I moved my mouth, everything would shatter into a torrent of stupid, self-centered tears.

And it did.

"Oh, Neens," I said, unable to control the hot tears that washed over my cheeks. "It was awful!"

I fell forward, my forehead plunking against a ballad about the UDA lunchroom. I felt Nina's cold hand on my shoulder, rubbing softly. "Oh, honey! I'm sure it wasn't as bad as you think it was. Come on." She snaked an arm under my chest and pushed me upright. "Tell me all about it."

I huffed, one of those half-hiccup, half-breath kind of wails locking in my chest.

"Did the girls make fun of your outfit?"

I looked down at myself. "What's wrong with this outfit?"

"How 'bout I get you some chocolate pinwheels?"

I groaned while Nina rattled away in the kitchen. "The girls are awful, Neens."

"They're teenage girls. Of course they're awful. It's their job."

I cast a frown at Nina and pushed out my lower lip pitifully. "It hurts my feelings."

Nina blew out a long, sisterly sigh, then threw her arm across my shoulders and hugged me close. "They're just kids, Sophie. And each one of them acts mean and nasty as a defense mechanism. They don't know who they are yet. Besides, what's that saying? They're probably more afraid of you than you are of them."

"That's a saying about wild animals."

Nina shrugged. "It's not like you don't have a defense mechanism of your own."

"What's that?"

"Me." She grinned and at that moment a tiny shard of sunlight crept through the window and bounced off her glossy black hair. With her impeccable makeup, incredible outfit and now this diffuse yellow halo, she looked like the quintessential popular girl.

"You'll come to school and be my friend?"

"I was thinking I'd eat them, but whatever works."

Chapter Four

I tried pulling my pillow over my head and then pulled ChaCha, my ever-trusty three-pound pup over that, but neither did anything to drown out the incessant pounding that was going on in my skull. ChaCha just rolled off me and went to work licking my eyebrows.

"Oh, ChaCha, stop. Mommy has a—" I was going to say headache, but once I sat up in the blackness, I realized the pounding wasn't coming from my brain—it was coming from the living room.

The pounding started again and ChaCha jumped to attention, a stripe of hair zipping straight up along her back. She curled her little black lips back, exposing frightening—if miniscule—incisors, and growled.

A stripe of fear went down my own spine and I stopped breathing, listening.

Another three raps.

"Go get it, ChaCha," I said, pointing. "Go defend your turf!"

ChaCha made a second fearsome growl followed by a pitiful yip as she disappeared under my sheets.

"Useless dog," I grumbled.

I was halfway through the living room, on my way to our sword closet (it's not *that* weird), when the pounding came again. It stopped and I stopped, my every living fiber taut with adrenaline.

"Nina?" I hissed.

There was no answer.

"Vlad?"

Again, silence.

Finally, the front door tore open in a Lucasfilm-style haze of whooshing wind and spitting fire.

"Holy crap!"

I stopped, dropped, and rolled. Somewhere in my subconscious I knew that was for earthquakes or bomb raids, but it didn't seem to matter as chunks of my doorframe blistered and turned to charred dust on the ground. I was being choked by smoke and my eyes stung, but I worked to keep them open until I saw the figure walking through the flaming frame coolly, as if he didn't feel the heat.

"Who are you?" I screamed. "What do you want?"

"Sophie?"

My heart was clanging like a fire bell and the soft voice saying my name only terrified me further. I knew that voice, I remembered that voice. I gulped, sour saliva dripping down my throat.

"O-o-Ophelia?" I asked, my lips burning from the heat. "Oh, God."

Ophelia was a fallen angel. One whom, until apparently right this minute, had been dead, killed by yours truly, staked with a trident to a UDA corkboard. The fact that she was the baddest of the fallen angel brigade made her death warranted. The fact that she was my half sister made the whole thing incredibly complicated.

"Oh God, ohGod-ohGod-ohGod," I mumbled to my hands.

"No, Sophie, it's me!"

The darkened form came closer and I could clearly make out slim hips, a tiny waist, and thick braids. I squinted. "Kale?"

She did some sort of Samantha Stephens move and suddenly everything—the fire, my charred doorframe—was fine. I took the opportunity to roll out of the fetal position and thank my lucky stars that in my last few years of being surprised, attacked, and *other*, my bladder was starting to strengthen up quite nicely.

"What the hell are you doing here at"—I glanced at the suddenly non-melted clock next to the door—"three a.m. and what"—I flailed wildly at the door—"was that? Why the hell are you trying to burn my apartment down?"

Kale seemed to shrink into herself and her blue hair as a Corvette-red blush blanketed her cheeks. "I'm really sorry, Soph. But look—" She knocked on the doorframe. "No harm no foul. It was all magik. An illusion."

"Great. Please tell that to my cardiologist because I'm about to drop dead. Why are you burning shit—illusion or otherwise—at this hour? And why my shit? I thought we were friends."

Kale rushed toward me and took my hand in hers. "Oh, Sophie, of course we're friends! This wasn't for you." It took a microsecond for the sweet, apologetic look in her eyes to change to one of fiery rage. "It was for Vlad."

"Vlad's not here," I said, my teeth gritted, my breath coming out in spitting gasps. "He and Nina are probably at Poe's."

Vlad and Nina—and the rest of their vampire brethren—have no need for sleep and, really, abhor relaxation of any kind (another reason I'm A-okay not being one of the pointy-fanged undead). As the majority of the breathing world fell asleep during the wee hours, some shopkeepers saw their niche in the market and started opening up a select group of shops—bars, coffeehouses, etc.—specifically for their all-night clientele. Vlad and Nina had a special fondness for a little hole-in-the-artery place called Poe's and spent at least a couple of nights there each week, brooding and drinking blood out of giant cappuccino bowls.

"So sorry about that. And you know, this." Kale's bottom lip started to wobble as I prayed for her to leave so I could drop back into my blissful dreams about sexy men and not murder. But I was a pushover. "Come in."

She did and immediately flopped onto the couch. "I'm just so mad at Vlad. Did you hear what he did?"

"Allegedly," I mumbled. "But Kale, it's the middle of the night. You're eighteen. You should save the blowing up of ex-boyfriends for daylight hours, young lady." I stifled a yawn. "Besides, aren't your parents going to be worried about you?"

Kale waved a nonchalant hand and sniffled. "My parents won't even notice I'm gone."

"Oh, Kale, I'm sure that's not true!"

"No, I put an oblivion spell on them." She turned her watery eyes to me. "Do you think I'm doing the right thing?"

I looked over her shoulder. "If you mean burning down doors at three a.m., no. If you mean trying to make Vlad pay his debts by throwing fireballs and whatnot at him? Still no. Ditto on the magical parental lobotomy. What's all this really for, Kale? What do you want from Vlad?"

She sniffled again and used the heel of her hand to push the mascara-edged tears away. "I just want him to notice me."

"Well, burning things might get you noticed, but not in the right way. Why don't you try talking to him? Or, possibly sending him a nice, quiet text message?"

Kale heaved a weight-of-the-world sigh. "I don't

know. That's really subtle. Do you think it would work?"

"I think it's worth a try."

She looked at her hands in her lap, shaking her head. A fresh round of tears rolled over her cheeks. "It has to work. You're right, Sophie. I'm already nineteen. I don't want to be alone forever."

I bit into my bottom lip as Kale looked up at me with those round, earnest eyes. Eyes that truly believed that eighteen was, apparently, approaching the crest of "the hill" of which I was most notably over.

"I just don't know how you do it. You don't have anyone and you're still just so confident."

My left eye started to twitch. I pressed my index finger to it in a vain attempt at stopping the thrum. "You should probably head home now, Kale."

Kale nodded and touched my hand softly. "Thanks, Sophie. You're really wise." She stood up and brushed her palms over her jeans. "And again, I'm sorry about waking you up."

I swung the lock on the door and crawled into bed after Kale left, intent on getting at least another three hours of sleep.

I wasn't going to be alone for the rest of my life, I reasoned. *My life was very full with two incredible guys. One who was supernaturally bound to me and another who could never be truly happy unless he killed me.*

Maybe I should go back on Match.com.

I tried to drift off to sleep—tried counting sheep

and reciting the Gettysburg address, both usually fail-safe knockouts—but twenty minutes later my heart was still slamming against my rib cage and my whole body was tense, humming with adrenaline.

Kale was willing to show up in a shower of fire to get Vlad's attention. She is willing to cut off his head due to jealousy, I thought. *Yes, but she's a teen witch,* I reasoned. *With non-witchy hormones.*

I sat bolt upright in bed a second time.

Jealousy.

I grabbed my cell phone and counted the rings.

"This better be a matter of life or death, Lawson."

I took a brief, fluttering second to absorb the velvet smoothness of Alex's voice—even as it was throaty and gruff with sleep.

"How'd you know it was me?"

"A thrilling combination of good detective work and caller ID. To what do I owe this pleasure?"

I sucked in a breath and began pacing. "Sampson said you're working on the Mercy kidnapping case, too, right?"

"Strictly the aboveground part of it. No creepy-crawlies or bump-in-the-nighties. Why?"

"Have you interviewed the girls' friends yet? Cathy and Alyssa's?"

I could hear the mattress groan as Alex changed position and I clamped my knees together and bit into my lower lip, scolding myself for thinking of Alex, position, and mattress all in the same sentence.

"So, Alyssa's disappearance. What if it's not the

same unsub who snatched Cathy? What if it's something entirely different?"

"I'm listening."

"What if it's jealousy? Alyssa was popular and friendly, everyone seemed to like her. She disappears and two days later another girl is sitting in her seat. Her clothes are burned *on campus*. That could be very significant. What if another girl is literally trying to be her?"

"Wait, wait, wait. What is this about Alyssa's clothes being burned? And on campus?"

My chest tightened. "Didn't Will mention that earlier? He was supposed to call you." A flash of guilt washed over me and burned at the back of my neck.

Alex grumbled. "I don't trust that guy."

Ever since Will had inadvertently stabbed Alex in an attempt to defend my life, the two weren't so keen on each other. And my Freudian slip—or my tossing of Will under the bus as it were—wasn't helping.

I tried to appease my guilt by making a mental note that once the universe stopped vaulting into hell and raining down dead bodies, I'd throw some kind of bowling party or something so they could really bond.

But now wasn't the time.

"I think I was supposed to call you. It wasn't Will's fault." It rolled out in one complete string and Alex's silence on the other end of the phone did nothing to make me feel better about coming clean.

"Where did you find Alyssa's clothes? When? Who found them?"

"We found them. Today. In the Dumpster. They were on fire. Well, the Dumpster was on fire, but we were able to save some of the fabric. Enough to at least be able to figure out what it was."

"How did you know it was Alyssa's? Aren't all the girls pretty much in the same uniform? Did it have her name printed on it somewhere?"

"No." My stomach churned and I could feel the slightly warm plastic sole of Alyssa's shoe in my hand. "We found one of her shoes. Her name was written on that."

There was another beat of silence. Then, finally, "Lawson, this isn't a game. A girl's life is at stake."

"I wasn't trying to keep anything from you—"

It could have been an innocent cough, but I was pretty sure it was a derisive snort from Alex's side of the phone. It wasn't too long ago I was sitting in the passenger seat of Alex's squad car, lying to his face.

I gulped and muttered weakly, "I promise."

I could hear Alex processing the information. "Fine. But bring me the burnt uniform and all the information you have tomorrow. And no more conveniently forgetting to relay information. Deal?"

I nodded, knowing he couldn't see me on my end. "Deal."

"Now can I get some sleep?"

I chewed the inside of my lip, considering whether or not to tell him my theory. "No. My theory."

Alex sighed.

"You said you wanted me to tell you everything."

"And I'm already starting to regret it. But go ahead."

"Well." I sucked in a steadying breath. "A girl who is jealous of another girl can be ruthless."

"Ruthless, sure. But murderous?" Alex sounded skeptical.

"People have killed for a lot less. It's not like when you were—" I caught myself before saying "alive."

"So you're vetoing Sampson's witchcraft idea?"

I sat back onto my bed and pinched my lower lip. "Not exactly. I'm just throwing a theory out there for you."

There was an audible, painful pause and I held my breath until Alex spoke. "Look, Lawson, I appreciate the tip, but you're with Will on this, aren't you? Working the Underworld angle?"

I could hear a strain of something—annoyance? jealousy?—in his voice, but I couldn't recognize it. "Yes, but—"

"How about you two stick to your end and I'll stick to mine, okay? Physical evidence—anything other than black cats or pointed hats—is my end. Bring me the uniform tomorrow."

The sudden change in Alex's tone hit me like a ton of bricks. "Uh, well, oh—"

But Alex's phone hit the cradle before I had a chance to respond.

I was determined the next day would be better. Nina laid out my clothes—a kicky combination of two items that I never would have thought to put together matched with a pair of shoes that were edgy enough to be cool, but not cool enough so that I'd blunder like an idiot and fall all over myself.

Nina was puttering in the kitchen when I walked in. She beamed when she saw me, her fangs tinged a faint raspberry red from her breakfast—O neg, I figured. Her face fell when I came closer.

"You look simultaneously ab fab and like your puppy just died." She immediately clapped a hand over her mouth, her eyebrows quirking. "Oh, no," she let out an aching whisper. "Not ChaCha."

At the utterance of her name, ChaCha came prancing in, nuzzling up to Nina. She scooped him up, chirped, "Oh, thank God!" then turned to me. "Then, what happened to you?"

I yawned and filled a Big Gulp cup with coffee. I craned my head over the kitchen pass-through and found Vlad—as always—perched behind his computer screen. "Last night while you guys were out gallivanting I had to deal with the ghost of Vlad's girlfriends past."

Vlad's eyebrows shot up over his laptop screen. "Kale?"

"Are you insinuating that there could be someone else blowing our doors off at three a.m.?"

Vlad shrugged and went back to sucking CGI blood.

"Anyway, Kale's easy enough to deal with. There's this popular girl at my school. I swear she's hell bent on making my life miserable."

Nina sat down across from me. "What'd she do?"

"Nothing. But you know the type. Super pretty, evil. Her name is Fallon."

Vlad choose that minute to walk into the kitchen and snatch himself some breakfast. "Fallon." He tried out the name, rolling it on his tongue. He must have decided he liked that because he nodded with a self-satisfied smile.

"She's evil and she must be stopped."

"Why don't you hit her with a spit wad?" Nina grinned while I poured myself a bowl of something non-sugar-coated and vaguely healthy. I took a bite and reminded myself that I was a responsible adult who ate responsible adult food and I would not be flustered by an oversexed sixteen-year-old in a push-up bra.

"Oh! I made lunch for you!" Nina plunked a brown paper bag in front of me.

"Aw, Neens!" I pulled open the bag and peeked in: apple, hard-boiled egg, granola bar, something that looked like a sandwich. "This might be the sweetest thing anyone's ever done for me.

She grinned, looking every bit like a sweet, doting mother and I felt a twinge of sadness, knowing that she'd never be able to have—or be—that. I slung an arm around her neck and pulled her to me. "You're the best."

She tossed a handful of her perfect Pantene hair over one shoulder. "You'd better believe it."

Like a sweet, doting mother with fangs.

I got to school so early that I met Heddy in the parking lot and Janitor Bud in the hall.

"He's taking a leave of absence starting tomorrow," Heddy told me as an aside.

"Isn't that a little suspicious with a girl having just gone missing from the school?"

Heddy looked at me, indignant. "Janitor Bud has been with us for sixteen years. And the police did a full background check just to rule him out."

"And did it?"

I thought Heddy's eyes would explode out of her head with a trail of steam. I immediately started to backpedal, to open my mouth in an attempt to help Heddy simmer down, but she held up a single finger to me, her orangey lips pursed, eyebrows diving down. "And, he's had this planned trip for seven months."

I gave Heddy a moment, then licked my lips. "I wasn't implying anything, Heddy."

She gave me an over-the-shoulder harrumph and walked away, her sensible heels clicking down the pristine hall.

I went into my classroom, first flipping on the lights and doing my precursory "what wants to kill me?" scan, then dumping my things on my desk.

I was still feeling wounded from my early morning phone call with Alex. I let my fingertips ramble over the Ziploc bag of clothing that I hadn't had the courage to drop off on my way to work, then felt a hint of smugness.

I didn't need Will to babysit me and I didn't need Alex's help. I'd put the puzzle pieces together— alone—and I would find Alyssa—alive.

I sat at my desk, my back ramrod straight, hands clasped in front of me. I had each of the girls' files spread out on my desk, the girls forever locked in open-mouthed joy. I revisited everything I knew about both of the girls—both abductions—in an attempt to force some kind of structure.

There were no witnesses to either of the girls' abductions. The words "vanished" and "thin air" punctuated the reports, and each time I reread the words, my stomach, and my hope for finding Alyssa alive in the diminishing timeline, plummeted.

I sighed, resting my face in my hands, my index fingers rubbing small circles on each of my temples.

I looked up and scanned the files as if something would have changed.

It didn't.

I was biting my thumbnail and drawing little circles in my sparkly unicorn notebook when Janitor Bud pushed open my door.

"Oh," he said when he saw me. "I didn't know anyone was in here. Heddy said to bring these in." The old man pulled a cart weighted down with yearbooks into the room. "Where do you want them?"

I stood up and Bud paused, then took a step back. "You're not one of the regular teachers, are you?"

"No, no, I'm just substituting."

He had a kindly smile on his face. "You look awfully familiar."

I felt myself blush. "I was a student here myself. It was nearly fifteen years ago, but maybe—"

Bud wagged his head. "No, that's not it." His eyes cut from studying my face to the case files open on my desk. His smile dropped, his caterpillar eyebrows weaving together under his lined forehead. "Terrible thing about those girls, isn't it?"

I hopped up on my desk in an awkward attempt to cover up the files. "Did you know the girls?"

Bud paused as if thinking. "I know all the girls here. Well, not by name." He smiled again, one of those soft smiles that pushed up his cheeks into little fleshy balls. "Least I know them by sight. I know they were both good girls, though."

I leaned forward. "Good girls? What do you mean by that?"

"Didn't get in trouble much. Sometimes the girls come to me for punishment."

Something shot through me. I looked at this man and had an instant image of his grin, terrifying and maniacal as hellfires shot up behind him in his basement quarters while he did unspeakable things to innocent girls. I was about to launch myself from my desk and into his chest for a severe pummeling when he continued.

"They get sent to me for cleaning supplies and they have to come back and clean up any graffiti or muck in the halls and classrooms."

My heart flopped back to a normal beat. "Oh. That's how they're punished?"

Janitor Bud shrugged. "These girls aren't like us, hon. Some of 'em have never seen a broom. They don't like to see themselves as lowly folk like us. Put a mop in their hand and put them on display. Some of those girls will do anything to avoid ending up on my spray gang." He pulled a spray bottle filled with blue liquid from his belt and pretended to shoot me. I could hear his laugh as he disappeared into the hallway.

I slid back into my desk chair and pulled my notebook closer to me, writing *Suspects* at the top of a blank sheet, with the name Janitor Bud right underneath. I chewed the top of my pen and wrote, *Spray Gang*. I felt quite accomplished and sleuthlike until I realized I had absolutely no idea how Windex and Janitor Bud fit into a ritualistic murder.

Feeling defeated, I pulled Bud's cart of yearbooks closer and grabbed the one on top, paging slowly. I was looking at six smiling girls in a makeshift pyramid when a thought hit me. In a *CSI*-fueled stupor I remembered reading that in cases like this one, leads often come up well after the fact. Details that weren't really anything—a slight memory of a car that looked out of place, a couple of kids rifling through a backpack they found shoved in the trash, a rivalry, a crush.

I went back to the file, shaking it now, willing something to fall out—a name, a location—anything that would rev me up, start me off, point me in any discernible direction. There was nothing. No screams. No strangers. Had Cathy known her attacker? Did Alyssa know her kidnapper? Trust him? It made my skin crawl just to consider the thought.

"Brought you a cuppa."

Will's cheery entry practically emptied my bladder and sent me to the ceiling. I clutched at my chest and tried to breathe.

"Holy crap, Will, you scared the crap out of me."

Will stood there, holding two steaming paper cups, his brow furrowed, eyes sympathetic. I wanted to run to him and throw my arms around his neck, telling him it was okay.

I wanted something to be okay.

"Thanks for the coffee."

"You sure you're not going to go all meerkat on me again?"

I smiled and sighed, reaching out for the coffee. "Scout's honor."

Will cocked a brow, his sympathetic eyes going immediately sultry. "Scouts, huh? Still have that uniform?"

"You're disgusting. And I was just going over Alyssa's and Cathy's files."

"That's what you needed to do so early this morning? Love, you know we're partners, right? This isn't a competition. We're supposed to share information."

I took a big swig of coffee and held up my hand, stop-sign style. "Don't worry. If this were a competition, we'd both be losing. Big, fat losers."

"Speak for yourself."

I snapped my fingers. "Hey, what are you doing after work school today?"

Will grinned. "I think I'm about to get an invite to the ice cream store."

I rolled my eyes. "No. You're getting an invite to go to Alyssa's house with me. And to Cathy's."

"Haven't the police already done that?"

I sucked in a sharp breath. "Yeah, but maybe

there is something we can see that they didn't. You know, maybe take an Underworld kind of look at some overworld kind of evidence."

It sounded good and supernaturally detective-like when I said it out loud, even though I really had no idea what Will and I could possibly find that the entire SFPD couldn't—magically veiled or otherwise.

I just knew we had to do *more*.

Will looked over my shoulder and poked Cathy's picture. "Isn't that like the pin that we found?"

I pulled the photo closer to me. There was a little lock-shaped pin—key and all—attached to Cathy's collar. "Lock and Key pin."

Will sipped his coffee. "Coincidence?"

"Probably. It's a big club. Everyone wants to be in it." I brushed my fingertips over the photo of the pin. "All the popular girls already are."

"So, our two girls were in the same club. Maybe we should figure out who else is in the club."

I closed Cathy's file and sighed. "Why bother? It's an academic club. People aren't killing to get in. And we already know the girls knew each other— they went to school together and it's a small school. Everyone knows everyone. I just think we might be wasting our time."

"You don't think it's worth our time?"

I stomped my foot, getting frustrated. "I feel like we're not doing enough to help Alyssa. Actually, we're not doing anything! At least the police are out there actually *looking* for her. I'm teaching a bunch of over-privileged stuffed bras about things they'll never care about."

"Seriously, love. Move on. High school is over. And how do you know what the police are doing? Talk to Alex?"

It was nearly imperceptible, but something flashed in Will's eyes when he said Alex's name. Something that clearly indicated how much he loathed him.

"No. Sampson told me." I didn't want to tell Will about Alex and my last conversation. About the fact that I had speed-dialed Alex twice since and twice gotten his voice mail. I was thrilled to see he called me back while I was in the shower, then crushed to hear his sterile, "I'll come out and pick up the uniform if you can't drop it by." No hello, no good-bye, just a click at the end of the message.

"And he said someone is coming by today to pick up the clothes we found in the Dumpster."

Will picked up the plastic bag, giving the uniform a cursory look before he laid it on my desk just as the first morning bell rang. He stepped into the hallway and I heard the first chirps of adoring greetings from the girls.

"Good morning Mr. Sherman."

"Hi, Mr. Sherman."

"Oh my God, is that a Mercy uniform?"

My eyes widened as Fallon appeared in the doorway, then made a beeline for my desk, snatching up the bags.

"It's all burnt. Where—oh my God—is this what was on fire in the Dumpster? Is it Alyssa's?"

I leaned a hip against the desk, crossed my arms in front of my chest. "What would make you think this belongs to Alyssa?"

Fallon suddenly seemed to realize that it was me, the repugnant substitute teacher, in her presence. She looked up, narrowed her eyes, and held her lips in something akin to a smile—or a sneer.

"Because Alyssa always wrote on her shoes." She held the bagged sneaker out toward me; I snatched it out of her hand.

"Were you good friends with Alyssa?"

Fallon matched my stance, crossing her arms in front of her chest. She kicked out a hip. "Am I a suspect or something?"

I shrugged, trying desperately to maintain my cool. "It was just a question."

Fallon shrugged back. "We knew each other."

"Is there a reason you're sitting in Alyssa's desk all of the sudden?"

Fallon seemed taken aback for a short second. Then she blinked, iceberg coolness floating over her once again. "I just sat down in an empty seat."

The second bell rang and Fallon cocked her head, listening until it ended. "This was fun. I'll see you in sixth." She gave me a little finger wave and flipped on her heel, her skirt and her thick black ponytail swaying behind her.

When the lunch bell rang, my last class practically toppled over each other trying to put distance between me and their Mercy skirts. I tried not to take it personally and tucked my head into Will's classroom, where every desk was still filled, each girl in rapt, awed attention. Not a single mascaraed eyelash blinked. Not a single pair of pursed, newly lipsticked lips parted. The silent air was thick with baby animal magnetism. I saw Will pacing in front of the chalkboard and groaned, then yipped when my cell phone vibrated wildly against my hip.

"Uh, Sophie Lawson," I whispered into it.

"Sophie, it's Officer Romero. You have some evidence for the Alyssa Rand case?"

My previous uselessness broke into a wave of validation and I actually smiled. I slipped into the ladies' room, doing a quick check for feet under the stalls as any good detective who was consulted by a major police force would. "Yeah. Did Alex tell you about the theory? I think I might actually have a little more to add if you want me to come by—"

Romero coughed lightly. "I'm here at Mercy to pick up some bagged evidence. Al—Detective Grace—sent me to pick it up. Do you have it?"

I felt like someone had punched me in the stomach. "What?"

"I'm in the front of the building by the main doors."

I blinked, still struggling to catch my breath. I knew Romero. Romero knew me. Romero even know *about* me—well, as much as he could know without his life being threatened. I believe I was listed on his Rolodex as *Sophie Lawson, Call When Weird/Unexplainable Things Happen.* And now he was acting like he didn't know me. Like we hadn't stood shoulder to shoulder on a crime scene just a few months ago. He was suddenly all business.

Just like Alex had been.

I cleared my throat. "Yeah. Let me just go back to the classroom and I'll meet you. Right out front."

Romero was in full uniform, pacing the steps outside the main door. He gave me a curt nod when he saw me and held out his arm. I held the uniform against my chest.

"Alex sent you?" I asked him.

"Yes." He gave me one more curt nod and avoided my eyes.

I put a hand on his arm and finally, he looked at me, discomfort all over his face.

"Is everything okay, Romero? You know, it's actually lunch hour here if you want to grab a sandwich across the street or something. We could talk." I tried a cheerful smile. "My treat."

"Actually, Ms. Law—"

"Sophie."

He cleared his throat and shifted his weight from foot to foot. "Detective Grace asked me to get the evidence and come right back to the station."

I hung back and popped out a hip. "Did you guys come up on a big lead or something?"

"Look, Sophie, you know I can't talk about an active case with a civilian."

"That never stopped you before. And we both know I'm not just a civilian. I work with Alex."

Romero looked at me then, a flash of hopefulness going through his eyes. "So you're back?"

"Back from where? I didn't go anywhere."

His cheeks went red.

"Romero, tell me what's going on."

He held up his hand. "Look, I don't want to get involved. I'm just doing my job. Alex sent me here to get the evidence from you and come back to the station. He said I'm not supposed to talk to any civilians about the case—"

I opened my mouth, but Romero rushed on.

"Especially Sophie Lawson. He said you two weren't working together anymore."

Relief flooded over me and I batted at the air. "Oh! On this case. He meant we're not working together on this case. But it's not like we're not friends—er, colleagues. We're just working different angles."

"All he said was he needed to disconnect from you. I've really got to get back to the station." Romero put out his hand again, and this time I didn't hesitate handing over the burnt uniform. He may have said good-bye to me, but I didn't remember. Suddenly everything was in a fog and my ears were full of cotton or rushing blood or whispers—just full of something that wouldn't let me process anything like a normal human being.

Alex wanted to *disconnect* from me?

Everything inside me ached. I slipped into an alcove and dialed his number. There was no answer—I expected as much—so I dialed the station and asked to be patched through. The dispatcher didn't ask my name.

"Grace."

"Romero was just here."

I could hear Alex suck in a slow breath. "Did you give him the evidence?"

"What do you mean, you want to disconnect from me, Alex? What is this all about? Is it just this case? Are you jealous because I'm working with Will?"

"Lawson, this isn't the time—"

"Then when is the time, Alex? When I try and call you again and you ignore my calls? When someone else drops dead?"

"Lawson, you don't understand. Things are—"

"Things are what?"

"They're complicated."

I didn't try to hold back my splitting laughter. "Really? Really? That's your excuse. Things are complicated. When have they not been complicated? I'm the freaking Vessel of Souls. You're a fallen angel. Your whole job is to kill me."

Alex didn't say anything, and suddenly every inch of me was on fire. My heart was thundering through my rib cage.

"You *want* to kill me now?"

"No. Of course not. That's not it. I just can't talk about this here."

"Were you not with me six months ago? Were you not the one who slapped the Some*bunny* loves you hat on my head?"

"Lawson, it was just a hat."

"This isn't about the headwear," I spewed, tears breaking over my cheeks. "I picked you, Alex. I pick you. I'm not with Will. I thought you knew that. You. I want to be with you." My voice was choked with big, body-wracking sobs. "I pick you."

"Yeah." Alex's voice was soft but edged with something distant, something cold that I didn't recognize. "Do us both a favor, okay? Don't."

The sound of his receiver clicking into the holder reverberated in my head over and over again.

I slipped into one of the upstairs bathrooms and locked myself in the handicapped stall in the back corner, crying until my chest hurt. After blowing my nose through an entire roll of toilet paper, I had mostly gotten a hold of myself and was about to put my feet down—I had braced myself against the stall—when I heard the ladies' room door open and snap shut. Someone was panting like they were out of breath—or like they were about to cry.

I held my breath and glanced under the stall long enough to see a pair of white socks slouching into a pair of well-used sneakers. Their owner let out a half-scream, half-grunt before breaking into a torrent of huffing tears—not unlike my own. I was about to open the stall door and offer some help when the crying abruptly stopped. The sneakers turned and headed directly toward me.

My mind raced. I couldn't spring out on the girl now that I had witnessed her obviously private moment. I thought about coughing or flushing the toilet when the sneakers veered left. There were a few short grunts and pants, then the sound of something hitting toilet water. I cringed. The toilet flushed. The sneakers went tearing out of the bathroom, the door snapping shut and leaving me with the sound of rushing toilet water. I quickly gathered my things, splashed some water onto my face, and hightailed it back to my room while I speed dialed Sampson.

I wanted to get out of Mercy. There was no coven, no witchcraft, no secret portal to hell on this campus and Will and I had now wasted the last two days—possibly the last two days of Alyssa's life—looking for paranormal activity when there clearly wasn't any. This was a normal school with normal school problems—girls crying in the restroom, cafeteria food that was as unrecognizable as it was awful, and queen bees who reigned with sneers and snarky one-liners.

I wanted to go back to work at the UDA. I missed my tiny, underground office with my perfect line-up of Post-it notes and pens. I missed Nina and Sampson and Vlad and even the hobgoblins with their constant fountain of oozy slobber.

And yeah, I even missed Steve.

"Underworld Detection Agency, this is Kale. What can I do you for?"

"Hi, Kale. It's Sophie. Can you put me through to Sampson, please?"

Kale smacked her lips and paused. I could practically see her mind working, weighing whether or not to ask me about Vlad.

"I don't know where Vlad is," I added.

The next thing I heard was a series of beeps while Kale put me through.

"Sophie! Tell me you've got something," Sampson said.

I blew out a sigh and caught myself, coughing so Sampson might miss my complete and utter dejection. "I was hoping you were going to tell me something."

Now it was Sampson's turn to sigh. "Everyone is coming up empty. The police force is stumped, there are no new clues, no fingerprints, no nothing. I was really hoping you'd find something,

Sophie. I feel like you and Will are the only chance Alyssa has."

I dug my teeth into my lower lip so hard I could feel the skin start to split. I didn't want to fail Alyssa. I *couldn't* fail her.

"I'll get ahold of Lowe and have him pull you out tomorrow."

"I'm really sorry, Sampson."

"Hey, if there was nothing there, then there's nothing there. We'll try and follow another lead."

I brightened. "There's another lead?"

"No."

The word hit me like a fist to the gut. "Um, can I call you back later?"

I didn't stay on the line long enough to hear Sampson's response because I heard the one sound that I would forever recognize since the first day it was burned into my own brain: a body slamming into a locker.

Chapter Five

Just down the hall from where I stood I saw the crowd and briefly wished for kick-ass leather and some kind of sword as I raced toward the students.

"Girls, girls!"

They scattered like billiard balls from a crack and left at their center was Miranda, eyes wide and terrified, and Fallon, lips pressed in a hard line, eyes sharp and accusing.

"What's going on here?"

Fallon snaked her arms in front of her chest but didn't take her eyes off Miranda. "Nothing, Ms. L."

"Nothing? Miranda?"

Miranda cleared her throat and pushed a fuzzy lock of hair behind her ear. "She's right, Ms. L. It was nothing."

"It wasn't nothing, Ms. L. I saw the whole thing." Kayleigh blazed down the hall, pointing. "Miranda shoved Fallon. I saw it. That girl is crazy—she needs to be expelled. And look, look, she ripped Fallon's shirt!"

There was a small tear at the collar of Fallon's shirt. She looked embarrassed or guilty—I couldn't tell which—and began pulling her long hair over her shoulder to cover it. "That happened a long time ago."

"So neither of you are going to tell me what was going on?"

Miranda and Fallon looked up at me and blinked. I watched the bright pink edge of Fallon's tongue poke out from between her pursed lips and slide across her bottom lip, leaving a glossy trail. "We told you," she said slowly.

My forehead started to pound and I pinched the bridge of my nose. "Okay, fine. Move on. You, too, Kayleigh. Go."

Kayleigh threaded her arm through Fallon's and tugged her away, throwing sinister glances over her shoulder and muttering to Fallon. Miranda's eyes were glued to Fallon's back and I could see her cheeks burn, her teeth clench. I put a hand softly on her shoulder.

"Ignore her, Miranda. Girls like that—"

"Only grow up to be bigger girls like that."

I smiled, despite my attempt to be adult and full of after-school-special wisdom. "Yeah, a lot of them do. Believe me: I know better than anyone what being bullied feels like. Especially because you don't fit in with the pretty girls or the popular girls or the smart girls."

I looked at Miranda hopefully and saw the crestfallen look on her face.

"Oh, no, not that I meant that you're not all of those things—pretty, popular, smart—it's just that, well, I was bullied in high school. Right here, in these halls." I pointed to the scuffed tile underneath us as though my tortured footprints would still be there as proof. "It was torturous and everyone hated me because I was different. And I stayed different. But when I became an adult, being different is what got me my job, my best friend, even my boyfrie—" I choked on the word, and the need to check my cell phone for a call I didn't hear or a text I hadn't read burned up my arms.

"You were a student here?"

I nodded quickly. "Yep."

"And your being different got you a job as a substitute teacher."

My mouth dropped open. My "being different" got me a job thirty floors underground and got me into a hell of a lot of scrapes. "Um, in a way, yes. You should probably get going."

Miranda nodded and stepped away.

"Oh, wait!" I swiped the book that had been laid flat on the floor, just behind Miranda's left foot. "You dropped this."

I held it out to her and Miranda's eyes shot over

it as though she'd never seen it, then up at me. I glanced down at the cover and my heart lurched.

"Protection spells?" I remembered my own desperation. I would have done anything to make myself invisible, to grant myself a few hours free from the demons in my high school hallways.

Miranda reached for the book and I eyed her. "If you need help, you need to tell someone. A silly book of spells isn't going to protect anyone."

She snatched the book out of my hand and shoved it in her bag. "I know," she said to her shoes.

I watched Miranda walk alone down the hall, trying my best to swallow the enormous lump that had formed in my throat.

"Everything okay, love?"

I jumped and grabbed at my thundering heart. "Oh! You scared the crap out of me. Someone should get you a bell."

"So you could ring every time you need your bell rung?" Will's grin was familiarly salacious, his hazel-flecked eyes slipping from my lips to my naked collarbone, to the cleave of my Nina-scaffolded breasts. I covered my chest and narrowed my eyes.

"No, that would mean that I would have a bell. And thanks, by the way, for ruining a very touching moment here. Have you dismissed your fan club?"

Will leaned against the bank of lockers, tossing a handful of peanut M&Ms into his mouth. "Can I help it if these girls are fascinated by history?"

I rolled my eyes.

"And your 'moment'? Saw it," he said, chewing. "Wasn't that touching? Nice with the 'I was bullied, too' stuff."

"I *was* bullied," I muttered, still staring down the hall.

"Anyway, ready to go? Oh." Will kicked at the ground. "Dropped this."

He handed me a receipt and I took it cautiously as though it were a snake about to bite. "This is a receipt."

"And this is a man, walking toward the door."

"It's from Simply Charming out in Marin."

Will shook another handful of candies into his mouth. "And I pegged you more as a Crate and Barrel kind of bird."

"Simply Charming is a shop for potions, spell books, candles. And this receipt isn't mine."

Will stopped then and turned, eyebrows raised. "So we have a witchcraft type killer and a receipt from a witchcraft type store."

"Yeah, but this must have fallen out of Miranda's book. She dropped a book of protection spells when she got in a scuffle with Fallon just a few minutes ago."

"So Miranda is dabbling in the dark arts?"

I put my hands on my hips. "No, Miranda was buying a book of protection spells because Fallon keeps bullying her and knocking her around."

Will came toward me, crushing the M&M bag in his hand. "And you don't find it the least bit coinky-dink that she went directly to a spell book rather than, say, the principal? Or her parents? Or a bodyguard?"

"We don't know that she went 'directly' to magic. She's probably tried everything else to get Fallon off her case and she knew if she went to the principal it would only get worse. She was probably too humiliated to go to her parents."

The rest of the school day passed uneventfully. After I scarfed the granola bar Nina had tossed in a paper lunch bag for me, I started topping each empty desk with the single-page pop quiz Heddy had delivered that morning. I paused when I got to the end of the room, brushing my finger over the carving on one of the last desks.

"Hello," I said, dropping the test papers and sliding into the desk. I bit my lip, still tracing the little round carving. I recognized it, but I wasn't sure from where.

After wracking my brain, I joined the twenty-first century and snapped a picture, sending it to Lorraine—my own personal witchcraft Wikipedian. As I waited for her response, Will poked his head into my classroom, did a quick sweep—obviously not seeing me in the back of the class—and sauntered in, snagging my cup of dry erase pens.

"Ahem."

Will made the exact same high-pitched yip that ChaCha made the time I had accidentally stepped on her paw. I broke down laughing, watching my collection of pens—cup and all—rain down on Will's head.

"Holy God, Sophie! There's a killer in our midst and you're trying your sodden best to add to the body count."

I sat back against the attached-chair's backrest and shot Will my best cop look. "Looks like murder might not be the only crime afoot. Why were you stealing my pens?"

Will strode toward me. "I think the real question is why weren't you protecting your pens?"

"You know that makes no sense, right?"

"Subject changed. What are you doing back here?"

I grabbed a few strands of my frazzled red hair and twisted them around my finger. "I'm waiting for Lorraine to call me back. See what I found?"

I pointed out the carving and Will craned his neck to look at it. "Looks like a circle."

"Look closer."

Will squinted, but obliged. "A circle with stuff in the middle."

"Really, you should share your brilliant powers of deduction with the world."

Will opened his mouth to respond, but my phone exploded into an annoying series of chirps. I glanced at the text.

"Circle with stuff in the middle my butt! According to Lorraine, that's a symbol of protection. It's usually found on talismans. The pattern is called

Luaithrindi, and these"—I drew my finger over each of the crossed lines—"are swords. The eight Ciphers of the Angels. This part where they interlock forms a—and I quote—powerful shield of protection."

Will crossed his arms in front of his chest. "So a girl goes missing a year ago. She turns up with carvings all over her body." He gestured toward the desk. "Do we know if this symbol showed up?"

I bit my lip and shook my head. "Not that I remember." My stomach roiled. "Not that I want to remember."

"One year to the day another girl goes missing. Her clothes are dumped and lit on fire. Same thing with Cathy?"

"No. I don't think Cathy's clothes were ever found."

Will pressed his lips together, using his index finger to tap his clean-shaven (a rarity) chin. "So, how do we know that this"—he mashed his finger against the symbol—"has anything to do with our case?"

I could feel the adrenaline beginning to well. "Sampson suspected witchcraft. We find a symbol of protection carved into the desk, and earlier today . . ." I raised my eyebrows, assuming he'd finish my thought.

"Earlier today what?"

Of course not.

"The book—Miranda's book of protection spells. She's afraid of something—or someone."

"So Miranda settles into her seat here in the back and carves herself some protection."

I stopped cold, clamping my mouth shut. Then, "This isn't Miranda's desk." I swallowed. "Up until last week, it was Alyssa's. Now its Fallon's."

Will cocked a smug grin. "Well, then I guess we know the school's not evil—just the students."

I blanched, thinking how any girl—especially one not even old enough to vote—could be warped enough to kidnap, murder, and maim, whether or not she thought she was a powerful witch or just wanted to be.

I rested my head in my hands and massaged my scalp. "At least, for the first time in years, I'm not the one they're aiming to kill."

"And now it's done." He threw up his hands.

I looked up at him; he stood with arms widespread, a look of clear disappointment marring his hazel eyes.

"What's done?"

"You. You are. You've essentially double-dog-dared every Vessel baddie in the known world to come take a swing at you." He shook his head, clucking his tongue. "I really didn't want to get these shoes scuffed."

"Fine. Change into your defensive shoes while I go to the bathroom. Then we're going to Cathy's house."

Will looked surprised. "On a bombardment mission?"

I rolled my eyes. "Her mother knows we're coming. I called her between classes and got her address." I produced the scrap piece of paper I had written the Ledwiths' address on. "There was no answer at Alyssa's, so we'll have to search her place another time."

Will left on a sigh.

My phone chirped just as I exited the classroom.

"Hey, Neens, what's up?"

"I have great news," she said, breathless.

"Really? Awesome. I could use some good news right now."

"Well, first things first, I dumped *UDA: The Musical.*"

A little starburst of joy shot across my heart.

"Aw," I said in my best that's-too-bad-voice. "What made you decide that?"

"I suck at writing music. And you know what rhymes with Underworld Detection Agency? Nothing."

"So . . ."

"So I have a new plan. And this one is legitimate. I am going to be writing, casting, and directing *UDA: The Documentary.*"

"Do you cast a documentary?"

"Sampson was muttering something about our need to drum up more business, so I thought what better way to do that than to advertise? And what better way to advertise than to make a commercial?"

I bit my thumbnail. "And the documentary comes in where?"

"See, that's the great thing. I'll have the camera people following me while I make the commercial. Isn't that going to be incredible?"

I knew better then to remind Nina of all the enormous loopholes in her new project—she couldn't be seen on film; the clients, and existence, of the Underworld were supposed to be kept under non-major-media wraps—so I just gave her my most enthusiastic, "That sounds amazing!"

She paused for a beat, and I knew that she was biting her lip on the other side of the phone line. "Just one totally little teensy thing."

My hackles were going up and my tolerance was going down. "What?"

"I just may need to use the apartment for some non-apartment-related things."

I was imagining hobgoblin slobber soaking the carpet and blood spattering every wall—Nina was nothing if not incredibly theatrical and the documentary would be that times a thousand. "Like what?"

"Writing, storyboarding, meeting with the crew, casting."

A whoosh of relief went through me. "As long as

I don't walk in on you on the casting couch with some hot little actor, that's totally fine with me."

"You're the best, Soph."

I clicked my phone off and put a little hop in my step. Things would work out. We were going to find Alyssa and solve this case and my alma mater would be no worse for the wear. High school was terrifying enough without adding a cache of teen witches—and Mercy didn't have any, anyway. I smiled to myself. By this time tomorrow I could be peeing in the comfort of the Underworld Detection Agency, right next to the tiny pixie stall, with Nina giving me advice from her perch on the sink where she stared at her non-reflection.

I was disgusted—yet slightly comforted—to see that the girls' room in the Junior Hall hadn't changed since my years of hiding from my tormenters there. The tile was still that same horrid, milky pink with once-white grout that had endured years of pens and fingernails being driven into it. I tried not to breathe in, lest the stench of canned potpourri and industrial-strength cleanser stick in my lungs.

I flushed, and was mentally picking out tomorrow's outfit when the overhead light started humming. It crackled, and my heart stopped beating while the light did one of those horror-movie flashes before going back to normal. I laughed at myself and yanked on the stall door, and nothing happened.

I jiggled the handle. I jiggled the lock. I yanked. I pushed. I pulled.

"Hello?" I called in the universal come-kill-me-now fashion.

The lights buzzed and flashed again, and heat zipped up the back of my neck. I started to panic, clawing at the cold metal door, kicking it, throwing my full weight against the chintzy lock. It gave at the same moment the lights went out. I stumbled over my own feet and barrel rolled onto the cold tile floor, gagging at the thought of bathroom floor touching skin and whimpering at the all-encompassing darkness. The room was pitch black and deadly silent, the only sound the heavy beating of my heart and my own open-mouthed panting.

And then came the sound. A bristling howl—primitive, inhuman—and deafening. I clapped my hands over my ears, trying to press the brain-numbing sound out, but it only got louder. I hunched down into myself as each stall door barreled open on its own accord, the metal slabs clanking against each other. The toilets were next—one, two, three—exploding pistols of water straight up toward the ceiling. A chilling blue light swirled with the water and I pushed myself up, steadying against a sink as water swirled around my ankles.

I gaped. The mirror was smeared with angry slashes of red, the words GET OUT scrawled across the mirror, hacking through my reflection. I was screaming and crying, tears and snot rolling over my chin, throwing my weight against the bathroom door when a heavy force pushed against me. My legs were matchsticks and I crumpled back to the horrible pebbled tile and Will looked down at me.

"Soph?"

In an instant the bathroom was bright and dry. The mirrors reflected the unscathed Pepto-pink stall doors and the only sound was the slight hum of the overhead lights and my own thrumming heart.

I could see that Will was geared to say something smart, but the second he saw me, he crouched down at my feet and pulled me to him, one hand on my shoulder, the other cradling my cheek. He thumbed a tear from the end of my nose. "What happened?"

I looked over both shoulders, expecting singing birds or a giant neon sign blaring CRAZY PANTS with an arrow pointing to me.

"There was, and then—" I sniffled. "Something happened in here, Will!"

Will stepped around me, poking his head in each stall, doing a quick check. He turned to me and shrugged, his expression surprisingly sympathetic.

"I—I don't know what to say," Will said.

I pushed myself up and used the heel of my hand

to wipe away the tears, then scanned the room myself from the safety of the doorway.

"Lights were blinking, and then they went out and there was—" I paused while Will studied me. I couldn't tell if he was listening hard or considering whether or not my family history of nuttiness and pure evil had seeped into my brain. "There!" I pointed to the ceiling, cocking my head. "There, you hear that, right?"

The ominous squeak-squeak-squeak sounded again. I grabbed Will by both lapels. "Tell me you hear that!"

Will slid his arms around my waist and carefully led me into the hall. His eyes were intense. "Yes, I heard that, too."

Part of me felt like collapsing in relief in his arms. The other part of me wanted to climb the length of his body and bury myself in his neck while we ran from imminent danger.

"What is it?" I whispered.

The triple squeak stopped, but my heart continued to hammer.

"Wait," Will hissed. "Listen."

Something heavy hit something hard. I could hear goo, something—blood?—sloshing and I started to heave. "That's a body. That's a body hitting the ground if I ever heard it."

Will took his hands off me and turned carefully.

"Go back into your classroom and lock the door. Don't come out until I tell you to."

I clung to his back, wrapping my arms around him and burying my forehead in the cleft between his shoulder blades. "No. No, no, no, no, no. I can't lose you, too. I won't sit by and watch you die."

He looked over his shoulder. "Thanks for your vote of confidence."

"There it is again!" I gripped fistfuls of Will's shirt and moved with him, my eyes clenched shut.

"This would go a lot more smoothly if you would let go of me."

"I can't." My muscles had seized up, my full body molded into the shape of ardent terror. "If I survive, I'm going to be in this position forever."

"Lucky me. Would you just—" He wedged his hand between my front and his back and I was forced to move a quarter inch. "I thought you were supposed to be some great crime-fighting asset. Weren't you learning to be tough or something?"

That's right! "That's right!" Adrenaline shot through my entire body and I imagined myself giving whatever terror awaited us the ass-kicking of a lifetime. I'd stake a vamp with the number-two pencil in Will's shirt pocket. I would stop a zombie with a head-removing scissor kick.

Squeak-squeak-squeak.

My bladder felt heavy, but I was ready.

Finally, I felt Will's body loosen slightly. He pulled my hands from his shirt. "This one's yours."

He stepped aside and I imagined myself jumping into my most Buffy-esque fighting stance before doing some sort of dive roll into a helicopter kick that would disable my attacker.

In actuality, I was crunched myself into a chair pose and held my fisted hands close to my sides, protecting my breasts. The smell of fear, adrenaline and fate hung in the air.

And it smelled like bleu cheese.

"Steve?"

Steve, the Underworld Detection Agency's resident troll and three-foot-tall stalker, grinned at me, baring all three of his snaggled yellow teeth.

"What the hell are you doing here? You almost got your ass kicked!"

"By him?" Steve motioned toward Will, who was doubled over, holding his gut, doing that silent, tears-down-the-face kind of laugh.

I wanted to slap him.

"What are you doing here?"

"Sophie needs Steve. Sophie is in danger, and Steve would never leave his Sophie in danger." He looked disdainfully at Will. "A true gentleman would never leave his woman in danger."

"I'm not your woman. And why do you have a bucket? Why—" Knowing—sickening, overwhelming knowing—crashed over me. "You're wearing a uniform. A janitor's uniform."

"Steve is undercover. Steve knows that's the best way to protect his woman."

Will stopped laughing and gasping for air long enough to say, "Does he always refer to himself in the third?"

"Steve does," said Steve.

"Okay, okay, wait. Both of you—wait. Steve?"

"Steve is filling in for the janitor on vacation." He looked at his bucket and frowned. "Steve doesn't like his job very much." He flapped nonexistent eyelashes. "But anything for my Sophie."

"Did you just start today?"

Steve nodded.

"So when you said Soph—I—was in danger, it was just general. You don't have any pertinent information, do you?"

A slip of Steve's forked black tongue washed across his bottom lip. "Steve always has pertinent information."

Will straightened. "Share it, mate."

Steve shot him a blood-curdling glare. "Steve only shares with his woman."

I pinched the bridge of my nose, hoping that would stop my new, suddenly pounding headache and the fact that my left eye was starting that twitching thing again. "Okay, Steve, what information do you have?"

He grabbed the wooden handle of the mop he had been slapping across the linoleum and pointed to the second floor with it. "Toilet's clogged."

I gaped. My eye twitched. "That's your pertinent information?"

"Steve fixed the clog."

Will blew out an annoyed sigh. "Fabulous. You've exorcised the crap out of the toilet." He clapped. "Brilliant job, mate."

"Steve, we don't have time for this. Will and I need to—"

"Doesn't Sophie want to know what clogged the toilet?"

I felt myself blanch. "Not especially."

He poked his mop into his bucket and laboriously fished out a sopping wet sweater. "Not even if it was this?"

I took a step closer. "Is that a sweater?"

Will took a step closer. "From here?"

Steve flicked the sweater end of the mop in Will's direction. "For Sophie's eyes only."

"Fine, Steve. It is a Mercy sweater," I told Will over my shoulder. "Where did you get this?"

"Steve feels like he's sharing a lot of information."

"Of course. What do you want, Steve?"

Steve puckered up. "Little kiss?"

"Not if you pulled Jesus himself out of the toilet."

Steve narrowed his eyes and started to sink the sweater again.

"Wait! Wait! I've got something even better. A kiss is so fast. It just comes and goes—"

"Not when Steve kisses."

I let that roll off me and kept going. "This is way better." I fished a tube of lip balm out of my pocket and held it in the palm of my hand. Steve poked his head forward, then tentatively came around his bucket, pulling my hand just under his nose.

"Lipstick?"

"Better." I uncapped the balm and spread it across my lips. "Lip balm. I use it everyday. All the time. If you take this, it's like your lips will be touching my lips all the time."

Steve cocked his head.

"That's awfully sexy. If the little man here doesn't want it—" Will went to reach for my hand, but Steve rolled up on his tiptoes, yanked the balm from my hand, and squirreled backward with it tucked against his chest. He glared at Will. "Steve's woman." He uncapped the lip balm, rubbed it across his lips. I looked away as his eyes rolled backward and a little moan of pleasure emanated from his thin black lips.

"Where'd you get the sweater, Steve?"

"Someone tried to flush it down the toilet in the bathroom upstairs." He rolled the balm over his bottom lip and closed his eyes. "Sweet kisses."

"The upstairs bathroom? When?"

"Sweet, sweet, Sophie kisses."

"When, Steve?"

He cracked open one eye. "After lunch. Took Steve a while to get it out. Not because Steve is weak." His eyes flashed open, panicked. "Because water is strong."

"Which toilet?"

"Huh?" Will asked.

"Which toilet was that stuffed in?"

Another swipe of the lip balm. Another ecstatic roll of his eyes. "Second from the wall. Next to the handicap."

I dug through my purse and yanked out a travel bag, covering my hand, plucking out the sweater and dropping the sodden thing into it. "Thanks, Steve. You're the best! Let's go, Will."

Once we were clear of Steve and the high school, Will turned to me. "So you traded some ChapStick for a toilet-soaked sweater? That's—that's horrific, love."

"No—I mean, yes, it's gross—but I was there, Will. I was there when this sweater was flushed."

Will looked mildly impressed.

"I was in the upstairs bathroom and someone came in. She was crying, but it sounded like she was angry. She screamed a little bit and then went into the stall next to me and I heard her throw

this"—I pointed to the bag holding the sweater—
"in."

"You heard it or you saw it?"

"I heard it because she—well, she didn't know I
was there in the bathroom. But I know I heard it.
She wasn't going to the bathroom because her feet
were facing the wrong way and it didn't sound like
someone going to the bathroom. And she was wearing sneakers and socks! I heard something hit the
water and then she flushed. And I thought it
flushed for a while, but then I didn't really think
about it."

Will's impressed look went to one of slight dis-
gust. "I think this is the most disgusting clue we've
ever found."

"Well, we have to look at the sweater. We have to
find out who it belonged to."

Will grimaced. "You didn't recognize the flusher
by the shoes?"

I brightened. "Well, I can certainly narrow it
down that way. I know it was a student. Who was
wearing white socks and sneakers."

"Excellent. That cuts out approximately six
people. Well done, love. Now take a look at the
sweater."

"I'm not going to look at the sweater. You look at
the sweater. I already told you the information. So
technically, it's your turn to do something."

"You *happened* to be taking a pee when someone
walked in and may or may not have tried to flush a

sweater. It's really *your* investigation. You started it."
He gestured toward the bag. "You should finish it."

I chewed my bottom lip. "Okay, how's this? We'll
let it dry out a little bit while we go to Cathy's and
then we can both figure out what to do with it."

Will didn't look convinced, but he agreed anyway,
and started the car.

Chapter Six

The closer we got to Cathy's house, the further my heart dropped toward my gut. I couldn't get her mother's voice out of my head—the slow, sad way she spoke, the overwhelming sense of hopelessness even when I told her that Will and I were looking at her daughter's case with new eyes.

"I think this is it," Will said, jutting his chin toward the tract home in front of us that looked like every other tract home in the neighborhood. I swallowed hard, looking at the two front windows that seemed to stare back at me, two black eyes accusing, burning into my soul.

"Do you really think we should be doing this?" I asked.

Will swung his head toward me. "You told me you talked to the girl's mum. You told me she was okay with it."

"I did and she is, but"—I massaged my palm

with my thumb and stared out at the house—"I feel bad now."

"Isn't this the proper way to 'work a case,' as you say?"

"Yeah, but I just feel so—like we're taking advantage of Mrs. Ledwith. She sounded so sad on the phone and now we might be using her daughter's death to bring another girl home?" I shook my head. "It just doesn't seem fair."

Will wrapped his big hand around my elbow and squeezed gently. His eyes were soft, a lick of hair blowing over his forehead. "A girl dead, another one missing—none of this is fair, love. But if Cathy's death could help another family to not go through the same grief, don't you think her mother would want that?"

I shivered; the idea of death and kids had once been so blissfully foreign to me. I liked it that way. "Yeah, I guess so."

I followed Will up the walk, still trying to assuage the guilt that welled in my chest. This was Cathy's house. Cathy had walked up this path everyday. Had her mother stood out here and waited the day Cathy didn't come home?

I was overwhelmed with a paralyzing grief. My stomach went heavy.

"You okay, love?"

I swallowed hard and took Will's arm when he offered it. I let him lead me to the porch. Cardboard boxes were stacked just to the left of the house's double doors. I squared my shoulders and rang the bell while Will peeked in the top box. "Kitchen stuff. Looks like someone is moving."

Julia Ledwith pulled open the door and offered Will and me a close-lipped smile. "You must be the investigators."

Will looked at me, slight question in his eyes, but went with it.

"You're Mrs. Ledwith?" he asked.

She opened the door wider and ushered us in, pulling on the neck of her faded Stanford University sweatshirt. "Actually, it's Ms. Foley, now, but you can call me Julia. Can I get you both something to drink?" Without waiting for an answer, she turned and left us standing in the foyer.

I did a quick scan of the entryway and dining room before us. Both were nearly bare and scrubbed clean, each with its own stack of carefully labeled cardboard boxes in the center.

Julia came back with two glasses, handed us each one, and looked around as though she had just noticed her surroundings.

"Oh, I'm sorry," she said. "The place is a mess. I'm moving, so . . ." Both her words and her eyes trailed off, her eyes scanning the walls, our clothes, looking anywhere except directly at Will or me. "We can sit in the kitchen."

A thick fog of uncomfortable silence set over us as we sat at the kitchen table. I sipped at my lemonade and wished that I were anywhere else on the planet, Will took in his surroundings, and Julia stared into her cup.

"Nice place here," Will said. "Had you been here long?"

"Sixteen years," Julia said without looking up. "It's too big now without Cathy. And Peter and I"— her shoulders slumped—"we're divorcing."

I shot Will a murderous look when Julia's voice cracked.

"I'm sorry," I said soothingly. "I'm sorry we have to be here and bring all this up again."

"You're not bringing anything up. It's not like 'it' has gone anywhere." She laughed, but there was no humor in it. "Do you want to know about the day she went missing?"

I was taken back at the abruptness of Julia's question. This woman who moved slowly, looked about questioningly, suddenly sounded like she was asking us if we wanted to see her Avon catalog. The lemonade I had been sipping burned at the pit of my stomach. "Yes. Please."

Julia cleared her throat and set down her glass. "There was nothing special about that day. Not a single thing. Cathy got up, got dressed, came downstairs. She probably poured herself a bowl of cereal and we probably glared at each other across the table as she ate it."

"You two had problems?" Will asked.

"What mom and her teenage daughter don't? It was nothing really terrible—I would ask her to do

things and she would tell me I was ruining her life."
Julia smiled, her eyes becoming glassy. "I drove her
to school, she got out of the car and—and"—she
looked down at her hands, sniffling—"that was
the last time I saw her."

"Again, Ms. Foley—"

"Julia, please."

"Julia, I'm sorry," I said, licking my lips. "I am
sorry to have to—"

Julia waved her hand. "The cops have been over
this a hundred times, but if anything helps save—
save another little girl . . ."

"Did Cathy have any problems at school?"

"Her grades were exceptional."

I edged forward. "Was Cathy in any clubs on
campus?"

Julia's smile was genuine. "What club was that
girl not in? She cheered, she sang, she was president of the French club—she even did animal
rescue on the weekends. Ran bake sales and things
at school to pay adoption fees. When it came to ex-
tracurricular activities, there was nothing she didn't
do. She was interested in so many things."

Julia's eyes teared up and she pressed a napkin
to them, then coughed. "Sorry."

I put my hand on her arm, my heart in my throat,
my gut reaction demanding that I find Cathy's killer
and Alyssa's kidnapper right now, today, and skin

him alive. Every muscle in my body was taut, alert, and the anger pricked under my skin.

"How about with other students?" Will asked. "Was she ever bullied, or, did she ever mention anything about having a hard time with some of her schoolmates?"

"No, no. Cathy got along with everyone. I mean, there were always little tiffs or 'drama' as the girls say—said—within her social circle, but nothing out of the ordinary."

I perked up. "Her social circle? Do you remember the girls she hung out with?"

Julia nodded. "Kristy Thomas. Kelly Peck. It was mainly the three of them. Kristy and Kelly have both gone off to college now. Oh, there was a new girl, a younger girl that used to tag along, too. She had a different name."

"Kayleigh?" I asked, my breath catching in my throat.

"No. Uh, Faith. No, that's not right. It was—Fallon—that's right, Fallon. Real pretty girl. Pretty standoffish, though. Didn't seem very friendly. Cathy said she was just shy. She was like that—would take girls under her wing who were new or she thought were having a hard time."

It was hard for me to imagine Fallon ever having a hard time at anything.

"She and this Fallon girl got very close." Julia's lips pressed against her gritted teeth and I could tell she was fighting not to cry. "Fallon came over once after—after. She brought flowers—Stargazer lilies, Cathy's favorites. She was very upset. I remember she went up to Cathy's room and curled up on her bed, crying. Then she fell asleep. I didn't have the heart to wake her. She was gone the following morning. She left a nice note, though."

I straightened. "A note? What did it say? Did you keep it?"

Julia nodded and stood, staring at the stacked boxes with her hands on hips. She skirted them all and pulled open a drawer of a curio cabinet.

"I don't know why I kept it," she said as she sat back down. "It's silly, I guess."

"No, not at all. May I see it?"

She put the folded piece of binder paper—one edge frayed from the spiral binding—into my hand. I unfolded it, my heart pounding, the blood pulsing in my ears. Will slid his chair closer to me; I could feel his shoulder brush mine.

Dear Mrs. Ledwith, I read silently. *I am so sorry for all the pain and grief you must be feeling right now. I wish I could bring Cathy back for you—for all of us. I loved her. I wish I could have done more. I should have done more.*

The breath that caught in my throat was now sucked out of my body along with all the air in the room. I shot Will a knowing glance, but he was too busy pushing the ice around in his cup to register my silent *Aha!*

I refolded the note carefully, blinking hard to hold back the tears.

"I don't think I can tell you much more, unless you want to know about the—the day she was fou—"

"No, no, that's okay, we don't need to—"

"Have you packed up Cathy's room as well?" Will asked, his accent ricocheting around the room—and knocking through my head. I tried to shoot him my most demonic look, but, as usual, he was focused on something else.

"No, Julia, we don't mean to—"

Julia set down her cup and wrung her hands in her lap. "Actually, I haven't touched Cathy's room since—since it happened. I keep telling myself I'll get around to it."

"Do you mind if we take a look?" Will wanted to know.

"No, of course not. Top of the stairs. You'll know the one. I hope you don't mind if I stay down here."

I pushed the note into her hands and Will and I trudged up the stairs.

"Did you read that?" I whispered, my lips against Will's ear.

"Yeah."

"I don't think we should be looking through Cathy's room. I think we need to be looking through Fallon's."

"Why's that now?"

"Why?" I gaped. "Were we not reading the same note? 'I'm sorry.' 'I wish I could bring Cathy back'? If those aren't the words of a guilty conscience, I don't know what is."

Will and I stopped on the landing. He looked down at me, the sympathy in his eyes quickly chased out by steadying logic.

"I thought the note sounded very much like a grieving, guilt-ridden survivor."

"'I wish I could have done more'? 'I should have'? That's not admitting anything?"

"No, love, it's not. Maybe Fallon wishes she could have done more to help find Cathy. Maybe she wishes she could have done more to help the Led-withs grieve."

I let out a whoosh of air, putting my hands on my hips. My eyebrows slammed together in one of those *Really?* looks. "You really think *that's* what Fallon meant? You know her!"

"Not really. And I know even less of who she was a year ago, just after one of her closest mates was found murdered."

I knew, intellectually, what Will was saying made sense, but I was having a hard time believing it.

"But—"

"But she's a teenage girl, Sophie. Who you're accusing of killing her best friend."

I narrowed my eyes. "I'm not saying she killed

her, I'm saying that Fallon may have had more to do with it than you think."

"And I'm saying she may have had less to do with it than *you* think."

"You don't know teenage girls, Will. You don't know what they're like."

Will took a step back from me, his eyes raking over me in a way that made me feel exposed. "Those are your demons, love. Not hers."

I stood, silent, dumbfounded, wounded—and not wanting to admit that Will was right.

"Are you two okay up there?" Julia was standing at the base of the stairs, one hand wrapped around the wrought-iron bannister, one foot on the bottom stair. She pressed her toes into the carpet, and I could see the muscle flick in her arm as she seemed to toy with whether or not she would take a step.

"You can't miss her door," she said, a slight catch in her voice. She turned and disappeared around the corner before we had a chance to answer.

Julia was right: there was no missing Cathy's door. It was the only one closed, the only one with any semblance of life—a big, glittery C nailed to it, a heap of hairbands choked around the knob. Will pushed the door open and sauntered inside, but I hung back in the hallway.

"Come on, then. What are you waiting for?"

I bit my bottom lip and Will turned on a sigh.

"Sorry about the demons crack, love. I just meant—"

"No." I held up a hand. "You were right." I eyed Cathy's door. "It just seems—wrong."

Will opened his legs slightly and crossed his arms in front of his chest. His eyes staring down at me. Whether the stance was his version of alpha male or Sigmund Freud I wasn't sure. "Why do you think it's wrong? We're investigators, remember?" There was the slightest hint of play in his voice. "We're investigating."

I toed the carpeted threshold. "I feel like we're violating Cathy's privacy. Her last bit of respite."

Before I could recoil, Will reached out and grabbed my arm, pulling me into the room. "With all due reverence for the dearly departed, we've got business to tend to and a rapidly pressing time line."

"Right. Yeah, sorry." I shook myself and did a three-sixty, my eyes sweeping the sweet-pea pink walls. Most of the paint was covered over with posters, photographs of smiling, beautiful teens, and glossy cutouts of sunken-cheeked models stomping down runways. Cathy's desk was cluttered with papers, makeup pots, and all manner of girlie tchotchkes—all except one thirteen-inch rectangle.

"What do you think went there?"

I brushed my hand over the blank spot. "A laptop."

"Was that mentioned in the evidence collection?"

I tapped a finger against my bottom lip. "Her backpack, I think two textbooks, a pencil case, and a notebook. Spiral not viral."

"We'll want to ask Julia about that. Are you just going to stand there or help me look for some clues?"

I raised my eyebrows. "Why, Will Sherman, when did you become a detective?"

He held up an admonishing finger. "Private investigator. Angel Boy is the detective."

"Noted," I said. "Don't you think it's even a little telling that Fallon was friends with both the girls who went missing?"

"Well, there are four-hundred-eighty girls in the entire high school. Everyone was pretty much friends with everyone, right?"

I snatched a picture of Cathy and someone who must have been Kristy or Kelly from Cathy's corkboard. Though she was shadowed in the background of the shot, I could still make out Fallon's low brows, the menacing purse of her lips. "Everyone may have known each other, but everyone definitely wasn't friends."

Will slugged an arm over my shoulder and pulled me to him, ruffling my hair and kissing me gruffly on the top of my head. "Aw, like a wounded bird."

I rolled my eyes and in my attempt to shove

Will and his lame attempt at comforting me, I dropped the photo. It wafted to the ground, fluttering just under Cathy's dust ruffle. I groaned, then dropped to hands and knees. I could feel Will move behind me.

"Did I ever mention—"

I swung my head and glared at him. "If you're going to finish that sentence with 'how much I love America,' I've heard it. You seem to become incredibly patriotic whenever my ass is in the air."

"Not just your ass, love."

"Even better. Hey." I swiped at the photo, then slid out the wooden box stashed behind it. "What's this?"

It was a plain rectangular box about the size of a jewelry box but with absolutely no adornment. I flipped it open and sucked in a breath.

"Oh. Well, that casts a bit of new light, don't you think?" Will said, pointing at the cluster of herbs in a plastic baggie. I picked up the bag, gave it a sniff, and frowned. "It smells like Thanksgiving."

Will took the baggie from me, squinted, then sniffed. "It's sage."

"You know about herbs?"

"Don't look so completely surprised. I can cook, you know."

"You store your cleats in your oven."

Will shrugged. "I said I *can* cook. I didn't say that

I *do* cook. So, is sage smoking the new black in SF? Or was our girl planning on cooking . . . secretly?"

I took the sage back. "No. Sage is used—especially bunched like this—to cleanse evil spirits from a room." I put the baggie aside and picked out a few other trinkets—another grouping of dried herbs with flowers mixed in, two orange votive candles burned down to the tin, and a quarter-sized charm hanging from a length of black satin cording.

"What is that?" Will said, taking the amulet end of the necklace in his hand. I chewed the inside of my cheek, my heartbeat starting to thud. "It's the symbol that was carved into the desk." I turned the amulet around and showed it to Will.

"Another girl who thought she needed protection."

Will pulled the last item from the box—a thin, fabric-bound book.

"That's the same book Miranda had," I said, taking it from him. "It's a book of protection spells. The exact same one Miranda had." I flipped it over, looking for some kind of discernible marking. "I wonder if it was from the same place." I could feel myself starting to chew on the inside of my cheek again and I shook myself. "Do you think Cathy knew what was going to happen to her? And if so, does that mean Miranda is next?"

Will took the necklace and the book from me, slipping them both in his pocket and slipping the box back under Cathy's bed. "Only one way to find out." He stood and opened the bedroom door. "Coming?"

"We can't just take that," I hissed. "It's Cathy's property. Shouldn't we at least tell her mother?"

"I think Julia has enough to deal with already," Will said without turning around.

It was nearly seven o'clock when Will and I left Cathy's house. I dialed Alyssa's home number, my stomach doing flip-flops with each ring. Finally, the voice mail kicked on.

"I guess we're out of the luck for the day, huh?" Will asked as we crested the Mercy High driveway.

I pinched my bottom lip, held up an index finger, and dove into my shoulder bag.

"What's that?" Will asked, gesturing with his chin at the thin book I pulled out.

I slapped on the overhead dome light.

"Hey! Careful! Nigella is a collector's item, remember?"

"A trash collector's item," I grumbled, trying to make anything out in the dim light. "Aha." I grabbed my cell phone and dialed the number. "It's the high school directory," I whispered to Will as I let the phone ring. "I'm calling Miranda."

"Why?" he whispered back.

"She could be next. She could be in danger right now."

Miranda's voice mail kicked on and I smacked the phone shut. "Damn it!"

"You don't want to leave a message?"

My eyes bulged. "Really? What would I say? 'Miranda, dear, this is your teacher. You're in grave danger, so try not to leave the house. Or maybe you should leave the house. TTYL!'"

"Well, I certainly wouldn't end with 'TTYL.' I was thinking more along the lines of 'can you call me when you get this.'"

I flopped my head back against Nigella's cracked maroon headrests. "I don't know what to do anymore, Will. I feel like we aren't getting anywhere. Maybe it's time to leave this one to the professionals."

Will was silent for a beat before he clicked off the overhead light. It took a moment for my eyes to adjust, and by that time Will had slipped my hands into his and pulled them close to his chest.

"You are a professional, love. The police department is doing what they're best at, and you're doing what you're best at. Sampson knows—this is not just about teenage girls. This is about witchcraft and you know how to deal with that."

"That's the thing, Will. Some toilets blew up. Some girls have spell books. What else proves that this has anything to do with witchcraft? And it is about the girls. We're looking for bedknobs and broomsticks and Alyssa is still missing."

He squeezed my hands and the warmth of his—his smooth palm, our fingers interlaced—shot a comforting warmth through me and I wanted to believe anything he said.

"We're going to find her, love."

Chapter Seven

Will and I sat in his car for a silent beat. My heart was hammering in my chest and I licked my lips, looking at the monolith of Mercy High in front of me. It was imposing in the daytime, but at night, barely highlighted by the silver slashes of moonlight, the building looked ominous, threatening. I half expected a flash of lightning to crack through the sky, an MGM warning that this particular building sat like a lightning bolt for all things evil.

"We need to go back in the building."

Will looked at me, eyebrows disappearing into his sandy hair. "Back into the high school? Why? We've checked it over twice."

I sucked in a slow, deep breath. "I don't think I was ready to see anything."

Will's brow furrowed and he pressed his lips together.

I rushed on. "I didn't want to see anything there

except for what I knew—in my head, in my—what is it? Repressed memories."

Will reached across the center console and took my hand tenderly in his. He cocked his head slightly and blinked, the honey-amber of his eyes warm and inviting. "You've never repressed a thing in your life, love."

I snatched my hand back and grabbed the door. "Are you coming or not?"

We stood in front of the glass double doors and stared, somehow both waiting for the ultimate evil to come barreling toward us or for a commercial break. The school remained silent, the double doors cloudy and revealing nothing, and there was no pause to regroup or offer some sort of cheery distraction. My heart was thundering in my ears and Will had been uncharacteristically silent the whole walk from parking lot to school entrance. A wind kicked up and a handful of skeletal leaves and garbage brushed past us.

"Ready?" I asked, my fingers closing around the administration key Principal Lowe had offered me.

Will shrugged and attempted to look nonchalant, but his eyes never left the keyhole. "I guess."

I unlocked the door and stepped aside, waiting for Will to push it open.

"What?" he asked.

I gestured. "You always open doors for ladies."

He cocked a brow. "I didn't know gender roles held firm even in the face of unspeakable danger."

I steeled my body and tried to sum up confidence I didn't feel. "What are you so worried about? You said yourself we've checked the place twice already and found nothing."

Will pushed open the door for me and I hesitated before stepping through. "Yes, but that was before your whole 'I see dead people . . . if I care to look' routine."

I huffed, crossing my arms in front of my chest. "I don't see dead people. I mean, I've *seen* dead people." I shuddered. "I've probably seen more dead people in the last two years than most people will see in their whole lives."

Will glanced at me before slapping a flashlight into my hand. "You're not the best at putting people at ease, you know?"

I flicked on the flashlight and shined the yellow bulb toward Will's face. "Hey, you're the Guardian."

He slung an arm over my shoulder. "And if there's a team of fallen angels lurking around this place, then you're in luck."

"Otherwise?"

Will flashed his light down the blackened hallway. "Otherwise? You're on your own."

"What a relief," I groaned.

"They don't pay me enough."

I rolled up on my tiptoes and glanced through the windows into darkened classrooms that looked as benign as they had during the day—desks in neat lines, unoccupied by witches, hobgoblins, or any other manner of creepy-crawly; stacked textbooks; glossy posters reminding girls to stay off drugs.

"I ask again," Will said as we approached the last room. "What exactly are we looking for?"

"I don't know, exactly. Just keep an eye out for anything that seems . . . off."

Will swung his light toward me, and I was enveloped in a bright yellow glow. I rolled my eyes.

"You're funny."

"You're off."

"Upstairs." I shined my light and took the stairs two at a time. By the time I crested the second floor my hackles had gone up. Something hung heavy in the air; there was a sort of buzz, a crackling electricity that hadn't been there before.

"Do you feel that?" I hissed over my shoulder to Will.

He just wagged his head, eyes focused on me.

My skin started to prick and I could feel the sweat start to bead at my hairline and over my upper lip. My heartbeat sped up, the thrum a solid ache in my chest.

"There's something here," I whispered, shaking my head. I clawed at my chest and pressed my palm against my quick, steady heartbeat. I was finding it hard to breathe. My eyes stung, and every muscle in my body perked, then stiffened. I felt like I was walking into something—something cold, something with icy fingers that walked down my vertebra bone by bone—something evil.

I paused and Will stopped behind me. I could feel his energy—warm and comforting—a hairsbreadth behind me.

"There." I didn't know when I did it, but I had turned and was facing a door, my arm extended, index finger pointing.

"We need to go in there."

Will obeyed wordlessly, slipping past me and pushing the door open. His hand went for the light switch, but I stopped him. "No."

I knew there was something in the room. I knew there was something that would be disturbed by the light. I clicked my flashlight off and Will did the same, the thin strips of moonlight coming through the window the only illumination in the room.

"This is the art room," Will said, looking around. "Haven't we been in here before?"

There were no desks in this room, just a circle of wooden easels surrounded by high stools. Some easels held canvasses in varying stages of completion, some were empty. There were half-canisters of paint, brushes scattered on a long table, nothing out of the ordinary. But still, something nagged at me.

"There," I said finally, pointing to a tiny scrape of white peeking out from underneath one of the easels. "Do you see that?"

Will's gaze followed the length of my finger, toward where I was pointing. "Nope."

I sighed, handed him my flashlight, and pushed the stool and easel aside. I could see another line now, thick, white, and arched, chalked on the floor. "You have to see that."

I saw him squint in the darkness, then sink down onto his haunches. "I have no idea what you're pointing at, love. It looks like cheap linoleum to me."

I groaned and pushed a few more easel setups aside, sucking in a surprised breath when I had uncovered an entire half-circle etched onto the floor.

"It looks like someone has made a chalk outline of a circle," I said, pointing again and now walking beside the arch. "You can't see it?"

Will shook his head, eyes still fixed. "I can't."

I frowned. "Help me push the rest of these out of the way."

He did as he was told, the look of confusion marring his features the whole time. "I'm sorry, I just don't see what you're seeing."

I stepped back and felt my mouth drop open. The front legs of the stools were set up on a large circle. The back legs of the easel were covering a slightly smaller inner circle, and inside that—a star.

"It's a pentagram."

Will swung his head yet again. "I'm sorry, Sophie, I just don't—"

I did a mental head slap. "It's veiled."

"Huh?"

I gestured toward the drawing. "It's veiled. It's been hidden—magically. I can't—you know—I can see through that stuff."

Will looked at me, and even though I knew that he knew that one of my "special" abilities is that magic can't be done on me—the characteristic also allowed me to see things hidden magically—I still felt weirdly exposed standing here in a high school classroom.

"You can't see it because it's veiled."

Will put an arm around me and pulled me to him as if he felt my awkwardness—and wasn't repulsed by it. The warmth of his body the length of mine was comforting.

"So, it's here." I pointed out the loop. I leaned down, brushed my fingers over the line. "And it looks like it's been drawn in chalk. Geez. It's—it's like the whole thing is vibrating."

The chalked circle looked almost animated— thicker, deeper than it should be, and almost as if the line itself were pulsing.

"It's definitely magiked. This isn't just a few kids playing with chalk." My stomach started to roil and the heat broke out again, all over me. "This is big, Will. There's more to this."

"Well, of course there is, love—"

"No. No. I mean this." I gestured to the circle. "There's more to this. Here. Now." I looked around the room. "I can feel it."

"Okay." Will's gaze swept the room. "So how do we deal with a 'feeling'?"

I chewed my bottom lip, then pulled my cell phone from my pocket.

"Tupperware, toads, or finance, this is Lorraine."

"Hey, Lorraine, it's Sophie."

"Sophie! You must have heard about the new salad spinners. They are ex—"

"No, thanks. I have a salad spinner, actually." Not that I'd ever used it. "I'm calling about a spell."

I heard Lorraine suck her teeth—whether she was angry about losing a potential salad spinner sale or the idea of imparting her witchy wisdom to me, I wasn't sure. I continued on anyway.

"I'm standing in front of a pentagram, chalked into the floor. But it seems like something—like something is underneath it, maybe? It's like it's pulsing."

"Ooh." Lorraine sounded interested. "It's active."

"Like in use right now?"

"Not necessarily right now, right now, but recently, likely. Or there is another more active one underneath it. That happens sometimes especially when legends of hallowed grounds brings out the fake teen witch crowd." She didn't bother to hide the disdain in her voice.

"Well." I pinched my bottom lip as Will pulled out a stool and perched himself on it. "If someone were to draw something on the floor and then erase it, is there some kind of spell that would bring it back up?"

"Um, like an anti-Mr. Clean spell or something? That's not really what we focus on—"

"No. If someone were to draw a pentagram on the floor and then clean it up. Like you said. Maybe one stronger than the other."

"Oh! Oh, of course. Anytime a circle is drawn in the earth it leaves a faint magical outline."

"Thank you! Will doesn't believe me." I glared at him as he bit his thumbnail, looking wholly uninterested.

"That's because he probably can't see it. If a pentagram has been used magically, it's veiled."

"Okay." I paced the perimeter of the room. "This one is really bright—to me, at least. Is there some kind of spell that could restore the other circle?"

"Oh, sure." I imagined Lorraine pressed back in her chair, scratching her hellacious cat Costineau between the ears. "Super easy. You're going to need four orange candles, some dust from the floor, and an eight-inch string."

I bit my lip, looking around the classroom. "I have two flashlights—one is almost orange, dust from the floor and"—I scanned, then brightened—"one of Will's shoelaces?"

"What?" Will snapped to attention. "These are my good shoes."

"Good shoes don't have laces," I hissed. Then, to Lorraine, "Will any of that work?"

"It's not perfect, but probably close enough. Place the flashlights torch-side-up on the opposite points of the circle. Sprinkle the dust in the center."

I relayed the instructions back to Will, who

growled at me, stomping around the room in one shoe, but did as he was told.

"Now you'll need to take the dust and the string—or shoelace—and go stand in the center of the circle."

A flutter of nerves rippled through my stomach as I crossed the threshold of the pentagram and found its center. "Okay, now what?"

"Sprinkle the dust and repeat after me: *Goddess Hectate, bringer of all we know, chants of the past bring a dazzling glow.*"

I slowly circled, dusting, and repeating Lorraine's chant.

"Now take one end of the string, and let it flow out as you circle, chanting." Lorraine cleared her throat and I did the same, pinching the string between my forefinger and thumb.

"Goddess footsteps shall never be stopped, bring me wisdom so I too may walk."

I stopped, Will's shoelace flopping to the ground at my feet. "Nothing happened."

"Give it a second," Lorraine said before hanging up.

"Well, that was quite a fun show," Will said, striding into the circle and snatching back his shoelace. "But—"

He paused, openmouthed, as a rumble emanated from the floor. I could feel the vibration through the soles of my shoes; it was as if hundreds of students were running through the halls.

I saw Will's mouth move, but any word he spoke was drowned out in the chanting wail that shook the walls of the art room. I couldn't make out one single voice or one single word; each blended into the others, creating a din so solid and loud that it pressed against my chest like a weight. A hot wind shot up, too, circling us.

I felt Will's hand slice through the air and grip me around the waist, pulling me so that my hammering heart was pressed up against him. A light kicked up—then a thousand lights—circling us and moving in time with the din.

"Oh my God, Will, look!"

The pentagram on the floor was slowly, painstakingly being formed. A line of chalk arched into the circle. Another one, slightly larger, moved faster. Star upon star upon star etched itself into the ground.

The etching sped up, the wail hitting an ear-splitting crescendo as the thunder of unseen footsteps shook every bone in my body. And then, as quickly as it had appeared, the sound, the movement, the hot wind, the chalk, all disappeared.

"What the fuck was that?"

I stared down at the circle around us. The lines were thick, heavy, well defined. My throat was suddenly dry and I tried to swallow, tried to talk, but my tongue was plastered to the roof of my mouth. Finally, I was able to point a single shaking finger toward the floor.

"It was them."

What seemed like hundreds of pentagrams—one on top of the other—were outlined around us. Some were exact, some were slightly skewed, but each had a point that formed a direct line toward the bay.

"You can see them too then?"

Will circled slowly, once hand clenched around his jaw. "Of course I can. There must be at least a hundred here. What is this? What is this room used for?" He gaped at me. "What the hell kind of classes do they teach here?"

I scanned the macabre graffiti, my stomach clenching with each new line. "I don't know. I'm pretty sure the only electives they offered when I was a student were jazz band and home ec."

When my phone rang, I went light-headed and Will dodged for the door. "It's only my phone. Were you taking off?"

Crimson washed over Will's cheeks. "I was securing the door to save you."

"Right. Hello?"

"So, did it work?"

It was Lorraine, and once my heart dropped out of my throat and into my chest, I spoke. "Yeah. Maybe a little too well."

"What does that mean?"

"There are pentagrams everywhere. The spell illuminated at least sixty—maybe more."

Lorraine paused for a beat. "Really?"

"Really. What does that mean?"

"It means that you're definitely not dealing with a couple of kids messed up with the occult. You're dealing with a legacy, Sophie."

I clicked the phone shut and looked at Will. He swallowed slowly. "So?"

"Lorraine says we're dealing with a legacy."

"A legacy? What does that mean?"

I picked my way across the room, careful not to step on any of the fading lines on the floor. My entire body ached and my skin felt pinpricked and tight. My heart dropped down to a normal beat, but the thuds were heavy and hard. "It means that Cathy Ledwith wasn't the first. And, unless we stop this, Alyssa Rand won't be the last."

I drove home with the heat blasting and the radio off, Will's taillights shining bright in front of me. Everything felt wrong—*I* felt wrong—and I tried a series of deep-breathing techniques I had seen on some late-night yoga set infomercial. Everything was churning in my head—was it the students or was it the school? Had other girls gone missing, girls we didn't know about yet? Who—or what—was to blame?

I was just starting to feel normal again when I crested the third-floor steps of our apartment.

"Christ."

And there it went again.

"What is this?" Will asked.

The little strip of public property between our apartment and Will's was set up like a waiting room, complete with a stack of long-expired magazines, my living room set, and the half-dead spider plant I had been trying to revitalize since the Bush administration. It would have been a nice little setup if I didn't have to throttle the arm of the couch and clear the coffee table to reach my front door, or, if it had been, you know, *inside* my apartment as it had been when I'd left this morning.

"Good luck with all that," Will said with a smug smile before disappearing into his furniture-on-the-inside apartment.

I groaned and grabbed my door, flinging it open. "Nina, what the hell is go—"

"Shhhh!" I was met by a chorus of angry hisses and then the business end of a megaphone as Nina yelled, "Cut!" directly into my face. She pinched her icy, bony fingers around my elbow and yanked me into the kitchen, which had miraculously gone from cozy mess to break room chic: our mismatched collection of hand-me-down mugs with unappetizing statements—*Carrie for Prom Queen, The Problem Is Gonorrhea*—had been replaced by an orderly heap of stolen straight-from-the-UDA Styrofoam stand-in mugs and brown paper napkins stamped with the Starbucks logo. Our sugar bowl was stuffed with pilfered packaged sweeteners and coffee stirrers, and bottled water bloomed from an ice bath in the sink. There was a hastily arranged basket of individually wrapped snacks that I recognized—basket, bagels, and all—from the Red Cross station on Second Street.

"What is all of this?"

Nina swept an arm toward the cleared out living room. "Auditions."

I scanned the room and frowned. "Auditions? For the UDA commercial?" I rolled up on my tiptoes and eyed the woman pacing my living room. She couldn't have been under five feet nine inches tall or over eighty pounds. She took short, careful steps, smacking a sheaf of papers against her bony hip as she spoke soundlessly, her eyes bright and batting, engaging the struggling kitten on my *Hang in There!* poster.

"Who is that?"

Nina produced a clipboard from somewhere and thrummed through a stack of eight-by-ten black and white glossies. "Um, that is Stella MacNeir. Don't you just love her?"

I pinched my bottom lip. "What department does she work in? I don't think I've ever seen her. Is she new?"

"Uh, new like just off Broadway."

I raised my eyebrows, impressed. "Like, Broadway, Broadway?"

"Like Broadway at Kearney, San Francisco."

"That's Big Al's porn shop."

Nina leaned through the kitchen–living room pass-through. "Thank you, Stella. We're going to wrap up for the day. We'll be in touch."

"Wait. You're auditioning people for the UDA commercial who don't work at UDA?"

"I need the best, Soph."

I gaped as Stella slid into a neon-pink leopard-print jacket and slipped one of my Frescas into her knock-off handbag before she slunk out the door.

"That's the best?"

Nina looked casually over her shoulder as though Stella would reappear, perhaps in even more thespian-slash-sex-store-worker glory. She looked back at me, using her index fingers to rub tiny circles on her temples. "Look, it's been a really long day. And we need Stella. You know how many actual Underworld employees show up on film? Two. Two! And one of them is a centaur. So as you can see, outsourcing this part was necessary." Nina's face suddenly brightened as her eyes slipped from the top of my forehead down to my toes.

"Unless . . ."

I stepped backward, mashing my hips against our cheap Corian counter. "No. Oh, no."

Nina framed me with her hands and grinned so widely, I could see the tip of her fangs and the tops of her gums. "Oh, you're perfect."

"No. I know what you're thinking and no. No, no, no."

Nina's arms dropped to her side and she pushed out her swollen lower lip. "You have no idea what I was thinking."

"I've lived with you way too long, Neens. I know exactly what you're thinking and the answer is a giant, loud, resounding, no. Scratch that—a no way in hell." I hopped up on the counter and plucked a mostly wrapped muffin from the Red Cross stash and eyed Nina, who said nothing.

"You were going to ask me to be in your commercial," I said then, fishing for a bottle of water to wash the sawdust muffin crumbs out of my trachea. "Right?"

"I was not!"

I paused, water bottle midway to my parted lips. "You weren't?"

"Oh!" Nina clapped a hand over her candy-pink lips as her eyebrows dove together in a sympathetic V. "Oh, now you're sad! Don't be sad! I can't believe I hurt your feelings. I didn't mean to do that." Nina paced dramatically while I looked on in wide-eyed confusion.

"Oh, honey, you know what? You're too important to me. I *am* going to put you in my commercial. You deserve, probably more than anyone, to *be* in this commercial. If anyone should be the voice, the image of the Underworld Detection Agency, it's you. It's Sophie Lawson."

"Wait, what? No, I—"

Nina held up a silencing hand. "Not another

word. It's done." She yanked me off the counter and toward her, my chest mashing into hers in an overzealous hug that nearly knocked the wind out of me. "You don't have to thank me, sweetie. You're my best friend. Of course I want to have you in my commercial. Oh, I feel so bad—it was almost an oversight."

She flitted out of the kitchen and I stood there, completely dumbfounded. "No, that's not what I meant. That's not—I don't want—"

But Nina was already out of the room and I was left with my day-old muffin and the *second* most horrible job in the world.

I shoved the last bit of sawdusty muffin in my mouth and upturned a can of something meaty and congealed into ChaCha's rhinestone-studded dog bowl, thinking that the only thing that could possibly alleviate the angst of high school and *UDA: The Documentary* was a hot bath and a cold Chardonnay. I drew my bathwater extra hot and sat on the edge of the tub, watching the steam waft up and coat the mirror in a fine, foggy mist. After adding a mammoth glop of coconut bubble goo and downing my first glass of wine, I stood in front of the mirror and wiped off the steam. I glanced over each shoulder and, finally, used my index finger to tap the edge of the mirror.

"Hello?" I whispered. "Gram?"

After my father abandoned me and my mother

killed herself, my grandmother had always been my rock, my one voice of sanity in an insane world. She was a seer, a mystic, and a regular at a mahjongg game that included a pixie and most of a centaur. She occasionally would pop up in shiny surfaces to offer me words of encouragement, advice, and the latest about Ed McMahon and the waffle situation in Heaven.

In our family, sanity was relative.

I tapped the mirror again, waiting, hoping. I hadn't talked to her in ages and I suddenly was feeling very alone.

"Gram?" I tried again. Then, desperately, "Ed McMahon?"

Nothing.

I poured another slug of wine and slipped out of my robe. I had a toe in my bathwater when I heard a little scratching tap. My whole body perked. "Gram?"

I rushed out of the bath and toward the mirror, my heart exploding with joy—she had answered! Finally!

I slapped that one dipped toe onto our old-school tile floor and went sailing. I saw the golden arc of my wine as it sloshed out of the glass. I saw my own bare feet as they slid out from underneath me. It was graceful, and silent. Soon the sun was overhead and my neck and shoulders were cuddled by something fluffy and soft. I had to close my eyes just for a second. . . .

"Ms. Lawson? Ms. Lawson?" It was a desperate, echoing whisper. I didn't recognize the voice, but everything inside me told me that I *knew* the voice. Something told me that I knew everything.

"Alyssa?" My own voice sounded weird—it echoed almost, like every syllable was bounding off a concrete wall and ricocheting through my head. I couldn't tell if the voice was inside or outside of me.

"Alyssa, is that you? I'm Miss—Sophie. Sophie Lawson. Do you know me? Let me help you. I can help you."

"Help me. Help me. . . please . . ."

I was panicked. I felt myself spin; I could hear the gravel crunch underneath my sneakers. "Where are you? You have to tell me where you are!"

"It's so dark."

I hadn't noticed that and suddenly I blinked. The darkness was all encompassing. I couldn't see my hands. I couldn't feel my limbs. I was sinking and it was suddenly getting hard to breath. Someone was squeezing my legs, my waist. Pinning my arms. Pressing against my chest.

"Alyssa!"

"She's awake now."

I sucked in a giant gulp of air that burned at my lungs and reached up, feeling my arms, my hands.

I was clawing, scratching, trying to get more air into my lungs.

"Whoa, whoa, just relax there."

It wasn't Alyssa's voice anymore. It wasn't dark anymore. The sun was overhead, beaming into my eyes.

"That's right, open your eyes."

"Will?" I squinted, then shivered, staring toward the sun. That was attached to the ceiling with the peeling paint. In my bathroom.

And I was naked.

"Ahh!" I kicked and squirmed, then yanked open the linen closet door and hid behind it. "What are you—" My eyes traveled over Will's shoulder to Nina and then Vlad. "All of you, what are all of you doing here?"

"We heard a crash," Nina said, inching around Will and handing me my robe.

"A loud crash," Vlad added.

"You had the door locked and you weren't responding. And I could smell blood." Nina's eyes were wide and terrified. She hugged her arms over her chest and I could see the edge of her fang as she nibbled her thumbnail. "I was worried."

I looked down and saw the blood smeared across the usually white bathroom tile. The grout was stained a deep rust color. "Where did that come from? Whose is it? What happened?"

Will pushed himself up from his knees and

crossed his arms in front of his chest. "Best I could tell, you were drinking and took a bit of a spill, landed smack on your back in a pile of glass and were murmuring about your grandmother, darkness, and waffles when I was able to get through the door."

"They called you?" I peered out from around the linen closet door. "You called him?"

Nina shrugged. "I couldn't open the bathroom door. I mean, I could have, but with the stab hole in the front door and the coat closet permanently smelling like Steve, I thought I should give Will a try first. Open things the human way."

Will grinned. "I used a butter knife. So what about the waffles, then?"

I gingerly touched the goose egg that was rapidly forming at the back of my head. "Nothing. No waffles. I—hey, how long was I out?"

Another shrug from Will. "Long enough."

"Was I naked the whole time?"

"I figured I could either save your life or your dignity."

I looked down at my left arm, which was miraculously bandaged, and tightened the belt on my robe.

Will nodded. "Couldn't risk you possibly bleeding out while I was choosing which panties you should wear."

"You're an absolute savior, Will Sherman."

He shot me an aw-shucks look, and Vlad and Nina went into the living room. I grabbed Will's sleeve just before he left. "I saw something, Will."

He turned and shot a salacious smile over his shoulder. "I saw something, too."

A shot of heat pinballed through my whole body, pooling just below my navel. "You're gross," I said, pulling a brush and dustpan from under the sink. "I mean when I was out. I could hear Alyssa calling for me. She knew I was looking for her."

Will took the brush and pan from my hands, crouched down, and swept up the remains of my wineglass. "How did Alyssa even know who you were?"

I shivered and pulled my robe tighter. "I have no idea. Maybe she just knew, you know? Knew I was looking for her."

Everything on Will's face told me that he was wondering whether to call the paramedics or the loony bin, but he surprised me.

"All right, then. Where was she?"

I bit the inside of my cheek. "That's the thing. I don't know. But it was very dark, and I felt confined. And it was echo-y. My voice echoed. I think."

"Did it echo like you were possibly mumbling while half passed out in a bathroom?"

Once Will was assured I wasn't going to pass out in the raw again any time soon, he went back to his apartment. Nina and Vlad went back to whatever it is vampires do, and I paced a bald spot in the carpet. Finally I sat down in front of my phone and stared at it.

"What's wrong, Sophie?"

Nina was standing in my doorway, her hip cocked against the doorjamb.

"I passed out naked on the bathroom floor."

"You and I both know that's pretty much par for the course for you." She stepped into my room and pulled me to sit on my bed next to her. "What's really going on?"

"I heard something, Neens." I explained, then looked hard at her. "Do you think I should tell Lorraine? Do you think it could have been some kind of spell or something?"

Nina paused, then took both of my hands in hers. "Honey, you're looking for a little girl."

I stiffened. "I know that. I'm not new to case-work—"

"Right. You're not new to chasing down killers and investigating dead bodies. This is a girl. A teenage girl. Alive."

"So what are you saying?"

Nina avoided my eyes and I pulled my hands from hers, tucking mine under my legs.

"I'm saying that your job is to investigate a coven at the high school. That's what you should be doing, not trying to find this girl. You're putting too much pressure on yourself, Soph. And also, you were passed out. In the bathroom. You hit your head. Don't you think it's a lot more likely that the voices came from you wanting so badly to help this girl, rather than from bathroom-tile-penetrating witchcraft?"

The funny thing was, it wasn't.

Chapter Eight

ChaCha was snoring away, making those little dream-doggy running motions with her tiny legs while I stared at the ceiling. Headlights from three stories down streaked across my ceiling and every time I tried to pull my eyes shut, they popped back open again, the voices in my head chattering, needling, telling me I was missing something. By 3:45 AM I gave up, clicked on my bedside light, and buried myself in my closet.

I found it behind an avalanche of polyester pants and Nina-vetoed hoodies, shoved in the farthest corner of my closet: a cardboard box, packing tape still pristine, the word SOPHIE printed across it. I sucked in my breath as bat wings flopped in my gut, then I pulled the tape off in one swift motion.

In the same instant, Nina was in my room, a quarter inch from me, staring down. No matter how many times it happened, I could never get over the vampire super-speed, super-stealth thing.

"God, Nina, you scared the crap out of me."

She flapped at the air, rolling her coal-black eyes. "I know, I know, I should get a bell. Just wanted to make sure you had your clothes on." She grinned, all Crest-white fangs. I rolled my eyes and she plopped her bony butt right down beside me on the floor, the chill from her skin sending goose bumps over my flesh.

"What are we doing?" she wanted to know.

"I'm checking something out and you're scaring the bejesus out of me."

"Oh, Soph, you're such a pansy." She pushed herself onto her knees; then her whole top half disappeared into the newly opened box.

"Well," she said from its depths, "I can see why you wanted to keep this particular expedition to yourself." She flopped back out, each hand clutching a framed picture of the Backstreet Boys in various just-dangerous-enough poses.

I yanked the frames from her grip. "It was a long, long time ago." I shoved the photos behind me, surreptitiously using the sleeve of my pajamas to wipe a leftover Bonne Bell Lip Smackers kiss from the glass. "Move."

"Oh my gosh. Did you wear this? Sexy!" Nina had a piece of my Mercy uniform in each fist. I ignored her and dug in the box myself, while she yanked on my old skirt and blouse, rolling the skirt to porn-star heights and tying the blouse over her smooth, perfect midsection. I glanced up.

"Yep, that's exactly how I wore it, too."

Finally, after pawing through a hideously thought-ful senior photo and seventeen wistfully dog-eared prom dress ads, I found what I was looking for. Nina's eyes went wide, the glee shooting from her mouth all the way up to her ears.

"Yearbooks!" She yanked one from me, sat down again and started thumbing through it. "You never showed me these before!"

I opened the top one left on my stack and sighed as seventeen-year-old me stared out from the pages, my hair a frizzy, barely-in-the-frame mess, my black eyes pleading for death. Or, possibly, that was just my interpretation.

"Self-preservation," I said without looking up.

"Aw, Sophie! You were adorable!" Nina cooed, holding the page with my junior-year photo up against her cheek. "Bless your heart!"

I narrowed my eyes. "Bless your heart is what people say to sugarcoat something ugly."

"Bless your heart," Nina said again.

"I hate you."

"I hate this beehive! Didn't anyone let this Heddy creature know the sixties ended a hundred and fifty years before this picture was taken?"

I smiled. "That lady is still at the school. I ran into her again. Sans beehive."

"Well, I suppose I should forgive a woman who dedicated fifty years of her life to high school girls."

I rolled my eyes. "I've been out of school barely ten years." Give or take.

Nina ignored me. "Who's Gretchen Von Dow?"

She turned the yearbook around, her finger pressed against the smiling, half-page photo of a very blond, very pretty student.

"Why does it say 'we'll miss you, Gretchen!'? She die or something?"

I bit my bottom lip. "I don't think so. She was a foreign exchange student." I took the yearbook from Nina and pointed to the smaller text. "See? 'Gretchen is a foreign exchange student from Hamburg, Germany, who shared her many traditions and sparkling smile with us for the past two years. She is now back home, but will never be forgotten! From the members of the Lock and Key Club.'"

"Touching," Nina said, bored. "What's Lock and Key Club? Some kind of bondage thing?"

"What kind of high school did you go to? Lock and Key is one of those honor society, public service things. You know, to look good on your college applications. They have them at tons of schools."

"Were you one of these Locked chicks?"

I pursed my lips. "Not exactly. I was more the locked-out chick."

"Isn't it weird for a foreign exchange student to be somewhere for two years?"

I shrugged. "I don't know. I guess not."

Nina tossed the book aside and grabbed another

one from my lap. "So, what brought on the three a.m. walk down memory lane?"

I sighed, leaning back on my palms. "Nothing. I guess I just thought there might be some kind of clue, something that would point me in the right direction. I filled Nina in on the day's activities—including my chat with Lorraine and the dozens of glowing pentagrams.

Nina shivered. "Those witchcraft things always creep me out with their symbols and their chalk and stuff."

I couldn't help grinning, watching my undead roommate flip yearbook pages, the tip of her tongue playing with the point of her angled fang as she fretted over witchcraft.

"Doesn't vampire trump witch?"

Nina cocked a brow. "Vampire trumps everything, toots. Except for sunlight. But we do what we do"—she splayed a hand elegantly against her pale chest—"because we have to. Essentially, we're not born bad, we're made bad."

I squeezed Nina's bare knee. "You're not bad."

"But witches?" Her upper lip curled into a disgusted snarl. "They *choose* to be bad."

"Some of them."

Nina cut her eyes to me. "Tell that to my nephew who practically got shish-kabobed today in the finance meeting."

"Kale's still mad?"

Nina flipped a page. "Madder. She hit the roof—

el kabob-o—because she saw Vlad talking to a Kishi demon in the waiting room."

"Kishi demons tend to eat the faces off the men who engage them."

Nina shrugged. "Not punishment enough in Kale's eyes. So you're strolling down memory lane, looking for the pentagram-drawing club?"

I closed the yearbook on a sigh. "I guess there's nothing in here. And you were right. I want to find Alyssa. I just keep feeling like I should be doing more than sitting around looking for clues. I should be out looking for her."

"And Sampson said stay put. Look for the coven only. Check yes for coven, no for no coven."

"And then what?"

"And then UDA goes in and tries to make them compliant."

"But they could be murderous witches!"

Nina fixed her eyes on mine. "Check yes for coven, no for no coven. Even if they're murderous, it's not your investigation."

I shrugged.

"It's Alex's. He does the normal, you do the para. Right?"

I shrugged again, looked away. "Like you're such a rule follower."

Nina cocked an eyebrow, then produced a blood bag from her robe pocket and pierced it with a fang. "I like the deeply contemplative senior pic," she said, holding it up for my inspection. "It looks like you're considering whether you should read Tolstoy or Nabokov next."

"Probably more like *Seventeen* or *Cosmo Girl*—I wasn't that deep. Or that smart. The only chick who read Tolstoy—and paid for it dearly—was Suri Lytton."

"Suri? Like Suri Cruise?"

"No, like the name Suri existed independent of the late Cruises. Look her up; she's probably right next to me."

Nina looked back at the book and frowned. "Nope. No Suri. Maybe she was younger?"

"No, we sat next to each other in every class. She's got to be in there."

Nina flipped back to the index. "Not here either."

I opened my book, thumbed a few pages, then pointed. "See, right here next to me. Junior year."

"And not here senior year."

I flopped back onto the carpet and yawned. "I don't know, I can't remember. I have to get more information."

Nina's head bobbed over me, her long black hair swishing over my cheeks. She grinned, her fangs pressing against her lower lip. "Spy trip?"

I bit my cheek to hold back my grin. "I need to get the police reports from Alex."

"Didn't Sampson give you a copy?"

"Of the preliminary report, but I know there's more." I pinched my bottom lip. "But how am I going to get it? Last time I broke into the police station—"

"You broke out with your left arm handcuffed to a desk chair."

"Yeah, that really slowed me down. We need someone here. We need someone who can get into the computer system. Someone who's good with technology and has no moral compass."

As if on cue, the front door slammed and we heard Vlad shrugging out of his duster and unloading his keys onto the counter.

Nina waggled her brows. "I think we've found our morally bankrupt companion."

"Vlad!" Nina and I went tearing into the living room, catching Vlad wide eyed, a half-smashed blood bag in one hand, a tiny trickle of velvet red dribbling down his chin. He caught it deftly with the tip of his tongue and my stomach lurched. "What?"

"Can you help me out with something?"

I yelped as Nina body checked me, shoving me aside. "Here is your mission should you choose to accept it," she said, hands on hips, legs akimbo. "And you have to accept it or we're kicking you out. You are to break in to the SFPD computers and filch a couple of case files for us."

"Please?" I said, poking my head over Nina's shoulder.

Vlad regarded us coolly, crossed his arms in front

of his chest, and cocked out a hip. "So you're asking me to break into the city's computer system."

"It's a matter of life and death."

"It's illegal," he said, as though he had suddenly sprung a conscience.

I gaped. "You care?"

"No, I just want to make sure you know what I'm risking."

"Can you do it?" Nina wanted to know.

Vlad scoffed. "Of course I can."

He crossed the room to his laptop, and I nipped at his heels behind him. "You can do it without anyone knowing, right? The police"—*Alex*, I thought— "absolutely can't know. Will they be able to trace this back to us?"

Vlad sat down, minimized the CGI vamps in the middle of his *BloodLust* game, and glared at me. "I need some space. You need some toothpaste."

I snarled, backed away, and did one of those huff-breaths into my cupped hands. I *was* a little dragon-breathy. But then again, it was nearing 4 AM.

As Vlad's long, thin fingers weaved deftly over his keyboard, my heart thumped, the adrenaline shooting like ice water through my veins. I paced, then finally grabbed my shoulder bag and upturned it on the table, spreading out the preliminary files that Sampson had given me, the receipt, my sparkly unicorn notebook containing all my notes, and an etching of the protection symbol carved into the desk. I sat down, grabbed a pen, and waited for

Vlad to feed me information. Instead, he poked his face around the side of his laptop screen and narrowed his coal black eyes at me. "What are you doing?"

"Waiting. You find the files, shoot me any pertinent information and I'm here"—I waggled my pen—"waiting for it."

Nina came up on my left, her arms wrapped around her as if she was chilled. "Are you sure about this?"

"What do you mean?"

"Alex, Sampson getting pissed at you?"

"Yes," I said, standing. "I'm way more worried about the forces of evil schoolgirls raining down on me."

Vlad popped around the computer again. "Schoolgirls?"

"Keep working."

Nina pulled out a chair. "So it's officially schoolgirls, not witches?"

I nibbled my bottom lip, considering whether or not to share my bathroom experience.

"Will said you got locked in the john," Vlad murmured.

Nina clapped her hands over her mouth, her small body collapsing in giggles. "Is that true?"

"It was magic! I was *magically* . . . locked in the john. Have you found anything yet?"

Vlad pursed his lips and crinkled his nose. "Okay, here they are." He looked up at me, his dark eyes fixed and steady. "You sure you want to do this?"

I looked from Vlad to Nina and back again. "For once I have the opportunity to help on a case in which I am not the deadliest catch. Print, dammit."

I took the pages out of the printer as it spit them out, stacking them carefully. I divided the two files on the kitchen table, laying the preliminary files I had gotten from Sampson next to them, and topping each side with a photo of one of the girls. My evidence pile looked substantial and Nina came up over my shoulder, nodding, impressed.

"Looks like you have a lot of information."

"Yes." I slipped into my room and came back with four years' worth of yearbooks. "And these, too." I started to pace. "Now we know that a student may have disappeared my senior year of high school, and that there is a legacy"—I glanced at Nina and Vlad to see if either of them were impressed with my witchly knowledge—"of spell casters. Cathy goes missing last year, Alyssa goes missing this year." I flipped open the files. "The dates the girls went missing are within days of each other and each feature the number seven."

I put the kitchen calendar in Nina's hands. "Look up these two dates. Did anything significant happen on the days the girls went missing?"

I took my seat and opened my sparkly unicorn notebook, ready to write.

"Yes," Nina said. "Cathy went missing on the

seventh, which was a Tuesday, and was officially declared Birds Eye Frozen Foods Day in 1957."

"I think I remember that," Vlad said with a nod. "There was a parade."

I pressed my fingertips to my temples. "How is frozen food significant to this case?"

Nina narrowed her eyes at me. "You asked for significant happenings. Not necessarily significant happenings in view of this case."

I groaned.

"So I suppose you don't care that the day Alyssa went missing is National Send a Card to Your Grandparents Day?"

I could feel the itchy buildup that started my left eye twitching.

I snatched the calendar from Nina and pointed to the square in question. "Half moon. That is slightly more significant than frozen vegetables."

"I was getting to that! You didn't let me finish!"

"Half moon the day Alyssa went missing, too." I raised my eyebrows. "Coincidence?"

"You people tend to do crazy things at the full moon," Vlad said with a cluck of his tongue.

"Us people?"

"Breathers."

"Right, we do. But witches tend to cast on full moons, too, right?"

Vlad waggled his head as if considering. "Depends

on the spell. Incantations, portals, protections, callings—usually done on full-moon nights."

"What the hell does a half-moon mean?"

Vlad shrugged. Nina looked blank. But I refused to be deterred. I was moving forward. I was taking steps in the right direction. I had my friends—my real friends. I didn't need Alex or Will.

I scrawled, *Half moons*, in my notebook, and started to hum.

I was going to solve this case. And I was, for once, going to do it without putting myself in danger.

ChaCha's yips broke through my pat-on-the-back revelry as she tore from my bedroom across the living room, her quarter-sized paws scratching the front door.

"What's up, ChaCha?" I said in the customary high-pitched voice one must adopt when talking to children or pets.

ChaCha allowed me to sweep her up, but she kept her little marble eyes focused on the closed door, growling fiercely, as her tiny paws scratched at the air.

"Guess she needs to go," I said, shrugging my jacket over my pajamas and grabbing her leash. I opened the door and was mid-step over the threshold when I saw it.

A shoebox. Wrapped simply in brown craft paper and stringy twine, settled up against the threshold.

Fingers of fear crept up my back, touching and

chilling each vertebra. My mouth went dry and a whoosh of chilled air seemed to wash over me.

"Are you coming or going?" I heard Nina yell.

I swallowed.

"There's something out here."

Chapter Nine

Nina poked her head over my shoulder. This time, her super speed didn't faze me. "What is it? Who's it for?"

She crouched down, poked the box. It moved an inch, the motion benign, not setting off a slew of knife-wielding Vessel thieves or rabid witches with skin-carving tendencies.

"It's probably from Amazon. Open it."

I frowned. "Amazon boxes have a smile on them."

And I got the distinct feeling that this box wouldn't make me smile.

I bent over anyway, picking up the box. It was surprisingly light and ChaCha sniffed at it, her little paw working its way under the twine. I set her down and slipped the twine off myself, the brown craft paper popping open and slipping to my feet.

I thumbed the lid open carefully, squinting my eyes and peeking in.

Then I slammed the lid down hard.

"Jesus Christ, it's a dead bird!"

Nina was back on the other side of the room, standing on the table, arms flapping like, well, a live bird. "Ew! Ew! Get rid of it!"

While garlic, holy water, and sunlight were the reigning terrors to most vampires, Nina had one more to add to the list: birds. Dead or alive, in any form. They terrified her.

I looked into the box again and my heart started to swell for the poor creature laying silent in the box. And then my heart dropped down like a fist to the gut.

"People only send dead livestock for one reason," I said, licking my paper-dry lips. "It's a warning."

Vlad looked up from his computer, his fingers still hovering over the keys. "About what?"

The little corpse shook in the box as my hands started to tremble. I clamped my eyes shut, thinking back to the horrendous clanging of metal, of porcelain, of the water shooting to the ceiling in the Mercy High bathroom—the words GET OUT scrawled in angry red across the mirror.

"About me getting any closer with this investigation."

"What now?"

My head snapped up to Will's door, cracked open, and Will, his eyes narrowed and caked with sleep. He stepped out of his apartment and raked a hand through his sleep-ragged hair, sandy brown streaks pointing in every direction. He was dressed in nothing except a pair of well-worn jeans, and he didn't look happy.

I was almost too distressed to notice that he was shirtless, his incredible abs tanned nicely, his jeans slung low enough that the muscles under his hip bones were exposed, sloping toward his groin, a glaring invitation.

"S-Someone left this," I said, tearing my eyes from the abs I wasn't staring at because I could be in the midst of a life or death situation and once again, there was a sexy-as-hell, half-naked man in the middle of it.

Will crossed the hall in two swift strides and gingerly took the box from me.

"Get rid of it!" Nina screeched from her table-top perch.

Will glanced into the box and then up at me, his hazel eyes clouded. "Are you upset because it's a terrible gift or because you didn't get anything?"

I frowned. "What are you talking about?"

"It's for Vlad."

Will upturned the lid. There was a thin, white envelope with the name VLAD scrawled across it.

"Oh."

"I don't care who it's for or who it's from. It's a dead. Freaking. Bird. Get rid of it! Those things carry disease! They carry the plague!"

I looked at Nina. "You're immortal. What do you care?"

Will shook the box. "It's just a pigeon."

Nina gaped. "A pigeon? It's not even a classy bird!"

Once we were able to dispose of the bird—which we soon learned was a warning from Kale, for Vlad—and lure Nina from her spot on the dining room table, Will and I sat down with two cups of tea.

"So, I take it that it wasn't just a dead bird that woke you up in the middle of the night?" Will said, wrapping his hand around his mug.

I wagged my head. "Couldn't sleep. I just don't feel like we're doing enough, Will."

"We're doing all we're supposed to do."

I pinned him with a glare. "And that's not enough. We're no closer to finding—" I paused, then snatched the papers Vlad had printed out for me. "I forgot."

"What's that then?"

"Police files."

Will cocked an approving brow and I handed him half the stack.

"Wait a minute—didn't the preliminary report say that they found Cathy in Marin?"

I nodded. "Yeah, Battery Townsley. Definitely over the city line."

Will looked up. "If you're going to drop a body anywhere around the city, that's the place to do it."

I nodded. "What else?"

Will scanned. "It says there was a preliminary search, but they didn't find any additional evidence and deduced that the Battery was merely a dump site. Subject was not killed there."

I bit my lip, thinking of Cathy, of her pink-and-cheery room with the frozen-in-time smiles and the deep, ridged lines on her mother's face. Hearing her referred to as a "subject" that had been "dumped" made my heart clench, became a tightening knot in my chest.

"Feel like going on a field trip?"

Will looked over my head, out the front window where the sky was even blacker than normal, the lights of the city barely punctuating the all-encompassing blackness. "I have a feeling there is absolutely no chance I'll be able to go back to sleep if I don't go."

I smiled and nodded. "You catch on quickly."

I don't think I'll ever be comfortable with San Francisco in the hours just before dawn. Normally, the city vibrates—it pulses with life, with people going about their day, with horns honking and smoke spewing and, just, *life*. But in these hours the entire city is still—but perilously so—as if something is slowly lurking, fingers of evil trailing through the night, claiming victims, claiming life.

I leaned forward in my seat and kicked up the heat, circling my arms around me and trying to shrug off a cold that was bone deep.

"It looks like the end of the world, doesn't it?"

Will looked sideways at me, the light from the

passing streetlights shining over him, then plunging him right back into darkness. "You mean because the streets are so empty?"

"Yes—and no." I shivered again. "It feels like something more this time."

Will guided Nigella toward the Marina, each mile toward the bay thickening the fog around us. "Something more?"

"You can't feel it? It's like . . ." I looked out the window, pressing my forehead against the freezing glass. "Unrest."

I didn't look at Will and he didn't answer me. We crossed through the Marina and coasted onto the bridge in silence. The fog was cotton-ball thick now, squeezing through the night-muted cables of the Golden Gate, wafting over our windshield, leaving spitting drops of moisture. Behind us, the city faded into it, the lights struggling against the haze. I knew there was a mountain in front of us, but all I could see were the two slashes of Nigella's headlights illuminating the fifteen feet in front of us.

"I'm thinking we probably could have done this in the morning."

I swallowed. "Probably. But we're running out of time, Will. And this"—I waved the sheaf of police reports Vlad printed out—"just proves that the police aren't any closer to finding Alyssa or catching her kidnapper either. There's something more. Girls don't disappear into thin air."

"And a dump site isn't just a dump site?"

We were turning off the bridge and beginning the steep road up and down toward Battery Townsley. I bit my bottom lip the whole way there, and let out the breath I didn't know I was holding when Will pulled into the deserted parking lot. He handed me a flashlight.

"Ready?"

My heart thumped. My skin felt too tight. But somewhere, in the back of my head, I could hear that voice. Alyssa, calling. Pleading. Begging.

"Yeah."

The ice cold hit me like a stinging slap in the face the second I pushed the car door open. It was a wet cold, heavy with salted sea air, and it snatched my breath away and clawed at my hair. I zipped my jacket to my chin, cursed myself for not changing out of my pajama pants, and yanked my hood up over my head. I jutted my chin toward the black blanket of grass leading to the battery.

"That way."

Will and I cut across the damp grass, walking in companionable silence, the round blobs of light from our flashlights bobbing in front of us. The wind howled and whipped and the water sloshed below us when I stopped, my flashlight hand dropping straight to my thigh, suddenly feeling as though it were tied there.

Will stopped and looked at me, his concerned face yellowed by the glow of the flashlight. "You okay, love? Cramp or something?"

My tongue was solid, stuck to the roof of my mouth. All I could do was shake my head and command my arm to move, but it didn't. I moved a finger, then two, then wrestled my arm a half inch from my side before wincing at a searing pain around my wrist.

"Sophie!" Will's arms were around me, but I couldn't feel them. All I could feel was the searing heat circling my wrist—both wrists now—and the terror that washed over me. Heat pricked at my hairline and burned the back of my neck. I struggled against invisible bonds that pressed against my shoulders, my rib cage. The pain was intense. I felt my skin splitting.

Finally, I fell backward, suddenly and without warning, expelled from whatever "held" me. Will ran to me and crouched.

"What the hell was that?"

I sputtered and coughed, pushed Will away and pushed myself to standing, righting my flashlight. "Let's go," I said, my voice a strangled choke.

I stomped across the grasses and Will trotted behind me before grabbing my left shoulder and turning me toward him. "What the hell was that?" he repeated, slowly this time.

"Cramp," I said, my eyes holding his.

I bit down hard on my molars so the tears wouldn't fall, and pulled my hands into my sleeves so he couldn't see the bruised, reddening marks that circled each wrist.

I needed to focus on Alyssa now.

I was breathing heavily by the time our flashlights swished over the entrance to Battery Townsley. We stopped and I flashed my light toward Will, who stared straight ahead, his lip curling into a scowl.

"That's it?"

The front side of the Battery (or the backside of the gun) was a plain cement opening half hidden in the edge of the bluff. The words BATTERY TOWNSEND were carved in the concrete above the opening, and a rusted metal gate hung gaping open at the mouth.

"What were you expecting?" I asked Will, taking a step forward.

He looked over his shoulders, then zipped his jacket up to his chin. "Something less sinister looking is all."

"It's a dump site for a body," I reminded him. "And it looks a lot less foreboding during the day."

"Remind me again why we decided it was absolutely necessary to come out here tonight?"

I glared at Will, challenging him, as I mustered the courage to take a step forward. Finally, I took a small one, then another, closing the distance between the mouth of the Battery and where we were standing. I flashed my light up and down the cement supports, examining every bar of the rusted-out gate.

"Find anything?"

"No," I said, my teeth starting to chatter.

"Where exactly did they say she was found?" Will wanted to know.

I swallowed, the fear welling up in me.

"There." I pointed through the gaping black doorway. "In there."

Will flashed his light in the direction I pointed, his meager light barely piercing the blackness. He looked back at me, then held out his hand.

"Come on."

I looked at his offered hand, the wind and mist slapping my face, chapping my lips. Behind me was San Francisco, the Underworld, Alex. In front of me was Will, hand outstretched, eyes clear and open. But there was a gaping blackness behind him.

"I—I—I'm not sure—"

The snap of the wind knocked the breath out of me and Will lurched forward, grabbing my wrist. He rolled me into him and we were both slightly airborne, his arms wrapped tightly around me. In a flash our lights were out and we were plunged in total darkness, standing in the concrete entrance-way to the Battery. Will flattened himself against the wall and pulled me to him, my body pressing up against his.

I listened to his heart thud in the blackness.

"What was that?" I whispered.

Will glanced down at me. It took a second for my eyes to adjust, but I was able to make him out, the slope of his jaw, his pursed lips, his index finger pressed against them.

We stayed like that for what seemed like hours, but I'm certain was only a few minutes. Finally Will poked his head into the Battery, the silver of the moonlight outlining his profile.

"Okay," he said, his voice audible, but low.

"What was that all about?" I asked, shaking my flashlight that refused to come on.

"I thought I heard something—someone."

I was going to say something smart, something about the crashing waves and the deafening wind, but I could see the slight sheen of sweat above his lip.

"Oh, God, Will, you're serious."

He instantly avoided my gaze, snatching my flashlight and pulling the batteries out. "Maybe I just wanted to cop a feel in the darkness."

But the lightness in his voice, the usual snark of sexy Will was gone. I looked to the sky.

"The clouds are moving. There's a lot more moonlight now."

Feeling emboldened by the bit of light, I walked into the Battery, toward the center. The second my sneaker crossed the threshold it was like I had been hit with a Taser. There was a crack of nearly blinding light and I doubled over, pain searing every inch of my skin.

"Something happened here," I whispered. "This is where she was found."

Will stepped toward me, lacing his arm around my waist.

"Come on. There's nothing here for us. Let's go."

"Wait," I said, pushing him away.

"Are you 'getting something'?" The way he said it let me know that he thought my "feelings" were right up there with revelations from Dionne Warwick and her Psychic Friends Network. "Come on out when you're ready."

He took off toward the mouth of the Battery and that creaky metal gate while I walked around and around the circle. Something caught the moonlight, something on the ground. I crouched and squinted and stood back, certain I was missing something. Finally, I crawled my way up the side of the bluff, using the moonlight behind me to stare down into the Battery. There, things became clearer.

And then completely dark again.

I felt the clamp over my mouth before I felt the crushing grip around my rib cage. My arms were pinned to my sides, but I clawed just the same, thinking that I would feel nothing but air as another feeling overtook me. But I felt the arm around me clench tighter, pushing the air out of my lungs in a silent whoosh. I tried to scream, but a leather-clad hand pressed against my open mouth, my assailant's thumb digging into my cheeks. I squirmed and struggled. He remained stalwart. He took a step backward and I fumbled with him before slumping and angrily digging my heels into the soft dirt.

I heard him huff, heard his heartbeat speed up

and his breath come in short bursts as he struggled with me.

"You. Have. The—" he huffed and I used the leverage of my heels in the mud to arch my back, giving my arms just enough play to land a solid blow to the groin. I heard the grunt and then the break of his arms as they fell from my mouth, from my sides. The wind slapped at my face as I ran, screaming into the wind, not daring to look behind me.

Where is Will?

It was the last thought I had before I felt the world slide out from under me. There was no extra give, no few seconds of Scooby Doo-like running on air—I went straight down.

My feet slapped at the mud and my shoulders banged against the earth.

And then everything stopped.

"Lawson?" I heard Alex's breathy call on the wind.

Angelic.

Oh. I had died. I had fallen off the earth or into the ocean and died, and Alex was there. In Heaven.

Or maybe I was in hell?

I tried to struggle, to move, but the cold was everywhere, around me, sinking into my clothes, through my sneakers and into my socks.

"Where am I?" It was an aching, gut-wrenching scream. I expected fire and brimstone or flying monkeys or the gates of St. Peter at any moment.

But all I got was the overwhelming stench of fresh earth and a pair of muddy Nikes right under my nose.

"What the—?"

A blinding wash of light poured over me and I tried to use my hand to shield my face—but my arms were still stuck by my sides. So I squinted, then sunk back against the dirt.

"Alex? Where are—why—what the hell is going on?"

He crouched down next to me, settling his flashlight on the ground so it wasn't blinding me anymore. "I could ask you the same thing."

I was about to answer him in some fashion—I still had no real idea where I was or what, exactly, had happened—when Alex went vaulting forward, the toe of his sneaker scraping across the top of my head. I heard the sickening sound of flesh hitting earth and I tried to turn, but I was stuck, held solid by this—dirt.

I stopped.

"I'm in a fucking hole," I mumbled, awed. "I'm in a fucking hole!" I craned my head over my shoulder as far as I could get it. "Will, help me!"

Will had pummeled my attacker and was on top of him now, pinning him into the dirt, about to land a blow.

"Will?" I heard.

"Alex?" Will asked.

"Alex? Alex!"

"Lawson?"

"Oh, holy Christ."

Will rolled off of Alex and pushed himself to standing, offering Alex a hand—which he didn't take.

"What the hell are you doing here?" Alex spat.

"Why the fuck are you attacking her?" Will returned, throwing a gesturing arm my way.

"You're trespassing at a crime scene."

"Guys!" I yelled from my hole. "Guys!" I tried to dig my toes against the wall of the hole, but without the use of my hands—still bound by the narrow hole to my sides—all I could do was wobble back and forth uselessly.

"Sophie and I were here looking for clues. We were assigned this job."

I rolled the abandoned flashlight with my chin so that both Will and Alex were illuminated. My stomach dropped when I saw the fire in Will's eyes, the hard clench of Alex's jaw. The guys were nearly nose to nose and spitting mad. Will's hands were fisted at his sides, and Alex kept one hand resting on his holster.

"Guys!"

"I'm on this case. The SFPD is on this case, not the UDA. You shouldn't be here."

"I'M IN A FUCKING HOLE, HERE!" I screamed.

Both Alex and Will swung their heads to look at me as though they had just realized I was there.

"Why are you in a hole?" Will asked, calm as ever.

"I fell in." I gestured with my chin toward Alex. "I guess you thought I was an intruder. He chased, I ran. I fell."

Alex's ice-blue eyes washed over me. "I was just doing my job. We were staking out the Battery." He jutted his head toward me in my hole, then cut his eyes toward Will. "Doesn't look like you were doing much of your job."

Will's nostrils flared. "I am doing my job just fine. She's not hurt. The Vessel is still intact." He took a half-inch step closer. "It's not like I lost it."

"Guys?" I asked, half to diffuse the spitting glares between Alex and Will, and half because I was still stuck in a goddamn hole on the Marin headlands in the middle of the night.

"I didn't lose it," Alex said, biting off his words—and completely oblivious to my stump of a head in the dirt.

They were talking about the Vessel of Souls—before it was me. Alex stole it, which caused his fall from grace. There is much more to the story as it's rather long and complicated and I was praying to God, Buddha, and Oprah that they wouldn't go over the details now, while I stood in my HOLE IN THE GROUND.

"Really?" I screamed. "Really, guys? I'm down here. IN A HOLE. I fell into a hole that's about as big around as my shoulder span. I'm in a hole!" I could hear the hysteria and panic rising in my voice, but I didn't care, because my mind was suddenly full of all the bugs and maggots that climbed around underground, mere centimeters from my exposed skin.

Suddenly, I was an upright corpse and I swear to God there was a worm on my arm.

"Get me out of here!"

"How'd you end up standing upright in a hole?" Will wanted to know.

"Just get me out!"

The guys stared at me and walked around the hole as if somewhere I was hiding a spring trap door.

When Alex and Will shared a shrug and a glance, I realized that I would likely have to spend the rest of my life in this hole, begging for people to bring me marshmallow pinwheels or dig me out with soup spoons.

"Can you get your arms out?" Alex asked.

My enormous, exasperated sigh was lost in ten inches of damp dirt. "I can't do anything. This"—I think I shrugged—"is what you have to work with."

"All right," Will said over my head. "I'll take this side. I think we can slide our hands in enough to reach under her arms and pull from there."

"From her armpits," Alex clarified.

Will nodded and counted to three, and suddenly I was being remarkably molested by four strong hands. I tried to help, squirming in one direction and then the other, but that only served to first lob one boob into Alex's hand, the other into Will's.

"Those aren't my armpits."

"Sorry."

On three, there was a larger-than-necessary groan, and I was free from my upright tomb. The fresh air whipping through my clothes was cold but freeing. I would have run, but the guys were still holding me, my feet six inches from the ground, dangling.

"You can put me down. I'm free. I'm okay." I swung my head, addressing Alex and then Will. "Nothing's broken or anything."

But neither Will nor Alex was focused on me. Each of their heads were bent downward.

"We're going to set you down, but keep your right foot raised, okay?" Alex asked.

"Okay, I guess."

The guys placed me down gently, my one sneaker touching the tuft of soft grass in front of me, my right leg bent, foot swung in front of me. I could feel my eyes widen. My teeth started a chatter that had nothing to do with the cold. My stomach folded in on itself.

"Wh-wh-what is that?" I asked, pointing.

"Don't freak out, Lawson."

Will still had my arm as Alex whipped a Ziploc bag from his pocket and used it to gingerly remove the thing that was hanging from the cuff of my jeans.

He moved his hand and I saw what he'd picked from me as it crossed the yellow beam of light.

"Is that a—"

Will's grip on my arm tightened and I heard Alex say again, "Lawson, don't freak out." This time his words were stern, but they did nothing to slow me down.

"That's a hand! That's a hand!"

I felt the heat shoot up the back of my neck and throb in my temples. Suddenly, I was doubled over, then on my hands and knees, my body jerking and heaving as I vomited.

I barely had enough time to register my rage when I heard Alex yell, "Keep it away from the hole!" because the sudden stench of moist dirt and decay assaulted my nostrils and I heaved again.

I felt Will's cool hand lace through my hair as he pulled it back from my face, his other hand touching the small of my back tenderly as I sputtered and coughed, hot tears mixing with snot dribbling over my chin. I sat back on my haunches and Alex handed me his handkerchief. It may have been my nerves or my recent assault by a disembodied hand, but I thought I saw a flash of jealousy in Will's eyes as I took the white cloth from Alex.

"What—whose—who does that belong to?" I croaked, dabbing at my nose and mouth.

Alex had the hand laid out on the plastic bag as Will shone a light down on it.

"Doesn't look too recent," Will said, squinting.

"Most of the flesh has been eaten away. Kind of hard to determine time of death at this point."

My stomach lurched and I prepared for another round of vomit that thankfully, never came.

"It's a female," Alex said. He pulled a pencil from his pocket and pointed it toward the hand's clawed index finger.

"Is that a ring?" Will asked.

"Looks like it."

I crawled over, unable to help myself, and stared. Among the dirt and muck was a tiny band of something silvery, pushed up against the knuckle. "It has a stone in it," I said, amazed.

Will pushed the eraser end of the pencil toward the stone that I pointed out and nudged the moist earth aside. A sliver of emerald green—muted and fogged—caught the light.

I swallowed heavily and sat back on my haunches, suddenly overcome with grief.

"Hate to break up the bio lesson but, wouldn't you say where there's a hand there's probably—"

Alex glanced up at Will, his eyes reflecting the light. "An arm?"

Will nodded solemnly and they both looked at me. My heart thumped. "What are you looking at me for? I found that, I'm done for the night."

Alex handed Will the flashlight as he pulled his

cell phone from his back pocket. "I'm going to call this in. There's probably a body in there."

"A body." I heard myself say it, the word dropping solid on the cold air.

Will rolled the extra flashlight to me. "Just take a look."

I chewed the inside of my lip and begged that this hand had come upon this hole independently. But when the yellow streak of my light caught the glossy mud walls I'd had leaned up against, my stomach went to liquid.

Suri. Gretchen. Cathy. And now—Alyssa?

"It's not a body," I said slowly. "It's a couple of bodies."

Fingers of color were just starting to streak through the night sky as the police began making their way toward the bluff. A news crew followed the cavalcade and onlookers came behind them; I shuddered when Alex directed a few officers with metal gates to hold back the sudden proliferation of people.

"You okay, love?" Will asked.

I swallowed and sighed. "Yeah. Just got a very unfortunate case of deja vu."

The last time I had been on a beautiful, grassy bluff overlooking the bay, I had also been at a crime scene. There, the bodies of two women had been found, decimated. And now, before the majority of the city even roused from their beds, the police were digging up the remains of more women. The realization was like a steel band tightening around my heart. I glanced toward Alex as he was meeting the coroner's van in the parking lot.

"Sometimes it seems like we're all under attack," I muttered.

Alex tossed a glance over his shoulder as Will and I made our way toward the parking lot. I wanted to say good-bye to Alex, to explain—something— but exhaustion and a numbness that seeped all the way to my bones prevented it.

Chapter Ten

Once home, I showered and changed in record speed—fast even with Nina's wrinkled nose and directive to "change into something that doesn't look like I buried my Aunt Fanny in it." I interpreted the Aunt Fanny crack to mean a never-been-worn pale blue cashmere sweater and a pair of charcoal-grey slacks that had miraculously become cigarette-slim while living in the back of my closet.

"Way better," Nina said, handing me a Fresca and a bagel in a brown paper bag. She shrugged. "You should probably go grocery shopping."

"We're out of detergent, too," Vlad chimed in, scaring the bejesus out of me. He poked his head over the top of the couch and grinned.

"Look, I was out all night—"

Nina held her hand out, stop-sign style. "No need to brag about your conquests with a C-H-I-L-D in the room." Her eyes cut back and forth from the top of Vlad's head to me.

"I'm not a child," Vlad snapped. "You're a child."

"I wasn't out conquesting. I was out." I took a deep breath, trying my best not to recall the image of that gnarled hand, of the makeshift graveyard the police were unearthing as we argued about my nonexistent sex life. "We found some bodies. Several, we think. Out at Battery Townsley."

Nina blinked and popped a straw into the blood bag she'd helped herself to.

"With Alex or Will?" Vlad asked.

"Both."

"Kinky."

I narrowed my eyes and took a big swig of my Fresca. "You're disgusting."

"My vote's for Will, personally," Vlad said as I gathered my purse.

"No." Nina hopped off the counter, following me into the living room. "Alex. The whole doomed love is so romantic."

Vlad snarled. "I don't like that guy. I'm so over his holier-than-thou shit."

I grabbed my keys. "You have no soul, Vlad. Everyone is holier than you."

He resettled himself on the couch. "Not everyone has to act like it."

I was still grumbling from Vlad and Nina's lackluster response to our break in the case—but then again, for a couple of undead vampires, the actually dead really did little to pique their interest—when

I crossed two lanes of screeching traffic and bolted into the Philz Coffee parking lot.

"Coffee," I mumbled to absolutely no one.

I yawned and blinked, my eyes stinging and dry from lack of sleep. "Code Thirty-three," I said to the perky, well-rested barista. "A big one."

She studied me intently for an uncomfortable beat before reaching out to touch my hand. "You look just like him," she said, her voice low and breathy.

"Excuse me?" I asked, heat pricking out along my hairline.

She snapped her hand back from mine, but her grin never faltered. "I said that will be $3.71, please."

I felt my mouth drop open and I worked to push the words past my teeth. "No—no. You said—you said that I looked just like him."

The barista cocked her head, the sweet smile still plastered across her glossy lips. "I'm sorry, you must have misheard me. Three seventy-one, please."

I handed over the cash without taking my eyes off her. She gave me my change and I stepped aside, far enough to get out of line, but close enough to hear her should she murmur something else.

She was all business with the next customer.

I must have imagined it or misread her. I really need to get some sleep.

I slurped the last of my Code 33 as I pulled into the UDA parking lot, the octane hitting my blood-stream in one hot, energetic explosion. Thirty-six floors later, the big silver elevator doors slid open on the familiar chaos of the Underworld Detection Agency. Kale was at the reception desk with a cheek full of Hubba Bubba as she cocked her head and listened to a voice screaming on the other end of the phone line. The velvet ropes were bulging with clients already annoyed—a couple of zombies with brand-new papers, a windigo who shot a cool breeze at the oblivious vampire behind him.

I hadn't even broached the UDA STAFF ONLY door when Sampson caught my eye and made a beeline for me.

"Sophie, great. You picked a perfect day to come back." He waved toward the crowd. "First of the month. Everyone wants everything renewed or reneged."

I stepped back. "Oh, I'm—I'm not here to work. I have to get back to the high school."

Sampson frowned. "But yesterday you asked me to pull you and Will out."

"Sorry, that was a mistake," I said, shaking my head. "That was before—we found bodies and symbols and—I think we might actually be on to something."

"So you have a lead about Alyssa?"

"Not exactly."

Sampson's shoulders slumped, the motion barely visible under his steel-gray suit.

"But I expect this thing to unravel really soon.

Really soon. I just came down here to see Lorraine."

"Well, Lorraine's not in yet and Principal Lowe has already called in your replacements for today so . . ."

I snapped my fingers, brightening. "That's okay. That's actually good. Will and I can observe and poke around the school and check out a few things." I stepped backward, edging my way toward Lorraine's office. "Thanks!"

I wasn't sure if my sudden thundering heart was due to actual adrenaline or still the Code 33 kick, but I took the opportunity to photocopy the receipt I had from Miranda's book and stack that, along with a second shot of the protection symbol from the Mercy desk, and a photo Will snapped looking down into Battery Townsley on Lorraine's desk. I clipped the stack together and slapped a *Need your thoughts on this* Post-it note to the top.

My thumb was hovering over the speed-dial button on my cell phone when I ran into Kale rounding the corner.

"Just the person I was looking for!"

I held up a hand. "I'm sorry, Kale, but I'm in the middle of something."

Kale clapped her hands together, prayer style. "Two seconds."

I dropped my phone hand to my side. "Okay, two seconds."

She immediately produced a square envelope

and began trying to push it into my hand. I stepped back. "No, sorry. I won't be the go-between for you and Vlad's lover's spat."

Kale's cheeks pinkened. "Vlad said we were lovers?"

"Kale . . ."

"Okay, okay, sorry. This isn't for Vlad, though. It's for Nina. Give it to her for me, please? It's just an apology for the bird incident."

I looked over my shoulder. "Nina works here. Can't you give it to her yourself?"

Kale paled and wagged her head slowly. "Vampires are so scary when they're mad. Especially Nina."

Knowing that my sweet roommate had once decimated an entire army for pissing her off, I couldn't really blame Kale.

I took the envelope. "Fine. But I don't know when I'm going to see her."

"You're such a sweetie, Sophie!"

I zipped past Kale, then paused. "Hey, make sure that Lorraine reads the stuff I left on her desk, okay?"

Kale pumped her head while her lips worked a giant orb of hot pink bubble gum.

"Will?" I screamed into the phone. "Will, would you wake up?"

It was the third time I'd dialed Will, and while it

did occur to me that I was leaving messages on a voice mail rather than an answering machine, I still couldn't help myself from screaming that he wake up and, "pick up, pick up, pick up!"

I was too frustrated once the doors opened on the police station vestibule to try again—and too frustrated to notice before I went chest to chest with Alex. He stepped back, steadied me, and furrowed his brow.

"Have you thought about getting glasses?"

"I don't need glasses. I see you . . . now."

Alex's lips cocked up into the familiar, panty-dropping half-smile that shot lightning through my veins. "Leaving already?"

"Actually, after everything last night—or this morning—I'm headed back over to Mercy."

Alex crossed his arms in front of his chest and sat back in that incredibly manly Abercrombie model kind of way.

"You picking up Will along the way?"

I batted at the air. "I can't even get him out of bed."

And suddenly, in that millisecond of recognition, it was as if someone had sucked all the air out of the room. Something flitted across Alex's eyes, marring the clear ice blue. He stiffened—just slightly—as heat snaked up my neck, washed over my cheeks and burned my ears.

"I didn't mean that I—that he—that we—"

"No." Alex held up his hand and took a step

back—a step that seemed to put an enormous chasm between us. "You don't owe me anything. You don't have explain."

"No." I bounced up on the balls of my feet. "No, I do. It just came out wrong!"

But my meager explanation was lost in the crackle of the overhead speaker calling all available cops into the briefing room.

Alex turned on his heel and I reached out for him, my fingertips brushing across the fabric of his Windbreaker.

"Alex, wait!"

"Later, Sophie."

Sophie.

My name—my *actual name*—rolling across Alex's lips hit me like a fist to the gut. I was Lawson to Alex. I always had been. Suddenly, the fact that he used my first name—more intimate, more familial—sent me reeling. My name on his lips sounded like a door slamming firmly shut.

I tried to put Alex—and the crazy barista—out of my head by blaring the latest *American Idol* winner–slash–pop star du jour as I drove to Mercy. Normally, perky pop beats and songs about chasing your dreams and young love could shake me out of any rut, but I just sunk deeper and deeper the closer I got to the school.

We still hadn't found Alyssa. My stupid, mindless mouth had hurt Alex. And here I was pulling into the parking lot of a school that had given me more questions than answers.

"Oh! Ms. Lawson!" Heddy said when I walked into the office, her orange lips a waxy O of surprise. "We've got someone covering you classes. Principal Lowe said that you and your friend were through with your little investigation."

Something niggled at me and I cocked my head, narrowing my eyes at Heddy. "Our investigation? Will and I are just substitute teachers."

Heddy paused for a beat, her lips slightly parted, crimson meshing with the red rouge already on her cheeks. "Principal Lowe told me." She clapped a hand over her mouth daintily. "Was I not supposed to say anything"—she dropped her voice to a throaty whisper and leaned forward—"here?"

It wasn't until Heddy's last motion that Fallon—standing at the back of the office with a stack of file folders in her hand—even seemed to notice us. I glanced up, feeling my heart do a little double thump, hoping she hadn't heard anything.

"Fallon," I said to her as she stared at me.

She crossed the office in three long strides, pressing the manila folders against her far-too-ample-for-a-woman-who-couldn't-yet-vote chest.

"I thought you were done here," she said, her eyes cold.

"And I thought Miranda was the office aide," I said, my eyes traveling back to Heddy.

"She is," Fallon said. "Third period."

In my mind, I knew Fallon was just a snotty kid. Her daddy handed her everything and she'd been blessed with Lolita-like looks and enough cunning to use them, but she was still just a kid. So I couldn't figure out why she put me on edge so much.

"Witch."

I didn't realize I'd said it out loud until I felt the hot press of air edge past my lips

Heddy looked up at me. "Did you say something, dear?"

The word ricocheted around my head until it was droning in my ear: *WITCH. Witch. Witchwitch witchwitch.*

"Nothing, Ms. Gaines. Where is the library again?"

I turned my back on Fallon, still feeling the heat of her eyes boring into my back as I left.

Fallon was a bitch. She was a bully. And an office aide. She would have had access to each of the victims' records, their home addresses, detailed confidential information about their family lives.

Did that make her a witch?

No.

There were bodies—multiple bodies. And if it was true that Suri and Gretchen had gone missing, Fallon couldn't have had anything to do with it. She would have been a toddler then. But if she . . .

I made a beeline for the Mercy library and the librarian pointed to a tiny nook in the back of the room. "The yearbooks are all over there," she said. "Every year. They're getting very popular lately."

"Excuse me?"

"You're the second person who's asked to see them in as many days." She smiled thinly. "I hope you find what you're looking for."

I settled myself in, pulled out my sparkly unicorn notebook, and yanked out a handful of books. I started with last year's, flipping back and forth between the sweet-smiled Alyssa and the broad-smiling Cathy. Then I checked the index, writing down every page where the girls commingled.

There was only one.

"Lock and Key Club," I said to myself in a low whisper. "They were in Lock and Key and one literature class together. Okay." I bit my bottom lip. "That's a start . . . I guess."

I reached for another book, opening it on my lap.

"Oh, holy crap!"

I didn't realize I'd screamed it until a selection of narrowed eyes squinted at me in a universal, "Shhhh!"

"Sorry," I mouthed, picking up my cell phone.

"Hello?" I whispered into it.

"Shh!" This time from the librarian.

"Let me call you right back."

I shoved the yearbooks back onto the shelf and

my unicorn notebook into my shoulder bag, then apologetically made my way into the hall.

"Will?"

"Nice to hear from you, love."

"What do you mean 'nice to hear from you'? I've been calling you all morning."

He yawned loudly into the phone. "Did you?"

"If you didn't get my messages, why are you calling me?"

"I'm calling you because the PD came back with some info from your hole." Will paused, then broke into a round of schoolboy giggles.

"Seriously, Will?"

"That came out wrong."

"I know which hole you meant. What did you hear—and how did you hear it?" Alex's pained face flashed in my memory and just as quickly skittered away.

"Not important. According to the bobbies, the bones of three different people were found there. All three women, all three seem to be in the range of sixteen to twenty-two."

I bit my lip, my stomach roiling. "Are any of those bodies Alyssa?"

"Not likely. The bones were old. The decomposition was natural, so they're placing the kills between fifteen and twenty years ago."

My saliva tasted like hot lead in my mouth. Had

our killer been working on his "project" for fifteen or twenty *years*?

"They were only able to identify one of the bodies. There was a bracelet tangled on her." Will sucked in a sharp breath. "A bracelet with her remains. She was called Gretchen. Gretchen Von Dow."

Chapter Eleven

The high-pitched, hysterical laugh that came out of my mouth echoed through the empty hallway.

"That's funny to you?"

"No." My heart thumped in my throat. "Gretchen Von Dow—we were at Mercy at the same time. She didn't go missing though. I'm sure of it. Nina and I looked it up just last night. She wasn't missing. Unless—unless it was far after high school."

"Clothing with the Mercy logo was dumped in the makeshift grave. How are you so sure that she didn't disappear when she was in high school?"

I licked my lips, confidence welling up inside me. "Because she was a foreign exchange student. From Hamburg, Germany. She went back during our junior year. It's in my yearbook. 'We'll miss you, Gretchen,' etcetera. Did someone try to locate her in Hamburg?"

There was a beat of pregnant silence on Will's

end of the phone. "I think you may have gotten some bad information, Soph."

"No, no." I started to tremble, started to *need* to be able to explain to Will. "It's in the yearbook. Gretchen Von Dow was a foreign exchange student. If something happened to her while we were in high school, I would have known. I would have."

I wasn't sure if I was trying to convince Will or myself.

"Sophie," Will tried again.

"No," I said, wagging my head. "Gretchen Von Dow left during our junior year. Legitimately. She was a foreign exchange student."

I could hear Will's fingers flying over a keyboard. "Open your iPad."

I paused, then slowly pulled the iPad from my bag and flipped it open. "Okay."

"Gretchen was a foreign exchange student?"

I nodded as though Will could see me. "You know, they come here, we go to their country. An exchange. For foreigners."

"Look, I know you people consider San Francisco its own planet or whatever, but I'm pretty sure the school system would step in and disallow exchange students from San Mateo."

"What?"

"I'm sending you the information now."

I forced myself to look at the text populating my page.

Gretchen was born in San Mateo County and lived there until she disappeared.

I swiped the screen and frowned down at the birth certificate that flashed on my screen.

"She went back to Hamburg," I mumbled.

"Gretchen Von Dow went missing the August before her junior year in high school." I imagined Will scanning the screen, the black words reflected in his hazel eyes. "There were no leads, no witnesses. She was filed as a possible runaway."

My legs went to jelly and I slid down the lockers, my butt hitting the floor, hard. "I can't believe this. How did we not know she went missing?"

"Apparently, because you thought she was a foreign exchange student."

"Well, yeah, that's what all of us at Mercy thought, but, but, a kid missing. That would have been in the paper, right? That would have been big news." I bit my lip. "Right?"

The keyboard clacked again on Will's end of the phone. "Open those," he commanded.

There was a little *plink!* then a message from Will. I opened it and files started popping up all over my screen.

"These are the local papers from the day after Gretchen was reported missing."

I scanned one after the other, a vague recollection of headlines blaring news about a Black Friday movement, the parks in peril. "There's nothing here."

I began clicking through page after page of the

paper, getting further and further away from blaring headlines and moving closer to the not-as-noteworthy news.

"Here!" I said, strangely triumphant. "The police blotter."

"'Sixteen-year-old high school student Gretchen Von Dow was reported missing by parents Lola and Howard Von Dow after failing to return home from school Thursday afternoon. Police are investigating.'"

My stomach turned in on itself. "That's it? That's all there is?" I yanked the article down the screen and maniacally scanned for something else, something with more meat on Gretchen and her disappearance. "There isn't even a photo. Or a 'she went missing from here.' Didn't anyone care?"

I could hear the crack in my voice, could feel the hot sting of tears behind my eyes. "Didn't anyone look for her?"

Will's voice was soft. "I'm sure someone looked for her, love."

"But—but—" I flopped the cover back on my iPad. "No one did anything. And I—I didn't even know her. I didn't even know she went missing. None of us did."

"It's not your fault, love," Will was saying, his voice soothing. "You were just a kid."

"And I was totally wrapped up in my own stupid issues. I was giving myself home perms and crying over the Backstreet Boys while my classmate was snatched. Probably hidden away somewhere. Tortured. Words carved into her flesh." The image of Cathy's ravaged body flashed in front of my eyes and I heaved.

"You need to relax. You couldn't have done anything even then. You thought she was a foreign exchange student."

I suddenly stopped crying and used the back of my hand to swipe at my wet cheeks. "Yeah. I did." I pinched my bottom lip. "Why did I think that?"

"What do you mean?"

I slumped back against the locker. "Well, why would I just assume—I mean, we had foreign exchange students, but Gretchen—" I squinted, remembering. "She didn't look all that foreign."

"Maybe she told you she was from a different county. I used to tell birds I was Australian. Upped the mystique. Every girl wants to bed a bloke from Oz."

"No." I shook my head, using my fingernail to trace a line of grout. "I was social napalm. No one told me anything. At least not directly. And you're disgusting." I sighed. "Maybe it was just a rumor."

"Who would start a rumor that a girl who had gone missing was actually just a foreign exchange student on her way back to the mother country?"

I bit my lip. "The person who made her disappear."

At that moment, the bell rang. I pushed myself up from the linoleum as students flooded out of their classrooms, the bell soon drowned out by the flurry of conversation and the general din of movement.

"A bunch of bodies," I heard someone say.

"Bones, like, thousands of them," someone else whispered.

"Hey, Ms. Lawson!"

I looked up from the sea of navy blue to see Miranda, arm raised, a wide grin on her face. I took one step closer to her and then she was gone, girls closing over the small hole she made in the crowd.

"Miranda?"

"I think she needed to sit for a spell." Fallon's lips were right at my ear, her voice serpentine, like a black snake winding its way into my brain.

Just as I was about to respond Fallon was washed down the hall, too, the only remainder of her a high-pitched giggle mingled with Finleigh and Kayleigh's.

"Miranda!" I yelled, pushing my way through the crowd. "Miranda!"

Miranda was on her butt on the ground—just as I had been—and probably with the same dumb-founded expression. Her books were strewn around her and I crouched down hurriedly, gathering her things, feeling every bit like I was stepping back into my own high school life.

Miranda pushed herself up, her cheeks blazing red. "Thanks, Ms. Lawson," she said, taking the books I held out to her.

I smiled. "You can call me Sophie. I'm not working here anymore."

Miranda's face fell. "You're not?"

"No. I'm needed elsewhere." I sounded like a dumb superhero, but Miranda didn't seem to notice. "Did Fallon just shove you?"

"No. No, I just tripped. I'm clumsy."

I crossed my arms in front of my chest. "I was clumsy in high school, too. You don't have to take that, Miranda. Bullying is a crime. Or, you know, a lot of what bullying has become is. You can talk to me."

Miranda took a step away from me, a cold front going up. "I'm fine. I can take care of myself. But thank you for the public service announcement." She whipped around and ducked into a classroom.

I sighed, and turned just in time to see the swarm of girls parting like the Red Sea, their voices dropping away until only silence remained.

And then I knew why.

Framed in the open doorway and against the mid-day fog was Vlad. His eyes scanned the crowd and he licked his lips, a tiny triangle of blood-red tongue running across them. As gross as it was, he was stunning against the gray backdrop, his usually helmeted hair slightly mussed by the wind outside, his thick, deep navy peacoat buttoned up over what I was certain was an unattractive Dracula-style puffy shirt. I saw his dark eyes scan over the sea of ardent adorers before he caught mine.

The door snapped shut behind him, and it was

like every girl had been released from her silent trap. The murmuring started and reached nearly deafening levels immediately, ponytailed heads snapping between Vlad and the girl he may have been looking at, a plethora of whispers of "how's my hair?" and a Sephora's worth of lip gloss being whipped out and applied.

"Sophie!" Vlad's deep voice cut through the crowd and all was silent again, though every mouth was open, every eye fixated on me, every onlooker completely floored that *he* was looking for *me*.

If he hadn't been Vlad—my manager, my roommate, Nina's *BloodLust*-playing teen nephew—I would have kept up the mystique, let the girls ogle me in wonder while I rewrote what never happened in my high school past. But it *was* Vlad and I was miffed.

"What are you doing here?"

Vlad edged his way through the girls and I held my breath, half-expecting a series of fainting spells as he made contact with the girls.

I bent my head when he approached me and pinched my lips together, trying to talk as discreetly as possible. "You better not be using a glamour."

Vlad grinned at me. "That's the funny thing. I'm not."

I rolled my eyes and cocked out a hip. "What do you want?"

"Nothing, but Lorraine said I should give you this."

He held out a royal-blue velvet shoulder bag. I wrinkled my nose. "I already have a purse."

"It's not the purse. She wanted you to have what's inside."

I frowned, then popped open the purse. I immediately snapped my hand over my mouth. "Oh my God, what is that?"

Vlad just shrugged and tossed some senior one of those "how you doin'?" head bobs.

The smell that was coming from the innocuous-looking bag was noxious to say the least. Kind of like a cross between Steve's socks and flaming garbage.

"She said you need it for protection."

"From what?" I pulled the bag shut. "From anyone with nostrils in a forty-five-mile radius? And why does she suddenly think I need protection?"

"I don't know." Another head nod as the girls went back to normal motion—although the majority of them seemed to find one reason or another to brush their breasts up against Vlad. "She said you put something on her desk and there was something dangerous in it or something."

I gaped. "She said there was something dangerous in the photos *or something*? What was dangerous, Vlad?"

He shrugged. "I don't remember. Something. What'd you put in the photos?"

"There was a picture of Battery Townsley, a picture taken here at the school, a receipt—"

"I definitely remember that she didn't say anything about a receipt."

I rolled my eyes. "Great."

"And I'm doing you a favor bringing this here."

I raised an eyebrow. "You're doing me a favor?"

Vlad nodded.

"Out of the goodness of your black heart?"

Vlad's eyes narrowed.

"And you got nothing out of it. Nothing except the satisfaction of knowing that I will now be safe against not-receipts."

Vlad blinked. "I may have gotten something out of it, too."

I waited and Vlad sighed.

"Fine," he groaned. "Lorraine is going to talk to Kale. Maybe try to smooth things out so I could talk to her without her, you know, cutting off my head and spitting fire down my throat. Oh, and Lorraine said there's something in there that you have to wear." He took the bag from me, reached in, and yanked something that looked like a cat horked up, tied to a piece of twine. "This thing. You're supposed to wear it all the time. Under stuff. It's supposed to touch your skin."

I took the charm from Vlad. As I brought it closer to my face, my mouth started to water with that familiar pre-vomit saliva. "I think I'm going to be sick."

"Lorraine said you would get used to the smell."

"Not likely."

I held my breath and put the thing over my head anyway, immediately pushing the cat-hork end under my shirt, hoping that would stamp out the smell.

Vlad smiled. "Gotta go."

He wound his way through the crowd and out the front doors. I briefly expected a rush of girls pressing their noses against the windows, pound-puppy style. Instead, I came eye to eye with Fallon.

"You know him?"

"Of course I do, Fallon. And you know what? I'm glad you're here. I want to talk to you about something."

Fallon looked over her shoulder and then back at me. She paused for a beat, then wrinkled her nose. "What smells?"

I took a deep breath and then instantly regretted it, visualizing my insides turning into withering blackness as the stench whipped through my lungs. "I don't know. Come with me."

I was surprised when Fallon did, falling into step with me. She pressed her palm against her nose. "It's like the smell is getting worse."

I pulled open the door to my old classroom and ushered Fallon in. She looked around as though she hadn't been in that room every weekday of her junior year. "You're not working here anymore. Are you allowed to pull students into an empty room like this?"

"Look, Fallon, I know what's going on between you and Miranda."

For the first time since I'd known the girl, Fallon's

eyes widened, her perfect façade cracking just slightly. She recovered almost immediately.

"I don't know what you're talking about."

I put my hands on my hips and did my best to stare down and intimidate her. "The hall the other day? And then today? You said she wanted to 'sit down for a spell.' What did you mean by that?"

There was a miniscule twitch at the edges of Fallon's mouth, the infinitesimal start of a smile. "She wanted to sit down."

I inched closer. "You said, 'for a spell.'"

"It means for a while."

"I know what it means. What I want to know is why you chose that particular phrase."

Fallon took a step back and waved her hand in front of her nose. "Is the smell coming from you?"

"Fallon, at least two girls have gone missing from Mercy High in the last two years. And according to things uncovered by the police—and by me— possibly a lot more. You know this is all tied to witchcraft."

Again that tiny, twitching smile. "I do?"

I cocked my head, pinning her with a glare. "Why would you say 'sit for a spell'?"

Now it was Fallon who stepped forward, suddenly uncomfortably close to me. "Are you accusing me of something, Ms. Lawson?"

"Tell me about Cathy."

"She was murdered. Before that, she was alive."

I blinked, and Fallon blinked back at me, as if daring me to ask her to elaborate.

"Alyssa?"

Fallon held her ground for a beat before turning stiffly, her hair fanning out behind her. "I don't have to—"

She stopped when I grabbed her arm. Her eyes sliced over her shoulder and narrowed, first staring at my hand on her arm, then looking directly up at me. "Get your hand off of me," she said sharply.

I let her go as if her skin had burned my palm.

Once Fallon disappeared into the hall, I slid up on my former desk, resting my face in my hands.

Did I really believe that Fallon was some kind of witchy serial killer?

At least three bodies . . . Will's voice echoed in my head. *Gretchen Von Dow* . . . I hopped off the desk and started shoving things in my shoulder bag, humming a riff from a Bon Jovi (my era) tune when there was a knock on my door.

I didn't look up when the door opened. "Nice, Will," I said, grabbing a sheaf of papers. "You knock on my classroom door but barge in on me in the bath—" I stopped, my eyes wide. "Tub. Kayleigh, hi. I was just—can I help you with something?"

I was fairly certain that the abject horror in Kayleigh's eyes—*Teachers have lives outside of school?*—mirrored my own. She went beet red from the tips of her ears all the way down to the tops of her UGG boots.

I cleared my throat and blinked at her, flashing a pleading "let's pretend this never happened" look.

"Can I help you with something?" I said again.

Kayleigh's hands went from fingering the strap on her crossover bag to fumbling in front of her. She licked her already glossy lips and took a tentative step forward without saying anything.

I laid my shoulder bag back down on my desk and practiced one of those "open stances" that supposedly welcomed communication—or so Dr. Phil said.

"Do you want to talk to me about something?"

Kayleigh glanced over her shoulder—quickly, nervously—before stepping all the way into the room and pulling the door closed behind her. She waited until it clicked shut to let out a shaky breath.

"It's about Fallon," she said, her voice a low whisper. "And Miranda, in the hall the other day."

I felt my ears prick as my hackles went up. I was instantly protective of Kayleigh, of whatever it was she needed to tell me.

"You can tell me anything, Kayleigh. We can keep it just between us."

"Fallon would murder me if she knew I was talking to you, but this—this is getting really serious. You—you don't know the whole story—everything that's happening with Fallon and Miranda."

"No, I guess I don't. Why don't you tell me about it?"

Kayleigh licked her lips and hugged the strap of

her bag tighter against her chest. She opened her mouth, but her words were drowned out by three hard, heavy raps on the glass. She whirled and my head snapped up, just in time to see Fallon's narrowed eyes, that slate-blue stare boring into me. She was in the hallway, her lips set in a hard, thin line. She disappeared from view, the snap of her gum echoing in the hallway before she pulled open my door. Her eyes regarded me coolly before zeroing in on Kayleigh. I was shaking for her, the sweat breaking out at the back of my neck, but Kayleigh dropped into the iceberg-cool mode I was sure I'd never master.

Fallon snapped another bubble.

"Do you want a ride home or not? I've been waiting for you for, like, ever."

I surreptitiously glanced at the clock: nine minutes since the last bell. I was about to let Kayleigh off of Fallon's barbed hook, but she spoke, shaking her long hair over her shoulder and turned her back on me.

"Old lady Lawson said my Beowulf paper lacked depth."

"She should know all about lacking depth," Fallon said in a low snark.

I rolled my eyes, then grabbed a page off my desk, scrawled my number down and stepped in between the girls, shoving the half-folded paper into Kayleigh's hands. I caught her eye, held it.

"Here's your paper back. If you'd like help, you can call on me, anytime."

I waited for a miniscule flash of thanks or apology to flit through Kayleigh's eyes but got nothing. She just snatched the page and edged past Fallon to get out the door. Fallon said nothing, but she shot me a look that was so icy that I actually shivered before she let the door go. I caught it before it snapped shut and stood there, considering. When I caught a mane of fuzzy dark hair out of the corner of my eye, I dashed toward it.

"Miranda?"

Miranda, her back to me as she sipped from the water fountain, straightened, then turned slowly.

"Um, Ms. L?"

I leaned in so our foreheads were nearly touching. "I need to talk to you."

Miranda tried to inch away from me, her butt up against the water fountain. "I told you—"

"It's not about Fallon," I said, shaking my head. "It's not about bullying or what happened in the hallway."

Miranda looked around. I realized we were circled now, girls strategically angled to look like they weren't paying attention to us, but every eyebrow was quirked, every glossed lip was pursed in a slick smile. Miranda looked part horrified, part pacified—as though being the center of unwanted attention was something she had gotten used to.

"Please?" I said on a whisper.

Miranda took a step forward and I led her to an alcove in the hall. I would have dragged her into my room, but after Kayleigh and Fallon, I figured it wouldn't be long until Heddy or Principal Lowe stationed an armed guard there.

"You're not really a teacher, are you?"

I started. "Well, no. I'm a substitute."

Miranda smiled. "Yeah?"

I felt an instant wave of guilt and I made a mental note to get my hormones checked. I was investigating a crime scene undercover, and feeling guilty for lying to possible major players.

"Yeah. Look, I know we talked a little bit before—about clubs and stuff on campus." I held her eyes, hoping my raised brows would convey what I didn't want to say.

"Yeah, so?"

I lowered my voice. "And the covens?"

Miranda shrugged. "Yeah, we talked about that."

I sighed and pinched the bridge of my nose. "Look, I don't work for the school, okay? At least not officially. But I really need to know, Miranda, are there girls who think they're witches here?"

Miranda didn't seem startled by my question, but she didn't answer, either.

"The book that you dropped in your scuffle with Fallon? This is it, right?" I unfolded one of the color copies of the book's cover.

Miranda gave it a cursory look, her shoulders rising a half inch. "Yeah, why?"

"It's a book of spells, Miranda."

"I know. You don't think that I—I'm not some kind of witch. I just—some girls . . ." Her voice trailed off, her eyes focusing on her shoes.

"It's okay. I know what they are."

Miranda's head snapped up, her eyes wide. "You do?"

"Protection spells. I know what this is, too." I unfolded the copy of the symbol carved into the desk in my classroom.

Miranda took the page from me and studied it. "Is this in the book? I didn't really read it."

"You don't recognize this symbol?"

Miranda swung her head. "Should I?"

"You said you weren't friends with Cathy Ledwith."

Miranda leaned against the alcove wall and yanked on the straps of her backpack. "Not really, no."

"You knew her from around school?"

She nodded wordlessly, her eyes skittering to mine, then going back to her toes.

"Did you know she had the same spell book that you have?"

Miranda looked up, but the "oh my!" expression I was wanting wasn't there. Instead, she shrugged again and said, "No. Was she one of the witches?"

I swallowed hard. "No, I don't think so. But the book is for protection. So is the symbol. Cathy had both and now you—you at least have the book. What—or who—are you afraid of, Miranda?"

Miranda kicked at the ground, the toe of her sneaker grimy and well worn.

I hunched so I was directly in her line of sight. "Miranda, this is important. You're not going to get in trouble if you tell me."

Finally she looked up, her cheeks blazing red. "I bought it by mistake."

I felt my eyebrows arch up. "By mistake?"

Miranda kicked at the floor again, checked her backpack straps a second time, and glanced at the ceiling—anything to avoid my gaze while the blush on her cheeks went all the way to the tops of her ears. "I thought it was a book on love spells."

"Love spells?" I said it out loud, then clapped a hand over my mouth. Then, in a whisper, "You wanted a book of love spells?"

"Yeah." It was barely a mumble.

"What for?"

Miranda looked up at me. "What do you think?"

Now I felt myself blush.

"Look at me, Ms. L."

"You're beautiful."

"Because I'm smart, funny, and some day some amazing guy is going to come along and realize it, once guys are mature enough to see over my current idiocy? Thanks, I've heard it. I'm sixteen. I've never even held hands with a guy."

"Well, you are at an all-girls school."

"I know it's stupid, but I don't have any friends at school so it's not like I can even go to one of the mixer dances. Like I'm just going to walk in there alone and stand there the whole night, waiting for Mr. Mature to throw someone like Fallon or Kayleigh aside and ask me to dance. Never. Going. To. Happen. Never! I thought maybe—I don't really believe in the stuff—but I thought maybe I could get a little extra help." Her smile was small, almost apologetic. "I figured, what could it hurt, right?"

I sighed, wanting to hug her, wanting to gush about all the dances I sat at home through, how the last actual date I'd been on ended with a jaw-snapping werewolf and a zombie pub crawl. But I also wanted to give this kid hope.

"You don't need any book of spells to get a boy to notice you. Maybe just—" I put an index finger under her lowered chin and gently tilted her head up. "Maybe just look up once in a while. Make eye contact."

Miranda smiled, her cheeks still pink. "I was so embarrassed buying that book that I walked into the store, went straight to the book shelf, and assumed any book with a red binding must be about love. I guess I picked wrong. I hadn't even opened it."

"So you didn't buy a book of protection spells because you thought you were in any danger?"

"Only in danger of being alone for the rest of my life."

"That won't happen. But no more spells, okay?"

"Okay." Miranda turned and was halfway out of the alcove before I stopped her.

"Hey—what do you know about Lock and Key Club?"

She shrugged. "Only that I can't get in. Ask one of the perfect girls." She waved, made a point to look me in the eye, and disappeared down the hall.

I went back to my classroom to gather my things and sat there, alone, until the school quieted as students filed out of the halls and into the parking lot. It was still early, but the fog had already rolled in, casting shadows through the large picture windows. I was in a silent, mourning stupor, which is why I nearly tossed my cell phone across the room when it started sputtering a jazz-heavy version of "God Save the Queen."

"You changed my ringtone again, didn't you?"

"And a good day to you, too," Will chirped into my ear. "Where are you?"

"What do you mean?"

"Simple question, love. Where. Are. You. I, myself, am sitting at your kitchen table enjoying a spot of tea."

I hopped off the desk, offended. "Why are you at my house? How did you get into my house?"

"A good Guardian shall always have access to his charge's place."

"A good Guardian wouldn't have to call to know where his charge is."

"Touché."

"I thought you'd come down here, to the school," I said, pressing my fingers against my just-starting-to-ache forehead.

"I have my every confidence in you. Besides, football's on."

I could hear the rush of the crowd from his side of the phone. "Whatever. I'm going to grab a couple of those yearbooks, maybe poke around a bit, then I'm on my way home. Be ready to go by Alyssa's house when I get there." I glanced at the closed door. "And maybe Fallon's. Okay?"

"Aye aye, love."

I hung up the phone on a groan.

I heard the clack-clack-clack of Heddy's shoes before I saw her. Then suddenly she was in front of me, all pudges and grins.

"Well, Sophie! I didn't know you were still here."

"Um, just wrapping up a few things. Actually, though, it's a good thing I ran into you. Does Mercy have a policy against bullying?"

Heddy's eyes were wide behind her big round glasses. "Oh my, yes. The bullying has gotten so bad nowadays."

I cocked an eyebrow. "So you've had bullying here on campus?"

"Heavens, no! The girls here all get along. They're just angels! Well, you remember that from your years here, don't you?"

I thought back to my cowering, terror-filled years,

the overwhelming silence and screaming into my pillows at night. "Yeah, sure. It was a big ol' love fest."

Heddy smiled at me and hiked up her bag, flipping up her collar as though she were heading into the Arctic. "I hope we get to see you around under better circumstances," she said as she pushed open the door.

I offered her a pressed-lipped smile and waved. The door snapped shut behind her and echoed through the silent hall.

Chapter Twelve

The semi-deserted parking lot shouldn't have been scary. There were splashes of light from poles that dotted the concrete, and five hundred feet away cars honked, tires squeaked, and muddled bass thumped as traffic eked down Nineteenth. But either way I was a woman who was aware, who watched all the "it could happen to you" specials and who had been pummeled by everything from a sweaty book agent to a rabid vampire. I walked with purpose, making a zippy beeline toward my car with my keys threaded through my knuckles—a makeshift set of eyeball-gauging claws.

It was these claws that tumbled from my hand when I awkwardly tried to stab them into the door lock. I bent over to retrieve them and my shoulder bag walloped me in the chin while my backpack clipped the back of my head. I steadied myself against my car door and pressed myself back up slowly (lest I behead myself on a side view mirror).

That was when an engine revved and the headlights from the car half a parking lot away clicked on and flooded me and mine in glaring white light. I was temporarily blinded, unable to see anything but the glowing white orbs. I squinted and the driver revved his engine again.

"Big engine, small dick," I mumbled, searching for my car key.

I heard the faint crunch of gravel and then the unmistakable sound of rubber peeling over concrete. My head snapped back and the white orbs were growing bigger and bigger as the car came hurtling toward me, its engine throbbing so loudly that the sound pinged through my bones, made my teeth feel weird and achy.

The driver saw me, I know he did. Or if by chance he didn't, there was no mistaking my car beside me, my smashed-up, *vampire*-scrawled car. But he didn't seem to care. The headlights didn't waver, didn't move a millimeter to either side. The driver knew where I was and was aiming right for me—quickly.

My brain told me to move, to dive, to swerve, to run, but my feet weren't mine. They wouldn't respond, *couldn't* respond, and kept me rooted to the vibrating concrete as the car closed the distance between us.

I could smell the exhaust from the car, the fast burn of gas on the chilled night air. I knew it couldn't have been more than a few seconds—five at the most—but it felt like a lifetime, me rooted to that spot, my meager offering of skin and bones and muscle and flesh against two thousand pounds of rocketing steel. Adrenaline shot through me in fiery waves and my legs gave out. I felt my hair whip across the flying car and I clenched my eyes shut, crushing my palms against my ears as the sound of metal pulverizing metal deafened me. I heard the pop of glass, saw the shards fall in delicate slow motion—like snowflakes, I thought—as they danced to the ground, glistening in the weakening light. I felt my flesh breaking, hot against the concrete.

And suddenly it was quiet. Dead quiet.

I couldn't feel anything. My heart wasn't beating, the blood that had been coursing through my veins was stiff and oddly silent. I dropped my head and felt the concrete grating into my cheek.

Then there was pain, and noise.

Cars honking, tires squeaking, the muddled bass of cars on Nineteenth.

Blood pulsed from my bottom lip, now swollen and tasting like dirt. I edged myself out from under my car, amazed that I had gotten there. My arms and palms looked like someone had taken a cheese grater to them and bloomed with fresh heat.

My heart started to thunder. The blood started to pulse. Suddenly, I was gasping, crying, coughing, doubled over with my arms wrapped around my stomach, hugging myself while fresh tears rolled over my nose and fell onto the ground in front of my shoes.

"Ms. Lawson? Ms. L, is that you?"

I heard Miranda's voice over the din of traffic. I inched my eyes up, and when hers met mine, she vaulted out of the doorway and sprinted toward me.

"Oh my gosh, Ms. Lawson, what happened to you? Are you okay? Should I call someone? The police or 9-1-1?"

I sucked in a deep, steadying breath and pushed myself to standing. Miranda's cheeks were flushed— whether from the short run from the school or her concern for me, I wasn't sure—and her eyes were glassy and wide.

"No, thanks, Miranda," I said, shaking my head slowly. "I'm okay. Really."

She shifted her weight and a shard of glass from my smashed side-view mirror popped under her foot. She jumped. "What was that? What happened?"

"That"—I used the toe of my shoe to nudge some errant glass aside—"is what remains of my mirror."

"Your car mirror?"

"Someone tried—" I paused, biting my bottom lip. I could feel the lump tightening in my throat, but I couldn't cry in front of Miranda, in front of my student. And I couldn't drag her into this. "Someone just cut a little too close to my car while they were leaving the lot." I felt my heart thunder, remembering the brush of metal against my hair even as I lied about it. "They must not have seen me." I managed a small smile.

Miranda studied me suspiciously. "You look like you were crying."

My hand flew to my face. "Oh, do I? Probably because I was thinking of how much my insurance was going to go up. You know, hit and run and all."

I saw Miranda's gaze go over my shoulder and examine my shit heap of a car. "You have insurance?"

"Um, what are you doing out here? It's late. Can't possibly have been in detention."

"I stay late a lot." She thumbed over her shoulder. "Heddy—Ms. Gaines—lets me do some administration stuff for her while I wait for the bus so I don't have to hang outside the whole time."

"You stay until"—I glanced down at my watch—"after six every day?"

"Oh, no. Not every day. Today I talked to you, and that made me a little bit late so I missed the earlier bus."

My near-death-experience emotional rush was replaced by an apologetic blush. "Oh, no. I'm really sorry."

Miranda yawned, then shrugged. "No big deal. Not the first time I missed it," she grinned, wide and genuinely. "Won't be the last."

"Why don't you let me drive you home?"

She shook her head with a sweet smile. "That's okay. It's probably out of your way."

"It's the least I can do for making you miss the first bus. And you may have saved me from a potential mow-down. I kind of owe you."

Miranda opened her mouth just as the Muni bus wailed to a stop at the curb. "That's my bus," she said, taking a step back.

She gave me a tight wave before turning around on her heel and sprinting toward the bus, backpack bobbing behind her. I watched until she boarded. She turned and glanced back at me, her whole body illuminated by the heavy yellow glow of the bus lights.

The bus belched out a puff of black air as it groaned away from the curb; I watched the illuminated trip board blaring HUNTERS POINT/BAYVIEW and sighed. Hunters Point was the most undesirable place to live in the whole city. Miranda wouldn't let me drive her home because she didn't want me to know where she lived.

"It never changes," I mumbled to myself.

I had almost managed to forget I that I had been a half-inch away from being a hood ornament until I opened my apartment door. Nina immediately jumped off the couch and slammed her pale hands against her open mouth.

"Ohmigod, Soph, what happened?" Her coal-black

eyes were huge and saucer wide. She was on me in a heartbeat, and the second she slid her ice-cold arms around me, I crumbled.

"Someone tried to kill me!" I wailed into the crook of her neck.

Nina stiffened. "Again?"

I pulled back and attempted an indignant huff, then fell back against my best friend. "Yeeeeeeees!" I hiccupped, then burrowed my face into Nina's neck. "I got run over!"

Nina took a few careful steps back, keeping one hand splayed against me while the other pressed against her perfect little ski-jump nose. "By a manure truck?"

I started. "Wha—?" Then I snaked a hand under my shirt and pulled off Lorraine's fetid "charm," tossing it across the room. "That was supposed to protect me." I fell into another heap of tears, this one due both to my recent dance with a Goodyear and the fact that I smelled like a giant cow pie.

"Oh, Sophs, it's going to be okay. No one's going to kill you, I promise. I mean, look how many times people have tried."

"But why do people keep trying? It sucks so much! I never try and kill anyone."

Nina cocked an eyebrow and I frowned.

"Okay, okay. But they were all really bad people." I clapped a hand to my chest. "I'm a good person and yet people keep trying to pummel the crap out of me." I pressed the pads of my fingers to my swollen bottom lip. "And they keep getting closer and closer."

Nina went to the kitchen while I settled myself on the couch. ChaCha circled me, looking concerned, and I cuddled her to me until Nina returned with an ice cube wrapped in a dishcloth. She pressed it gently to my lip. "You have a swollen lip and a couple of scratches. That's so not a big deal. Remember when you almost got staked? And you got stabbed in the leg? Those were way closer. And you escaped a fire! Goodness, Adam was hell bent on taking you out and you survived that."

"For some reason, none of that makes me feel any better."

ChaCha whined on my behalf and shoved her little dog muzzle in my armpit.

The door clicked open and Vlad walked in, shaking off his duster and narrowly missing hanging it up. "Hey, what's going on?"

"Sophie's upset that people keep trying to kill her."

"Still?" Vlad's lip curled.

"Again."

Vlad shrugged and picked up the mail on the table. "Try being a vampire. They make movies about all the people who want to kill us."

I peeked over the edge of the couch, my eyes narrowed. "Yeah, but you're immortal. It really has much more weight when you're full of blood and can actually die from being pummeled by a car."

"Potato, potah-to. Do we have anymore O neg?"

Proof positive that even at a hundred and thirteen, a sixteen-year-old never changes.

I stepped into the shower and scrubbed every inch of myself until my skin hurt, trying in earnest to get rid of the feelings of parking lot and imminent death. When I was nice and pink and warm, I slipped into my bathrobe and padded into my bedroom, ChaCha trotting happily on my tail.

I yanked open my top drawer and frowned, poking around at what should have been a sea of silk and lace. Or, more accurately, cotton and elastic stretched to the hilt.

Either I was woefully behind on laundry duty or there was a panty prowler afoot.

"Um, Neens?"

Nina came floating into my bedroom trailed by a cloud of pale pink silk and marabou. She was also wearing kitten heels, and her eyes were made up with thick swaths of black liner that winged at the sides, fringed with the most enviably long eyelashes I'd even seen—boxed or otherwise. The heavily lined lashes and lids only served to make the flat red color on her lips even more dramatic. She blinked at me and gingerly patted her hair—a spectacular waterfall of glossy waves the size of juice cans.

"Did you just do that while I was in the tub?"

Nina flicked an imaginary hair from her eye. "Maybe."

"Wow. And here I thought you were directing a commercial, not starring in the *Whatever Happened to Baby Jane* biop."

Nina crossed her arms in front of her chest, a rainstorm of marabou feathers showering her wrists and my carpet. "You have no vision."

"I have no underwear, either."

She cocked a slightly interested—if overtly confused—brow. "What are you talking about?"

I gestured to my knicker-free drawer. "I did laundry two days ago. Suddenly, I have nothing. Have you seen my underpants?"

"I try not to keep too tight an eye on your undergarments, Soph. That's just disgusting."

I yanked the pants I was planning to wear from where they lay on my desk chair and waggled them in front of her. "Not as disgusting as going commando in a poly-blend. Do you know what happened to my underwear?"

I could tell by the slight flash in Nina's eyes and the delicate way she pinched her upper lip that there was something she wasn't telling me.

"Nina?"

She went from tugging her lip to tapping her sleekly manicured index finger against her nose. "I may have had a few people over. Investors, mainly, for the shoot. If you really want high quality, you can't just shoot the thing on an iPhone. I know they say you can but—"

An annoying heat stirred in my belly—while a cool breeze wafted through my bare legs. "Did you sell my underwear for financial backing? Who would do that? Who would *buy* that?!"

"Don't be ridiculous! I wouldn't sell your underwear because you're right, who would buy it? Perhaps you've just misplaced it." Nina looked at the blank spot on her wrist and tapped it. "I'm going to be late. I have to dress. You should, too. We can get to the bottom of this later. Here." She picked through the meager remains of my lingerie drawer and handed me what appeared to be a sequined Chinese jump rope. "Panties. Now quit being such a baby."

I yanked on the underwear, assuming each string was going in the correct direction, then dressed quickly and did an "are you kidding me with this butt floss?" duck walk toward the bathroom, rubbing my scalp with a towel.

"Aren't you a vision of soppy wet loveliness?"

Will's fat, grinning face reflected back in my mirror, and I almost hauled off and bludgeoned him with my hair dryer.

"How did you get in here?"

"I'm not a vampire, love. No one has to invite me in."

I rolled my eyes and clicked on my hair dryer.

"You ready to head over to Alyssa's?"

I yanked the cord from the wall and began wrapping it around my still-warm dryer. "You obviously didn't hear what happened to me just a few short hours ago. Hand me that comb."

Will grabbed the comb, edged me aside and ran it through his own hair. I snatched it out of his hand and used my hip to shove him aside.

"I almost died!"

Will didn't show the proper amount of horror or concern. Instead, he cocked a sandy eyebrow and asked, "Again?"

I crossed my arms in front of my chest. "Just because it happens fairly often doesn't make it any less dramatic."

He slid an arm out and pulled me to him, pressing his lips against the top of my head. "I'm sorry, love. It is serious."

I shoved him off one more time. "Yeah, and as my Guardian, you should have been there. Or, at the very least, I should not have so many almost-murdering-me incidents, now should I?"

"Actually, love, I'm contracted specifically for fallen angels and all the baddies who want to cut the Vessel out of you, remember? Anything else really isn't in my jurisdiction."

My mouth dropped open. "That's what's wrong with Americans today! Slackers. No one willing to do anything more than their job description allows."

"I'm not American, love."

"Still!" I was fuming. I turned on my heel and

marched out of the bathroom, stopping only to narrow my eyes at Will. "See this spot on the ground?" I screamed, feeling the hysteria growing in my chest. "This could have been me!"

"It happened here?"

"No, at the school. In the parking lot."

"Did you upset the bathroom ghost again?"

"This. Is. Serious. And you know what? I'm going to file a complaint with the Guardian department. I'm going to get a new Guardian! Who do I call?"

"W-w-w-dot-guardian-dot-com."

I paused. "Seriously?"

"No."

"Ass!"

I stomped toward my bedroom, watching Nina and Vlad's heads swinging back from me to Will like they were watching a tennis match.

"I think this one's way funnier," I heard Vlad tell Nina.

Will caught up with me and threaded his arm through mine. He pulled me along with him. "We'll go ahead and wrap you in bubble wrap the second time allows."

I rolled my eyes. "So. Not. Helping."

I was far less steamed by the time I was dressed and settled in Nigella. Partly because I had found a clean pair of non-stringy underwear and partly because Will apologized with a hunk of Galaxy chocolate.

"Are you sure we're going in the right direction?" Will wanted to know.

"Well, if you would break down and buy a car from this century, we could be following a GPS. Right now, this"—I waggled the directions Vlad had printed out for me, complete with the *Some roads may no longer be accessible or exist* warning— "is all we have."

Will sighed, but leaned back into the driver's seat. "Okay."

"Oh, right up there. That's the street we need."

We turned off the main road and were immediately plunged into a mecca of large houses with actual lawns and perfectly manicured landscaping. Hulking trees laced over the streets, but the cheery, mega-watt streetlamps made everything look like it was a Martha Stewart setup rather than anything encroaching or smothering.

"Nice neighborhood," Will said, nodding. "Quaint."

"If you consider five thousand-square-foot houses quaint. This is it."

The doors in front of me were the largest I had ever seen. Like, behemoth, leering, laughably big. They, along with the carefully coifed swirls of juniper in pots the size of my bathroom, dwarfed me physically and mentally, everything telling me that I was a tiny, unsavory fly in the ointment of the posh. I tried to steel myself, to steady my shoulders and give myself the kind of self-talk that included bon mots like "money doesn't buy class" and "no one has the power to make you feel small but you," but even with such great bumper-sticker nuggets it was more than obvious that I stuck out like a sad, sore thumb among the carefully cultivated perfection here, and I almost felt sorry for Alyssa, for having spent her formative years as a showpiece in this gilded cage.

My fingertip on the doorbell released a series of clock-tower bells. The hunchback-esque crescendo shouldn't have shocked me, but it did and I hopped back, hand on my chest, Will's arms quickly snaking around my waist.

"It's just a doorbell, love."

I quickly righted myself, feeling heat zinging through me. I blinked and stuttered. "Um, right."

The open door sliced through my awkwardness with Will and a one-dimensional image of a perfect, upscale soccer mom poked her dewy, Botox-young face through the opening.

"Yes," she said, blinking red-rimmed eyes that seemed to bulge around her pulled skin. "May I help you?"

I cleared my throat and mustered up courage from somewhere, offering a teeth-baring smile that I hoped was more welcoming than grimacing. "My name is Sophie Lawson and this is Will Sherman. We're teachers from your daughter's school.

I appreciate this is a difficult time, but would it be possible to speak with you about your daughter, Mrs. Rand?"

Mrs. Rand seemed to shrink into the slit of open doorway. I could see her hand go to her throat, her bony knuckles pressing against her breastbone. "You have the wrong house," she said, her voice suddenly hoarse. "The Rands don't live here."

The woman clicked the door shut before I had a chance to respond.

I sighed, pushing out my bottom lip. "Well, that was useless."

Will licked his lips and grinned, looking nothing less than smug. "Not exactly."

I rolled my eyes, sighing. "Oh, let me guess? Your plan is to bat those sexy hazel eyes at Mrs. Rand in there and she's going to roll over and give you anything you want, huh?"

Will's grin went from smug to mischievous in a single, panty-melting second. "You think my eyes are sexy?"

I felt the blush roll into my eyeballs. "Uh, so, what was your plan?"

His eyes washed over me and cut over my shoulder. He jutted his chin and I looked. "What's she doing here?"

Fallon was cresting the hill on a white and mint-green bicycle, spotlighted by the streetlights. She was still in her uniform, her Mercy skirt tucked between her legs, the heavy fabric brushing against her thighs, catching the breeze, exposing the edge of her white, boy-short panties. Her hair sailed behind her in long pigtails, lazy s-waves that licked her shoulder blades and tumbled down her back. Her lips were pursed, her eyes a steely blue. She zig-zagged down the street, commanding the blacktop as though a car would never dream of clipping her, of stopping her slow ride.

Even I was taken by her, and I felt myself scowl. Fallon Monroe was a lollypop and an Aerosmith song away from a Nabokov novel.

I jumped back as Fallon skittered to a stop in front of Will and me. Her eyes never left his and her front tire grazed my pant leg. I would have been certain that her pigtails and push-up bra had resulted in a stunning case of tunnel vision had she not flicked an apathetic, "Sorry, Ms. L," my way.

Fallon pressed her feet to the ground, the bike balanced lewdly between her thighs. "What are you doing here, Mr. Sherman?"

Will's eyes were firmly lodged on Fallon's fore-head and I appreciated that, given the fact that Fallon's perfectly manicured forefinger and thumb were playing with the top button on her blouse. A hint of white lace peeked out, stunning against her tan skin.

"Actually, Ms. Lawson and I were looking to speak to Mrs. Rand."

"Ms."

"What was that?" I asked.

Fallon kicked at the dirt. "Ms. Rand. She's not married. And she's not here right now. She's probably on her way home."

"Home? Doesn't she live here?"

Fallon's laugh was halting and bitter as she swung a leg over her bike seat. "She doesn't live here. She works here." She grabbed the handlebars and pushed the bike up the walk, dropping it unceremoniously on the porch. The bike dropped in a huge clatter, and Fallon was walking through the front door that had just been slammed in our faces.

Will's eyebrows shot up. "Well, how about that?"

"How about nothing." I was striding up the walk, about to knock, when Will grabbed my arm.

"What are you doing?"

I whirled, suddenly angry for being jealous of a teenage girl's sex appeal, angry that Fallon got to live in a house like this, angry that I would always be the outsider with the heavy, gorgeous door to fabulousness slammed in my face.

"I'm going to find out some answers." I whipped Alyssa Rand's records out of my purse. "How come the address Mercy has on file for Alyssa is Fallon's address? And what did Fallon mean that Ms. Rand doesn't live at this house. She—" I paused, feeling dense. "Alyssa's mother works for Fallon's family."

Will nodded and took Alyssa's papers from my hand. "And Alyssa's mother must have used the Monroes' address to keep her daughter at Mercy."

"I feel like this blows everything wide open."

Will eyed me. "You're thinking that address masking led to Alyssa's kidnapping? Or Cathy Ledwith's? Wait." He splayed both his hands as though he were about to lay something deep on me. "You've discovered that the demon our little criminals are trying to summon is the Antichrist of desegregation, right? Satan's own school administrator?"

I narrowed my eyes, clenching my fists and jamming them into my pockets so I wouldn't wallop Will right between his sexy hazel eyes in the middle of the goddamn street. "Go to hell."

"Okay, I'm sorry. Go ahead." Will held up his palms. "Tell me your theory."

I thrummed my fingers against my hip bones, the cogs in my head spinning but coming up with little.

"Well, there is only one reason why a student would have to use another address to attend a private school. Frankly, if you have the money and the grades, you could live on Jupiter and still attend—as long as you show up, right?"

Will shrugged blankly. "This is your thing, love."

"Every year, a certain number of scholarships are made available. The girls have to do well on the entrance exam and have the grades, but they all have to live within a certain radius of the school."

"So?"

"So, Alyssa, likely on scholarship, used Fallon's address to qualify."

"Aha!"

I turned. "Aha, what?"

"Nothing. I just don't see how your little theory here changes or, let's just say, 'improves' anything. But I wanted to be supportive."

I rolled my eyes. "I'm thinking out loud here. What if someone caught on to Alyssa's false address and threatened to not only have her expelled, but have"—I dropped my voice to a hoarse whisper and cut my eyes toward the house—"Fallon exposed, too."

Will blinked at me, expression completely unchanged. "Is being on scholarship really that bad? Like, murderously bad?"

I shook my head. "Only for your social standing. I was on scholarship and hid it like it was some kind of oozing lesion."

"I'm going to have good dreams tonight," Will said with a grimace.

"Everyone teased me anyway, but when they found out I was a scholarship, too . . . oh, God. It was like a feeding frenzy."

I remembered walking down the hall as slowly as possible so that the school would be empty by the time I got to my locker, but no one was budging.

I could hear their muffled giggles. I didn't dare look at anyone because the giggles were easier to stomach than the narrowed, challenging eyes of Jessica and her gang, but worse were the eyes of

*the other students. They almost seemed to flash
sympathy, but no one spoke up or offered me a re-
assuring glance. Most just looked away, thankful
it was me and not them.*

*The thump of my heart got louder with each step
I took and by the time I was ten feet away, I could see
that something was pasted all over my locker.*

*Coupons. An application for public assistance.
The Goodwill logo torn from a paper bag.*

*Jessica Bray sashayed up to me, a fresh coat of
orange-scented gloss on her lips. She batted those
huge, doe-innocent eyes at me. "Heard about your
situation. Thought these might take some of the
burden off you. Who knows? Maybe you can save
enough to get yourself a decent pair of shoes."*

More than a decade later I could still smell the
faint scent of orange blossom and it turned my
stomach and shot an embarrassed heat down my
spine.

"Maybe someone was willing to exterminate the
issue to keep her status secret?"

Will crossed his arms in front of his chest and
cocked his head. "You really think someone would
go to such lengths?"

I groaned and rubbed my forehead in a vain attempt to cull the throb that had begun. "No. I just
feel like we're running in circles. There may or may
not be a coven on campus. Are some girls witches?

Or just bitches? I should have just got out of this when Sampson gave me the chance."

Will shrugged and pulled out his keys, leaving me behind to sulk. I trotted after him. "Aren't you going to tell me that we really are making progress? That I'm not a total failure?"

He gave me a quick once-over before disappearing into the car. I snatched the passenger-side door open and slid in. "Well?"

"Well, nothing. We've come up against a dead end. I haven't time to tend to your bruised ego. There's an Arsenal game on and I fancy a pint."

I felt my lower lip press out and my bruised ego was starting to grate.

"Coming with?" Will asked me as we coasted along a surprisingly un-crowded Geary Boulevard.

Though drinking myself into a beer-addled oblivion sounded particularly pleasurable at that exact moment, my pulse was still thundering and the mass of puzzle pieces that never seemed to fit nagged at me.

"Can you drop me at the police station, please?" Will's brows went up.

"I think I'll just go into work and see if there's anything pressing."

Will bobbed his head once as though he were considering the validity of my answer rather than agreeing with me in any way.

I had my hand on the glass double doors at the entrance of the police station as Nigella coughed into reverse behind me. She and Will were halfway down the street when my body seemed to seize up. Everything locked tightly; even the blood pulsing through my veins seemed to freeze solid.

"Help me!"

Chapter Thirteen

It was a whisper at first, then louder, more insistent. I tried to turn my head, wanted to lean toward the sound, but I was still frozen—bound, somehow. Red washed over my eyes and I could see bits of light in front of me. My shoulder blades ached as they pressed against something wet and cold; I could feel the moisture seeping through my shirt. Now I was the one who wanted to beg for help, but my lips were cracked and dry and my throat was sandpapery and hoarse. I knew—somehow—that it was from hours of screaming.

A figure leaned over me, his edges blurred. I blinked and then blinked again, trying to clear my eyes, trying to get a better look. A coarse cloth brushed over my bare arm and I strained to shrink away from it—but I was still frozen, still bound.

My lips parted and I winced at the needling pain as the skin at the corners of my mouth slit and tore. Blood trickled past my lips.

"What do you want?" I heard myself whisper. "What do you want from me?"

But when I saw the edge of the blade catch on the moonlight, I already knew.

"Whoa, Sophie!"

I felt like I had been underwater and suddenly broken the surface. I gasped, and Officer Romero grabbed me by both arms, his eyes the size of dinner plates. "Let me call Grace."

"No!" I stumbled backward. "No. I—I'm sorry, I was just daydreaming and you surprised me."

Romero's dark brows went up. "You were daydreaming in the doorway of the police station?"

"I'm fine, really," I lied, as my heart hammered like a fire bell. "Fine." I squeezed by Romero into the safety of the vestibule. "I've just got to get—" I forced a smile, relief crashing over me when Romero kindly smiled back. "I've just got to get my head on straight."

"Yeah," Romero said, finally grinning. "I can respect that. Have a good night."

I stayed rooted in the vestibule until Romero crossed the parking light and disappeared into his squad car. By that time, I could feel little beads of sweat prickling at the back of my neck while I mashed my finger against the elevator's down button twenty times over.

The Underworld Detection Agency waiting room was deserted. The rows of blocky chairs and tattered magazines looked benign under the sodium chloride safety lights, but the calm façade did nothing to settle my nerves. I headed directly to my office, shoved the stack of papers and messages on my chair to the floor, and sat down on a sigh, holding my head in my hands. Finally, I steeled myself and picked up the phone.

"'Lo?"

"Lorraine? It's me. It's Sophie. Can I ask you something?"

Lorraine sounded like she was chewing on her end of the phone, and she didn't bother to stop. "If it's quick. I have six orders to drop off tonight."

I licked my lips. "Can a witch—can a witch make someone see—or hear something? I mean, like, could someone like you remotely make someone—"

"Someone like you?"

I sucked in a breath. "Yes, someone like me. Can someone like you remotely make someone like me hear someone's voice?"

"Tell me exactly what happened."

I relayed the details of my police station parking lot experience, cringing with each new word and each new thought that I was finally losing my marbles.

"Oh, God, Sophie. You're dealing with someone pretty powerful. This is from the school case, huh?"

I pinched my bottom lip. "Yeah. Look, Will and I found a couple of spell books—just protection spells. Is this the kind of spell that someone can learn?"

"From a book?" Lorraine snorted. "No way. There are some spells and incantations that can be learned from a book and some that are only passed down through families and covens. The spell that overtook you? It's the latter. Its not the kind of thing someone just messes around with."

"But why would someone—this mysterious, powerful witch—want to show me something incriminating? Or at least something that could possibly help me find Alyssa?"

"Could it help you find the girl?"

I frowned. "No. But there was someone in a robe and a knife. That's got to be pretty specific to a certain spell, right?"

"Absolutely. With a robe and a dagger, a witch can bind another being, call dark forces into their servitude, and ensure that a herd of cattle stays fertile. Among other things."

"Great. So I'm not even a tiny bit closer to figuring out who—or why—or anything."

Lorraine paused for a beat. "I'll come by tonight. I can run a few clarification spells, do some star mapping—maybe I can shed some light on what's going on."

A little sliver of hope pierced my heart. "Yeah. Yeah, okay."

* * *

I rode up the elevator and when the big silver doors opened, I stood there mutely until the door began to slide shut again. Then I took a few tentative steps into the police department.

It was late enough that the majority of standard business was done there, and the only people left in the office were the nightshift and their newly caught, grumbling against their restraints or wailing that the police "got the wrong dude." Eventually, I found myself heading directly for Alex's office and hoping against hope that he was momentarily away while his office door was wide open, all the evidence in the Mercy kidnapping case spread out wide for me to take.

No such luck.

I rounded the corner and found myself in a standoff with Alex.

"What are you doing here?"

It wasn't the warm, fuzzy, possibly kissy greeting that I always hoped for, but it was pretty much becoming standard Alex Grace.

"Can I talk to you in your office, please?"

I watched Alex suck in a deep breath, his cut-crystal eyes sharp and suspicious.

He sank into his desk chair and I perched in the visitor's chair across from him. "So, how are you doing?"

Alex leaned back in his chair, the leather groaning underneath him. "What do you want, Lawson?"

I swallowed. "I want you to look up these names.

They were students at Mercy with me, and well, suddenly, one day they weren't. I think they might be part of this."

I handed the page across the desk to Alex. He glanced down at it, his eyes giving it a quick glance before he moved it aside. "Thank you."

"Aren't you going to do anything about it?"

Alex blinked. "Right now? No. I'll get around to looking at this after we bring Alyssa home."

I felt a flicker of anger growing at the pit of my stomach. "But this could help. If we find out what happened to these girls, we might be able to find out who—or what—is responsible. I'm trying to *help* you, Alex."

"Look, Lawson, we're doing all right, okay? Believe or not, the police department here can function without your help."

The sting shot through me and my cheeks burned. "Wait, what?"

"We have plenty of leads. We know we're looking at a serial."

"But the carving—and the witchcraft!"

"Probably happened after the fact." He slid my paper into a manila file folder and laced his fingers on top of it. "There really isn't any evidence that Cathy Ledwith's killer and the person who desecrated her corpse are the same people."

"You know that they are!"

Alex shrugged. "There's no evidence to support that."

"Let me just take a look at your files. I can show you mine." I yanked my notebook from my shoulder bag. "We found spell books and a pentagram. And a carving." Even as I said it, I knew how weak Will's and my "evidence" really was. "I didn't believe it either, but there's something there, Alex, I'm sure of it. Check the names. Look at this."

"Lawson, what do you want me to do? We're"— he pointed from himself to me—"not working together. And we're"—this time he circled a finger, indicating the police department—"not interested in finding a group of witches."

"A coven."

"What was that?"

"A coven. A group of witches is a coven." I zeroed in on Alex. "I can't believe you won't let me help you. We're friends, remember? Maybe even more than friends. Some *bunny* in San Francisco loves me?" I quoted the cheesy words from the plush hat he had given me, doing my best to squelch down an embarrassed burn.

"You had a concussion."

Heat snaked up my spine and I gritted my teeth. "What's with you? One day, you're kissing me and saving my life, the next day you're all fallen, no angel."

His expression stayed hard. "I'm sorry I'm not everything you dreamed of."

"What the hell is that supposed to mean?"

"That's supposed to mean that you and I have a

working relationship. Period. You remember what that means, right?" He narrowed his eyes, the tiny muscle at the side of his jaw jumping.

"Are you—are you accusing me of—"

"What else can I help you with, Lawson?"

I was too angry to sputter back at him, to throw his own on-again, off-again behavior back in his face. "What happened to you?"

"You know what I am, Lawson. You've known since the beginning."

I stood up, seething. "Yeah, but I didn't peg you for such an asshole." I turned on my heel, but not before seeing Alex's cheeks flash red and something—sorrow, apology—flit through his eyes. He opened his mouth but closed it again, silent.

I stomped through the police department, livid.

"Who does he think he is? I mean seriously, who? He just—he just—and cast me aside like—like—"

Nina pushed a glass into my hand.

"What is this?" I wanted to know.

"Booze. It will help stabilize you."

I took a giant glug, then winced. "Uh, what kind of booze? Where did you get it?"

Nina frowned. "From the cabinet. It's sherry."

"It's cooking sherry!"

Nina shrugged. "Same thing." She sashayed past me, the cool breeze that wafted from her marble skin sending goose pimples all over mine. "I think the whole thing is really romantic, actually."

I gaped before swiping up ChaCha and flopping on the couch. My little pup did her requisite three circles, then curled up in my lap. "What the hell is romantic about this? Alex acts like an ass after acting like an actual romantic hero?"

Nina popped up on the coffee table, and sat down hard, Indian style. Her dark eyes glittered. "Don't you see, Soph? That's the only way he *can* react. He can't be with you because you are the one thing that is keeping him from grace. See?"

She sat back, awash with candy hearts and hope, her hands clasped against her cheek.

"So he has to be pissed at me because I'm some sort of supernatural roadblock to where he wants to go. Sorry, but I'm just not seeing the romance."

Nina rolled her eyes and kicked her legs out in front of her, resting her bare feet in my lap, pushing her toes under ChaCha's warm fur. "He can't have you. And he can't kill you, because he loves you. And you've got Will—the other romantic hero. Oh my God, it's so amazingly romantic, I think my uterus is going to explode!"

"I'm still not seeing the slightest romantic element here." I wrinkled my nose. "And less so should your uterus explode."

"Romance?" Vlad thundered through the door. "Fuck romance. You know what I got today?" He shook the thin, flat box he was carrying.

Nina shriveled. "If that's another dead bird . . ."

"It's a summons," Vlad spat.

I raised my eyebrows. "A summons?"

Nina bit her bottom lip and looked apologetic. "I did tell you if you kept up with those stupid ascots, the fashion police would eventually catch up with you."

Vlad snarled and threw the box at my feet. "It's a summons from Kale. She's suing me."

"For what?"

Nina leaned forward and grabbed the box, pulling out a thick stack of papers and blinking. "Apparently for everything in the world. You've encroached on her right to liberty and happiness. Ooh, you've caused her pain and suffering, emotional distress—" She blanched, her marble skin going a sallow shade. "I don't even want to know where the damage to her soft tissue is." She held up a silencing finger before Vlad could answer. "Or what part of you may have damaged it."

"Who the hell would take the case of an eighteen-year-old jilted witch?"

Nina dropped a single page in my lap, the fancy heading in an expensive-looking raised font.

"Steve Elpher, attorney at law."

My eye started to do that twitching thing again.

I startled to giggle. Tiny little waves first that grew to maniacal ones. Vlad whirled and glared at me. The murderous look in his dark eyes should have— usually did—chill me right down to my beating heart, but just served to bring on another gale of unstoppable giggles.

"You think this is funny?"

All I could do was nod, point, and laugh harder when I started to snort and tears rolled down my cheeks.

A hint of a smile played on Nina's heart-shaped lips. "It's not that funny, Soph."

I shook my head, trying to catch my breath. "I know. I have no idea what's so funny."

"I think she's lost it."

Vlad snarled. "I'm not sure she's ever had it."

I flapped at the air, then used the heel of my hand to swipe at my tears. "Okay, okay, I'm sorry. But Steve? As an attorney? Twenty-four hours ago he was a janitor. And you're being sued. Sued! And as usual, I'm in the middle of an investigation and I've got diddly-squat."

Nina leaned back suspiciously, her eyes narrowing. "And you find that hilarious."

I stopped laughing. "No." I sniffed, scratched ChaCha behind the ears. "I think I just needed to let a little crazy out."

"So what are you going to do about the whole Alex/Will thing?"

Vlad looked desperate enough to self-combust. "Are we on that again?"

I sat up straight on the couch and ChaCha whimpered, moved from her soft spot. "No, no. I'm fine. I'm dedicating my life to serving the people of this great city."

"And your lady bits? Serving the people, too?" Nina asked smugly.

I rolled my eyes at Nina. "You're gross."

"You're crazy."

Vlad's nostrils flared. "You're both idiots."

"And you're being sued by a teen witch," I said with a dagger glare.

As if on cue, there was a sharp knock on the door, then Lorraine's voice wafting through. "Sophie? It's Lorraine and Kale."

Vlad's eyes seemed to swallow his whole face. "Did you do that? Did you make her come here?" he hiss-whispered.

"Sorry, Vlad," I said, crossing the living room. "I don't have that kind of power. You've got three seconds to decide what to do with yourself before Kale decides it for you."

His nostrils flared and I could see him press his jaws together, the tips of his razor-like fangs slicing in front of his lips. I had my hand on the doorknob and he whirled around, silently disappearing into Nina's closet-slash-bedroom. She rolled her eyes.

"Teenagers."

I snatched open the door just as Lorraine started to pound again. "Sorry. Thanks so much for coming, though."

Lorraine placed a Tupperware sandwich keeper topped with a floppy red bow in my hands and wordlessly pushed through the door, Kale in tow. Both ladies were loaded down with carpetbag-style luggage and serious expressions.

"I hope you like that," Lorraine said, edging her chin toward my new sandwich storage. "It's from the spring line. Now let's get busy."

She set to work clearing everything off the dining room table while Kale stood back, her eyes searching the apartment, finding, landing—and staying—on Nina's closed bedroom door. Nina popped directly into Kale's line of sight.

"Can I get you ladies something? Water, tea, eye of newt?"

Lorraine shot her a slightly annoyed look. Kale pressed her satchel to her chest and took a step toward Nina. Nina held up a hand, stop-sign style.

"He's not here."

Kale blinked, her kohled-over eyes suddenly going doe-innocent. "Who?"

"Okay, okay," I broke in, taking Kale's carpetbag in one hand, her arm in the other. "We need to focus on this case. Or, this spell. It's gotten worse since we last talked. The pentagrams and the spell books, Cathy last year and—" My stomach roiled, thinking of the disembodied hand hanging from my pant leg at the Battery. "And we're pretty sure there are others." I looked from Kale to Lorraine and lowered my voice. "And I think someone might be playing with my mind." Lorraine and I exchanged a look. "Making me see and hear things."

Lorraine nodded sympathetically and took my hand, giving it a tight little squeeze. "Like I said, we might be dealing with someone very powerful."

Kale turned to face me, arms crossed in front of her chest. "But you're immune to magic, right? I mean, aren't you?"

I worried my bottom lip, looking to Lorraine but receiving no help. "Maybe we're dealing with someone even more powerful."

Lorraine seemed to avoid my questioning glance, and Kale joined her at the table. They began spreading out all manner of maps and curl-edged, ancient-looking scrolls. Kale took her bag from me and upturned it, unloading a series of benign-looking garden rocks, a cache of half-burned candles, and a matchbook from Big Al's. She must have seen my eyebrows go up because she palmed the matchbook and blushed. "Someone left it at the office."

Will chose that moment to stick his head through the front door. He looked from Nina, still soldiering in front of her bedroom door, to Kale and Lorraine, then finally, to me.

"No one invites me to the party?" He stepped into the apartment and shook an enormous bag of potato chips. "I brought crisps."

"This isn't a party, Will," I said, pulling him into the apartment and throwing the lock behind him. "Lorraine and Kale are trying to help me—help us—find Alyssa."

He cut his eyes to me, the displeasure evident. "Thanks for calling on me."

I pinched the bridge of my nose. "Sorry, it was sort of last minute. Lorraine?"

She turned to me. "Are you still wearing the talisman that I gave you?"

I felt the blush crash over my cheeks. "Yes. I mean, right now, no, because I just got out of the shower. But I was."

"Put it on. And bring me the bag, too."

I went to my room, Will following a half-step behind me. "What's this all about?" he said, closing the bedroom door softly.

"I don't follow. What's what all about?"

"You call in the witch brigade on our assignment, but you don't call me?"

I shoved aside the heap of laundry on my chair and dug around for the talisman. "It wasn't like I was trying to cut you out of anything, Will. It just happened that way. I would have called you."

I brushed past him and he reached out, his hand closing around my elbow. He pulled me to face him. His lips were pressed in a thin straight line. "When would you have called me? When you were in grave danger?"

I took a step back, trying to shake his grip, but he held on for a silent beat, then finally let go. "I know I'm not Alex, but I'm your partner, Sophie. I'm here to help you."

There was something about the earnest look in

his eyes that stung my heart. There was Alex, his eyes cold and hard, pushing me away, and here was Will, begging to be a part of my life. And there was me, straddling the chasm between them both.

"I really am sorry, Will."

I walked out of my room leaving Will behind me, a lump growing in my throat. I wasn't entirely sure what I was apologizing for, but I knew it had nothing to do with not calling him tonight.

I cleared my throat and approached Lorraine and Kale. "I really appreciate you giving me the bag and . . ." I reached into my shirt to show off the talisman, than was immediately sorry I did so. "This thing. Like I said, other than the shower, I haven't taken it off." I said the last part while holding my breath. "But I'm not really sure it's exactly helping—"

Kale took the bag from me and upturned it on the dining table. Another series of rocks poured out, along with the rolled scrolls and herbs.

"I think what Sophie means to say is that we've got a girl missing, a hole full of bones, a hell of a lot of hoodoo voodoo going on in the schoolhouse, and no idea why you've given us a stinky bag full of rocks and wallpaper samples."

I was startled that he was defending—or explaining—on my behalf as Lorraine and Kale paused and looked at him. He had his hands on hips, eyebrows raised, obviously expecting an answer.

I was expecting them to turn him into some kind of amphibian.

Lorraine ignored him. "Star maps and calendars, Soph. Remember when I taught you about those?" Lorraine was bent over the table while Kale was clearing it. She piled my stained place mats and the coupons I would get around to using someday on the floor while Lorraine threw out the star maps and secured them with a polished rock at each corner.

"I need a picture of the girl," she asked without looking up at me.

Will shrugged and handed me Sampson's file. I took a guess and laid Alyssa's grinning mug in her hand.

"No," Kale said, taking the photo from Lorraine. "We need the picture of the one who was sacrificed. The one with the carvings."

My throat went dry, but I sifted through the stack, pulling out the photo. I wouldn't let myself believe the ruined flesh could be Cathy's; that what had happened to this lifeless thing had anything to do with the smiling girl I had seen in her mother's photograph.

"You guys should get back," Kale directed us as she lit the two candles and positioned the photograph on the star map.

"With pleasure," Will said, moving onto the couch.

"I'll leave you to this," Nina said, opening her door three inches and shimmying through.

Lorraine stood in front of the table, which had quickly become a kind of altar. Candles flickered and the stars on the maps seemed to glitter as Lorraine's palms went over them. Soon the chicken feathers were unbound, their edges burnt. They were scattered and dotted with oil from a tiny jug Lorraine produced from her pocket, and everything was tossed as Lorraine began to mumble. Kale joined her from the other side of the table and both of their voices dropped to the same octave and soon became the same throaty whisper. It got deeper, heavier, and I wasn't sure if I was hearing it or feeling it as the words reverberated through my chest. My heart started to match the pulse of their speech. My breath rose and fell with theirs. My eyes may have been closed, but I couldn't tell. Everything I saw was in a deep, red haze and the smell of blood—metallic, thick—was suddenly overwhelming. It was in my nose, I felt it pressing against my eyes, on my lips. I felt the heat dribble in, a tiny drop at a time, until the blood was pouring over my bottom teeth, filling up my mouth. My whole body started to shake and then it was like I was breaking apart—inch by inch.

I heard someone cough and sputter, then felt heat on my cheeks. I opened my eyes and the candle flames seemed to have amassed into one giant orange roar. Lorraine and Kale's voices rose to a crescendo and the flame seemed to follow. Will's face was drawn, the dancing firelight flickering in his eyes. I was mesmerized until I heard the crack—so loud, so unholy that the entire building seemed to tremble under the vibrations and all of my friends—Will, Lorraine, and Kale—were lifted off their feet and thrown backward. In an instant, the fire went out, the apartment was blanketed by a bone-chilling cold, and the only sound was the heartbreaking crush of body against wall. Will shot backward, his head smacking the edge of a framed photograph with a sickening crunch. Glass showered over him as he slumped down the wall and huddled on the ground. Lorraine was launched sideways toward the kitchen, her spine crushing against the countertop and bending so far backward that her skull scraped against the tile while her legs folded uselessly underneath her. And Kale tried to brace herself by digging her nails into the table, but whatever was pushing was too strong. There were bloody grooves where she'd dug her nails in, and now she lay like a crumpled rag doll against the baseboards.

I heard myself scream. I felt myself yanking handfuls of hair as my legs turned to useless rubber. My mind warbled as I tried to think of who to go to first—Will, bloodied and unmoving;

Lorraine, silent, eyes frozen wide with terror; or Kale slumped and whimpering.

But I wasn't moving. And I hadn't moved. The explosion had done nothing to me. I wasn't singed by the mammoth flame or pierced by the shower of broken glass. I was spared.

"Oh my God!" Nina shouted as she flung her bedroom door open. "Oh my God, what happened?"

Vlad raced out beside her and cleared the overturned table in a single leap. He silently landed a hairsbreadth from Kale and fell to her, gingerly brushing her hair aside, his voice low and soothing as he worked to cradle her. I saw her blink, the confusion in her eyes, the tiny splatters of broken blood vessels spider-webbing.

Nina had her palms pressed against Lorraine's ruined back and she was looking at me, her mouth moving, color pulsing in her cheeks. She was saying something, she was screaming, but it was all a muffled blur.

Will. "Will!" I could finally make my lips work. I could finally make my legs work, pushing them, taking steps that seemed achingly slow. I tried to close the distance between us, I tried to reach his silent, crumpled form, but I couldn't move fast enough. The air in the room seemed to push against me until finally, I was there, dropping to my knees, feeling his warm flesh underneath my palms. I pushed his arms aside and pressed my ear against his chest, praying silently to hear a beat.

There was silence. Dead silence. And then, a beat, and a second one, and I was crying. I raked my hands through his hair and murmured his name, relishing the steady sound of his heart until his eyelids fluttered and opened.

"What?"

"I don't know, I don't know," I wailed, the tears rolling down my cheeks.

"She's okay," Vlad said, and even without looking I could hear the smile in his voice.

"Sore," Kale croaked.

I straightened, my hands still cradling Will's head. "Lorraine? Lorraine?"

Nina's coal-black eyes were heavy with emotion. She said nothing. There was no rhythmic rise and fall of Lorraine's chest. No triumphant gulp of air or even a pitiful moan. There was just . . . nothing.

I remember the beeping because it was the only thing I could hear outside of the blood pulsing in my ears. People talked to me and jostled me, and I signed something and nodded a lot. I wanted to cry, but I couldn't anymore. My entire body felt papery thin and sucked completely dry.

We were in the hospital and Nina had both of my hands in hers. There were flashes of light and my head was cold and Will was looking down at me. I sprang to my feet and threw my arms around his neck and crushed myself to him, finally feeling his warmth

*as it seeped through me, made every fiber of my being
hot and awake and alive again.*

*"Will, Will, Will," I was mumbling into the crook
of his neck, feeling the edges of his hair on my cheeks,
inhaling his sweet, cut-grass-and-soap smell. And
then the picture skewed and fish eyed. I could hear
nothing but a deafening sizzling and hideous crackling, and the overhead lights were popping and
smoking. . . .*

*I heard someone cough and sputter; then I felt the
carpet against my knees, the heat of it as it brushed
against my palms.*

"Move her!" someone yelled.

*I wanted to cry out as someone pinched my skin, as
they tried to extract me from the ground I had melded
to. I felt my head bobbing backward and was vaguely
aware of movement, no blood now, then something
cool washing over me and finally, softness.*

I woke up sputtering in the darkness.

"Where am I? What the hell—where am I?"

I heard ChaCha's surprised little yelp and felt
her paws pitter across my bare skin. I shivered, then
was finally able to push against what held me down
and sit up. There was a click, and a tiny slice of
yellow light. I squinted.

"Will?"

"She awakes!"

I heard a shuffle in the darkness and then the
bed depressed. Will was next to me, sitting on my
bed, his thumb brushing over my wrist as he

counted. I tried to struggle free, but he was strong—and it was nice.

"Am I in my bed?"

"You are, and you're alive." He let go of my wrist. "Properly so."

I leaned back against my pillows and rubbed my palm over my head. "What happened?"

"I was hoping you would tell me. What do you remember?"

"Stars. Darkness. Did Lorraine come over?"

Will nodded.

"And Kale, she was here, too, right?"

"Yes, Kale, too."

I ran my tongue over my lips—they were dry and cracked. "So Lorraine and Kale—they're okay." I smiled, giggled. "They're okay."

The soft smile that played at the edges of Will's lips was gone. "They will be."

"What?"

"You passed out at the hospital, Sophie. As far as places to pass out, that was a capital choice, but we were there—do you remember any of this?"

My heart did a little half-beat as I reached out and gingerly threaded my fingers through Will's hair, stopping just short of the bandage. "The spell."

Images of Kale vaulting across the apartment and the shower of glass breaking over Will filled my vision, and I pinched my eyes shut, pressing my palms against them. "Kale—Kale. Is she—?"

"She's fine," Will said calmly, pulling my hands from my eyes. "I can't say the same for your little otter mate though."

I tried to sit up, but Will lulled me back down. "I have an otter?"

"Little plaster guy in the bookcase out there?" He jutted his chin toward the living room. "Kale used it as a thank-you gift on Vlad's forehead."

I frowned. "Oscar Otter?"

"I'll pick you up some epoxy later."

I snuggled back into my pillow and then sat bolt upright. "Lorraine!"

She was suddenly all around me, her body crumpled in an impossible S shape. Her eyes closed so gently, her lips slightly parted. The rivulet of blood at the edge of her lip burned into my vision and I gasped, breaking into a heartbroken sob. "Lorraine. Is she—is she—"

I couldn't push the word *dead* past my lips. I couldn't attach the two—Lorraine and death— but I couldn't get the image of her pale face so peaceful, so calm—so marred by that velvety drip of blood out of my mind.

"She's going to be fine. She has a broken back, but there doesn't seem to be a whole lot of internal damage." Will chuckled. "It was an interesting one to try and explain away, though."

I let the tears drip silently. They slid down my cheeks and into my ears, and I couldn't stop them.

"She'll never forgive me," I whispered. "And Kale, Kale will never forgive me."

Will pressed a thumb across my cheek and picked up a tear. "Neither of them will blame you. They knew—probably better than any of the rest of us—what they were getting into. Lorraine said herself that we were dealing with someone very powerful."

I sniffed. "And we still don't even know who it is. Do we?"

Will shook his head and brushed another tear from my cheek. "No, love, I'm afraid we don't. The whole being blown across the room then having our star investigator pass out on us kind of flattened the investigation."

I sat up. "Okay. Okay." I shoved down my blankets and went to swing my legs over the side of the bed before being hit with a solid wall of Will's well-muscled arms.

"What are you doing?"

Will gently took my bare legs, pinned them together, and swung them back under the covers. "I'm taking care of my charge." He tucked the sheet tightly—cozily, if I had to admit it—around my legs, up around my hips, and then paused at my waist.

"Will!" I squealed. "We have a case!"

"And you had a blackout. Lorraine is with Kale; she's is resting, and Nina and I are working out there." He jerked a thumb over his shoulder toward the living room. "Vlad is off licking his wounds somewhere and you are in here, getting some sleep."

"I passed out, Will. It's not a big deal. I've been tired and I—"

Will pressed a single hand against my shoulder and looked at me, his eyes like liquid amber, swirling, churning, and pulling me in. "You didn't just pass out, love. We couldn't revive you. The doctors couldn't revive you for seven minutes. They couldn't even tell us what happened." I watched his Adam's apple bob as he swallowed. "It was terrifying."

I blinked, feeling the weight of his eyes.

"I am not kidding around with you, Sophie Lawson." His fingers went around tucking my blankets tighter. "You're staying in this bed." There was a flicker at the edge of his mouth as he hid a smile. "Get out, and I'll be dragging you into mine—if only to keep an eye on you."

"Will!" I started to sit up again, but there was something in his eyes that let me know that he really wasn't joking. I closed my mouth silently and let him gather me to him as he carefully laid me down and pulled the blankets up to my chin. Will had always been the goofy, cheeky one so his tenderness was a surprise—and I was surprised how much I was enjoying his arms around me.

"Come on, now," he whispered. He curled himself behind me and I could smell his cologne—the cut-grass scent faint, but clean smelling—on his chest as he pressed against me. He made me feel small and, if only for a few moments, safe.

I wasn't sure exactly when I drifted off to sleep.

Chapter Fourteen

I could still hear his breath when I woke up. It was fast and hot, and had just the slightest scent of . . . Alpo.

"ChaCha?"

She jumped up happily on her Popsicle-stick legs and pranced over my shoulder, nuzzling the spot between my neck and chest and giving me an enormous, salutary lick from chin to eyebrows.

"Thank you, baby," I grumbled, scratching my pooch behind the ears. "Did I imagine you were a big, strong man last night? Did I dream that you were Uncle Will?"

"Uncle Will, huh?"

He was in my doorway in a towel slung so low around his waist it should have been a sin, with a bare chest and a decadent smile. I was face forward on the carpet, feeling the draft from my nightshirt shoved up around my waist when I fell out of bed. I scrambled over, yanking my Giants nightshirt down toward my ankles.

"Why did you shower here? You live right across the hall."

Will tousled his damp hair. "But my shampoo doesn't smell like mangoes."

I rolled my eyes as he gestured to my hands holding fistfuls of black and orange fabric. "You know I've seen all that before, right?"

I blushed right up to my eyebrows.

"You may have, but that was a long time ago."

Will grinned, and the heat kept up. He tapped an index finger against the side of his head. "Good thing I've got a hell of a memory, huh?"

I yanked my comforter from my bed and rolled myself up in it, standing. "Shouldn't we get to work? We still have a case to solve, don't we?"

Will raised his eyebrows. "We were all just sitting around waiting for the queen to grace us with her consciousness."

He walked in and I walked out, even though everything from my nipples downward screamed at me to stay in my room and to suddenly get very interested in collecting errant towels.

The *Indiana Jones*–looking spread on the dining table brought back a vague recollection of the night before.

"Hey," I said to Vlad, who was stretched out on the couch watching something on mute.

Vlad blinked up at me, and I could see the

enormous dent—and the angry-looking bruise surrounding it—on the side of his head.

"How did that happen? And how is it still like that?"

Vlad's upper lip curled and he sunk into the couch a small bit farther. "Kale hit me with an otter."

"Ooh," I muttered. "Oscar. But how's it still all—" I did my best intimation of an obnoxious, blood spurting bruise.

Vlad touched two fingers to the wound and winced. "I had just eaten—a lot." He patted his belly. "I'm still pretty full. Once the blood wears down it'll go away. Damn that woman. I can't go out looking like this."

"Why? All the other vamps on the playground going to make fun of you?"

I thought I heard a low growl from the direction of the couch.

"I don't remember everything," I said, curling myself into my robe. "But I do remember the way you went to her after the crash."

He avoided my gaze, grabbing the remote instead and turning the volume up high.

"So, make any sense of the thing?"

I spun as Will stepped out of my room, jeans on now, T-shirt thrown over one shoulder, towel thrown over the other.

"Of what thing?" I wanted to know

Vlad poked his head over the couch. "Before the pummeling. Lorraine and Kale and that star map thing." He jutted his chin toward the table.

I leaned over the map and frowned, pushing my finger over charred masses of what had once been star patterns. "It wasn't like this last night, was it?"

"No," Will said, closing the distance between us. "Lorraine was doing some spell—well before the group walloping. After, the sodding thing caught fire. She wrote these notes down before I had to save the day with the fire extinguisher and wrestle the otter from the bird."

"Wait—you were walloped. I was fine. Did I put out the fire?"

Vlad snorted and put the TV on mute again. "No, you were pretty much useless, *mate*. I put out the fire and saved what was left of Lorraine's writings. Then we all went to the hospital, this one pitched to the floor." His eyes cut to me. "Lorraine went into surgery, the doctor said Kale was fine, and she beat me with an otter once we came back home."

"So just another quiet night at home," Will said, kicking his feet onto the coffee table and lacing his fingers behind his head.

I took the notes from the table and read out loud. "'Spell chanted on the seventh calendar day when the zodiac and the stars'—we knew all this. Cathy was found seven days after her abduction.

We're working on the same timeline with Alyssa." I pushed the burnt star map aside and brushed my hand over the blond tabletop, now marred with black blossoms of charred wood. "We ruined a perfectly good table to figure out information we already knew?"

"Seemed like the information was pretty powerful to you. How's that goose egg?"

Will rubbed a hand through my hair and I winced when his fingers went over a sore spot. "Ow! What was that?"

"I told you, love. You passed out."

I shook Will off me and began cleaning the debris from the table. "So we know—again—that Alyssa's kidnapper and Cathy's"—I cleared my throat, still somehow unwilling to say the word—"assailant were—or are—using the girls as sacrifices to call on Satan. Both Cathy and Miranda have books of safety spells. Great." I sat down in a dining room chair. "We are absolutely nowhere."

"Why is someone trying to sacrifice girls to gain favor with the devil?" Vlad chuckled. "That's lame."

I felt myself pale. "I don't know why I'm asking, but why is that lame?"

Vlad rolled his eyes as if I'd just asked his opinion on Justin Bieber. "Because first of all, no one uses human sacrifice anymore. And everyone knows that blood isn't used for summoning, it's used for opening."

"Uh, opening?" Will asked.

"Blood, fluids, whatever—used for opening portals. Bodies are offered in reverence or thanks."

"So our dude is thanking your pops for something?"

I pinched my upper lip. "We're not entirely sure that Satan is my father."

"Right," Will said, picking up a magazine. "It could still be a dictionary salesman from Skokie."

"*Anyway,* Lorraine specifically said the carving was an incantation. It was a calling."

"So he used the girl as a bit of lovely stationary *and* as a thank-you gift? Is that what we're thinking?"

I put my hands on my hips. "Blood opens a portal. The incantation was a calling of something."

Will looked from Vlad to me. "Opening the door to hell, kind of like a Pied Piper thing drawing the devil out? That makes sense, right?"

Vlad barked out one of those "as if" laughs.

"Hey, stop with your brooding and moping, and help us, would you?" Will yelled, giving him a thump with the rolled-up magazine.

Another eye roll by Vlad. Wouldn't kids ever come up with something new?

"Try opening up a portal and then drawing something to it. That's what your perp is doing," Vlad said, glaring at us as though it were dead obvious.

"Why didn't you say something sooner?"

He sniffed. "No one asked me."

I groaned. "Vlad! Okay, okay, tell me this. If our guy is opening a portal and calling something to it, why is he doing it again?"

"He could be calling something that is only out for a limited time."

"Like the holiday china you get from Burger King?" Will asked.

Vlad scrunched up his nose. "Kind of like that. Or, it's not working."

"I don't understand. Why wouldn't it work if he's got the incantation and the girl?"

Vlad launched himself off the couch and into the kitchen, knocking over a series of long-expired condiments before finding himself a blood bag. He pierced it, took a swig and glanced up at it. "Because he just hasn't found the *right* girl."

Will and I exchanged a look as heat walked up my spine, vertebra by vertebra. "This is going to keep going unless we stop it."

I flopped down onto the couch, feeling incredibly defeated. "We can't ask Lorraine who or what this witch is trying to summon. She said some of the incantation was wrong on the original—" I swallowed, my throat dry. I didn't want to say "body," but that was the image that sparked in my mind's eye. "It was wrong in the original case." I paused, considering. "Hey, Vlad, what do you know about a store called Simply Charming?"

Vlad closed his laptop and shot me a narrowed

glare. "I know that you can't get me near that place with a ten-foot pole."

"Why's that?" Will wanted to know.

"Because that's the kind of place where Kale shops and I do not need another wallop to the head anytime soon."

"Bitches be crazy, right, cuz?" Will said in a spot-on American accent as he gave Vlad a fist bump.

"It's like I'm in the *Twilight Zone*," I muttered.

Simply Charming didn't stand out on the retail block where it sat, but once we were inside, it was a world unto itself. Will pressed a hand over his nose and leaned down toward me. "Why do all these places smell like crappy incense?"

"Blessed be!" A doughy woman with bottle-red hair came floating toward us in a sea of gypsy style silks. I knew she was one of the knock-off witches that drove Lorraine crazy and I gave a short smile, knowing that Lorraine would innocently turn her into a barnacle if UDA law would allow. "I'm Meadow. Is there something I can help you with?"

"Yes, actually, uh, Meadow," I said, taking the lead. "We're investigating a case with the SFPD. One of our victims had a book of protection spells in her possession that we believe is from this store."

The woman clasped her hands in front of her chest and nodded, her cornflower-blue eyes wide but only semi-focused. "We do have a book of protection spells that we keep in stock."

"Our victim was a fifteen-year-old girl."

"Oh, no." Meadow's hands went to her throat. "That's awful."

"Do you get a lot of teen girls in your store?" Will asked.

Meadow pumped her head. "Yes. Mostly for love spells, sometimes protection spells."

"Do you think you could recognize some of your teen customers?"

Meadow blinked. "I'm sure I can try."

I held up Cathy Ledwith's photo and the color immediately drained from Meadow's cheeks. "That's Cathy Ledwith."

"You know her? Was she a regular here?"

Meadow shook her head, her long hair bubbling around her. "Oh, no. I'd never met her, but we did prayer circles after she went missing. Such a tragedy."

"So you don't remember her ever coming into this store and purchasing that book?" I pointed to the spell book on Meadow's shelf.

"No, I'm sorry, I don't."

"What about this girl?" Will held up a photo of Alyssa.

"I don't recognize her. I'm sorry."

Will opened the manila file folder he was holding and went to slide Alyssa's photo in. Meadow grabbed his hand, stopping him. "I know her, though. That's Fallon Monroe. She comes in here from time to time."

Heat zinged up my neck. "You know Fallon?"

"I do. Nice girl. Came in with her father the last time. Or maybe it was her grandfather." Meadow looked up as though the answer were floating in the ether. "I think she called him her buddy." She smiled. "Very sweet."

I shifted my weight and steadied myself. "What did Fallon buy?"

Meadow pointed to the book of protection spells. "That book. Some candles. A charm. And her grandfather bought something, too. I know he came in before—without his granddaughter—and talked to Bronwyn. She owns the store."

Will and I exchanged a glance. I was sure he was feeling the same intense zing of adrenaline as I was. "Can we talk to Bronwyn?"

"Not for another six days. She's meditating at Green Gulch."

I chewed the inside of my lip. "Can you do us a favor? If Fallon or her grandfather come in, could you please give us a call?"

Will produced a business card and handed it to Meadow. She took it in both hands and examined it. "Didn't you say you were with the police? This says you're a fireman."

"Uh, she's the police. I'm the fireman. And this case is quite arsonistic, if you will. Very dangerous. Very secret. Can't divulge too much. Probably said too much already. You've been a big help."

Will and I backed out of the store with Meadow's huge eyes following us.

"Arsonistic, Will?" I said as we slid into my car.

"Credit me one for thinking on my feet. We got what we were looking for, didn't we?"

I looked back at the shop as we drove away. "Kind of. Fallon comes to the magic shop with a grandfather."

"Maybe that's the legacy we're looking for?"

"But why would she buy the book of protection spells? I mean, if she's partnering with, say, her grandfather—"

"That's one horrible family tree now, isn't it?"

"Why would she feel the need for protection?"

Will swung his head. "Don't know. Also, is the geezer really her grandfather or just a crazy old bloke she hooked up with? Some birds kind of like that May-December thing you know."

"Will, ew."

"Oh, and it's much less disgusting for you to think the girl is kidnapping her friends and delivering them to gramps for a little carving party?"

"The whole thing is just so messed up."

"Okay, so what now? We go back to Fallon's house, bust down her door, and demand she produce her grandfather? And by the way, why didn't we ask the garden bird about Miranda? She had one of those spell books, as well."

"Meadow. And we didn't need to ask about Miranda because we know that she purchased the spell book and we know she purchased it there."

Will sunk back in his seat. "Right. You told me

she said it was a lapse in judgment as she was going for a love spell book."

I nodded. "Right."

"Did you notice where Chaparral kept the love spell books?"

"Meadow. And no, I just assumed they were right next to the other books."

"They weren't. The lovey books were all the way in the back. Big pink heart over the rack. Awful thing, really."

"So? What are you saying?"

Will shrugged. "Just saying that it seems a little odd that your girl could miss a giant pink heart."

I pulled the car to a stop at a red light and turned to face Will. "There is no indication—zero—that Miranda has anything to do with this. She has no connection to the girls other than knowing them through school."

"And Fallon's big connection is that she was friends with the girls and you think she's a giant bitch. Seems a little weak to build a murder case on, love."

"Are you defending her?"

"No, I'm standing up for parliamentary procedure. Innocent until proven guilty and all that."

"We don't have parliament," I growled. "And there's plenty more to indict Fallon. She works in the office and has access to all the girls' personal information and class schedules. She's a bully. Bullies are sadists. And she came in to the store multiple times with her grandfather."

"She went out on an outing with her grandpa."

"That's a pretty creepily specific outing, Will. I— well, I went to magic shops with my Gram all the time, but my grandma—"

"I know, I know, love," Will said, holding his palm toward me. "Your grandmother played mah-jongg with a pixie."

I pressed the gas pedal down. "We'll investigate both girls just to cover all our bases, but I'm pretty sure Fallon's our perp. Or, one-half of our perp team. I just don't get a good feeling about her."

Chapter Fifteen

I turned the corner toward our apartment building and slid into a parking spot just as a carpet-covered van vacated it.

Will looked at me and smiled as I pushed the car into park. "Rock star parking. Maybe things are looking up for us."

I had my hand on the door when a bolt of heat shot through me. "I'm not so sure. Look."

Will followed my gaze to the girl sitting on the stoop in front of our building. She had her knees pressed up against her chest, her hands buried in the enormous sleeves of a charcoal-grey hoodie. Her head was down, and a very recognizable, fuzzy shock of hair slid out from under her beanie.

"Is that Miranda?"

I pushed open the car door. "Miranda?"

Her head rose slowly, the majority of her face hidden in the shadows. "Ms. Lawson? Mr. Sherman?"

"Yeah." I rushed toward her. "What are you doing here?"

I could see from the slice of light over her beanie and hair that she was trembling.

"I probably shouldn't have come here," she said finally. "But I didn't know where else to go."

"No, no, it's fine."

Will slid an arm through Miranda's and helped her up. It was then that I could see her face clearly. My chest tightened painfully and the familiar prick of tears itched behind my eyes. "My God, Miranda, what happened to you?"

A purple-red bruise peeked out from under her beanie and marred the left side of her forehead. Puffed red scratches shot dangerously close to her swollen eye. Her cheeks were flushed red and slick with dried tears. There were neat slices at the edges of her lips, and dried blood was caked all over. Though Miranda did her best to shrink back into her sweatshirt and shrink back into the cover of night, I could still see purpling fingers of puckered skin under her chin and circling her throat.

"Can you walk? Do we need to get you an ambulance?" I asked.

Miranda shook her head, her hair swinging. "No, thanks," she said, her voice a near-whisper.

"Let's get her inside," Will said before Miranda had a chance to elaborate.

Nina snatched open the door before I had a

chance to sink my key into the lock. "Lorraine?" she asked, before her eyes set on Miranda.

"Nina," I said, steering Miranda and Will around her, "this is Miranda, a student from my class."

"Here, Miranda." I led her to the couch and she sat gingerly, wincing. "Would you mind giving us just a second?"

Her dark eyes went from me to Will and finally to Nina before she nodded silently. I pushed Nina toward my room and Will shut the door behind us.

"What happened to her?" Nina wanted to know.

I chewed my bottom lip. "We just found her downstairs like that."

"We do plan on asking, right?" Will asked.

"Of course. It's just—" I looked at Nina, who sucked in a breath and patted the air.

"I know, I know. I'm just your normal flesh-and-blood roommate who is not salivating in the least at the overwhelming scent of dried blood."

"Can you let Vlad know about Miranda before he gets back?" I said.

Nina shrugged. "He never left." She cocked her head, listening. "And I'm pretty sure he's already discovered your student."

"Christ." I pushed out my door and was momentarily taken aback by Miranda sitting primly on my couch. It was like my two worlds had crashed together.

"Sorry, Miranda. Can I get you anything?"

"You probably could have offered her a glass of

water before you disappeared on her," Vlad said as he appeared from the kitchen, tall, filled glass in his hand.

"Thank you," she whispered to him, before downing the whole thing.

I sat across from Miranda. "Can you tell us what—or who—did this to you?"

She turned to me and tears began to pour over her lower lashes. "I don't know," she said. "I don't know who it was."

"She said she—"

I held up a hand. "Vlad, it's okay. I'd like to hear it from Miranda."

I'd expected him to growl or grumble something inappropriate before settling back behind his laptop to explode human arteries, but he sat next to Miranda—close to her—body-brushing close.

My heart thumped. He *liked* her.

Before I could swoon for teenage love and recoil at the vampire-breather consequences, Will quickly sat next to me and addressed Miranda. "I've got some paramedic training. What do you say you let me take a look and maybe clean up those injuries?"

Miranda looked around blankly, her eyes wide and heartbreakingly innocent. She pulled herself into her sweatshirt again. "It probably looks worse than it really is."

I looked at Nina, who was perched on the chair-and-a-half. Even across the room I could see her nostrils twitch. She steeled me with a glance letting me know that the blood she was smelling was not fresh—or flowing—enough to be dangerous.

"Can you tell us what happened, Miranda?" I asked.

Miranda clasped her hands in her lap and stared at them for a bit before she cleared her throat. "I was leaving the school."

I glanced up at the clock. "Wait. You were just leaving campus now?"

She shook her head. "No. No, I was trying to get on the three o'clock bus. I realized I left my book back in your classroom so I went back for it. But I still had enough time to make it back to the bus stop. Or I should have. Anyway, I went back to the main door. Janitor Bud let me in and I got my book. It's *Wuthering Heights*—the one you saw me reading in the cafeteria. But it was weird—the door to your classroom snapped shut while I was in there. Like there was a breeze or something, but there wasn't. I mean, all the windows were closed. And then . . ." Miranda shook her head and the tears started to fall again. She let them go and I could see Vlad watching as they rolled over Miranda's nose and fell into her lap.

"It's okay, Miranda." I squeezed her hand.

"It's going to sound crazy. You're all going to think I'm crazy."

Will and I exchanged a glance. "You have a long way to go before we would even consider that thought."

"A long way," Will added. "Your Ms. L there got locked in the toilet, and I didn't think any less of her."

I tried hard not to roll my eyes. "Just tell us what happened."

"So the door shut, and I tried to open it. But it was like it was locked. I tried to fiddle with the lock, but that didn't help. And then—all of a sudden—it was dark. Like, pitch black. I couldn't see anything. Then there was a wind—a howling wind. Everything went floating around me and things were hitting me. It felt like fists—like people were there. Pulling my hair and"—she heaved, then pressed a hand over her bottom lip—"and punching me. There was like, lightning or something cracking and every once in a while that would make it light. There was no one there, Ms. L—no one but me, but I could feel people. And something was written on the board—it looked like, it looked like—"

"Get out?" I offered.

Miranda nodded, her eyes the size of teacups. "How did you know?"

"Just a lucky guess."

"Then what happened?" Vlad asked her.

"Well, there was a giant crack. I was yanking on the door and as soon as I heard that, everything stopped. The room was normal again, there was nothing on the board, no wind. The door opened right up and I ran. I ran all the way out of the school and to the bus stop. I didn't even know there was—" Miranda gingerly touched her fingertips to her puffed eye. "I didn't even know there was anything on my face until the bus driver asked what happened."

"What made you come here?" Will asked.

Vlad shot him a scathing look. "She was traumatized."

"I'm just asking."

"Yeah, what—I mean, I'm glad that you did—but why did you decide to come here?"

Miranda's lower lip trembled and she looked into her lap again. "My mom works nights. I didn't want to go home." She looked up at me, her eyes desperate and imploring. "I didn't have anywhere else to go."

"Not to a mate's or something?" Will asked.

Vlad gritted his teeth. "She said she didn't have anywhere else to go."

Miranda started to sniff again—another round of heavy tears.

"Look what you did!" Vlad snapped.

I nudged him away and slung an arm around Miranda, pulling her toward me. "You did the right thing coming here, Miranda. Everything is going to be okay. You're safe now."

Will steadied his gaze and I avoided it.

"There's something else, Ms. L," Miranda whispered into my hair.

"What is it, honey?"

Miranda pulled back and looked at Will and

Vlad, then back at me. "We can go to my room," I said, taking her hand.

I closed the door behind us, and Miranda started when ChaCha sprang from the covers and growled.

"Oh, don't worry about her," I said, snatching her up. "She's my half-pint attack dog."

The edges of Miranda's lips quirked up into the beginning of a smile. "She's cute."

"You can pet her," I offered, swinging ChaCha within arm's reach. Miranda reached out tentatively, but ChaCha growled again, showing off her Tic Tac–sized bottom teeth.

I rolled my eyes. "Don't worry about her; she's very protective of my bed." I set ChaCha down and the terrifying thing buried her way into my covers, her little butt and stub tail disappearing last.

"Animals always seem to hate me," Miranda said wistfully. "Even my gerbil ran away."

We sat in silence for an uncomfortable beat until Miranda sucked in a breath. "I didn't want to tell them." She jutted her head toward the living room. "I didn't want to show them."

"What?"

She swallowed slowly and I could see her hands tremble as she pulled up her hoodie— slowly, painfully. There were fresh scratches on her hands, the deepest ones across her knuckles where blood had pooled and dried. Miranda dropped her sweatshirt on my floor, then slowly began to unbutton the blouse underneath.

Suddenly, there was no air. Everything pressed against me and the beating of my heart threatened to shatter me, to break me right open.

"Oh, Miranda."

I couldn't tear my eyes from the puckered flesh on her abdomen. The skin at the edges of the fresh cuts was turning up, the edges purple and fragile like the torn edges of paper. Everything swirled into a watery mess, and I stepped back, feeling my way to sit back on the bed as bile burned up the back of my throat and my own blood pulsed through my ears.

Miranda's abdomen pulsed when she breathed, the freshly carved words, *you're next*, a ghastly, skin-deep warning that chilled me to my core.

I cleaned Miranda's wounds and then set her up in a pair of my old sweats. She was now huddled with Vlad behind his laptop, his hand over hers as her brand-new *BloodLust* avatar sunk its fangs into its first human flesh.

"So your mom was okay that you're spending the night?"

Miranda looked over the laptop and nodded before breaking into a gale of teenage giggles. "Your hands are freezing!" she murmured to Vlad.

If she only knew the half of it.

"So, what are we going to do about this?" Will jutted his head toward Vlad and Miranda.

"He won't make any moves on her. Vlad knows the rules."

"No, I don't care about that. Unless he starts to floss his teeth with her. I mean about the bippity boppity in the classroom. We going to go check that out?"

"Pssst!" Nina stuck her head through her bedroom door and hissed at me. "A word with you, dear roommate?"

"Speaking of someone about to floss their teeth with—what do they call us? Breathers?" Will's eyes glittered.

"And you, too, Union Jack."

He didn't bother to contain his fear.

We shut ourselves into Nina's room. Will pressed himself up against the door while I faced Nina down.

"So?" I asked.

Nina narrowed her eyes. "So? So? That's what you say to me? Sophie Annemarie Lawson. I have tried to be good. I have tried to be malleable."

"Malleable?" Will asked, brows raised.

"But this!" She threw her arm out dramatically. "This is something else completely. You just can't bring your work home with you, Sophie."

"My work? Miranda is a person, Nina. And I didn't bring her home with me. She came here because she needed help. She needed help and she knew that I would be able to help."

Nina swung her head. "Fine. She needed help. She's helped. Send her home."

"I'm not going to just—"

"Sophie, she's a breather. With fresh cuts."

"They weren't bothering you a half hour ago."

"A half hour ago they were caked with stale blood."

Will wrinkled his nose. "Stale?"

"Dried," I clarified.

"And the smell of Windex or something was pretty much overpowering. Now she smells like you and fresh blood. And you've got two vampires in close proximity."

I felt my nostrils flare. "Aren't you the one always telling me that vampires can handle themselves with decorum? That you guys have the ability to see breathers as people, not just tasty snacks?"

"Whoa." I heard Will step back until his shoulders were pressed against the door.

Nina pinched the bridge of her nose. "Look, Sophie. I need to get things done. How am I supposed to get anything done with her out there?"

My gut roiled with white-hot anger. "Are you kidding me? You're concerned about your stupid project? This is a human being. A young girl! Who was attacked. She needs us, Neens. I'm sorry if you've been without a soul too long to *feel* anything for anyone. But I have a soul and I have feelings and so does that girl out there. This is my apartment too and she's staying."

Nina didn't bother responding to me. She didn't bother to look at me, either. I heard Will suck in a sharp breath; I heard the muffled voices of Vlad and Miranda in the other room. I didn't hear Nina when she slipped out the window and down the fire escape.

"Hey, love, you know Nina kind of has a point. There are two vampires—"

I whirled and pinned Will with a glare. "Stay out of it, Will."

When I walked into the dining room Vlad looked up at me, his coal-black eyes hooded, accusatory. He had heard every word we said. Miranda kept tapping away, blissfully unaware, her avatar cheering when she made the next kill.

Vlad and Nina slipped out to spend their remaining nighttime hours at Poe's while I pulled a blanket up over Miranda's shoulders as she snored on the couch. I straightened and cocked my head, then pulled open the front door.

"What do you need, Will?"

"Whoa, love, how'd you know I was out here?" He sunk into his sly, sexy grin. "Been keeping an eye on me, have you? Can't say I'm surprised."

"Miranda's asleep on the couch," I whispered before stepping into the hall and softly clicking the door shut behind me. "And I heard you being English out here. What is it?"

He shifted his weight, pulling his bottom lip into his mouth. "I haven't been able to sleep since our little visitor popped in."

I ran my hands over my arms, a cold shudder going over me. "I know. I feel so responsible."

"Well, don't." Will plopped down onto his chaise longue, the plastic patio slats groaning under his weight. He gestured for me to sit. I tossed aside his needlepoint *Home Sweet Home* pillow and two pairs of cleats, and sat across from him.

"What are you talking about?"

"Don't you think it's odd that Miranda shows up here, at your place, after what happened to her?"

I shrugged. "Her mother works nights. She didn't want to be alone. I get that."

"Wouldn't a teenage girl rather have gone to a friend's house than a teacher's? A substitute teacher at that."

I shifted in my chair, stung. "Most girls would go to a girlfriend's house—if they had a girlfriend to go to. Miranda and I had a connection. I told her I would help her if she needed anything."

Will pushed his fingers into his belt loops and stared off into space, a hard, thoughtful look on his face.

"What?"

He snapped to attention. "What, what?"

"You're thinking something. You have something to say. So, out with it."

Will cocked an eyebrow but said nothing. I gave him the universal "well, come on" scowl and he blew out a sigh. "She had a lot of detail in her story."

"Who? Miranda? Of course she had a lot of detail

in her story. It happened to her. She was telling us. The details are important."

"Is that common?"

I paused, thinking back on all of the eyewitness accounts Alex and I had sat through. Generally, the first time the story was told, the witness had very little to say other than the most general overview: "I was attacked. It was dark."

"Not really. But she had had some time to process it. And, she's kind of a loner. More of an observer. Not everyone reacts the same to trauma."

"Yeah . . . but she was out of breath, crying, terrified. And yet she remembered all these small, unnecessary details."

"People cling on to weird things when they're traumatized. You read about it all the time. There's even a name for it."

Will crossed his arms in front of his chest. "What is it?"

I opened my mouth and then closed it again, cogs spinning in my brain. "Traumatic Unnecessary Brain Focusing . . . Syndrome."

Will's lips quirked up into a smirk.

I threw up my hands. "Okay, there is no name for it. Just what the hell are you getting at, anyway?"

"Nothing, love. I was just pointing out that it seemed odd that a young bird coming from such a stressful situation would have a story with that much detail."

"You know what your problem is, Will? You just

don't understand women. We're complicated. We're varied. We're not 'birds'"—I made air quotes—"or 'lasses.'"

"I don't believe I've ever called a bird a lass, and as far as whether or not I can figure a bird out . . ." Will's eyes sliced into mine and he licked his bottom lip seductively. The action, paired with the steady heat of his eyes, shot fireworks off in my veins and my entire body perked to attention. "I haven't any complaints yet."

Somehow, all the breath was sucked from my body. Somehow, all of my bones had congealed into a wobbly, untrustworthy jelly-like material.

Get it together, Sophie.

Will closed the distance between us and his arm brushing past me—the light wisp against my nipples—was on the verge of making me purr. It was hard to be angry and confident when all I wanted to do was collapse against his chest and do the bodice-ripping things that Harlequin novels were famous for with just a hint of *Fifty Shades*.

He was so close now that I could feel his breath on my neck, could feel his lips against my earlobe. Goose bumps shot up like spikes all over my flesh when he breathed and my heartbeat went slow and heavy, my entire body aching with desire. I knew he wanted me, too. The way his hazel eyes skimmed over my cheeks and settled on my lips for an extra second, the way his fingertips grazed mine . . .

I closed my eyes as his lips came toward mine, waiting for that moment of soft flesh on flesh.

"There we go."

I started, every hormone crashing into a brick wall. "What?"

Will sat back in his chair, now with a yellow notepad in his hand. "I was reaching for my notepad," he said, waggling it for proof. "What did you think I was doing?"

I cleared my throat and straightened up. "That. I thought that's what you were doing."

There was a hint of amusement in his eyes and a bit of a sly smile forming at the edges of his mouth. His eyes broke from mine and scanned the notepad. Suddenly, all play and sex appeal was gone, replaced by an all-business look.

"Did you think it was strange that Miranda said Janitor Bud let her into the building?"

My sex-starved heart thudded to a stop. The saliva in my mouth went bitter. "What?"

"She said that Janitor Bud let her in the building tonight so she could go get her book. Janitor Bud who has gone on sabbatical and been replaced by your stinky troll mate."

"He's not my mate, and maybe she was just mistaken."

"Veil or not, do you really think someone would mistake a little person they've never seen before for someone they've seen in their environment for the past three years?"

"I don't think it's all that likely, but it's not impossible. And maybe she did actually see Steve, but in her recollection—with all the *trauma*"—I stressed the word—"maybe she just assumed it was Janitor Bud when it was actually—"

"A three-foot-tall gray fellow?"

I pressed my lips together thinking about Nina— about the snarl in her lip as she said that Miranda smelled like "stale blood and something like Windex."

"Do you think Janitor Bud did this? Do you think his sabbatical was a fake?" I stood, considering. "Oh my God, Will, Bud could be the guy we're looking for. He fits—it fits, right? He has close ties to campus, he could—he could hate the girls and want to exact revenge." My heartbeat started to speed up. "Think about it—Meadow, Meadow from Simply Charming, said that Fallon came in with her grandfather. Or someone she thought was her grandfather, but she said Fallon called him something like her 'buddy.' Maybe she just called him Bud. They're working together. They're partners. It's Janitor Bud. It has to be—that's the only thing that makes sense!"

Will was silent for beat. "I don't think Bud is the only thing that makes sense." He looked at me hard until I sat down again.

"What are you talking about?"

"Think about it, love—"

"Miranda? You think Miranda—what? Did this to herself? How dare you! Did you see that child? She has no friends. Basically has no family. And she was *beaten*, Will. There were words *carved into her flesh*. She didn't do that. No one would do that to themselves." I could feel the heat zinging through my veins. I knew I was yelling, clipping my words, but I didn't care. "It's not possible. It's just not possible."

"You're certain?"

I nodded before I could think otherwise. "Absolutely."

Will and I were nearly nose-to-nose, his arms crossed in front of his chest, my fists on my hips in a sort of Guardian-Guardee stand-off. We were still huffing into each other's faces when my cell phone split off into a crazy Latin beat. I slid it out of my pocket and held up a finger.

"It's Sampson. What do you think he wants?"

Will cocked an eyebrow. "I bet if you answer the call, he'd be willing to tell you."

I rolled my eyes and slid the phone on.

"Hey, Mr. Sampson."

"Sophie."

He had barely finished saying my name when the chill ran through me. "What's wrong, Sampson?"

There was a pause—it must have been for just a beat, but it seemed to stretch on as the sound of my own blood rushing through my ears filled up the room, punctuated only by the thud-thud-thud of my heart.

"Another girl has gone missing."

Fear, like a gnarled fist, unwound in my stomach.

I could feel the cold fingers reaching every part of my body. "Another girl, missing? That's not possible," I heard myself say. "That can't be."

I could hear Sampson breathe on his side of the phone and I wanted to be there to shake him, to tell him he was wrong.

"That's not the pattern," I mumbled dumbly. "That's not the pattern."

"It was another Mercy girl."

I was shaking my head now, stunned and numb. Somewhere, a thousand miles away, I could hear paper rustle and I knew that it was Sampson, bringing police files closer to him. He cleared his throat.

"Her name was Kayleigh Logan. She was a junior."

My whole body began to tremble and my lips felt impossibly swollen and weird. "I know Kayleigh. I know her. She's not missing. She was in school today. I saw her. I saw her," I repeated, somehow hoping that could change anything.

Sampson breathed slowly. "It happened after school. She was riding her bike and she just vanished."

I thought of Kayleigh sitting in the back of my class, snapping her gum and batting those thick, heavy eyelashes. She laughed when Miranda choked on her speech, the high, tinkling laugh of someone with no cares, and her blond hair fell in a perfectly glossy cascade of face-shielding curls when she leaned over to whisper something to Fallon.

Had they made future plans?

Had she told Fallon she was going away? *Had she known?*

"Are there any details? Are they sure she didn't just leave on her own?"

"A witness said she saw Kayleigh approach a car—a blue sedan." Sampson paused for a beat. "Not a really good description. The woman said she was working in her garden, saw Kayleigh stop her bike to talk to the driver of the car, she looked back to her plants and then heard the tires squeal and both Kayleigh and the car were gone."

I chewed my bottom lip. "Well, how did they know Kayleigh didn't get in willingly?"

"She left her bike."

I frowned. "Hey, wait a minute. The witness said she heard the tires squeal. Is that what she said?"

Sampson spoke slowly, probably reading from the police report. "Witness: 'I heard the squeal of tires and that made me look up.'"

"So Kayleigh didn't scream. If the driver nabbed her, she would have screamed and then the tires would have squealed. So maybe Kayleigh wasn't afraid of her kidnapper."

Sampson sighed. "She must have known him."

I nodded numbly and Will took the phone from my hand, murmured a few words to Sampson, and ended the call.

"Kayleigh," Will said.

I felt the tears stinging behind my eyes, but

before I would let them fall, Will wrapped me in his arms, his lips warm against the part in my hair.

"We're going to get her. We're going to get both of them home," Will said.

I looked up and caught his eyes—they were fixed, hard but open, the golden flecks dancing like firelight. I don't know if it was my scrambled emotions or the steadiness of Will's gaze, but suddenly, it was he and I against a kidnapping murderer and we were going to do whatever it took to bring Alyssa and Kayleigh back—regardless of who was willing to help us.

"All right, then," he said, breaking the silence. "You going to wear that?"

He gestured to the sweats I was wearing and I cocked an eyebrow. "To do what?"

Will grabbed his keys, his jacket, then turned to face me. "To prove that Janitor Bud is the man we want."

Chapter Sixteen

Other than navigating from the printed sheet Will handed me, Will and I didn't speak for the entire car ride over to Bud Hastings's Fillmore-area apartment. My whole body was humming by the time we entered the vestibule. My mind was on a constant spin cycle trying scenarios and considering locations. Will was energized and as chipper as a robin. He buzzed number seventy-four and we both waited, silently.

No answer.

Another buzz—this time Will mashed his index finger against the buzzer and held it there. Still, no answer.

"Probably because he's out looking for another girl to attack," I told him.

Will mashed another button.

"What are you doing?" I hissed.

"Manager."

"Yes, sir, Mr. Centuri, is it? My name is Will

Sherman from Scotland Yard and I'm afraid we need to get into apartment seventy-four, currently rented by a gentleman by the name of William 'Bud' Hastings?"

Mr. Centuri launched into a significant series of horrible-sounding coughs, further cementing my desire to never, ever take up smoking.

"Scotland Yard?"

"Yes, sir."

Another cough. "You guys have, uh, what's that? Jurisdiction out here?"

"I'd be happy to show you my credentials if you'll just show me into Hastings's domicile, sir."

Centuri clicked off the intercom and another series of coughs and labored breathing began, this one coming from the door of the apartment right in front of us. The door snapped open halfway and a squat man built like a fireplug leaned out toward us.

"What'd you say your name was, again?"

"Holmes, Doctor, and this is my associate Mrs. Malaprop."

Centuri's beady eyes scanned me suspiciously and I broke into a polite smile and a heavily accented, "Good evening, fine sir."

Will shot me a look, but it went right over Centuri's head as he apparently assumed Will's credentials were in my bra.

"Bud in some kind of trouble?" Centuri asked my tits.

"That's what we're trying to find out," Will said, his English sharp and clipped.

"He's a good tenant. Always pays his rent on time, never been no kind of problem. On vacation or something right now."

"The key, sir?"

"Yeah." Centuri disappeared into his apartment and reappeared with a single key pinched between forefinger and thumb.

"Aren't you going to escort us?"

Centuri waved a handful of Vienna sausage fingers through the air. "Eh, you're cops. *Jeopardy*'s on. Just lock up after yourself and give a knock when you're leaving. Drop the key through my mail slot."

"Brilliant."

"Pip, pip," I put in.

"Pip, pip?" Will asked, once Centuri shut his door.

"I was playing a part. Trying to make it believable."

"Thanks for going to the trouble, but I don't think our landlord there is going to mull too much over."

"He could. He asked you your name and about Scotland Yard."

"And he bought that I was first Will Sherman and then Dr. Holmes and that you were a wily English woman from a Sheridan play."

"Hence the pip, pip."

"This one's seventy-four."

Will knocked. "Mr. Hastings? This is Dr. Holmes from Scotland Yard. Please open up."

I crossed my arms and cocked out a hip. "You're really digging the Scotland Yard thing, aren't you?"

"Pip, pip," Will said over her shoulder as he sunk the key into the lock.

I sucked in a sharp breath, feeling my eyes widen. "Oh my God."

"What? Looks like a regular ol' place to me."

I pumped my head. "I know. Regular. No to-the-ceiling collections of doll heads or empty terrariums. There's a couch and a coffee table and an old television set."

"I don't want you to bust through your knickers, but there's a kitchen table and a refrigerator, too. Even a newspaper." He swiped the paper from the table and waggled it at me. "Yesterday's."

I poked around the living room as Will checked out the kitchen. "So, this guy seems awfully regular. He's got milk in the fridge. Some take-out that looks like it's from—" Will reached into and pulled out a Styrofoam carton. He popped it open. "Ugh, 1974. Nothing crazy. No disembodied heads or anything like that. Does that mean he's not our kidnapper?"

"No, no, not at all. What do people always say when they interview the neighbors of a serial killer?"

"He had a shrunken head in the linen closet?"

I snorted. "No. They say, 'He was just a regular guy.'" I picked up a magazine and flipped through it. "Or they say, 'He kept to himself, mostly.' Find anything interesting?"

Will turned around and handed me a framed photograph.

"Well, I'll be."

"The geezer from the front office."

"Heddy is not a geezer," I said, pulling the frame open and sliding the picture out. "Nothing special about this picture. Looks like it was taken at school, pretty recently. Not that Heddy changes much."

"So we've got Janitor Bud in an affair with the school secretary. If they weren't both a thousand years old, it would almost be sexy."

I rolled my eyes and tapped the glass. "Do you think Heddy knows about Bud's . . . side activity?"

"Whoa, love, we haven't found a single thing here that indicts Bud as our kidnapper, other than his incriminating normalness."

"But, Miranda!"

"But Miranda nothing. We've broken into a regular guy's regular old apartment. Other than a fetish for the office bird, nothing is incriminating. Nothing is even slightly out of the ordinary."

I put my hands on my hips and swung my head. "No, there's something here. Something that we're missing. I can feel it. Look for methods of restraint—duct tape, handcuffs, zip ties."

Will waggled his brows and grinned. "Ooh, kinky. I didn't really fancy a shag, but okay, I'll go with it."

"I mean things that Bud may have used to restrain

the girls, you sicko. Look for anything out of the ordinary."

I heard Will step into the bathroom and pull open the medicine cabinet. "No knockout drugs or Viagra, nothing like that."

"Keep looking. Bud can't be that smart. We should also be looking for any evidence of a secondary hiding place. There's no way he could be keeping Alyssa in here without his neighbors knowing about it. She's got to be somewhere else. See if you can find a storage container receipt or hotel matches or something. Bud's our guy, Will, I can feel it. We'll gather everything we can here and send Alex and the PD in for the kill."

"You mean, if we can find Bud."

"We will."

My chest was feeling light and the blood pulsing through my veins shot a new, hopeful energy through me. We were going to track Bud down. We were going to find Alyssa. And, God as my witness, we were going to find her alive.

I found Bud's bedroom at the back of the apartment. It was a simple as the rest of the place—a full-sized bed, a bureau, a television set that was probably brand new in 1957, and a single shelf lined with books.

"Bingo."

Will came up over my left shoulder. "Bingo, what?" I pointed to the shelf.

"Mystery buff." A pause. "Oh. That's different."

He reached over and slid a slim volume from the shelf. "*The History of Witchcraft.*"

I slid the rest of the questionable books into my hand. "*Coven and Craft. The Twenty-first Century Witch. Incantations and Spells.*" I paused, holding the last book up. "And the coup de grace."

"The book of protection spells."

"Still don't think Bud is our man?"

"All right, all right." Will nodded. "I don't think the books are definitive, but it certainly puts ol' Bud in the running." He sat down on the edge of the bed. "So, ol' Bud lures the girls into his car, brings them—somewhere—strangles them, does the carving and reads from his little spell books here? What was he trying to accomplish?"

"Well, let's see." I pulled *Incantations and Spells* book from the stack and began thumbing through it. "Hm."

"What?"

"Nothing. Just thought that a spell book for a guy like Bud would be a bit more worn, is all."

I turned the book over in my hand, checking the spine, then flipping a few more pristine pages. "Well, Lorraine said we were dealing with someone very powerful. Maybe he didn't use this much because he didn't need it. It does seem pretty simple for someone so advanced."

"So our guy is an all-powerful wizard?"

"No, a wizard is something totally separate."

"Ah, warlock then."

"No!" I shook my head in a panic, then dropped my voice as though Janitor-Witch Bud would suddenly materialize and turn us into toads or Kardashians. "No, male witches are just called witches. The whole warlock thing? Bad form. It's an insult. Literally means 'oath breaker.'"

Will nodded, impressed. "You know a lot about it."

"You tend to learn quickly when you call Lorraine's Christmas party date a warlock and he repeatedly dunks you in the punch bowl."

"Sounds like a lovely fellow."

"I had a piece of pineapple lodged in my ear until New Year's. Come on, let's see what else we can find."

We worked in companionable silence until Will pulled out the bottom drawer of Bud's bureau. "I suppose there could be some truth to your theory."

I rushed over and gawked. Will had last year's yearbook spread out on his lap. The spine was broken down the center from heavy use, the book flopping open to a photograph of Cathy Ledwith. The smiling, black and white photo was circled in black, but there was a heavy red slash through it. A date was written in the same black ink.

"Oh." My hackles went up and fear, like an icy breeze, shot down my spine. "That's the day Cathy went missing."

"You mean the day she was found."

"No. When she went missing."

Will turned a page; two newspaper clippings

were carefully folded and pinched in the crease. I didn't need to open them to know they were from the day Cathy disappeared and the day she was found.

"Trophies?" Will said grimly.

"Could be. What about these?"

Four loose photos were tucked in the back of the book. They were each the standard, posed picture-day photos—bright smiles, heads cocked, fuzzy blue background, Mercy uniforms pressed and impeccable. "Fallon, Alyssa, Kayleigh, Miranda," I said, as I flipped through each shot. "It's like a roadmap."

"Or a catalog." Will took the photos from me and laid Alyssa's and Kayleigh's out on the bed. "He's got these two." He picked up Fallon's photo and eyed me. "Still think they're partners?"

I swallowed hard. "I—I don't know."

Will placed the photo next to Miranda's. "Then I guess we need to figure out which one of these he is after now."

I waited outside while Will handed Bud's key over to Centuri. He hadn't been gone for a minute when I snatched my phone and hit the speed dial.

"Grace."

"Why didn't you tell me another girl has gone missing? Why didn't you tell me it was Kayleigh Logan?"

I heard Alex suck in a breath just as Will stepped out to meet me. Will's eyes raked over me as I stood there with the phone pressed against my ear. Suddenly, his lips were pressed in a thin, sharp line and I knew he wasn't happy. From the sound of Alex's sharp breathing, it was apparent that he wasn't, either.

"Did Sampson tell you about Kayleigh?"

"Of course he did. You and me and Will are supposed to be working together on this, Alex. How are we supposed to do that if we're not sharing information?"

"Actually, Lawson, me and Romero are working on this case. I don't know what you and Will are doing, and frankly, I don't care. I've got two missing girls to find."

I could hear him pull the phone away from his ear and something inside me swelled and broke. "Bud Hastings."

He paused. "What?"

"You need to be looking for Bud Hastings. He's the janitor at Mercy."

I could hear the sound of shuffling paper on Alex's side. "We interviewed him. He's got an alibi for the time Alyssa went missing. And, actually, for Kayleigh's, too. He's on sabbatical. So thanks, but—"

"Where?"

"What?"

"Where did Bud Hastings go on his sabbatical? Do you know? Because Will and I are at his apartment right now and Bud's not here, but pictures of four teenage girls are—and two of them have gone missing."

"Lawson." I could tell Alex was gritting his teeth by the tight, stiff way he said my name. "We're handling it."

"Not well enough, you're not."

I hung up the phone and jammed it in my pocket while Will stared at me for a moment of stunned silence. Slowly, a sly, impressed grin slid over his face.

"For some reason, I'm incredibly attracted to you right now."

I wanted to grin despite our dire circumstances. My pants also seemed to have no conscience as I felt the desperate need to take them off.

"No," I said as much to Will as to myself. "We're getting Alyssa and Kayleigh back. Then we're stringing up Bud by his sicko neck."

"I don't understand why he'd take another girl right now."

I pointed upward. The moon was hanging low over the bay, an enormous silvery orb half sliced by the night. "That's why."

Will's gaze followed mine and he let out a low whistle. "The seventh day of the moon cycle."

I gaped. "What?"

Will pointed. "The moon is half full on the seventh day of the moon cycle."

My insides went to liquid. "The seventh day. He wasn't holding the girls for seven days, he was waiting for the seventh day of the moon cycle."

"What exactly does that mean?"

"It means that Alyssa and Kayleigh are running out of time."

"Can't you go any faster?" I growled as Nigella huffed her way through town.

"First of all, we're going fast enough. And second of all, we don't even know where Bud is."

"But we do know that Miranda is in danger. Whatever Bud us going to do, he's going to do tonight. Go, Will!"

My heart was banging through my rib cage by the time we turned the corner. I had the car door open and my feet on the ground before Nigella sputtered to a full stop. Everything inside me was firecrackers as I listened to the soles of my shoes slap the concrete, then take the inside stairs two at a time.

"Miranda! Miranda!" I was huffing and out of breath by the time I crested the third-floor landing; I could feel the heat well in my cheeks as I gasped.

"Oh my God," Nina said, flinging the door open. She sped out into the hall and crushed me to her, pulling me through the door. "Running for your life?"

"No," I gasped, doubling over with my hands on my knees. "Just running. Where's Miranda?"

"She's with Vlad," Will said calmly, coming through the front door.

"What?"

He held up his cell phone. "While you were busy on your sprint I called Nina, who told me that Miranda was no longer at the apartment, as she has gone off with Vlad." He gave the phone a little shake and shot me the most annoyingly self-congratulatory grin I had ever seen.

I swore to myself I would pummel him if I were ever able to catch my breath again. "Okay, so we know Miranda's safe. Well, safe enough. What now?"

"Fallon."

I felt instantly guilty for not springing into the same, lung-exploding action over her.

"We're not entirely sure these girls are in danger *right now,*" Will said, his expression placating. "I'll give Fallon's house a ring, tell her to keep a look-out. You've already called Alex and gotten the police department on Bud."

My stomach burned at the mention of Alex—even more so at the idea of Alex listening to anything I said.

"And then you should take a nap. Yes?"

I started. "Wait, what? A nap?" I said, frowning. "I'm not a child. Why are you treating me like a child? I found the clue that cracked this case wide open."

Will crossed the living room in two quick strides and gave me a soft pat on the head. "Of course you did."

"I'm going after Bud. Now." I took a step forward, but Will caught me and held me a hairsbreadth from him. I was staring into his eyes; I could smell the slight scent of mint on his breath. My heart thumped. My nipples sprung to attention, and I vaguely wondered if I would ever be able to be aroused in circumstances that didn't include a possible serial criminal or imminent danger.

"Let Alex handle it."

He gave me a peck on the forehead and sauntered out the door.

Chapter Seventeen

I could feel Nina's eyes on me, and when I turned she had her arms crossed in front of her chest, one hip cocked, and an expression on her face that meant she was about to shake up the world. "You're not planning on taking any kind of nap, are you?"

"Oh, so you've met me before."

She grinned. "Okay, out with it. I need to know what harebrained scheme I'm going to have to pull you out of. You're my commodity, you know."

"Is this about my underwear again?"

Nina rolled her eyes and straightened her directorial beret. "No, this is about you being my star for the UDA commercial."

I gave her a once-over, for the first time that night taking in her knee boots, jodhpurs, and the enormous ecru scarf knotted around her neck. "Nice outfit."

"You've got to dress the part to be the part," she

said with a slick, fang-bearing grin. "Or fake it 'til you make it."

I wrapped a piece of hair around my finger. "Fake it 'til I make it, huh? Yeah, yeah, Neens, you're totally right. I don't need to wait for Will. I don't need to take a nap. And I sure as hell don't need Alex. All I need are his files."

Nina picked up the stack heaped on the dining room table. "These are the ones Vlad printed out for you."

"These are the official files. They were good enough, but I need more. Alex keeps his notes—handwritten ones, stacked with info—in his office. But now that I don't have him to rely on, I need to get a hold of those notes."

Nina's eyes lit up like a campfire, her heart-shaped mouth curving up, showing off her fangs. "Field trip?"

I took in my breathless, weightless, fingerprint-less best friend. "Absolutely."

Nina's face fell as quickly as it lit up. "Oh. Should we get Vlad?"

"Isn't he with Miranda?"

"I guess they're still together. She was dragging him out of here by the arm, but that was a couple of hours ago. He hasn't called or anything."

I shrugged. "We'll leave a note. This is an all-girl mission. Besides, he's big and burly and hard to hide."

Nina cracked a grin. "And you're so stealthy?"

I narrowed my eyes and poked her cold, hard chest. "Don't cross me." I grabbed my jacket and keys.

"Okay," Nina said, following me out the front door. "But we're running lines in between heists."

I like to think I was making Batmobile-type progress, slicing through town while the reflection of the yellow streetlights bounced through the spitting rain. But in actuality, Nina and I were pinched in my Honda and stuck at a traffic light while we waited for the half-naked, half-leathered Folsom Street Parade to march through.

"I thought they banned public nudity," Nina said, snarling.

"That's why they're marching," I said.

We pulled into the police station, and Nina and I shared a look. My heart was pounding and bat wings were flapping fire in my stomach, but Nina was cool as a cucumber in a pair of half-glasses, marking a script with her red pencil.

"Are you ready?"

"Say, 'No pulse, no breath, no problem!'" she asked, holding the eraser end of the pencil to her lips.

"No pulse, no breath, no problem," I deadpanned. "Now can we get in there? I really prefer to commit my felony offenses before midnight."

Nina blew out a sigh and crossed something off

on her script. "It's going to take a lot of work with this one," she said to the car's interior. "Take a note." She put down her pencil and tucked her hair behind her ears, then went through a brief series of random vocal warm-ups.

"Nina?" I screamed, when she went into a frenzied series of "Toy Boat" enunciations.

"Watch and learn."

Nina went into the police station first to get things rolling while I waited in the shadows of the parking lot. I had to clamp a hand over my mouth to keep from laughing as she went from a dainty walk through the parking lot to a spastic run into the station, screaming, crying, tearing at her long hair. I had to give it to my roommate: she played a splendid madwoman.

As every available officer raced to assist—and possibly subdue—Nina, I was able to sneak into the foyer.

"Excuse me—"

A pup officer whom I'm glad I didn't recognize was about to stop me when I heard Nina's feet stomping and her bellow, "Oh sweet Jesus, I got the devil inside me!" The pup's eyes went wide and right over my head as Nina scratched and clawed, shouting things about Corinthians and her need for an "old priest and a young one."

I was in Alex's dark office before she launched into an impressively deep baritone and the first few lines of "Ol' Man River." As she hit the chorus, I hit the jackpot—Alex had never fully embraced file cabinets or any particular system of organization other than "put stuff in box," and the Mercy file box was open on his desk. I had it under my shirt like an incredibly boxy pregnancy belly and was out free in the police station parking lot before Nina stopped, blinked, pressed the back of her hand to her head and made some excuse that left the five officers surrounding her open-mouthed and stunned enough to let her walk right out of the station.

I started the car and drove carefully out of the parking lot while every nerve in my body hummed.

"That was great. That was great! We really should do stuff like that more often; it makes me feel so alive," Nina said, kicking her feet up on the dashboard.

"No way," I said, flicking on my blinker. "We are only doing the sneaking-into-the-police-station thing when it is absolutely necessary. It might make you feel alive, but if Alex ever finds out, I'm the one he's going to make dead."

"Well, what'd you get?"

I wasn't able to answer because the seat-belt warning starting pinging furiously as Nina unbuckled hers and started to climb into the backseat, her butt mashed against my ear as she tried to climb. "What'd we get? Ew, papers?"

"I told you, this is business. I had to get the police files for this case. I'm not going to dodder around on this stupid witch hunt when there's a girl"—bile rose in my throat—"*two girls* in danger."

"Okay, but why are you turning here?"

"I've got a theory."

Nina's eyebrows went up. "Ooh, a theory. Lay it on me, Sherlock."

"Remember that girl I told you about, Fallon?"

Nina pursed her lips. "The pretty, mean one?"

"Yeah. I think—when Kayleigh disappeared, Sampson brought up the idea of a partner. Someone that Kayleigh—and maybe Alyssa and Cathy—knew."

"And you think this Fallon girl is in on the act?"

I paused for a beat. "Maybe. Kayleigh was riding her bike when she went missing. When Will and I went over to Fallon's house, she was riding her bike, just coming back from somewhere."

Nina looked at me, clearly expecting more.

"It's just a theory."

"Because two girls were riding bikes?"

"Two girls who knew each other. One that went missing. One that, I know, was scared of the other. We found Fallon's picture in with the other one's at Bud's place, but I'm not convinced she might be one of the victims. I think she might be a partner."

Nina pursed her lips and scratched at her chin, considering. "I don't know if I'm buying that. Don't get me wrong, I know how evil we ladies can be, but . . . what else you got?"

I told Nina about Kayleigh coming in to my

classroom, about the way her hands worked the strap of her bag as she struggled to get anything out of her mouth. I told her about Fallon interrupting.

Nina sat back, her jaws working as though she were tasting her thought. Finally, she looked at me. "Fallon's a teenager who still rides bike. Girls are afraid of other girls in high school. Hell, you're still afraid of high school girls."

I shifted in my seat, my eyes tight on the road.

Nina leaned forward, hanging on to the two front seats as she pushed herself closer. "These girls go missing, Soph, and they die."

I held up a single finger. "One of them. One of them died." That little, niggling voice in the back of my head wanted to correct me, wanted to tell me that it wasn't just Cathy—it was Gretchen Von Dow, too, and at least two other girls. And now maybe Alyssa and Kayleigh, as well.

I pushed the gas pedal down a little harder.

We had cleared the city and were closing in on Fallon's exit when my phone bleeped out "God Save the Queen." Nina picked up the phone and glanced at it.

"Will. Want me to answer?"

"No. Ignore it."

She punched the button and the cheery song died away. Nina frowned. "He's called three times."

I gripped the wheel. "Let him call three more."

I was still in my kick-ass, take-charge stance when I turned the corner onto Fallon's street. My kickassedness turned into a roiling stomach and sour saliva when the blue and red police lights washed over our car.

"Oh my God," I murmured.

My heart started to thud as the car slowed down and my blood became ice as I pulled aside and swept the scene. A handful of police cars were parked at jagged angles, an open ambulance in between them. A fire truck was blocking the driveway, the hose, like the discarded skin of a snake, flopped and ignored on the driveway. A wisp of smoke came from somewhere and the smell of something charred hung in the air.

"Why aren't you answering your phone?" Will bellowed the second my car door opened an inch. He was dressed for work—firefighting, not the Guardian stuff—and the entire scene stunned me.

"I was—what's going on here?"

Every light in Fallon's house was on, the warm light flooding into the front yard, mingling with the flashing lights of police cruisers and the steady headlights of the ambulance and fire truck.

Nina came around the side of the car and put her hand on my arm, the chill just shocking enough to shake me. "Why are you here? What's going on?"

"Call came in about twenty minutes ago," Will said, his voice low.

"Lawson!" Alex's voice cut through the general din of idling motors, barking orders, and my pounding heart. My body stiffened as he marched across the street and clamped a hand around my wrist. "I need you for this."

His eyes were stern and hard, in complete business mode. I stared at him blankly and started to move until I felt a hand on my other arm.

"Soph and I are working on this together. I need her to see something."

Alex's eyes went over my head and locked with Will's. "This is official police business, Will."

"And this is Underworld criminal activity. Sophie and I have been dealing with Fallon for a week."

I knew I should have said something, but I was still in a weird stupor, leaning toward Alex, leaning toward Will. Finally, I felt a tight tug and heard Alex say, "Sorry about that, but police business trumps your stuff."

Nina's eyes cut to the house and then back to me. She shook her head and took a step back. I handed her my keys. As far as I knew, Nina had never broken UDA protocol. But adding a vampire—even an adherent one—to a crime scene, where there could be enormous amounts of blood and a plethora of warm cop bodies, was begging for a rule to break.

I stumbled aside and glanced over my shoulder long enough to see the anger flicker across Will's face.

"Hang on, mate," Will said, following us quickly.

"Soph." Nina's eyes were wide.

"Both of you, stop!" I shook my arms free and turned on my heel, going directly to the ambulance, where a paramedic was wrapping a heavy blanket around Fallon's shoulders. I didn't know if the guys were following me and I didn't care.

"Fallon, what happened here?"

Fallon looked up at me, her eyeliner smeared, black rivulets of mascara laced with tears sliding down her cheeks. Her hair was still in pigtails, but they were lopsided now and somehow, she looked like a regular kid: vulnerable, sad—scared. She blinked up at me, her lower lip trembling.

"I—I'm not sure."

"Miss?" The paramedic put an arm up between Fallon and me, his other hand pumping a blood pressure monitor. "Please don't upset her. She's had quite a scare."

I was stunned to dead silence when Fallon looked from me to the paramedic and said, "That's okay, she's a friend."

The paramedic finished his reading and backed away with a shrug. I sat down on the tailgate next to Fallon. We were silent for a full moment, the lights of the police cars washing over us, first responders rushing around, eventually getting in their cars or making notes.

"I went out to get something to eat. When I came back . . ." Fallon's lip started to tremble again and her eyes filled with tears. I expected her to shake it off, to blink back the tears. The Fallon from school would have. This one just let the tears fall.

I put a hand on hers, squeezed gently. "What happened, hon?"

"Every light in the house was on. Blazing, like it is now." She gestured absentmindedly toward the house. The doors were wide open. I went inside and—and—"

"There was a pentagram on the dining room floor." It was Alex now, in front of Fallon and me, arms crossed in front of his chest, legs akimbo.

Fallon nodded and sniffed. "Someone had pushed aside all the furniture and drawn—drawn it in—in chalk or something. There were candles and—" Fallon closed her eyes and bit her bottom lip before whispering, "There was blood."

I looked up at Alex and he nodded solemnly.

"I screamed and ran out. I guess I kicked over one of the candles because the curtains caught on fire."

"Where are your parents?"

Fallon didn't look at me. "Gone. My mom left for Portland tonight—that's why I went out to get something to eat."

"And your dad?"

"My dad is . . ." Her voice went thin again and I could almost see the wheels turning in her head, deciding what she should tell me. Exhaustion must have won over. "We don't really know where he is. We haven't for a while."

My heart ached for her.

"Lawson?" I glanced up and Alex was right in front of me, eyes imploring. Will was twenty feet behind him suited up in his gear, soot streaked across his face, ax thrown over his shoulder. I felt my heart start to pound as Alex held out a hand. I saw Will shift behind him.

I swallowed hard, my stomach starting to roil. Finally, I stood. "I'm going to go in and check out what you saw, okay?" I was speaking to Fallon. She hugged the blanket tighter over her shoulders and frowned.

"What were you doing here, anyway?" She sniffed. "I mean, thanks, but you're a substitute teacher. Why are you like, fighting crime?"

I sucked in a breath. "You have no idea what it takes to get teaching credentials in California. I'll be right back, okay?"

Fallon nodded and rested her head on her knees.

The inside of Fallon's house was opulent—more so than I expected—with a swirling staircase wide enough for my car and slick walnut carved everything. Pictures were spaced equidistantly apart, each one showing the same family of three in stiff familial poses, their surroundings and smiles imitating the perfect, happy family, while their eyes stared out vacantly. The kitchen had the same pristine, model-home feel, with glossy industrial ovens that looked like they had never been used and a bunch of fresh bananas that were the exact hue of the trim.

I wondered if Ms. Monroe would toss them once the color changed.

"It's in here," Alex said, ten feet in front of me.

The dining room was the only room so far with its lights off, but there was enough light coming from the bouncing flames in the fireplace to give me a view of the whole room. I immediately started unbuttoning my jacket as the roaring fire ratcheted up the room temperature by fifteen degrees. An entire half-wall of the room was scorched, long fingers of soot crawling up to the ceiling. The remains of elegant drapery were gnarled rags on one side, Dupioni silk in a calming blue on the other. The window they were protecting was blown out and shards of glass littered both sides of the wall.

"What do you think?"

Alex was gesturing to the wood floor. Furniture hugged the walls, but the center of the room was bare. The pentagram that Fallon said was made of chalk had been ground into the lush wood, its luster covered by what looked like years of wear. A smear of red—blood, I supposed—was washed across the center circle. The candles set at the pentagram's five points were out, and the one closest to the charred wall was still on its side, a little ripple of form in a pool of black melted wax.

"Anything significant?"

I snapped a picture and turned around, careful not to step on any of the dust. "I don't see anything that screams out of the ordinary. Unless, of course, you count this giant pentagram on the floor."

Alex let out a whoosh of air that let me know he was annoyed. "I mean, is this real?"

"It's real." I bent down and brushed across a white line with my index finger. "It's here, isn't it?" I tugged at my collar. "Did Fallon make this fire? Did she do it before she saw the pentagram?"

"There's no way Fallon made that fire." Will stepped through the broken window and shot the licking flames with an extinguisher.

"Hey, that's evidence!"

"No," Will corrected. "It's a fire hazard."

I coughed at the ash that kicked up and took a step back, realizing a second too late that I was standing in the center of the pentagram, my feet firmly planted on a smear of blood.

"Oh, God!" I jumped forward, feeling instantly nauseous.

I paused when Will turned on the overhead light and the whole room lit up like it was day.

"That blood looks awfully thin." I grimaced. "I can't believe I said that. I can't believe I *know* that."

Alex crouched down and pulled a Q-tip from the evidence pack he carried in his windbreaker. He rubbed the cotton tip over the stain and frowned. "It's definitely not blood. Hey." He glanced over his shoulder at Will. "Why do you think the girl didn't make the fire?"

"You mean how do I know she didn't make the fire?" He used the poker to push around the debris. "An accelerant was used. You can smell it. It wasn't on Fallon's hands or clothes, and there was no soot or residue. The container's not here either."

Alex stiffened. "She threw it away."

"Not in any trash can in the house or the ones outside."

I saw Alex press his lips together, still unconvinced.

"When this fire was started, it would have been a near fire ball." Will pointed to spots on the fireplace façade with seeping black burn marks. "And I know the bird." He fished something out of the fireplace. "If she was going to burn her clothes, she wouldn't do it in her family fireplace."

I felt my mouth drop open as Will laid out what remained in the ashes of the fire.

"It's another Mercy uniform."

Alex stepped forward. "Does it belong to the victim?"

"Fallon, her name is Fallon. And I'm going to find out."

The second I walked out of the dining room, the cool night air broke over me and I realized I was sweating.

"Fallon."

She was still sitting on the edge of the tailgate, still wearing the gray blanket. A few people—neighbors, I suspected—were huddled around her, looking on sympathetically. She looked up at me, her eyes red-rimmed and tired looking.

"Tell me the truth. Did you start the fire?"

She shrunk back into the blanket and the sympathetic eyes were turned on me—but they were angry now.

"Leave this girl alone," someone said, shoving toward Fallon.

Fallon held the woman off. "It's okay. Yeah, I told you I started the fire. I knocked over the candle. It was an accident—I was freaked out."

"Imagine," another woman said, "a Satanic cult breaking into this child's house. Breaking into our neighborhood!"

"I mean the fire in the fireplace. Did you start that?"

Fallon frowned. "Of course not." Her eyes were hardening, the old Fallon showing through now that she had her entourage—albeit a less stylish one. "I don't even know how you make a fire in there. Isn't there just some kind of switch? Maybe I did when I was running out, I don't know."

"So was the fire going when you went into the dining room?"

Fallon's eyes rolled skyward. "Um, maybe. It was hot. Wait, yeah, yeah, I guess so."

"You're not sure?"

Now she rolled her eyes. "I was kind of in the middle of a major trauma. Someone broke into my house and made one of those Satan things and there was blood. I wasn't paying attention to whether or not my potential killer wanted to make the room warm and cozy with a fire. One of my best friends just disappeared, you know."

"So you didn't know that someone was burning a Mercy High School uniform in your fireplace?"

Her eyes went wide, her surprise seemingly genuine. "What?"

"One of the firemen found the remains of a school uniform in your fireplace."

Fallon clutched at her throat. "Mine?"

"I don't know. Is your uniform up in your room? Would you allow us to check?"

Fallon sucked in a long, dramatic breath. "I suppose so. I mean, if there was a killer pawing through my things—oh my gosh." She clapped a hand over her mouth. "What if he's still there? What if he's in my closet, lying in wait? Maybe he didn't even want Alyssa or Kayleigh—maybe he was after me the whole time!" She seemed to crumble as enormous tears rolled over her cheeks. The women closed in on her, soothing and clucking. I stepped away, grateful for a few moments alone.

I was on the front porch when Alex and Will caught up with me.

"What'd the girl say?" Alex wanted to know.

I glanced up. "She didn't start the fire. She didn't know anything about the uniform."

I could see Will's chest bolster a tiny bit.

"But I'm going to check her closet just to be sure."

"I'll go with you." Both guys said it in unison and both immediately bristled.

"Grace!" one of the perimeter officers called out to Alex and I could see the annoyance in Alex's eyes as they cut toward the officer, then to me, and finally narrowed and set on Will.

"Don't let anything happen to her." He turned on his heel and the cold air at his exit—and in his tone—highlighted the blaze of anger in my gut.

"Hey," I yelled, pushing past Will. "I don't need anyone to take care of me."

I could hear Will snicker behind me. "*Anyone*," I said, turning on Will. "There are two girls missing right now and there could have been a third. I need you to stop beating your chests or measuring your balls or whatever it is you think you're doing and start focusing on this case. Girls are missing. Girls are dead. Alex, go see what the officer wants and see what physical evidence your guys have come up with. Will, come with me."

I could see Alex's nostrils flare, the little muscle in his jaw that let me know he was angry, jumping. Will opened his mouth to say something—smart, I guessed—and I held up a finger. "And you shut your trap."

I stomped up Fallon's stairs, Will in tow, and was too angry to comment or stand in slack-jawed awe when I found Fallon's bedroom. It was easily the size of my apartment, and likely as big as Will's and mine combined, with an attached bathroom stuffed with more frilly scents and loofah sponges than an entire Bath and Body Works megastore.

"Damn."

The walls were painted a pretty rose pink and glittery fairy wings hung from the four-poster bed. There were crowns trailing ribbons and silky ballet shoes and a heavy pile snow-white rug.

"It looks like My Little Pony exploded in here," I said.

Will flicked a set of the fairy wings. "My Little Pony and her fairy friends."

"Not exactly what I expected from Fallon."

"What did you expect?"

"Something darker. More of a German dungeon type theme."

"I hear that sells big at Pottery Barn Kids."

I pulled open some dresser drawers and poked at the neat stacks of starched white blouses and a carefully folded navy-blue sweater. The drawers Will sifted through held little bits of neon and leopard-print skirts or tube tops or headbands—it was hard to tell.

"Well, it doesn't look like she's missing any shirts, and there wasn't a sweater in the fireplace." I bit my lip and went to the closet, pulling back double doors to expose the second-largest clothing collection (Nina's being the first) that I had ever seen outside of a retail establishment. One whole section was a sea of blues—four navy jumpers, four regulation plaid skirts, every manner of high school booster wear, and the whole thing repeating in a sea of greys. I groaned.

"For all we know this could be every uniform she has and the one in the fireplace could be someone else's, or this is all she has minus one." I nodded in the general direction of the dining room.

"The one in the fireplace was a size two. At least the skirt part."

"Yeah," I said, glad my snarled lip was hidden amongst the plaid. "Just like mine."

"Wait," Will said, pausing. "Did you say she's short a sweater?"

I shrugged. "There was only one in there. So, maybe yes, maybe no."

"Didn't your little stinky friend find—"

My eyes widened. "A sweater. Someone had tried to flush a sweater down the toilet." I paused, my previous revelation falling flat. "Why would someone try to flush a sweater down the toilet?"

Will pursed his lips. "You didn't think to ask that at the time?"

"Well, neither did you."

He held his hands up in obvious surrender. "Touche."

Alex came up the stairs and knocked on the doorframe. I stiffened when I saw him, immediately feeling the annoyance well up inside of me.

"We're still working in here," I said, going into my best *CSI* stance.

He crossed the room to me and held out a Ziploc evidence bag. "Do you recognize this?"

I took the bag, tentatively, somehow certain it was a trap. His fingertips brushed mine and I shuddered—I had never remembered his hands being so cold. When I looked up at him, I realized just how tired he looked—heavy bags under his eyes made the crystal blue of his irises seem washed out and dull. The usually rosy skin over his cheeks seemed papery and sallow. His lips were dry and cracked.

"Are you okay?" I whispered.

Alex just shook the bag in my palm. I snapped my attention to it.

"It's a Lock and Key pin," I said. "Where did you get this?"

"Romero found it. It was attached to the collar of the shirt in the fireplace."

Will and I exchanged a glance. "Fallon wasn't in Lock and Key," I said. "But Kayleigh was."

"Actually . . ." Both Alex and I looked to where Will was standing. A floor-to-ceiling bulletin board was in front of him. He plucked a single photo from the collage and held it out to me. I took it, and everything inside me stopped. "This is Lock and Key Club. From this year."

"And Fallon's in it." Will squinted at the photo. "Alyssa, Kayleigh—that Miranda bird. And the advisor there, isn't that the geezer from the principal's office?"

"Heddy's not a geezer. And Miranda told me she wasn't in the club." A cold stripe of fear shot down my spine. "The uniform downstairs could be hers. Fallon and she were constantly at each other's throats."

"I'm going to go downstairs to check on the girl."

"Ask her where Bud is."

Alex's lips went into a pale straight line. "Lawson . . ."

"Do it, Alex. I don't care if he was alibied or not. Fallon is in on this and she'll know where Bud Hastings is."

Alex eyed me. We were face to face, but I had my shoulders thrown back, my fists on hips, and was ready to shut down anyone who tried to placate me.

"You want us to go after Hastings on a hunch?"

"You want two girls to die because you were too proud to follow a hunch?"

I squared off my hips and kept Alex's gaze. Finally, he broke. "Yeah. Okay."

I pulled my cell phone out of my pocket while Alex left Will and me alone in the bedroom.

Will's eyes narrowed as he considered. "So you think Fallon did this? She made the pentagram, got nervous when the candle caught the drapes, then called the police?"

"She didn't have to make the fire to toss in Miranda's uniform."

I dialed Miranda's number and listened as it

rang repeatedly. I frowned, hung up, and tried Vlad.

"Direct to voice mail."

Will's eyes locked mine. For the first time, there was real concern in them. "You can't find Miranda?"

"Let me try Nina. I'm sure she's talked to Vlad."

Nina picked up on the second ring.

"Hey, it's me. Is Vlad there?"

"I haven't seen him all night. Your little friend came back though."

My heart stopped. "Miranda, really? Is she there? Let me talk to her."

"She's not here anymore. She just forgot a coat or something and took off."

"Without Vlad?"

"She said he peeled off for Poe's or something. She got in a car downstairs. Some guy was driving, but it wasn't Vlad. Although the car looked like something from our era." She gave a small, snorting chuckle at her own joke. "Anyway, I wasn't completely paying attention because I was on the phone with Scorsese's assistant."

"Wait—Martin Scorsese's assistant?"

Because even in the midst of peril, I could be not only horny, but starstruck.

"No, Neil Scorsese. He runs the soundstage down by the Presidio. Werevamp. Nice guy."

"Look, if either Miranda or Vlad come back, keep them there." I hung up my phone.

"Miranda took off with some guy who wasn't Vlad."

"Young love burns fast and hot, but fades fast."

"Nina said the car was old." My skin started to prickle. "What if the guy was Janitor Bud?"

"So, Fallon is working in cahoots with this janitor bloke. She sets fire to her own house so the police are tied up here, so Bud can go out and get Miranda?" Will shook his head. "Something's not adding up. The police had already cleared Bud."

I paced, stringing a piece of hair around my index finger. "Maybe she sent Bud out to get Miranda while she set up the sacrificial altar downstairs. She really did knock over a candle and a neighbor called the police and fire department. She probably heard the sirens and intercepted Bud."

"Kind of a stretch. What about Alyssa and Kayleigh? Why would he—or even Fallon—suddenly start collecting the girls rather than killing them? It can't be easy to hide one teenage girl, let alone three."

"Remember what Vlad said? Maybe he just hasn't found the right girl."

"But to deal with three?"

My stomach was leaded and my saliva bitter. "We don't know that he hasn't killed the other girls yet."

I took the stairs two at a time, Will following close behind. I pushed the front door open only to see the taillights of the ambulance fading into the darkness, the squad cars falling into line behind that. Alex was leaning into the open window of a squad car, and Fallon was gone.

"Alex! Alex, where's Fallon?"

Alex looked around as if just noticing his surroundings. "We were able to reach her mother. She gave permission for the girl to go with the neighbor."

My heart started to thud.

"Which neighbor?"

"I'm not sure. Wasn't my jurisdiction. What's going on?"

"She's the one you're looking for," Will spat.

Alex straightened, his eyes darkening. "Lawson, you need evidence to accuse someone of a crime. Especially of a crime like this."

My frustration and anger were reaching boiling points. "I know. Bud Hastings has an alibi, and there is absolutely no reason that you should go after Fallon except for the fact that she is in on this. She and Bud are partners. She lures the girls, he carves them up in an attempt to open some portal or do some kind of witchcraft. And it's going to happen tonight. No one broke in and made a pentagram on Fallon's floor. She did it. She did it for him! Look at the moon! It's the seventh phase. They're trying to open a portal and they need to do it tonight."

Alex leaned back and cocked an eyebrow. "Bud Hastings is some kind of warlock?"

"Warlock?" Will thumped me on the shoulder and rolled his eyes. "Can you believe this guy?"

"Bud Hastings is taking these girls and Fallon is involved. And I think I know what this"—I waved my arms, doing my crazy best to indicate—"is all about. I think I know who the next victim is."

Alex crossed his arms in front of his chest. "Why?"

"What do you mean why? She's crazy? She's the—the bad seed? Why? She just is. You have to get her!"

"These girls are her classmates. What makes you think Fallon is involved or that she's after another girl? That's not this perp's pattern."

I gaped. "Not the pattern? Kayleigh has gone missing, too, Alex. *That* is not the pattern, but it happened. It's just a matter of time—a matter of hours—until Alyssa's body turns up. Her *body*, Alex. Bud's gone off half-cocked—or Fallon has. We have to do something!" My whole body was thrumming and I tugged at the collar of my jacket, feeling hot again. I could feel the sweat trickle down my back and I squirmed, fisting my hands so I didn't grab Alex and force him to go find Fallon.

"Will, find her!"

Alex shot out a hand and grabbed Will's arm. "Wait a minute."

Will started to shrug Alex off. "Don't touch me. I'm not in your jurisdiction, either."

"I'm going to go find Miranda and Bud." I spun,

then slapped my hands to my head. "Nina took my car."

Will took my hand and folded his keys in my palm.

"Nigella?" I whispered.

"Just find the girl."

My heart was slamming against my rib cage and tears were stinging at the back of my eyes. I furiously dialed Nina, Vlad, and Miranda at every stoplight, getting nothing but a busy signal, a direct to voice mail, and no answer.

"Where would he take her, where would he take her, where would he take her?" I mumbled to myself as tears flooded my vision.

"The Battery!"

Adrenaline shot through me, hot and pulsing, and I stamped my foot on the gas, blowing through a red light on Kearney, my tires squealing as I took a left on Columbus. I was trembling, using the back of my hand to push away tears as I gripped the steering wheel with one hand. I was focused on my mission, focused on getting to Battery Townsley before Miranda, Kayleigh, and Alyssa could become another set of bones, tossed like so much trash, forgotten in some godforsaken hole. The thought hit me with another round of sobs, which is why I probably didn't notice the car inching up behind me. It may have been there when I rounded the corner, may have been waiting at the last inter-section. I caught its lights—and its driver—in my rearview mirror just before I heard the metal crunch, the ear-splitting pop of windows shattering. I felt myself vault forward; my teeth chattered and my brain seemed to ramp against my skull. Something ripped across my chest and my flesh was on fire. I could taste fresh blood in my mouth, hear the squeal of tires and someone screaming.

And then everything went black.

Chapter Eighteen

Everything hurt—my eyes, my face, my stomach, my hips. My hair hurt.

"There she is."

I blinked, the effort causing a painful spasm that reverberated through my skull. "Will?" My throat was parched and my lips felt dry and cracked. I tried to touch them with my fingertips, but a piece of tape pulled at my skin. "I can't move. Why can't I move?"

Will's face came into focus. His eyes were kind, but his brows dipped down into deep Vs. "You're in hospital."

"You had an accident."

I tried to sit up, tried to angle my gaze toward the other male voice. "Alex?"

"We're all here," Nina said, lacing her cold fingers through mine. "Will, Alex, and me."

I looked around at my friends, a brief, warm sense of comfort washing over me. As soon as the calm feeling settled, it was chased away by a bitter cold and I sat up. "Bud! Miranda!"

Alex came over to my left side and very gently guided me back toward the pillows. "We followed up on Bud, Lawson."

"And?"

Alex pressed his lips together, the muscle in his jaw jumping slightly. "He's dead."

"What?"

Alex slipped his leather notebook from his pocket and flipped it open, his ice-blue eyes going over the pages. "We found him at Battery Townsley. Someone called in an anonymous tip—they heard a gunshot."

"But who—?"

"We're thinking self-inflicted."

My stomach roiled and had I been attached to a heart monitor, it would have flat lined. My eyes went from Alex to Will. "The girls?"

Will avoided my gaze. Alex swallowed hard. "We had Fallon in protective custody. She doesn't know anything about Bud. And while we were securing the crime scene, we found Alyssa—alive— wandering in the parking lot. She was badly beaten and so far, hasn't said a word."

"She's catatonic," Will said. "They have her in the trauma ward upstairs. She didn't even react when her parents came."

I licked my lips. "Kayleigh?"

Alex looked down, studying the pattern on my

blanket. "We haven't found her yet. We've got men at Bud's place. We're going over it with a fine-toothed comb, trying to find the secondary location."

I looked to Will, hopefully. "But Miranda's okay, right? He let her go?"

Will hung his head but didn't answer. He didn't need to.

"We failed." A sob lodged in my throat. "We failed all of them, Will."

I sunk into my pillow as Will reached under the blanket, his hand finding mine and giving it a tight squeeze.

"We did the best we could."

I snatched my hand back. "No. That's not good enough."

He fisted his hands, his eyes going from Alex to me. "I'm going to get you a cup of tea, okay?"

I lolled my head on the pillow, avoiding him. Nina popped off the bed. "I'll go with you."

Alex waited until the door closed behind them.

"I can't believe that Kayleigh is still out there—somewhere. And maybe Miranda."

Alex cleared his throat. "We're not going to let this go. We're still working," he said. "We brought in the yearbooks you had in the back of your car." His smile was tight. "As well as the box of files that went mysteriously missing from my office."

I threw myself back on my pillow, tossing an arm

across my forehead. "Oh! The pain!" I watched beneath lowered lashes while Alex rolled his eyes.

"Right. Anyway, I was hoping you could go through them and let me know of any other girls you think may have gone missing."

I screwed up my brow. "You suddenly want my help? What happened to distancing yourself?" The anger was simmering in my gut, and I was mad at Alex for his continuous flip-flop behavior, at myself for not finding Bud—and Kayleigh—sooner.

"Lawson, you don't understand."

"No, Alex," I said, swinging my head. "I don't understand. Why don't you explain it to me?"

His eyes raked over me and I could see immediately that the clear crystal blue was marred and flat. He still looked exhausted and pale. He opened his mouth and then closed it, as if thinking better of it. "This isn't the right time."

I was seething.

"I'd like to be alone now."

Alex closed his notebook and shifted his weight. He paused for an uncomfortable beat before patting my leg awkwardly over the blanket.

"Take care of yourself, Lawson."

Alex met the nurse in the doorway. She poked her head in. "Visiting hours are over."

Nina edged her way past the nurse and perched herself at the end of my bed, her weightless body leaving no indentation. "I'm family."

Will blinked at me, but I turned from him, too. I heard him sigh.

"Hey, angel boy, can I catch a ride? The bird decimated my Nigella."

Nina ruffled my hair when the room was emptied out. I closed my eyes and sunk into my pillows. "I really screwed this one up, didn't I, Neens?"

"You can't save them all, Soph."

I swallowed hard, my throat aching. Tears pricked at the back of my eyes and I let them fall. "I don't know what made me think I could do this. It just doesn't make sense, though. If this was all Bud, why the pentagram at Fallon's house? Why the burned-up uniforms? Something is not adding up. If he wanted the girls for sacrifice, why would he just let one go? I mean, the spell books, the candles? Someone had to be keeping the girls. Someone had to be helping him."

"Why? Men kidnap girls all the time."

"Men who are in their sixties? He could have taken down each girl on her own, but how was he keeping them? And Alyssa was alive—and with him—when he took Kayleigh. How does a sixty-year-old man manage that?"

Nina popped off the bed and paced, her fangs straining against her lower lip. I straightened. "There's something you're not telling me. Oh, God—is there another girl? Did Bud take another girl? I'm telling you, it can't just be him."

Nina batted at the air. "It's nothing. It's just that

I called Vlad like, sixteen times. He never even called back."

I harrumphed and poked at the bowl of green Jell-O sitting on my bedside tray. "He's sixteen years old. Does he ever call back?"

Nina puckered her cherry red lips, her perfect façade unmarred. I briefly wondered what it would be like to look perfect all the time or be eternally sixteen.

"I told him you were at the hospital. He still didn't call."

I frowned, stung. "Sixteen," I said again.

Something nagged at me.

"Heddy."

"What?" Nina asked, pausing her pace.

"Heddy's not a geezer. Hey, Neens, pass me one of those yearbooks."

Nina did as she was told and pulled one out for herself, curling up next to me in my bed. She flopped open the book, her face immediately breaking into a grin. "Ah, the seventies. Everyone looked horrible."

"Look up Heddy Gaines."

Nina went to the index, her finger going down the line of names. I did the same, and we both flipped our books open to Heddy's smiling mug at the exact same time.

And it was the exact same picture.

"Wow, she hasn't changed a bit," Nina said.

"No, she hasn't changed at all from 1971 to 1994." I grabbed another book. "Exactly the same in 2010."

I pulled it closer, studying it. Finally, I flipped to the other indexed page. "Heddy Gaines, Lock and Key Club advisor."

My heart started to thump. "Heddy hasn't aged in thirty years."

"A lot of women look good for their ages. Look at me." Nina modeled her perfect mug.

"You don't age, Nina." I yanked another book—this one from '63—and flipped it to show Nina. "Neither does Heddy. Not at all."

Nina blinked, not quite absorbing.

"You know who else doesn't age? Kale or Lorraine."

Nina's eyes went saucer-wide. "Heddy's the witch."

"She's the faculty advisor for the Lock and Key Club. She was handpicking her victims."

"So what about the dead janitor guy?"

"Maybe it was too much for him to handle. Maybe the guilt got to him. She's got to do the spell tonight—the seventh night. We've got to get to them, Neens. She's got Kayleigh and whatever she's going to do to her is going to happen tonight."

I kicked the covers off my legs and yanked the tape from my hand, wincing as I removed the IV.

"What are you doing?" Nina wanted to know.

"I'm getting dressed. Um, where are my clothes?"

Nina bit her bottom lip, the blood she had just drunk just barely coloring her cheeks. "I took your clothes home by mistake."

"What? How do you take someone's clothes by mistake?"

"Will put them in your shoulder bag and told me to take them home. He figured you'd stay in the hospital until the doctor let you go if you had no clothes."

"Some mistake." I put my hands on my hips and paced for a half a minute before I pointed at Nina. "Go. Downstairs. Go to your car and get me something to wear."

Nina opened her mouth to protest, but I pinned her with a glare. It was widely known that any free space that Nina had or could find was stuffed with emergency couture. Her UDA file cabinets were stocked with high-end shoes and intricate bustiers. Her earthquake kit held Band-Aids, a ham radio, and a selection of gowns from Carlos Miele's winter collection—and the trunk of her car was nothing less than a closet on wheels.

"Get. Me. Something."

Nina held up her hands. "Okay. Okay! But most of what I have are gowns or dressy."

I gritted my teeth. "Find me something to wear."

She skittered out the door without another word.

I dialed Will and paced while it rang. "Will? Will! Answer the phone! Fine. I need you to meet me at Battery Townsley. Bud wasn't working alone. I think he was just the fall guy. Call me when you get this."

Nina came back through the door, lugging a log-shaped Louis Vuitton with one hand and pressing a pair of stiletto-heeled black boots against her side with the other. "I brought everything I had in the mobile armoire. But I'm warning you—there are none of your things in there. Lexus and poly-cotton blends don't mix."

I rolled my eyes and took the bag from her, dumping its contents onto the bed. A heap of black leather, hot pink lace, and tiny skirts or possibly large belts flopped out. I looked skeptically at the pile and briefly wondered if I could possibly kick butt while mine was hanging out. I picked up the hot pink hunk of tulle. "You don't have anything any little more authoritative looking?"

Without saying a word, Nina dove into the pile and fished out the black leather pants. One more shot and a matching shirt-possibly-headband came out.

"You can't expect me to wear that."

"Look, you asked for clothes and I got you clothes. You asked for authoritative and I got you authoritative. If you'd rather hunt down that crazy caught-in-time witch in your hospital gown, be my guest."

I sucked in a deep breath and stepped into the pants. "You didn't happen to bring in a can of Pam, did you?"

It took a tremendous amount of pleading, squirming and bending myself into angles that I'm not wholly proud of, but the leather pants were on. The top was, too, mostly, and now Nina was behind me working on the complicated lace-up detailing. I looked at myself in the mirror.

I wore slick black leather in my mind. I wielded a sword, kicked serious ass, and did it all without mussing my mid-back-length flowing red hair. Tonight, my legs looked a mile long in the leather boot-leather pant combination and a little pouch of chocolate pinwheel belly bubbled over the waistband. Nina had hoisted my boobs to my chin with the little strap-up apparatus and my cheeks were flushed—not exactly with the strength and confidence of a superhero—more like the angst of squeezing into the getup. But still, I looked reasonably badassed even if my hair was neither mid-back-length nor flowy.

"Okay," I said.

Nina hiked up her shoulder bag. "I'm coming with you."

I put a hand on her shoulder and shook my head. "I'm not letting anyone else get involved or get hurt. I can do this."

She silently handed me her keys.

I slammed myself into Nina's car and gunned the engine. I was midway to Battery Townsley when a call came in from Vlad.

"Vlad?" I screamed into the phone. "Vlad, Nina is worried sick about you. Where are you?"

But Vlad didn't respond. Instead, there was some

muffled speech, a high-pitched scream, and the thunk of something being hit. I pressed the phone against my ear, listening for some clue—until I heard the cry.

Desperate. Terrified. Young.

I slammed my foot onto the gas pedal, pressing it as far down as it would go. After a full block, the light turned red in front of me and I slammed on the brakes, tapping my fingers on the steering wheel.

"Come on, come on, come on," I huffed to the sleek black interior. "Ugh!" After what seemed like hours in idle, I clicked on the radio.

"This is Heather Idello reporting from Battery Townsley where Mercy High School janitor Budd Hastings seems to have taken his own life. Further down the bluff, police encountered fifteen-year-old Alyssa Rand. The teen has been missing for five days and appeared out of nowhere. Police Chief Conway will be releasing more information at a press conference on the hour."

I snapped the radio back off and made a squealing U-turn the second the light turned. Whatever Heddy was going to do tonight, she wasn't going to do it at the Battery.

"Okay, okay, okay," I said to the steering wheel. "If Battery Townsley was just a dump site, where would Heddy take her sacrifices?"

I snapped my fingers as the dozens of illuminated pentagrams burned in my mind. I barely had a moment to catch my breath before I was pulling in to Mercy High.

The building was bleak, the parking lot deserted save for one dented Rambler parked in the back corner. I didn't have to move closer to know that the car was Janitor Bud's—and likely the one Nina had seen Miranda disappear into. My heart lurched into my throat, but I steeled myself, sinking my administrator's key into the lock before it occurred to me that I was approaching a powerful, murderous witch, weaponless. I hesitated there for a quick second—but when I heard a scream—high-pitched, tortured, I pushed through the doors, thundering through the darkened hallway.

"Kayleigh! Miranda!" I screamed.

"Ms. L?"

Miranda turned out of a darkened alcove. Her eyes were wide and glassy.

"Oh, God, Miranda, I'm so glad I found you. We have to get you out of here."

I yanked my cell phone out of my bustier—the only place I could fit it—and speed-dialed Will.

"No," Miranda said. "You've got to help me. We've got to save Kayleigh. She's up there!" She grabbed my hand and stepped up, yanking me to her. "Come on!"

"Miranda—your hand—your arm. You're covered in blood!"

She glanced down at me one more time, her eyes pleading. "Please, there isn't much time!"

I shoved my phone back into my bust just as I heard Will's muffled. "Hello? Hello? Sophie?"

I was halfway up the stairs when I heard the sound of crushing metal behind me. Someone was kicking and growling and screaming. I took a step backward and Miranda ran behind me, pressing her palms against my back.

"No, upstairs!"

I held her off. "Miranda, what is that?"

"Please Ms. Lawson! We've got to get to Kayleigh!"

The desperate terror in Miranda's eyes clawed at my chest and I took the steps two at a time until I was on the second landing. The hall should have been dark, but a blinding yellow light was bleeding through the cracks in the art room door. I went for the handle, then burst back, my hand singed.

"You have to get in there. You have to!" Miranda was clawing at her hair, tears rolling over her cheeks.

I sucked in a sharp breath and prayed to God the leather would stretch as I center kicked the door, launching it open. I saw the glint of Heddy's eyes as she looked up at me, startled. Her hair was blown back by the wind that swirled out from the spinning vortex in front of her—the center where the pentagrams had been.

I felt myself gape. Then I felt the wind being

knocked out of me as something came down hard, pressing against my lower back, knocking me off my feet, and shooting me right to the edge of the black hole.

"Look what I brought you."

My head snapped up as Miranda sauntered in, a wide grin cutting across her face. It was only then that I noticed that most of her wounds had healed. The enormous purple-blue bruise that marred one whole cheek was gone, the skin pink and perfect. I must have been staring because she dragged an index finger down her cheek and said, "Oh this? It was all stage makeup. If you had really paid attention, you would have known I was a drama geek, too. A few necessary blows, and grease paint the rest. But thanks anyway, you made a swell nurse."

"Miranda," Heddy snapped, "lock that door and get into your robe. We don't have much time." Heddy was standing at the head of the pentagram and seemed to be controlling the swirl of the vortex. She was wearing a hooded robe that screamed every bad Druid movie ever made and carried a lit candle in one hand and an expression that clearly said that she wasn't as pleased with Miranda's gift of me as Miranda had been.

"What?" I pushed myself onto hands and knees. "Miranda—you?"

She just smiled silently.

"What the hell is going on here?" I pulled myself to my feet. "What is this?"

"Portal," Miranda said simply.

"Like a hell mouth? At a high school?" I cocked out a hip. "Hate to tell you, ladies, but it's already been done."

"Silence!" Heddy yelled. "Lay down where you are. The Dark One will appreciate a second sacrifice in his honor."

"The Dark One?"

"He will be very pleased." Another voice came out of the perimeter of darkness around the room.

"Finleigh? You're in this, too?"

"Sacred order," Miranda said, slipping into her robe. "Me and Finny are legacies. Those two"—she pointed to two girls I had never met—"were perfect additions to the old Lock and Key Club." Her eyes cut to the closed door of the supply closet. "So was Kayleigh." She wrinkled her nose. "But Kayleigh's special."

I licked my lips as the two girls I didn't know grabbed my arms and pinned them to my side. "And what about Fallon?" I asked Miranda.

Miranda shrugged and picked a piece of invisible lint from the sleeve of her maroon-colored robe. "She wanted in. Don't like her. She bugs me."

I narrowed my eyes. "She bullied you."

Miranda grinned. "Did she?" She checked her nails. "She and that stupid Janitor Bud."

"So Bud was a part of this."

"Uh, no." Miranda cut her gaze to me, laser sharp. "Bud thought he could stop this." She held her arms out, indicating the creepily robed girls, the vortex. "He really thought that he could change ol' Heddy. Bring her back from the dark side. Ain't that right?"

"Stop talking, Miranda," Heddy commanded.

"But he killed himself. Tonight."

"He had to go," Miranda said with a shrug. "And he got all over me."

My stomach folded in on itself and I had to look away, unable to consider how much evil was housed in Miranda's teenage body.

"We haven't much time!" Heddy yelled again.

Finleigh took a step forward and pulled open the supply closet door. Kayleigh let out a terrified shriek that was muffled by the gag around her mouth. Her eyes were wide and darting; her skin was filthy and her ankles and wrists were bound. Finleigh grinned at her friend before grabbing her by the feet and sliding her across the room. She dumped her at the edge of the pentagram. Kayleigh curled herself into a tight ball and pressed her eyes shut, crying softly.

"Oh God, Kayleigh." I wanted to offer her some comfort, but she kept her eyes fixed low, refusing to make contact with any of us.

Heddy looked at each girl; each girl in turn stepped to a point. I stood there, completely free, feeling stunned and numb as they each lit a candle and began chanting around me. The vortex seemed to ebb and flow with the rise and fall of the chanting voices. I cut my eyes to the door, judging the distance, but Miranda took a miniscule sidestep, glaring down at me as she broke my easy escape.

The voices rose in their chant and Heddy took a step toward me. She slipped a long, narrow sword out of the sleeve of her robe. I unfortunately recognized it as the Sword of Bethesda—a sweet little instrument of death that had once before been used in an attempt to gut me. I slid away as Heddy brought the knife dangerously close to my ear.

"Wait!" I held up my hands and looked from girl to girl to Heddy. "It's obvious I'm not getting out of here. So just tell me why. Tell my why you took Kayleigh if you already had Alyssa?"

"Alyssa was worthless," Heddy spat. "Not even as a morsel to appease the Dark One. But Kayleigh . . ." Her eyes glittered with a hunger so fierce it shot ice water through my veins. "She's the key."

Kayleigh began trembling, her whimpering more panicked.

"The key to what?"

Heddy ran her tongue over her teeth, forcing a grotesque smile. "The key to this world and the next. The key to finally freeing me from this plane. She is the key to Heaven and Hell. The keeper of souls." Her voice had gone from secretary sweet to a grainy, desperate pitch. She bellowed something else and the swirling vortex in front of her expanded and rose, reacting to her voice like a hellish version of Fantasmic. And maybe it was me being

mesmerized by the swirling vortex or me waiting
for a savior, but I didn't register what she said until
right that very moment.

"Wait. Do you mean the Vessel of Souls? That
Kayleigh is the Vessel of Souls?"

Heddy couldn't hide her surprise—then her
disdain. "What do you know about the Vessel?"

"I know that it's the preternatural Vessel—not
key—that houses all human souls in what we know
as limbo."

I widened my stance and crossed my arms over
my chest, shooting her my best "beat that" expression. Heddy seemed to shrink considerably.

"Wikipedia?" she asked, eyes narrowed.

"I also know that Kayleigh is not the Vessel. If you
use Kayleigh, you're going to fail again."

Heddy seemed to regain a little of her bravado
and she narrowed her eyes into angry little slits.
"And how do you know that?"

I caught my reflection as the vortex swirled and
blew my hair around my shoulders, which were
thrown back and strong. The leather that seemed
to chafe and pucker hours ago was like a second
skin now and all I saw was me—and my power. My
"bulging thighs" were pillars of strength. My belly
disappeared as I stood up tall.

"Because I'm the Vessel of Souls."

I guess I thought the vortex would swirl and rise
to the voice of its rightful owner or at the very least,
suck Heddy the infidel in, but nothing happened.

And then it did.

Heddy's eyes started to tear and wrinkle. She doubled over and held herself. Then she howled like a hyena. She laughed so hard that tears rolled down her face.

"Oh, Sophie. Do you think I don't remember you from high school?" she said when she regained her composure. "You were a lovable dolt back then. Now you're just nosy, delusional, and frankly, kind of a bitch. You're not the Vessel of Souls. Kayleigh's father is the most powerful witch in a hundred years. The Vessel needs protection like that. Careful watching over. Who watched over you? Your nutcase Grandma?" Heddy took a step toward me. "The Vessel comes from a place of power, Sophie. Kayleigh has that power." Heddy looked down at the terrified, trembling girl and huffed. "Though you wouldn't be able to tell it now. It's in her blood. You have no one. You're worth nothing. Never were, never will be." She grinned, her teeth gray and pointed in the dim light. "High school never ends."

I felt myself bristle. My insides roiled and heat shot through me, rage invading my every cell.

"You don't know a thing about power, Heddy. What it is, or where it comes from. People don't watch over me, they guard me. And while Kayleigh's dad may be able to pull a rabbit out of a hat? My dad can drag you to hell, where you belong."

Before I had a chance to think, my boot was square in the center of Heddy's chest as she was vaulting backward, screaming as the vortex sucked her in and closed around her.

The girls' screaming started when the door to the room was vaulted open. Will crashed in and the girls ran out, dropping their candles and stripping out of their robes as they did. Paramedics pressed in behind him, rushing to Kayleigh. I vaulted over them and followed Will out the door.

"Miranda killed Bud," I huffed. "We have to find her!"

It didn't take long. She had cut across the back hall and was already on the first floor, reaching for the double doors when they flew open in a haze of licking flames and smoke.

"Another witch?" Will asked me.

"Where is he?"

I took a step forward, coughing and squinting. "Kale?"

She was outlined in a crackling flames. Her hair was wild and her face was drawn. Eyebrows pressed into a furious V. Eyes as black as night.

And she was talking to Miranda.

"I don't know what you're talking about," Miranda said coolly.

Kale's nostrils flared and I half-expected steam to come shooting out of them. She took a step forward and Miranda's hand went up. Her lips were moving and I knew from watching Kale and Lorraine that she was chanting.

Kale just smirked. "Are you done yet?"

Miranda took a step back. "What do you want? I'm not the witch. I'm not the real witch."

I took a step forward. "Kale—"

And then it hit me. The thundering beat of metal. The growling. The screaming. I cocked my head toward the bank of lockers to my right.

"Vlad?" I asked.

"Uh-huh."

Miranda's head snapped to me, her lip curling into a snarl. "Go away, Ms. L."

I continued walking forward, talking to the lockers. "Where are you?"

"Nowhere!" Miranda growled. "He's nowhere!"

Kale cocked a single eyebrow and threw out one arm almost nonchalantly. A locker door—crushed and badly dented—flicked open.

Vlad poked his head out.

"Seriously?" I asked.

He was handcuffed to the top rail and he looked sheepish, then shrugged.

Miranda ran in front of the locker and splayed herself in front of it. "You can't have him. He's mine! He loves me. We're together and he's going to make me immortal. Get out of here! Get out or I'll send you to the depths of hell, do you understand me?"

I had never seen such fire in any woman. Miranda's eyes were lit and dancing. Spittle shot out of her mouth as she screamed. Her knuckles went white as she clawed at the ruined metal of the locker. I almost felt bad for her, having just lost her witch-mentor to a giant gaping hole in the ground, and now her undead love. Almost.

Kale paused, the brimstone and fire fading away behind her. She crossed her arms in front of her chest.

"Let me get this straight: You are going to be with him," she said, her voice calm.

"And you are going to leave us the hell alone."

Kale cocked her head, considering. "So you're saying that Vlad, the man that I've dedicated the better half of my year with, is going to be with you? Is that what you're saying?"

Miranda seemed to lose a little bit of her swagger, but she pumped her head anyway.

"Cuz if that's what you're saying"—she took another step closer and narrowed her eyes—"you better back off, bitch."

Will and I both dropped to the ground. I had my palms pressed against my ears and my eyes pinched shut. There was smoke and heat, and fire alarms wailed. Sprinklers rained from the ceiling. A wisp of smoke sailed up around the singed outline of what used to be Miranda.

"I probably should have stepped in," I said, as

Kale broke Vlad out of his cuffs and threw her arms around him.

"Nah," Will said, shaking his head. "I think you did the right thing." He slung an arm over my shoulders. "Don't you just love young love?"

Chapter Nineteen

It only took twenty-four hours for things to go back to normal. Kayleigh was back to reigning with Fallon, the other girls were in counseling, and no one, conveniently, wanted to know where Heddy Gaines or Miranda Shepperd were. I had my shoulder bag hiked up and was ready to go back to work at the Underworld Detection Agency when I opened my front door and caught Will standing there, mid-knock.

"Good morning," I said with a smile. "Did you forget we're not working at the school anymore?"

"No," he said, handing me a paper cup that percolated with the aroma of hazelnuts and whipped cream. "But I thought I could walk you, just for old time's sake. And also because you totaled my car."

I bit my bottom lip. "Yeah, Will, I'm really, really sorry about that. The thing is—"

"You don't have insurance?"

"I have insurance. Not American insurance."

He rolled his eyes, but there was still a hint of playful smile behind his coffee cup. "The thing is, I actually want to talk to you about something."

He stepped aside and opened the vestibule door for me. I tugged my jacket tighter around my shoulders. "Let me guess—you're really digging the supernatural crime fighting and want to come on board officially? UDA offers great dental."

Will stopped on the sidewalk and faced me. "Sophie, I'm serious. This whole Guardian thing. It ends, you know?"

I took a step back. "No, I don't know. Aren't you going to be here, guarding me?"

"As long as you're the Vessel of Souls."

I frowned. "And if I'm not?"

He shrugged. "Then I get reassigned."

I had never wanted Will in my life, but now I couldn't imagine my life without him.

"Why are you telling me this, Will? Why are you telling me this now?"

He sucked in a deep breath and looked down at me, his eyes the color of honey and warm. "Look, I know you've got a thing with Alex—"

"No." I held up a hand. "I don't have a thing with Alex."

At least I was pretty sure I didn't.

Will looked at his feet, then up at me again. "Well, that's good, because I lov—"

His voice was drowned out by the sound of horns honking as a woman zigzagged her way across the street, making a direct path through the cars for Will and me. She grinned when she crested the curb in front of me, a wide, thrilled smile that cut across her wrinkled face and pushed up her ruddy cheeks. She reached out and wound her fingers through my hair, still smiling.

Everything inside me told me to bolt, to put distance between this crazy woman and me, but I couldn't. My legs were leaden and I was rooted. Her eyes raked over me and finally locked on mine— hers a filmy, water blue.

"He's been looking for you for a long time, Sophie. He's been looking and he's so happy that he's finally found you. It's only a matter of time, now."

I pulled back, stunned. "Who's found me? Who are you?"

Immediately, the smile dropped from the woman's lips and they went to a tight purse. She stepped back from me as if I had burned her and yanked her hand out of my hair, breaking a few strands as she did so.

"Get away from me," she said, her voice sour, her eyes frightened. "I don't know you. Get away from me!"

She reeled backward, then was swallowed up

by the crowd. She was gone, but her voice kept swirling in my head: *He's been looking for you for a long time, Sophie. He's been looking and he's so happy that he's finally found you. It's only a matter of time, now. Only a matter of time . . .*

Please turn the page for an exciting sneak peek of the next installment of Hannah Jayne's Underworld Detection Agency Chronicles coming soon from Kensington Publishing!

I could feel the cold stripe of fear going up my spine-like icy fingers walking slowly up vertebra after vertebra.

"Is she dead?" The voice was a faint whisper but it throbbed through my head, singeing the ache that was already there.

"Maybe we should go."

I hoped that they would. I prayed that they would. I remained as still as possible, breath barely trembling through my body, willing my heart to thrum silently because I knew that vampires can hear everything. Every little whisper, every little thought. *Please go, please go*, I pleaded silently.

And then the icy breath was at my ear. "Sophie!"

Now the voice was incredibly loud and I jumped straight up until the tops of my thighs mashed against the underside of my desk. I missed the chair coming back down and flopped unceremoniously onto my ass.

"What do you want?" I glowered, rubbing my tailbone and seeing Nina and Kale through narrowed dagger-eyes.

"Were you asleep?" Kale asked, cocking her head so that her newly pink hair brushed against her cheek.

I pressed the pads of my fingertips against my temples, making small circles. My head kept aching. "I was trying to. I have a headache."

Nina rolled her eyes and hopped up onto the corner of my desk, her tiny butt and weightless body not making a sound. "Are you still trying to claim PTSD for the whole back to school thing? It's over, all right? You closed up the hell mouth or whatever, and never even had to wear the school uniform."

"What do you guys want?"

Nina whipped out a nail file from I-don't-know-where and began working on her right hand. She blew a bubble from the wad of gum she was chewing and after twelve years with Nina LaShay as my co-worker, roommate, and best friend, I'll never get comfortable seeing a vampire blow purple Hubba Bubba bubbles. It just looks *weird*.

"I'm hiding out from Vlad. He's got an all-fangs-on-deck VERM meeting and I have much better things to do than sit in a stuffy conference room with a bunch of dead guys talking about ascots and their graveyard dirt and glory days."

I grinned despite the nap interruption. The

Vampire Empowerment and Restoration Movement (or VERM, for short), was Vlad's baby. Vlad, Nina's 16-slash-113-year-old nephew, my boss, Kale's paramour, and the roommate who would never leave, pushed the movement that sought to restore vampires back to their broody, Count Dracula countenance and insisted its adherents wear fashions that Nina couldn't abide by. She was a member by virtue of being a vampire and being Vlad's aunt, but she studiously avoided their meetings.

"And I came in to tell you that Sampson wants to see you."

I straightened, my heart dropping into my stomach. Pete Sampson, resident werewolf and head of the Underworld Detection Agency, wanting to see me could only mean one of two things: I was fired, or yet another mysterious, gory, and seemingly supernatural murder had happened within San Francisco's seven square miles.

I would much prefer the former.

I'd like to say Sampson called on me for those cases because I could sniff out bad guys like a mouse sniffs out cheese, but that wouldn't be quite right. I find the bad guys all right, but usually just seconds before they try to bleed me dry, blow me up, or stake me through the heart. That last one is particularly bad since I am not a vampire. Or a werewolf. I'm just me, Sophie Lawson, sole breather in the Underworld Detection Agency, runner of the Fallen Angels Division, Sub-Par Napper.

I headed down the hall toward Sampson's office, holding my breath as I passed the break room where the VERM meeting was in full swing, then avoided the sweet, sparkly little pixie who made a cut-throat motion when I glanced up at her.

Pixies can be total bitches.

I went to make my usual shimmy around the hole in the floor where a senile wizard blew himself up—like everyone else, the UDA was low on funds so the hole was last on the fix-it list—but stopped dead, my mouth dropping open.

"What's this?"

There was actually a piece of "caution" tape up, jerry-rigged to a couple of folding chairs to make a work zone. A guy in a hardhat was up to his knees in the hole, diligently sawing away at one jagged edge.

He looked up and I could see from his gaunt, slightly green face and the hard cleft in his pointed chin that he was a goblin. From what I heard, they were brilliant at precision work.

"We're fixing the hole," he told me, his gray-green eyes widening as he took me in. I flushed, sudden embarrassment burning the tops of my ears and, I was certain, turning my pale skin an unattractive lobster red.

"So, it's true." The goblin pushed back his hardhat and scratched at the little tuft of hair on his head. "The San Francisco branch really does have a breather on staff."

The Underworld Detection Agency is like the clearinghouse for everything that goes bump in the night or bursts into flames during the day. We service everyone from Abatwas (teeny, tiny little buggers who could unhinge their jaw and swallow you whole) to zombies (who most often leave a hunk of their jaw while trying to eat a Twix in the lunchroom). What we don't serve, however, are humans. As a matter of fact, the UDA—and all of its clients—are relatively unknown to the human world. I know what you're thinking—*how* do people miss a three-foot troll walking down Market Street? The answer is a thin, mystical veil that prevents humans from registering what they see in terms of the para-not-normal. You see little person, I see troll. You see a homeless guy pushing a shopping cart full of cans, I see zombie pushing a shopping cart full of zombie body parts (seriously, they drop their stuff *every*where).

So what makes me so different? I can see through the veil. And in case you're thinking I'm some medium or Carol Ann or ghost whisperer, let me tell you that I am not. I'm a one-hundred-percent normal breather who is immune to magic: I can't do it, it can't be done to me.

Okay, so maybe I'm only ninety-nine percent normal.

"Ah, Sophie!" Sampson looked up when I walked

into his office. He grinned widely, tugging at the collar of his button-down shirt. He's a werewolf, but only after business hours. Right now he was regular old Sampson, close cropped, salt and pepper hair, sparkling eyes that crinkled at the sides when he smiled, pristine dark suit.

I sat down with a nervous smile pasted on my face.

"You okay?"

I nodded, fairly certain that if I opened my mouth the words, "who's dead now?" would come springing out.

Sampson went immediately business-y. "So I was going over your third quarter performance review and I have to say—"

I felt my spine go immediately rigid. Vlad was my boss at the office, but I screamed at him to pick up his socks at home. He may be one hundred and thirteen chronologically, but he would always be a sloppy, leaves crap all over the house, sixteen-year old boy in looks and at heart (if he had one). Weren't teens revenge seekers?

"Uh, sir," I said, toeing a line in the carpet and working up a viable explanation.

"—I have to say that I am really impressed with your progress. Not just in the community, but in the office, and personally as well."

I let out a breath I didn't know I was holding and every bone in my body seemed to turn to liquid. "Really?" I grinned.

"Of course. You've worked on cases diligently and successfully, you've got glowing reviews from two of your clients which is especially good because—"

"I know," I wrinkled my nose. "Because most of our clients give me a wide berth, thinking that I bring death and destruction to creatures of the Underworld."

I had a very hard time convincing my previous clients that I didn't bring death so much as it followed me around, like I had some sort of hell-fury GPS tracker shoved in my gut.

"So, taking all that into account, I'd like to congratulate you on another successful year."

I gaped. "That's it?" The words tumbled out of my mouth before my brain had a chance to examine them or reel them back in.

Sampson's eyebrows went up. "Uh . . ."

"No, no!" I jumped up. "I didn't mean that, Sampson, like, that's it how about a raise. I meant, *that's it*? You know, every other time you've called me in here someone was dead or I ended up back in high school."

Sampson shot me a relaxed smile. "That's true. Why don't you take the rest of the day off since I terrified you, and I'll see what I can do about that raise?"

I was stunned. "Really? Really, Sampson?"

"Yeah, take a long weekend."

No sea of death, murder weapons, or crazed schoolgirls *and* a long weekend? My eyes went to the ceiling.

"What are you doing?" Sampson wanted to know.

"This can't be right," I told him. "I'm looking for the piano that's going to fall on my head."

I grabbed my shoulder bag, said something that may have sounded like, "see you Monday, suckas!" and hopped into the elevator. As the Underworld Detection Agency was a cool thirty-six stories *below* the San Francisco Police department, I used the long ride up to mop my red hair from "business chic" into "reality TV marathon ponytail," and shrugged out of my suit jacket. I was halfway to couch bound.

When the elevator doors slid open at the police station vestibule, they perfectly framed Alex Grace.

Alex Grace—fallen angel, delicious, earthbound detective—the man I had an on-again, off-again, more off than on or something in between relationship with over the last few (mortal) years. We had moved past that awkward, bumbling, he-caught-me-in-my-panties stage of our relationship and into a more mature, open, adult one.

But I tended to have a habit of crashing us back down to bumbling and awkward every spare chance I got.

"Alex!" I said, trying to keep my cool as every synapse in my head shot urgent and improbable messages: *kiss him! Tear his clothes off! Maniacally mash the* CLOSE DOOR *button and hide under your desk!*

Alex had his hands on his hips, his police badge winking on his belt, his leather holster nestled up against the firm plane of his are-you-kidding-me chest. His shoulders looked even broader, even more well muscled if that were even possible, making his square jaw look that much more chiseled. His lips—full, blush-pink lips that I had pressed mine against more than once—were set in a hard, thin line. His ice blue eyes were sharp.

"We need to talk."

While normally those words would make me swoon and rethink today's lingerie choices (white cotton panties dotted with pastel pink hearts, no-nonsense [and no cleavage] beige bra), the set of his jaw let me know that this wouldn't be a tea-and-cookies kind of chat.

My stomach flopped in on itself.

Alex led me to his office, one hand clamped around my elbow as if I might dart or steal something at any moment. It was awkward and annoying, but I guess he had just cause: I may have occasionally pilfered a cup of coffee, a jelly donut, or a piece of pivotal evidence in an open investigation once or twice.

I sat down in the hard plastic visitor's chair and he sat behind his desk in his I'm-the-boss chair, arms crossed, eyes holding mine.

"What do you know about Gerald D. Ford?"

Heat pricked all over my body. I had just finished a case at a local high school, going under cover as a substitute teacher, but I "taught" English, not Social Studies.

"Uh, he was our twenty-sixth president and, uh, something about his teeth?"

Alex cocked a brow. "That's Gerald R. Ford and he was the thirty-eighth president. Our Ford was a homeless vet who took up residence at the bottom of the Tenderloin."

My saliva soured. "Was?"

Alex opened his ever-present manila file folder and handed me a photograph. "He was burned to a crisp two weeks ago Sunday."

I glanced down at the photo—a half-charred body sitting on the sidewalk, what remained of his torso propped up against a pink, stuccoed wall advertising *Panadaria Chavez*. Bile burned at the back of my throat. I slid the photo back to Alex.

"That's awful, but what does it have to do with me?"

"He was ultimately identified by his dental records." Alex passed me that sheet then, stamped with a military ID and government info. There was the standard image of disembodied teeth—top set and bottom—teeth randomly marked by ballpoint ink x's for a missing molar and a handful of cavities. But the ballpoint pen was used for something else, too—Ford's dentist had drawn two narrow images, one on each incisor. Rounded at the gum line, then each tapering to a fine point.

"Vampire."

Alex nodded.

I stood. "I'll bring this down to Sampson. I can't recall a Gerald Ford in any of our records."

Alex's face remained unchanged. "That's not why I asked you here, Lawson."

Fireworks shot through my body as thoughts pinged through my brain. *Let's get back together! Let's make wild monkey love on this desk!* Yes, my pre-pubescent twelve-year-old boy mind could go there sixty seconds after seeing a photo of a charred dead guy.

I wasn't so much sexually morbid as I was sexually frustrated.

"When the paramedics initially got there, Gerry was still alive, still talking."

I stepped back, interested. "What did he say?"

"He said, 'Find her.'"

I slipped back into the chair and leaned forward. "Find who? An estranged wife, a daughter?"

Alex shook his head, blue eyes intent on me as he handed me a scrap of paper sealed in a clear-plastic evidence bag. I looked down at the paper; its edges were curled, licked by fire, but the words were clearly legible. A cold stripe of needling fear made its way down the back of my neck as the words swam before my eyes, then burned themselves into my brain: Sophie Lawson, Underworld Detection Agency, San Francisco, California.

Find her.